Also by Sharon Sala

The Next Best Day

DON'T BACK DOWN

SHARON SALA

sourcebooks
casablanca

Published by Sourcebooks Casablanca, an imprint of Sourcebooks
P.O. Box 4410, Naperville, Illinois 60567-4410
(630) 961-3900
sourcebooks.com

Printed and bound in the United States of America.
OPM 10 9 8 7 6 5 4 3 2 1

Prologue

Hyatt Regency Dulles, Herndon, Virginia

A TALL, DARK-HAIRED SOLDIER WALKED INTO THE HYATT Regency, pausing just inside the entrance long enough to locate the front desk, then headed toward it, unaware he was being watched.

A young woman had just stopped beside a potted palm in the lobby to respond to a text when she spotted the soldier walking in.

When he paused to take the lay of the land, the hair stood up on the back of her neck. It was like watching a panther scoping out its prey. When he shifted his deployment bag higher up on his shoulder and started moving through the throng with a cautious stride, the first thing that crossed her mind was "stealth."

She watched him as he checked in, saw him pocket the key card, and then as he turned to walk away, he did that thing again—taking that long look before moving forward. She wanted him to see her. She wanted to know what his first reaction would be, so she moved away from the palm and into his line of vision and waited.

He'd already seen the potted palm, and then he saw her—motionless. Watching him. And his entire body went still.

She sighed. *Yes. He feels it, too.*

Conscious thought fell away as she started toward him. The need to be in his space was as strong as her need to breathe, and then they were standing face-to-face, searching for something, anything, that would explain what was happening.

She scanned the arch of his brows. The curve of his lips. The slight flare of his nostrils.

He saw the steady pulse throbbing at the side of her neck.

And then she spoke, and the sound embraced him. The instant shock of wanting to be inside her rocked him to the core. Was this what happened in love at first sight?

"Hey, Soldier Boy, are you coming or going?" she asked.

He was watching the way her lips shaped the words when he realized she was waiting for an answer.

"Going," he said.

She shivered. His voice was as deep as his eyes were dark.

"Got someone waiting for you back home?" she asked.

He shook his head. "No. I think I've been waiting for you."

"Do you have time for a drink?" she asked.

"I have all night."

A wave of sadness moved through her. One night. Was that all?

"So do I," she said. "But if one night is all we have, then

no last names, no boundaries, and no regrets. Can you live with that?"

"I don't think I will live without it," he said softly.

━━━━━━━

He stowed his bag in her room and then followed her down to the bar. They drank and they ate, and then engaged in the foreplay of lovers. Soft whispers. Quiet laughs. The back of his finger tracking the curve of her cheek. Her knee pressed against his thigh. Her skin was so soft, but the untamed curls of her red hair were what intrigued him. Making him wonder if she was as wild and unruly.

She was in the middle of telling him about the randomness of this happening, and how if her meeting hadn't run late, she would never have seen him, when he stood abruptly and held out his hand.

Startled, she looked up, saw the want on his face, and went with him.

They made it to her room without so much as a glance at each other—without saying a word. It was the click of the dead bolt after the door closed behind them that broke the spell.

They began tearing off their clothes, and then she was in his arms and they were falling, falling down onto the bed, and the rest of the way in love.

In heat. Lust. Passion.

Call it what you will, they were there.

They couldn't get enough. They couldn't find a place to slow down.

She feared she'd never see him again.

He didn't know if he would come back alive to even look for her.

She was his gift.

He was under her skin.

They would never be the same.

Even after she finally fell asleep in his arms, he lay watching her, storing up this memory for the bad times he knew were coming as he headed into his second tour of duty in Iraq.

―――――――

His flight out of Washington Dulles left at 8:00 a.m., and he was dressed and walking out the door at half past six. He paused on the threshold and looked back, needing that last sight of her. She was curled up on her side, sound asleep and clutching his pillow.

He couldn't bring himself to tell her goodbye.

She'd laid down the ground rules. No boundaries. No last names. No regrets.

But even as his plane was taxiing down the runway for takeoff, he was filled with nothing but regret. If only he'd known her last name.

―――――――

She woke up suddenly, and even before she opened her eyes, she knew he was gone. His scent was all over her, and she could still feel his mouth on her body and his hands in her hair. She was only twenty-four years old, and he'd ruined her for ever wanting another man. He was in her blood, and she didn't even know his last name.

Chapter 1

THE SUN WAS BARELY ABOVE THE HORIZON. SERVICE PERsonnel were already preparing breakfast in the galley of the *Aquatic Adonis*, an eighty-foot luxury yacht belonging to Gianni Rodini. Gianni and seven of his friends had been partying onboard for days, but this was their last. Within hours they would be heading into port.

Fancy yachts like his had been disappearing for months up and down the southern seaboard. From the Pacific coast. From the bay area of Houston, and along the Florida coastline. It was assumed the boats were being boarded by pirates who then sailed them to the Bahamas, repainted and refitted them, and then used them to ferry contraband from port to port, or sold them outright to unsuspecting buyers.

The pirates left no witnesses, and the few bodies that had been found all had execution-style wounds. There was nothing on them that would lead the authorities to identify the people responsible.

The feds were getting flack. The ATF was getting flack. And the DEA was getting flack. When the FBI learned of

Rodini's plans to take his yacht out for a weeklong cruise among the Keys, they planted one of their best undercover agents onboard with a sat phone and a gun.

Her name was Rusty Caldwell. She was twenty-nine years old. Average height. Physically fit. A sharpshooter with blue eyes and red hair. She went in as a sous-chef for the galley chef and did what she was told with as little comment as possible. She'd learned long ago that the quieter people were, the more invisible they became to others. And being invisible mattered in her line of work.

The crew knew they were sailing into port today, but instead of the usual morning chatter, they were unusually quiet, and Rusty noticed. She kept following the chef's orders in a quick and proficient manner, never looking up. Never meeting anyone's gaze. But every instinct she had was on alert. Something was going down. She could feel it.

She had gone to the cooler with a basket to get mangos and pineapple for the breakfast service, and was coming out with the produce when she overheard two of the crew at the other end of the hall. Sound carried in that corridor, and even though their voices were low, Rusty heard enough to make her skin crawl.

"Inbound. ETA four minutes. Same orders. TNP."

It could have meant anything. More guests arriving. Or maybe a fuel carrier. But in her world, TNP meant *take no prisoners*. That gave them away.

She went straight into the kitchen, put the fruit on a counter, and then glanced up at the chef. "Making a quick trip to the head, Chef."

"Fine, but don't dawdle! Service is in thirty minutes," he snapped.

"Yes, Chef," Rusty said softly, and slipped out of the galley.

Moments later she was in her cabin. She grabbed her sat phone and made one call to her contact on the outside.

He answered on the second ring.

"Browning."

"It's me. Get a fix on this location. Someone is inbound. ETA four minutes. And the last thing I heard was "Take no prisoners." I think our link to the pirates is the crew. Whoever is providing crews for these yacht owners has to be in on the thefts and murders. There's a speedboat anchored just off the starboard bow. I'm going to try and get to it before this all goes to hell. Get somebody here ASAP. I can't die looking like this. My hair's a mess."

Browning grinned. Caldwell's wild red curls were as unforgettable as she was. "Roger that."

Rusty grabbed her jacket, stuffed the phone into an inner pocket and zipped it in, then palmed her Glock, pocketed two fifteen-round magazines, and bolted out of the cabin, locking it behind her. If they thought someone was locked inside, the time it took for them to shoot their way in might be the difference between her life and death.

And then she began hearing a lot of shouting and screaming, and gunshots coming from above.

Shit! They were already onboard.

Now she had a decision to make. She was on the lowest level of the yacht and needed to get up to the main deck to escape.

There were two staircases, one at each end of the galley level, that led to the upper decks. She needed to know how many intruders had boarded and where their boat was—and pray to God they hadn't already taken possession of the speedboat. If they had, she was going to fight them for it.

She paused for a moment, her heart pounding as she listened.

One man was ordering Rodini and the others to move to the edge of the deck. There was more screaming and crying, and Rodini was telling them how rich he was and how they could ransom him for money, when Rusty pivoted and ran the other way.

She could hear men coming down the stairs behind her, but she kept running toward the opposite staircase and then up and out into the sunlight.

The pirates had lashed their boat to the opposite side of the yacht from where she was standing. That gave her the fighting chance she needed as she began to sprint toward the speedboat. And with every step, she kept hearing screaming and begging from the other end of the deck, and with every shot, a splash ensued. She was only seconds away from escape when she heard shouts. They'd seen her, and she'd just run out of deck!

Without a second of hesitation, she leaped. Only after she was in midair and looking down did she realize she was going in the water.

Then fate handed her a miracle.

A wave hit the speedboat, rocking it back against the yacht just as she came down. She landed in the boat on her hands and knees, popping her neck and biting her tongue from the jolt of the fall. Her body was one solid ache, and she was spitting blood, but there was no time to think about what she may have done to herself.

She scrambled to her feet, threw off the rope securing the speedboat to the yacht, and ran for the controls. Rodini had insisted on keeping the key in the ignition after someone misplaced it onboard days earlier. She had been counting on it being there. And it was.

She slid into the seat and turned the key. The engine fired at the same time the first bullet sailed past her head. There was no time for an engine warm-up as she grabbed her gun and turned, firing off a round of shots at the same time she pushed the throttle forward.

The sudden burst of power lifted the nose of the speedboat so high out of the water that for a moment Rusty thought it was going to flip over, but then it came down with a thud and she was flying, leaving a four-foot wave of water in her wake.

They were shooting at her again, the bullets zinging past her like a swarm of angry bees. She turned sideways, making herself a smaller target, and began firing back at the armed men lined up on the deck. She saw some of them fall and others ducking for cover, but she knew their faces. The men shooting at her were part of the crew. Her suspicions had been correct.

She emptied the first clip and shoved in a second clip before moving out of range. Even though she'd taken three of them out and wounded a couple of others, the fight was far from over. The pirates had the yacht, and their boat, and they didn't leave witnesses.

Rusty turned back to the stretch of water before her to get her bearings. They'd dropped anchor at Big Key. The sun was at her back, so she was moving west. Club Key was the small island to her right, which meant the Florida coast should be somewhere ahead.

She pulled the sat phone from her bag and made one more call, with salt spray in her face and the roar of the engine in her ears.

Again, Browning answered. "Backup is on the way, and we've got someone in a speedboat on radar."

"That's me. Don't shoot. I made it off the yacht, but I'm going to have company ASAP."

"Copy that. Choppers in the air and closing in. Less than two minutes out. Are you hurt?"

"Not so it shows," Rusty said, and then glanced over her shoulder. "They're coming after me. Can't talk now. My daddy always told me to keep both hands on the wheel."

She dropped the phone back in her bag. The speedboat was hitting the tops of the waves so hard it kept bouncing her out of the seat. There was a life jacket at her feet, and she needed to be wearing it, but the best she could do was get her foot between the straps. Maybe if she went into the water, it would go with her.

The wind was burning her eyes and tearing at her hair, but she didn't look behind her again. She was focused on the faint green shoreline of the Everglades ahead of her when the image of a man's face flashed before her.

Soldier Boy! That shocked her and then scared her. Was this her life actually flashing before her eyes? Was this some celestial sign that she wasn't getting out of this alive?

Then she saw a Coast Guard cutter in the distance and two choppers in the air above her, and when the choppers roared over her, she lifted her arm in jubilation. But it wasn't until the Coast Guard cutter blew past her, too, that she eased back on the throttle.

She'd made it. Home free again, but how many lives did she have left?

Each time she got into a situation like this, it felt like the end of her, and yet she kept going back in. She still hadn't decided if that was a death wish, or because she was so alone in the world that it didn't really matter.

Now that she had the power of the FBI and the Coast Guard behind her, she began to breathe easier. But coming down from the adrenaline surge of what had just happened was beginning to make her shake.

Every muscle in her body was throbbing. The coppery taste of blood was still in her mouth, her fingers wouldn't uncurl from the steering wheel, and the wind was drying the tears on her cheeks faster than she could cry them.

A short while later, the Coast Guard picked her up and towed the speedboat into port. Rusty was taken to a hospital for treatment and then, later that same day, returned to her home in Virginia to recuperate.

A week passed. She finally graduated from soup and pudding after her tongue had time to heal, but she was still suffering from whiplash, a swollen knee, a twisted ankle, and daily headaches from the hard landing in the boat.

It wasn't the first time she'd given thought to reconsidering her career choices.

———————

Jubilee, Kentucky

It was just after sunrise when Cameron Pope left his house, still wearing the shadow of last night's whiskers and the clothes he wore for his daily run. He wasn't one of those guys who needed earbuds and music blasting in his ears while he ran. Although his cell phone was zipped in an inner pocket of his windbreaker, he didn't need to listen to motivational speakers or the news of the day. He'd been a soldier too long to be stupid enough to cut off one of the senses that had kept him alive. He was aware of every aspect of his surroundings, as was the big dog at his side.

Fog was still rising as he came down from the porch of the sprawling, single-story home he'd grown up in. The air was as still as the big white dog beside him. Where he went, Ghost went. It's how they rolled.

A hawk took flight from a nearby tree as they started up the gravel drive, and by the time Cameron and Ghost reached the blacktop road at the end of his drive, they were running.

It was the feel of foot to earth, the blood racing through his body, the little clouds his breath made coming out of his mouth, the sting of cold air up his nostrils that reminded him to be grateful he still lived. Two tours of duty in a war-torn land and still coming back with all his limbs and senses was everything.

Ghost always ran a few yards ahead, unaware that this country did not have IEDs planted at the sides of the road. Always on the alert. Always clearing the way for his human. Their bond was deep. Unbreakable. Their faith in each other unwavering.

The road up the mountain was steep and curving and bordered on both sides by trees older than the humans who now lived on it. It was the land of the Pope and Glass and Cauley families. Their sprawling generations populated the Cumberland Mountains and the town of Jubilee in the valley below.

The blood of Cameron Pope's Choctaw ancestors ran true in his dark eyes and black hair, but it was his Scottish great-great-great-grandfather who'd put the breadth and height in the DNA of the Popes who came after.

Cameron towered over most people, just like Pope Mountain towered over Jubilee, and his long legs carried him far and fast as he ran, chasing Ghost up the mountain, outrunning the ghosts of the war they'd left behind.

They ran up, then they ran back down and all the way home.

Cameron's day had just begun.

Back inside the house, he fed Ghost, then headed up the hall to shower and shave. He came out dressed for the day and turned on the TV to listen to the morning newscasts as he made breakfast. Then a news bulletin interrupted the morning show, and he stopped, his focus shifting.

"We've just been alerted to an ongoing riot inside Abercrombie Penitentiary. Guards have been taken hostage. At least four prisoners are unaccounted for and are suspected to have escaped. The warden is in negotiations with the prisoners regarding the release of hostages.

These are scenes from within the prison moments after the riot began. It is unknown how the inmates were able to get out of their cells, so at this time, it is all supposition. We'll keep you updated as more information comes in. Authorities are asking everyone in the vicinity of the penitentiary to lock their cars and houses and, if possible, stay inside."

Cameron frowned. Every time somebody in this part of the state made a jailbreak, they headed for the most heavily wooded areas. Like these mountains.

He thought of his sister, Rachel, and her family who lived a couple of miles further up the mountain. He sent her a text, then plated his food and sat down to eat.

A few minutes later he got a reply.

Saw the same bulletin. Locked in. 👍

Satisfied he'd done his brotherly duty, he finished eating, cleaned up after himself, and headed into town with Ghost riding shotgun.

The day progressed. He thought nothing more of the bulletin as he bought groceries, then swung by the hardware store for nails and caulking. There were some loose boards on the porch steps, and he needed to recaulk some windows before winter set in.

It was nearing midnight.

Rachel Glass was waiting for her husband, Louis, to come home from work and had fallen asleep on the sofa. She was so tired from her busy day and taking care of her lively toddler that not even the laughter and chatter from the late-night television show was penetrating her sleep.

It was the sound of footsteps on the porch that woke her.

Thinking it was Louis, she opened her eyes just as the glass in the front door shattered, scattering all over the floor. She leaped up screaming as a man burst into the room, and then everything stopped.

The man was staring at her in disbelief. *Holy shit! Rachel Pope?*

Rachel was in shock. *Oh my God! Danny Biggers?*

The last time she'd seen him, she had been in court, testifying against him for rape and assault. She grabbed the poker from the fireplace, and as she did, he jerked like he'd been slapped and came at her.

"Get out! Get out!" Rachel screamed and swung the poker at his head.

He ducked. "Can't," he muttered. "You got somethin' I want."

She screamed and swung at him again, but this time he was ready. He grabbed the poker out of her hand and threw it across the room, then doubled up his fist and hit her on the jaw so hard it knocked her off her feet. She flew backward, hitting her head on a corner of a table as she fell, and didn't get up.

Danny Biggers frowned at the blood pooling beneath her head, unable to believe this was where they'd sent him. Then he stormed through the house until he found the nursery and the little girl asleep in her bed. There was a moment when he second-guessed his actions, but then he thought of the money she was worth and shrugged it off.

"Whatever," he muttered. He wrapped her up in the blanket she was sleeping under, and took off with her.

Three-year-old Lili Glass was tiny, but when she woke up in a stranger's arms, she let out a shriek that brought tears to Danny Biggers' eyes.

"Son of a bitch!" he shouted, and all but threw her into the front seat of his car, buckling her in as she was still shrieking for her mama.

He handed her a bottle of milk, thinking that would silence her.

Still shrieking, she threw it at the floor.

Cursing, Danny backed up, then spun out on the grass as he drove away.

Louis Glass worked the closing shift at Trapper's Bar and Grill on Main Street in Jubilee. He was tired and cold as he left town and headed up the mountain toward home. All he could think of was a hot shower and crawling into bed beside Rachel.

When he turned off the road onto their driveway and saw a couple of lights still on, he smiled. Rachel was waiting up for him again. But when he pulled up and parked, he saw the front door standing open. Panic hit, and then he was out of the car and running into the house, calling Rachel's name. She was lying on the floor between the fireplace and the sofa, with blood pooling beneath her head.

His heart stopped as he dropped to his knees beside her, desperately feeling for a pulse. The moment he realized she was alive, he rocked back on his heels with relief. He was reaching for his phone when it hit him.

The baby!

He ran down the hall to her room, turning on lights as he went. The little bed was empty. Lili was gone!

"Oh God, oh God, oh God!" he cried and grabbed his phone, his hands shaking so hard he could barely hold it, and made the call to 911.

"911. What is your emergency?"

"This is Louis Glass, at 33972 Winding Road on Pope Mountain. I just came home from work and found the front door open and my wife on the floor. She's unconscious and bleeding from a head wound and our three-year-old daughter is missing. Help me! Please help me!"

He could hear the 911 operator dispatching an

ambulance and relaying the same message to the county sheriff as he was running back to Rachel.

"Mr. Glass, is your wife still breathing?" the operator asked.

Louis dropped to his knees and felt again for a pulse. "Yes, but I'm afraid to move her," he said, and jumped up and ran to get a wet cloth.

"Okay, just stay on the line with me," the operator said.

Louis ran back to Rachel, put the phone on speaker as he laid it aside, and began gently wiping her face. He could hear the 911 operator dispatching services, but Rachel was his total focus.

"Rachel, baby…wake up! It's me, Louis. Can you hear me? Wake up, love. I can't do this world without you."

He was still wiping the cold cloth on her face and neck when he heard her groan, and then her eyelids fluttered and she opened her eyes.

There was a moment of confusion when Rachel saw Louis's face above her, and then his frantic expression registered along with the pain in her head, and she remembered. "Louis! He broke into the house!"

Louis groaned. "Don't move, sweetheart. You're hurt."

Rachel started sobbing. "He said I had something he wanted." And then it hit her. "Is Lili okay?"

"She's gone, Rachel. Who took her? Who broke in?"

Rachel was sobbing. "Danny Biggers. It was Danny. I fought him, but then he hit me."

The shock of hearing that name again—after all this time.

"I thought he was still in prison," Louis muttered, and then he began hearing sirens.

Sound carried in the mountains. It would be a bit before they got here, but at least he could hear them now. He picked up the phone. The dispatcher was still talking when he disconnected the line to 911 and called his father.

———

Marcus Glass was a big man. A strong, youthful-looking man in his midfifties. He'd been a widower going on three years now and still hadn't gotten used to sleeping alone, which was why he was dawdling about the house and folding laundry to keep from having to go to bed.

He frowned when his cell phone began to ring. A call at this time of night was never good news, and then he noticed it was his son, Louis.

"Hello, Son. You're up late," Marcus said.

"Dad! Rachel was attacked and Lili is missing. She said it was Danny Biggers. I don't know which way he went when he left with her, but we need help. The police and ambulance are on the way, but they're not going to start searching until they've talked to us. Call our people. Tell everyone on the mountain to be on the lookout. I don't know how long he's been gone, but not long because the front door was open but the house isn't cold inside. Rachel's head is bleeding and there's a big bruise on her jaw."

Marcus was in shock. "Lili's gone? He hurt Rachel? What the hell? I thought he was in prison!"

"So did we. Whatever Biggers's plans are, he'll be up to no good. And if he's on the run, he won't go back through Jubilee. He'll disappear in the mountains."

Marcus heard the panic in his son's voice. "Hold the faith, Son. I'm calling people now. If there's a strange car on the mountain this time of night, we'll find it."

"Thanks, Dad," Louis said.

The line went dead.

The law came up Louis and Rachel's driveway with sirens screaming and lights flashing and an ambulance right behind it. Officers and EMTs spilled out into their yard and came swarming into the house.

While the EMTs were treating Rachel, Rance Woodley, the county sheriff, did exactly what Louis feared he would do and wasted precious time grilling both parents, even as they kept telling him *they knew who took Lili*, demanded to know why they hadn't been notified Biggers was one of the escapees from the prison riot earlier in the day, and begged the police to go after him.

It was a nightmare of confusion, and then they caught a break.

John Cauley, Rachel's uncle, lived near the peak of the mountain, and when he got the call from Marcus about what had happened, he flew out of bed, dressing in haste as his wife, Annie, scrambled to get his rifle and ammunition, handing it off to him on the way out the door.

He took off in his old Land Rover and headed for the main road. As soon as he reached the blacktop, he started down the mountain, thinking Biggers would not have had time to get up this far this fast and hoping maybe he'd meet up with him on the way. But he saw nothing, and his worry grew.

And then a few miles down he drove up on an abandoned car with two doors standing open.

John grabbed a flashlight as he got out and then looked inside the car. The first thing he saw was a Styrofoam cup with droplets of milk still in the bottom. Then a baby bottle half-full of milk on the floorboard and a pile of uneaten cookies in the passenger seat. After a quick search around the car, he saw tracks in the ditch leading into the woods and followed them, then found a scrap of blanket caught on brush and more tracks in the forest leading up the mountain. It had to be Biggers!

John's heart was racing as he ran back to the road. His hands were shaking as he pulled out his phone, praying he'd get a signal strong enough to make a call.

━━━━━━━

Rachel was holding an ice pack against her forehead. Her eyes were swollen from crying, her head was still bleeding, and she was shaking so hard she could barely speak when her phone suddenly rang.

The sheriff jumped up, shouting. "Put it on speaker. If it's the kidnapper demanding ransom, we'll—"

Louis turned, shouting in anger over the sheriff's orders. "Ransom? Have none of you heard a word we said? You just told us Danny Biggers broke out of prison. We should have been notified! It's your fault we were unprepared! Biggers knows we don't have money. He's on the run, not hanging around waiting for ransom. He already got what he came for."

Rachel took a deep breath and then screamed, "Stop shouting! All of you!" Then she answered the call and put it on speaker. "Hello?"

"Rachel, honey, this is Uncle John. I found an abandoned car on the road about four miles up from your place. There's a baby bottle with milk in it and a pile of uneaten cookies in the passenger seat. I also found tracks and a piece of blanket caught on some bushes. He took to the woods, sugar. I'll let the other searchers know."

"Oh my God, oh my God… Thank you, Uncle John."

"You rest easy, darlin'. We'll find Lili and the bastard who took her."

Rachel was sobbing. "Thank you, Uncle John, thank you."

Woodley stared in disbelief. Let the searchers know?

"What searchers?" he shouted.

Louis snapped, "Our family. Our friends. I called them while I was waiting for you people to even show. They've been looking for a stranger's car for the better part of thirty minutes now, while you've been here arguing with us."

"Son of a bitch," Woodley muttered. "Amateurs on the mountain at night. God knows what will happen now."

At that point, Louis lost it and pointed at the front door.

"Nobody up here is an amateur at anything to do with hunting or tracking. Between them and their dogs, if Biggers is still in the woods, they will find him. If you're interested in helping, then get the hell out of my house and go do it!"

Woodley's face turned red as he began issuing orders to his men. Within moments they were exiting the premises and heading up the mountain to catch up with the search party.

But the searchers were already on the mountain with guns and dogs when they got the update from John Cauley. They came out of the trees and crossed the road to the other side and began looking for signs, while Louis went out to his shop, got a piece of plywood, and came back and nailed it over the broken window on their front door.

Chapter 2

CAMERON POPE WAS DREAMING OF AN ANGEL. RELIVING the moment in the hotel lobby when he'd first seen her.

She smiled at him and that was all it took. He'd never believed in love at first sight, but it felt like he knew her—had always known her. Through a thousand lifetimes she'd been his.

Now it was his last night on American soil before shipping out for a second tour in Iraq, and all he could think was This can't be happening. *It had taken so long to find her, and tomorrow he'd be gone.*

One of them moved first. He still didn't remember if it was him or her, but they were suddenly face-to-face and she was looking at his fatigues and the duffel bag on his shoulder, and a strange look came over her.

What happened next was the stuff miracles were made of.

He could still remember how they fit, body to body, and the tears in her eyes as she came apart in his arms.

And then his phone rang, yanking him from the dream. The scent of her perfume was nothing but a memory as he rolled over in bed. He heard Ghost leap to his feet and the click of toenails on the cold pine floor as he came into the room.

Cameron groaned as the phone continued to ring. "I hear it," he said, patting the head of his huge German shepherd as he turned on the lamp.

But then he saw his sister's name pop up on caller ID and frowned. This time of night? It couldn't be good. When he answered and heard her sobbing, his heart stopped.

"Rachel? Honey? What's wrong?"

"Danny Biggers was one of the men who escaped from Abercrombie! He broke into our house tonight before Louis got home and took Lili. We called the sheriff. Louis called his dad. Our people are on the mountain with the hounds. You know Danny. He knows the mountains. The law will never find him on their own. Uncle John just found an abandoned car about halfway up the mountain. Biggers is in the woods with my baby."

Cameron was already out of bed and getting dressed.

"Did Biggers say anything to you?" Cameron asked.

Rachel hiccupped on a sob. "It was weird. When he first saw me, he was shocked. Like he hadn't expected to see me, and then we fought. He knocked me out. Louis came home from work and found me on the floor and the baby gone. Find my baby, Cameron. You and Ghost. Please find my baby. Louis put the little shirt Lili wore yesterday in our mailbox for you. You'll need it for Ghost."

A quiet rage washed through Cameron so fast he had to take a breath before he could speak.

Danny Biggers put a hand to Rachel again? And took the

baby? God! Lili. Up the mountain. In the dark. With a man who'd already sold his soul to the devil.

"Are you okay? Did he hurt you bad?"

"I'll be okay. Just find my baby."

"We'll find them, Rachel. Ghost and I won't stop until we do."

He hung up, buckled on his holster and handgun, shoved his sat phone inside the inner pocket of his black jacket, and then grabbed a backpack from the floor of his closet. It had a first aid kit, extra batteries for the LED lantern, and hiking gear. It was his habit—a holdover from his military days—to always be ready.

Then he looked down at the white dog standing at his feet.

"Ghost. With me."

Moments later, they were in his Jeep and headed up the mountain. Two miles up, he stopped at Rachel's mailbox to get his niece's shirt, and then they were gone. He kept driving until he saw the open doors of an abandoned vehicle and a number of other cars parked nearby.

The searchers were already ahead of him.

He got out of his Jeep with Ghost at his heels, buckled on the backpack, then held the little girl's shirt beneath his dog's nose.

"Seek, Ghost! Seek!"

The German shepherd caught the scent, then went nose to ground outside the abandoned car before taking off into the forest with Cameron running behind him without caution, desperate to keep up.

The woods were silent. The air was cold. Cameron

couldn't let himself think about Lili out here with Danny Biggers. He'd raped Rachel and gone to prison for it. How the hell did he get out? Why come all the way back here just to kidnap Rachel's daughter years later?

But there were no answers. Only questions, and none of it mattered right now but finding Lili. Cameron just kept moving upward, running as fast as he could through the brush to keep Ghost in sight.

He heard the hounds long before he saw the LED-powered lanterns the searchers were carrying. The hounds were in the woods, but he could tell by the occasional bay that they had yet to strike a trail.

He could see Ghost a few yards ahead of him, moving at a lope through the trees, and then all of a sudden Ghost whined and took off running.

"Jesus," Cameron whispered, and kicked into high speed, desperate to keep the dog in sight.

They were behind the searchers, then running through them. There was no time to talk. To explain. He just kept running. He couldn't afford to lose sight of Ghost.

━━━━━━━━

Lights were bobbing through the trees on Pope Mountain like drunken fireflies in the dark as the searchers moved upward.

Men's voices.

Hounds on the hunt.

Two-way radios keyed up and then silenced.

Breath clouded, dissipating as quickly as it had formed, while the men who'd exhaled outran it.

All of a sudden there was the sound of someone coming up behind them—of dry leaves crunching and breaking twigs, and then something white moved between them and disappeared into the forest in front of them. A ghost on the mountain?

Before they could react, the black shadow of a man shot through the line of searchers and disappeared into the night.

A sheriff's deputy shouted as he reached for his gun, "What the hell was that? Was that our man?"

Before the deputy could get the pistol out of his holster, Marcus Glass grabbed his arm. "No. He's one of us. That's Cameron Pope, and it appears his dog, Ghost, has struck a trail," Glass said.

"But the dog isn't barking like your hounds," the officer said. "It isn't making a sound."

"Because it's not a hound, and the man we're after won't even know Ghost is there until it's too late. We run now. Ghost will find them. Cameron will need us," Glass said, and took off through the trees after them with the searchers at his heels.

Nothing was going according to Danny Biggers's plan. When he'd told his old girlfriend Lindy that the prison break was going to happen, she'd told him to call her if he made it out. She'd have a job for him that would get him the money he needed to disappear.

And then he'd made the escape, and the first thing he did was break into an old couple's home, tie them up, steal their car and the money they had on hand, and trade his prison duds for some of the old man's clothes. On the way out, he took their phone and called Lindy. He could tell by the sound of her voice she was surprised he'd made it out, but she made good on her promise and gave him the info on the job.

It was the last thing he expected to come out of her mouth, and he was so shocked he almost rejected the job, but then she told him what they'd pay him to do it, and he caved. Kidnap a little kid. Take it over the cutback on Pope Mountain to a bar called Fuzzy Fridays. She'd be waiting with ten thousand dollars, and he'd be on his way.

When she gave him the family's name and directions to the house, he realized it was on the actual mountain. The home was the residence of a man named Louis Glass. Except Rachel Pope had been there. And it was her kid he snatched. What were the odds that would happen? That he would come face-to-face with the woman whose testimony had put him in jail?

But he had not completely followed through on his orders. He did not kill the woman to get the child like he'd been told. Instead, he left Rachel unconscious, hoping it would give him time to get over the mountain before she came to and before Louis Glass came home.

Only he hadn't counted on all the shit with the kid.

She'd done nothing but scream since he'd picked her up. He'd planned on giving her a bottle loaded with something to put her to sleep, but she wouldn't take the bottle, so he'd dumped a bag of cookies in her lap and stomped the accelerator. Finally, she began eating on the cookies, snuffling and hiccupping through tears.

"Want a drink, baby? Want some milk with your cookies?" he asked.

She nodded, so he pulled over on the side of the mountain road, unscrewed the top off the bottle, and poured some of the drugged milk into an empty Styrofoam cup he'd picked up off the floorboard. She drank until she was full and handed it back.

"Get your blanket and lie down now," he said.

Tears rolled. "Want Mama."

"Okay, then. You lie down and close your eyes and we'll find Mama."

And with all the innocence of the toddler she was, she did as she was told. Within a few minutes, the drugs kicked in, and she went limp.

He felt for a pulse to make sure she was still breathing, and then nodded with satisfaction. All he had to do was get over the mountain to Fuzzy Fridays, meet up with Lindy, and get his money. He didn't know what they wanted with the kid, and he didn't care. His cut would be enough to help him disappear.

He put the car in gear and floored it, but he didn't get far before the engine began missing. His gut knotted. Then something blew beneath the hood—a mini-explosion that scared the shit out of him enough that he almost wrecked. He steered the smoking car to the side of the road, letting it roll to a stop. And when smoke began pouring into the interior of the car, he started cursing and pounding his fists on the steering wheel.

He tried to call Lindy, but couldn't get a signal. He didn't know if the smoke was coming from wiring, or if the car was about to explode, but he had to get out. He grabbed the kid and her blanket, dug a flashlight from the console, then clutched her limp body tight against him.

He stared up the road and then into the trees, debating which route to take, then opted for the route with the most cover, jumped the ditch with the deadweight of the kid in his arms, and disappeared into the forest. When the blanket snagged on a bramble, he yanked it free and kept moving.

After the first minutes of frustration and panic subsided, Biggers was finally able to focus on the child in his arms. Even though there was a three-quarter moon, the forest was so thick that very little light came through the treetops, leaving him with little more than a faded and blurry view of her features.

The air was cold, and the higher up he went, the colder it got. It was quiet. Too quiet. No night birds calling. No sound of foxes. It was too cold to worry about snakes this time of year, but the abundance of black bears was a threat, and it was too early for them to have gone into hibernation.

He stopped long enough to shift Lili's weight, then aimed his flashlight into the trees and kept moving upward.

If he could get to the switchback before daylight, he would be able to get a cell signal and call Lindy. She could come get them, and they'd be home free.

———— ——

Cameron was on autopilot, moving without thinking—heart hammering in his chest, muscles burning from extreme exertion, sweat pouring down his face despite the cold.

Ghost was his touchstone. He kept his focus on the glimpses of the dog weaving through the trees. All he could think was *Stay with him. Don't lose him. Lose Ghost, and you lose Lili.*

He'd rather die.

And then all of a sudden, he caught a glimpse of light. One single flash in the trees ahead and then gone. He'd outrun the line of searchers. The only person ahead of him had to be Biggers.

Then he realized Ghost had disappeared. Shit! He'd keyed in on Biggers, too.

Cameron shot forward with renewed speed, dodging low-hanging limbs, ignoring the briars tugging at his clothes and the brush slapping at his face. His gaze was focused on the dark before him, desperate for another flash of light or anything to tell him where they were.

And then he heard the screams.

———— ——

One second Biggers was upright and walking, and then something hit him in the back so hard it sent him to his knees. He heard growling only seconds before it began ripping at his legs, tearing clothing and flesh, and trying to rip the coat off his back.

All he could think was "Bear!" He was going to die!

He dropped the kid and began trying to crawl away, hoping the animal would take her instead, but it had a death grip on him and wouldn't let go. He began screaming—and screaming—and screaming, fearing the sound of his own voice would be the last thing he'd hear.

He was wrong.

Suddenly, a man was behind him shouting, "Stay, Ghost! Stay!"

As quickly as the animal had taken him down, the weight of it was gone. Danny thought he'd just been rescued, and then someone grabbed him and rolled him over. He opened his eyes to the giant shadow of a man looming over him, shining a flashlight into his face. And then the man pulled a gun and Danny started begging.

"Don't shoot! Don't shoot! For the love of…"

One shot rang out, followed by a second.

———

The searchers heard.

The first shot stopped them in their tracks.

Cameron! It meant he'd found something.

Then the second shot followed.

He'd found her alive! They let out a whoop and started running.

━━━━━━━━

"Ghost! With Lili! Stay!" Cameron said, and shed his backpack as Ghost immediately dropped beside the toddler and began licking her face. Cameron was so focused on disabling Biggers that at first he didn't realize Lili was unconscious. He pulled a coil of nylon climbing rope from his pack, and while Biggers was bawling and begging for help, Cameron dragged him to his feet.

"Help me," Danny wailed. "I'm bleeding bad."

"You're lucky I didn't shoot you, and if you've hurt Lili, I'll kill you anyway," Cameron said. He tied Biggers upright and standing to a tree, his face smashed sideways against the trunk as Cameron kept winding the rope around and around him until he was tied so tight the bark was cutting into his face.

As soon as Biggers was secure, Cameron ran to Lili.

Danny couldn't move his head, but from the corner of his eye, he saw the man scoop the kid up in his arms, and then when the man turned on him, he finally saw his face.

Oh God. It's Rachel's brother.

"She's unconscious! What the fuck did you do to her?" Cameron shouted.

"Nothing. Nothing, I swear. It's just something to make her sleep. I didn't hurt her. I didn't do anything to her," Danny whined.

Cameron unzipped his jacket enough to get Lili swaddled inside before zipping it up around her. Her body was like ice, her breathing too soft…too faint. Two tours in Iraq had not scared him as bad as the fear running through him now. He left Biggers's flashlight shining straight at the tree where he was tied, took a lantern from his backpack, then slung the backpack over his shoulder.

"Ghost. With me!" Cameron said, and headed back down the mountain, walking as fast as he dared, cradling Lili against him.

"Don't leave me! The bears will smell the blood!" Danny screamed.

Biggers was still screaming and begging for help as Cameron and Ghost disappeared into the forest.

The searchers were on the run when Ghost shot out of the trees, running toward them. When they saw the dog without Cameron, they froze. Where was he?

They were aiming their flashlights into the darkness just as Cameron appeared, cradling a small body beneath his jacket, with the top of her head just below his chin.

"Who's in charge?" Cameron asked.

Sheriff Woodley stepped out of the crowd.

"Biggers doped her," Cameron said. "She's barely breathing and hypothermic. Send an ambulance up the mountain. Tell them I'm headed down. I'll meet them on the road."

"Where's Biggers?" Woodley asked.

"Tied to a tree. You can't miss him. He's screaming for help. Something about blood and bears. Oh…and you'll need an ambulance for him, too. Ghost beat me to him."

Then he pulled his sat phone out of his pack and handed it to Marcus.

"Call Rachel and Louis. Tell them I found Lili. Tell them to get to the hospital in Jubilee."

"Will do, Cam. Good job," Marcus said.

"Ghost, home! With me," Cameron snapped. He made a sharp turn to the north and headed for the main road with Ghost leading the way.

Part of the searchers followed Cameron out of the forest, while the rest of them led the sheriff and his officers to Danny Biggers.

The ambulance driver and the EMTs were getting ready to leave Rachel and Louis's house when they got the call. Instead of going back to Jubilee, they headed up the mountain at the same time Marcus was calling his son.

Still in a panic about the ambulance's hasty exit, and not knowing what was going on, Louis answered with a shaking voice and put the call on speaker so Rachel could hear.

"Hello?"

"Son…Cameron and Ghost found them. He's headed to the road with Lili now to meet the ambulance. He said to tell you and Rachel to get down to the hospital. They'll be bringing her in to the ER."

Louis's gut knotted. "Is she hurt?'

"Biggers drugged her. She's not breathing so good, and she's suffering from hypothermia," Marcus said.

"Ah, Jesus." Louis groaned. "Thank you, Dad. Thank everyone! We'll be leaving now," he said and hung up, then grabbed Rachel's arm. "Sit still, baby. I'll get your coat and purse," he said.

They left the house minutes later, flying down the blacktop, desperate to get into town.

———

The urgency to get Lili to the ambulance was paramount, but her breathing was so shallow Cameron was afraid to run with her, so he lengthened his stride, turning his body to use as a shield as they moved through the brush. He didn't know if she could hear him, but he wanted her to hear a familiar voice—to let her know she was safe.

"Hey, baby girl. It's Uncle Cam. Remember how we go outside to look at the moon? When everything around us is dark except the stars and the big moon up in the sky? If you were awake, you could see how big it is tonight. Almost full. Only a little piece is missing. Looks like someone took a big bite out of it. Was it you? Did you take a bite of that moon? Like you always take a bite of my cookie?"

And so it went, with Cameron talking and walking, until all of a sudden they were out of the trees, crossing the ditch, and moving up onto the blacktop road. The moment his feet hit the surface, Cameron lengthened his stride and started down the mountain, with Ghost still trotting at his side.

The faint sounds of sirens were echoing all around him, so he knew the ambulances were coming, but it was hard to tell how far away they were. He knew some of the searchers were still behind him, but he didn't bother to look back. They were all on the same journey—to hand Lili over to a medical team. He and Ghost had done their part by finding her. It was up to God and the doctors to make her better again.

Cameron kept patting Lili's back and stroking her little head. "I hear sirens, Lili. They're bringing angels to take you to Mama and Daddy. Don't be scared, baby girl. You don't have to be scared anymore."

And then Ghost began to whine.

Moments later Cameron caught a glimpse of flashing lights about a mile down the mountain and then they disappeared around a curve. A huge sense of relief washed through him. He knew that curve. The ambulance was almost here.

It was like getting his second wind. Adrenaline kicked in as he glanced down at the top of Lili's head. She was warmer now, lying close against his body, and she was still breathing. He had to believe she was going to be okay.

All of a sudden, the sound of sirens turned into a scream as the flashing red and blue lights appeared, coming toward him at breakneck speed. Cameron immediately moved to the side of the road and held up his hand. The driver killed the sirens as the ambulance pulled up in front of him.

Cameron swiftly moved to the back of the vehicle as the driver jumped out and both EMTs came out on the other side. He knew them all. He'd gone to school with the EMTs, Fagan Jennings and Billy Jackson. And he'd known the drive, B. J. Kelly, for a good twenty years. He'd never been so glad to see them in his life.

Kelly opened the back doors. Fagan climbed in, and Billy took Lili from Cameron's arms and passed her off to Fagan.

"Jesus, Cameron. You guys pulled off a small miracle here tonight finding her so fast," Fagan said, then realized the little girl wasn't just sleeping. "What happened to her? She's unconscious! Has she been injured?"

"Biggers drugged her. I don't know what with. Her breathing is shallow, and she was hypothermic when I got to her. She's not allergic to anything we know of, and her parents will be waiting for you in the ER when you arrive. That's all I know," Cameron said.

He watched Billy Jackson climb inside. His last glimpse of Lili was Fagan putting a stethoscope on Lili's chest and Billy buckling her onto the gurney. And then B. J. Kelly closed the back doors and climbed up into the cab, turned the ambulance around, then gunned it back down the mountain as loud and fast as they had arrived.

Cameron could still see taillights when the second ambulance appeared on the way up to get Biggers. As soon as it passed him, he dropped to his knees and put his arms around Ghost's neck.

"You did it, Ghost! You found Lili. You are such a good boy."

Ghost whined and licked Cameron's chin. When Cameron stood, the dog moved a few steps ahead to lead the way until they reached where he'd parked.

A county officer was standing guard at Biggers's vehicle.

"Waiting for a tow?" Cameron asked.

The officer nodded. "Yes. Taking it in to the forensics lab. Good job finding the kid."

"Team effort," Cameron said, then opened the passenger door to his Jeep. Ghost jumped in, settling in his spot as Cameron closed the door and circled the vehicle to get in.

The relief of sitting down, and knowing they had accomplished what they set out to do, was huge. It felt like he'd lived a lifetime from Rachel's phone call to handing Lili over to the EMTs, but when he glanced at the time, he was shocked. Less than four hours had passed. It would be dawn soon. He shuddered, thinking what might have happened but for Ghost.

He laid a hand on the big dog's head.

Ghost looked up at him and then began licking his paws.

Cameron sighed. He wanted to go straight to Jubilee, but his face was burning from the cuts and scratches of running through the woods, and he needed to get Ghost home. He passed the mailbox where Rachel had left her baby's shirt, then another two miles down before turning up his drive.

Seeing the porch light still burning and the lights he'd left on was the only welcome he was going to get. There was no one waiting for him except the angel in his dreams.

Ghost sat up in the seat as Cameron pulled up beneath the carport. "Hey, buddy, we're home," he said.

He opened the door and got out, expecting Ghost to leap across the seats and follow, but instead he just sat, whining.

Cameron frowned and then circled the Jeep and opened the other door. Ghost still hadn't moved, and then Cameron saw all the blood on the seat and the floor, and dark stains on the white hair on one of Ghost's front paws.

"Aw, man...what did you do?" he muttered, then slid his arms beneath his dog, lifted him out and carried him into the house through the side door, and laid him on the kitchen floor.

It didn't take long to find the deep cut on the paw pad. Cameron ran back to the Jeep to get his backpack and rifle, then knelt beside Ghost and pulled out the first aid kit. After sluicing the cut with water to remove debris, he applied antiseptic cream.

Ghost yelped once, then continued to state his objections with soft, intermittent whines until Cameron began wrapping the injured paw with gauze.

When he finished, Ghost tried to lick it again, but Cameron put his hand over the bandage. "No, Ghost. No licking."

The dog looked up. Cameron cupped Ghost's jaw, gazing down into the deep black eyes of the animal before him, and then leaned down—foreheads touching.

"Thank you for your sacrifice, buddy. You ran hurt. You didn't stop because of what I asked of you. You have more courage than most men I know. No chewing your bandage off, okay? Now let's get you some food and water."

He carried Ghost to his food and water bowl, then went to clean up the mess he'd left on the kitchen floor while Ghost ate. Cameron knew he'd gotten scratched, but he had no idea it was so bad until he saw himself in a mirror. It looked like he'd gone four rounds with a bobcat and lost the fight. Still, there was nothing to be done but wash up and apply antiseptic. He would heal. He wasn't as certain about Lili.

Anxious to get to Jubilee, he stripped, washed his face and hands, applied antiseptic to the scratches that made them burn like hell, then quickly dressed in clean clothes before going back to check on Ghost.

The big dog had finished his food and had found his way to his bed by the fireplace, near the warmth from dying embers. But to Cameron's dismay, the bandage he'd put on Ghost was blood-soaked. The cut was worse than he'd thought. He couldn't leave him like this. He had to get him to the vet.

"Okay, buddy, this isn't good. I've gotta go check on Lili and then you're going to see Sam. You like Sam, remember?"

Cameron ran out to the Jeep, pulled an old blanket off the back floorboard, grabbed a handful of wet wipes to clean up all the blood, then put the blanket down in the front seat and ran back inside.

Ghost whined again when Cameron carried him out to the Jeep. Then Cameron went back to get his coat and locked the door behind him as he left.

Night was already fading, giving hints to the arrival of another day as Cameron passed the city limits of Jubilee. Streetlights were still burning. Delivery vans were already making rounds.

On a good day, Cameron would be running errands and checking on family who had their own shops here. But not this morning. The charm of the mountain village that had become a thriving tourist destination was lost on him today. The only things on his mind were Lili and Ghost.

Chapter 3

It was just after midnight and Ray Caldwell was in the penthouse of the Serenity Inn, the twenty-story hotel he owned in Jubilee. He was still awake when he began hearing sirens. He got up from his desk and moved to the windows overlooking the town below. When he saw a parade of flashing lights heading up the mountain, he turned away. What happened up there did not concern him.

About an hour later, he crawled into bed beside his wife, Patricia. Careful not to wake her, he soon fell asleep, only to be awakened in the early hours of the morning by more sirens going up the mountain. He pounded his pillow and turned over, thinking some meth head had probably blown up his lab.

Still mentally cursing the noise, Ray settled in and closed his eyes. He'd just gone back to sleep when he began hearing sirens again—but this time coming into Jubilee.

His twenty-four-year-old daughter, Liz, was asleep in her suite down the hall when the sounds of sirens reawakened her, too. "What the hell is going on?" she muttered, and rolled over onto her back. Sirens had been sounding on and off all night.

She glanced at the time and groaned, but when the sirens kept getting louder and louder, it dawned on her that they were coming down from Pope Mountain. Her heart skipped a beat, and then she was flinging aside her covers and running to the windows.

Cameron Pope lived up there—along with a whole host of other people he was kin to. It didn't have to mean it had anything to do with him. And he didn't know she existed. But that didn't mean he was no longer on her radar. Liz Caldwell had never wanted for anything that money could buy—except Cameron Pope. She'd tried flirting once. He'd never even noticed her. But it didn't stop her fantasizing about taking him to bed.

She watched the ambulance lights flashing red and blue as the emergency vehicles and police cars wound their way through the streets, and then they disappeared. Moments later, the sirens went silent. The ambulance must be at the hospital.

She fidgeted, wishing she knew what was going on, and then shrugged it off, crawled back into her warm bed, and closed her eyes.

Across town, Marshall Devon had been experiencing a similar night. He'd been hosting some of his investors in the penthouse of Hotel Devon when the first sirens sounded. Several of his guests went to the windows to look down into the town, wondering if something was on fire or if there had been a wreck. But when they saw the flashing lights driving through Jubilee and going up the mountain, Marsh commented.

"Likely some hillbilly blew up a still or a meth lab," he said, which elicited a roar of laughter from his big-city friends, and the party went on.

Much later, when everyone retired to their rooms to spend what was left of the night, they were too out of it to hear the second and third round of sirens.

Cameron was sick with worry by the time he pulled into the hospital parking lot. He recognized nearly a dozen vehicles, most of which belonged to family members. He parked near the ER entrance, then glanced down at Ghost. The dog was panting and whimpering, his tongue lolling to one side. It was a sure sign of the dog's pain and anxiety, and he hated that he was suffering.

"Stay, Ghost! I'll be right back. I just need to check on Lili before we get Sam out of bed, okay?"

Then he got out, locked the door, and ran inside, searching the faces in the lobby as he stopped at the desk. "Lili Glass. Where did they take her?" he asked.

The clerk looked up, recognized him as more of the family, and pointed. "Through the double doors, Cameron. At the end of the hall."

Still moving in haste, Cameron pushed the doors inward. He saw B. J. Kelly at the nurses' desk signing paperwork, and Fagan and Billy carrying fresh supplies to their ambulance. And then he saw the family, filling the entire north end of the corridor. All of them standing in total silence, watching the closed door to Room 7.

They turned en masse at the sound of Cameron's footsteps, then engulfed him with hugs, quick pats on the back, and whispered murmurs of "God bless you."

Cameron went straight to Marcus.

"How is she?" Cameron asked.

"We don't know. Rachel and Louis are in with the doctor," Marcus said.

"You're more patient that I am," Cameron muttered. He pushed past the crowd and slipped inside.

The sight of Lili's tiny body lying motionless beneath the covers and hooked up to all manner of machines and IVs was overwhelming. He stopped, in shock at the sight.

The doctor was still talking when Rachel heard the door open behind her. She turned, her eyes widening when she saw Cameron, but she said nothing.

Cameron saw the bandage on the side of Rachel's head and the darkening bruise on her jaw, and for a moment, he was sorry he'd let Danny Biggers live, but then he made himself focus on what the doctor was saying.

"Breathing is better. Blood pressure is stronger, but we're going to have to watch for other side effects. We'll know more in the next twenty-four hours," he said, and then noticed Cameron was in the room. "I'm sorry. And you are?"

Rachel answered for him. "Dr. Leeds, this is my brother, Cameron Pope. He's the one who found Lili."

"Good job, Mr. Pope," the doctor said. "You saved her life. Another hour and we'd be having an entirely different discussion here."

"Ghost did it," Cameron said.

Leeds was taken aback by the comment, and it showed. "A ghost?"

Cameron shook his head. "No, a dog. His name is Ghost. He was a bomb-sniffing dog in Iraq. He saved my ass more than once there. We came home together."

"You both did it," Louis said. "We'll never be able to thank you enough," and he gave Cameron's shoulder a quick squeeze.

The doctor eyed Cameron's face. "I'd say your face needs some attention, too. What happened?"

"It's just scratches from running through the woods in the dark. I'll heal. Is Lili going to intensive care?"

"Yes, for now," the doctor said.

Cameron frowned. "What about Rachel? Does she have a concussion?"

"A slight one," Dr. Leeds said.

Cameron eyes narrowed angrily as he turned to Rachel and Louis. "The sorry son of a bitch. This didn't have to happen. I want to know why you and Louis weren't notified he had escaped."

"I've already had that same discussion with local authorities," Louis said.

When Rachel moved back to Lili's bedside, Cameron followed.

"Rachel, honey, now that I know Lili's in good hands

and is going to recover, I won't stay. I need to get Ghost to the vet. He has a bad cut on his right front paw. I don't know when it happened but he never slowed down and never quit running. I didn't even know about it until I got him home and saw blood in the car seat and on the floorboard."

"Oh no! I'm so sorry," Rachel said. "That dog is amazing. He loves you so much, he'll do anything for you."

"Works both ways," Cameron said, and gave her a quick hug. "Give Lili my love. Tell her Uncle Cam says as soon as she's all better, he'll bring her cookies."

Rachel smiled through tears. "You two and your cookies. I'll tell her. And just so you know, Louis and I owe you forever."

"You owe me nothing. Call me to keep me updated on Lili, and go easy on yourself for a few days, too."

"I will. Now go see to Ghost. Between Louis and me, we have all kinds of extra help at our disposal."

Cameron passed the doctor on his way out of the room, but the moment he emerged, he was inundated again by the waiting family.

"The doctor says her prognosis is good. They are giving her something intravenously to offset the drugs Biggers gave her. She's going to the ICU out of caution. That's all I know. They'll be out soon and you can talk to them yourselves," he said, then walked back up the hall and disappeared through the double doors.

Still concerned about Ghost, he ran back to the Jeep, but he needn't have worried. Ghost was curled up in the passenger seat, and the bandage was still seeping fresh blood.

"Good boy," Cameron said as he slid in behind the steering wheel. "Now to get Sam out of bed."

He glanced at the time. It was just after 6:00 a.m. as he pulled up the vet's number and made the call, hoping Sam was not out on an emergency somewhere.

The call rang several times, and just when he thought it was going to voicemail, Sam Carson answered. "Hello. This is Sam."

"Sam, this is Cameron Pope. I hope I didn't get you out of bed, but Ghost is hurt and I'm in Jubilee. Can I bring him to the office?"

"Yes, of course. I was in the shower. What happened?"

"He's got a bad cut on his paw. It's a long story."

"Give me fifteen minutes. I should be at the office by then."

"Thanks, Sam. I really appreciate this," Cameron said, and hung up. Then he started the engine and drove away.

It took ten minutes to get across town to the vet's office. He was just pulling up in the parking lot when the lights began coming on in the office, and then Sam was standing in the front door, holding it open.

Cameron breathed a sigh of relief. Sam would know what to do.

"We're here, boy. I know you hurt, but Sam will make it better."

———

Sam Carson knew nothing about the kidnapping or the terror that had been on the mountain in the early hours of the morning. But when Cameron said it was a long story, he guessed something serious had happened.

He called Leslie Morgan, his vet tech, told her they had an emergency coming in and to meet him at the office, then quickly dressed and left his house on the run. He crossed the parking lot between his house and the clinic, unlocked the back door, and went inside, locking it behind him and turning on lights and turning up the heat as he went.

A few minutes later, he saw headlights through the front windows as they swept across the back wall. That would likely be Cameron. Leslie lived on the other side of Jubilee and it would take longer for her to arrive.

Sam went to the front door just as Cameron got out and circled the Jeep.

"Need help?" Sam called out.

"No, I've got him," Cameron said, and came toward the office carrying Ghost like a baby.

"First room on the left," Sam said, pointing across the lobby, then followed Cameron into the exam room.

Cameron laid Ghost on the table as Sam entered. Ghost wagged his tail when he saw Sam, but Sam was focused on the blood-soaked bandage on Ghost's right front paw.

"I washed it out as best I could and wrapped it so he wouldn't lick it, but the cut is deep and won't stop bleeding. I don't know how long he ran on that cut, but he never slowed down," Cameron said.

"Your face doesn't look so hot, either," Sam said as he

approached the exam table. "Hey, Ghost. I need to look at your paw, okay? Let's get this gauze off."

Ghost whined.

Cameron put his hand on Ghost's shoulder. "Stay, Ghost. You're okay. I'm here."

Sam frowned. "What the hell were you two doing?"

"Chasing a kidnapper up Pope Mountain."

Sam gasped. "What? Who got kidnapped, and how did you wind up in all that?"

"Remember Danny Biggers?" Cameron asked.

Sam paused, looking up in shock. "You mean the man who... Uh, your sister's attacker?"

"Yes. He was one of the inmates who broke out of Abercrombie. He attacked Rachel in the middle of the night and took Lili. Louis came home from work a few minutes later, found Rachel unconscious on the floor and Lili gone. They called the sheriff, and then they called the family, and every able man on the mountain came running with their dogs, including me and Ghost. I don't know when Ghost got hurt, but he never stopped running. He found Biggers with Lili, and by the time I caught up, Ghost had him begging for mercy."

"Oh, my God! Are Rachel and the baby okay?"

"Rachel's okay, more or less...and we think Lili's going to be okay, too. I just left the hospital. They're putting her in the ICU but she's showing good signs of recovery. Ghost is the one in need now."

"Absolutely," Sam said, and went back to unwinding the bandage from Ghost's paw. "Can you get him over on his side, please?"

Moments later, Cameron had Ghost stretched out on the table.

"That will do," Sam said as he stroked Ghost's massive head and moved closer. "I still can't get over his size. He's one of the biggest German shepherds I've ever seen. Now. Let's take a look at what's happened here."

Sam worked slowly, anxious not to cause undue pain, although when the big dog kept whining, he knew he was hurting him. A thorough cleaning of the wound revealed a deep, jagged cut and a continuous seeping of blood.

"This doesn't look good," Sam said. "I don't think it's going to heal properly without stitches, and that's going to mean putting him under."

"Whatever it takes," Cameron said.

They heard the front door open, then slam shut, and footsteps running through the lobby.

"That will be Leslie," Sam said, and he was right.

The young vet tech appeared in gray sweatpants and a matching sweatshirt, with her long blond hair in a messy ponytail on top of her head. She looked like she'd just crawled out of bed. Her eyes widened when she saw Cameron's scratched face and Ghost stretched out on the exam table.

"Hey, Les," Cameron said.

"Hey, Cam. Lord, what a night you've all had."

"You mean it's already common knowledge?" Sam asked.

Leslie smiled. "I may live in the valley, but my family is still on the mountain. Dad was one of the searchers."

And then her gaze shifted. "Dr. Sam, what do you need me to do?"

"Scrub up, then get a tray ready. We're going to have to put Ghost to sleep to stitch up the cut on his foot. I'll need you to monitor his oxygen levels and heart rate after he's out."

"Yes, sir," she said, and raced into the adjoining room.

Cameron stayed beside Ghost until they got him to sleep and then moved out of the way, letting them do their job.

He glanced out the window. The sun was up. Then he looked at the clock as Sam began trimming hair away from between the toe pads on Ghost's paw. It was just after seven, and yesterday felt like an eternity away.

———————

Sam Carson finished the surgery on Ghost and gave him a shot to reverse the anesthetic and another shot for pain, then handed Cameron a small bottle of antibiotics as Ghost was coming around.

"Keep him off his feet as much as possible, and bring him back in three days to get the bandages replaced," Sam said.

"Thanks to the both of you," Cameron said. "Sorry to get you up so early."

"That's what we do," Sam said. "Take care of yourself while you're at it. Some of those scratches on your face could qualify as cuts."

"They'll heal," Cameron said, then scooped Ghost up in his arms. The dog was still groggy as he carried him out.

Leslie ran ahead of them opening doors and then helping get Ghost settled in the front seat of Cameron's Jeep.

"You tell Rachel and Louis we're all praying for Lili."

"I will. Thanks for helping out," Cameron said, and drove away.

Leslie sighed as she watched him leave.

Cameron Pope was gorgeous, and single, and just the teeniest bit intimidating. Everyone knew he'd spent two tours of duty in Iraq and Afghanistan, yet he never talked about it. Still, Ghost was a daily reminder because when Cameron Pope finally came home from the wars, Ghost was with him.

Her daddy said Pope had been Special Forces.

Her uncle said Ghost had been a bomb-sniffing dog and had saved Cameron's life.

All Leslie knew was that the boy she remembered was not the man who came home.

By the time Cameron got home, he was exhausted and Ghost was asleep. He got out quietly and once again lifted his dog from the seat. As he did, Ghost whined.

"I know, boy. I know. But we're home, and you're going to be okay," he said, and carried the dog into the house, then took him into his bedroom and laid him on a pile of blankets on the floor beside his bed.

The moment Ghost was among familiar surroundings and next to his human, he went limp and closed his eyes.

Satisfied that all was well for now, Cameron went back through the house, locking everything up and turning out lights. He checked his phone to make sure Rachel hadn't called, then stripped down and showered before crawling into bed.

The sheets were cool. The room was warm. He rolled over on his belly and fell asleep.

Once Biggers had been taken into custody, Sheriff Woodley had been forced to accept Rachel and Louis's story about the abduction. He knew he needed to make peace with the Glass family before he returned to the office, so he drove to the hospital to check on the child's condition and found both parents in the waiting room of the ICU.

"Louis. Rachel. How are you doing, and how is your daughter?" he asked.

"I have the headache from hell and, no thanks to any of you, my baby is alive," Rachel muttered.

Woodley flushed, but he had the good sense not to challenge her.

Louis could tell Rachel was too angry with the police to talk. He was disgusted with how they'd been treated, but he wanted details.

"Where is Danny Biggers right now?" Louis asked.

"He's being treated for his wounds, but he'll be going

back to prison. We were contacted by federal marshals who've been on his trail, and we now know that the car he was driving was stolen, as was the phone he was using. The owners were found tied up in their home but unharmed."

"There's something about this whole incident that makes no sense," Louis said. "Biggers had no relationship with Rachel. He had no bond whatsoever with Lili. And yet when he escaped, this was where he came. How did he know where we live, and why come all this way after *our* baby?"

Woodley leaned forward, resting his elbows on his knees. He was tired and ready for bed and had a mountain of reports to write. "We don't know, but the kidnapping moves this into the hands of federal prosecutors. The FBI will take over this case."

Rachel shuddered. "I don't get why Danny Biggers would target me again. He was shocked it was me. I saw it on his face. He didn't know or care who the child belonged to and wasn't expecting to see anyone he knew," she said. "This is a nightmare."

Louis hugged her, pulling her close. "But Biggers didn't succeed, honey. And all of the laws he broke after he escaped will be added to his sentence. He'll still be behind bars when we're old and gray," he said.

"Again, I'm sorry for all the misunderstanding, but in my business, everyone is suspect until proven otherwise," Woodley said.

Rachel glared. "Misunderstanding? Bullshit! You knew the connection between me and Danny Biggers before you ever arrived on the scene! So now I'm thinking you're the biggest fool walking to think I'd be in on my own daughter's kidnapping with the man who raped me. And if it hadn't been for Uncle John finding the abandoned car, and our people and my brother searching, my baby girl would be gone."

Then she got up and walked out of the room.

Woodley's face was an angry red, but he didn't have a decent rebuttal and he knew it.

Louis wasn't about to apologize for what Rachel had said, because she'd spoken nothing but the truth. He waited until Woodley left, then went to look for Rachel. He found her in the chapel on her knees, her head down, praying.

Without saying a word, he knelt down beside her and lowered his head.

Frankfort, Kentucky

Special Agents Jay Howard and Dan Pickard of the FBI were part of a team investigating human trafficking. They'd been staking out a certain group for months, trying to link them to more than a dozen missing person cases in a tri-state area, and more recently to a surge of missing babies and toddlers.

One suspected member of the group was a woman named Lindy Sheets. The FBI team believed she was working as bait, befriending teens and single women, then luring them into traps. They knew Sheets was also a regular visitor to an inmate named Daniel Lee Biggers, who was serving time in Abercrombie Penitentiary for assault and rape.

When the team learned Biggers had been one of the escapees, it was nothing more than a point of interest, until they found out some hours later that Biggers had stolen a car and a cell phone from an elderly couple in Frankfort and left them tied up in their house, then drove all the way to Jubilee, Kentucky, where he assaulted a woman and kidnapped her three-year-old child. That's when the FBI agents' internal radar pinged.

It was just after daylight when they learned Biggers had already been caught by some local searchers, and both he and the child were being treated in a small hospital in Jubilee. Within minutes, Howard was on the phone.

———

Jubilee Police Chief Sonny Warren hadn't gone home last night. Even though County had been in charge of the assault and abduction, Sonny had been born and raised on Pope Mountain. He'd been shocked by what happened and worried sick until he found out Lili Glass had been rescued and Danny Biggers captured.

Relieved, he thought that would be the end of it. He was about to leave the office long enough to go home to shower and change clothes before beginning his day when his phone rang.

"Jubilee Police. Chief Warren speaking."

"Good morning, Chief. This is Special Agent Jay Howard of the FBI. I'm out of the state headquarters located in Frankfort. I understand there is an escaped prisoner named Danny Biggers being treated in your hospital. Is that correct?"

Sonny blinked. "Uh, yes, sir."

"We need to talk to him regarding an ongoing case. I need a hold and multiple guards put on him until we arrive. We're coming in by chopper from Frankfort, and we'll need a car at our disposal for a few hours. I take it you have a heliport somewhere?"

"A few," Sonny said. "One behind the police station. One at the hospital, and a couple at the area hotels. I'll make sure there's a car waiting for you."

"Do you have Biggers's personal effects and the vehicle he was driving?" Howard asked.

"They would be with Sheriff Woodley, who headed the pursuit."

"Then I'll be needing the sheriff's contact information," Howard said.

"Yes, sir. Shall I text it to the number you're calling from?"

"Please," Howard said. "See you soon."

The line went dead. The chief pulled up the number for County and sent it to Howard's phone. He already had a guard on Biggers's room, but now it seemed one was not enough, so he made a quick call to one of his officers and sent him straight to the hospital to double the guard.

Back in Frankfort, Howard was organizing a helicopter

to get them to Jubilee, while Special Agent Pickard was on the phone with Sheriff Woodley.

———————

Woodley was in his office still writing up reports when his phone rang. He paused, and then turned away from the computer to answer.

"This is Woodley."

"Sheriff Woodley. This is Special Agent Dan Pickard, Frankfort FBI. We understand you headed the search for Danny Biggers and the recovery of a child he'd kidnapped. Is that correct?"

Woodley sat up straighter. "Yes. That's correct."

"I've also been told that you have Biggers's personal effects."

"Yes, but there wasn't much on him. We confiscated the stolen car he'd been driving and the stolen phone he'd been using."

"We'll be sending a forensic team to go over the car, and we'll be needing everything you confiscated, including that phone. My partner and I are on our way to Jubilee to talk to Biggers. If you could get all that to Chief Warren as soon as possible, we would appreciate it. We're operating on a really tight schedule here, and time is of the essence."

"Yes, sir. I'll bring it myself," Woodley said, and then his skin crawled when the line went dead in his ear.

He hit Save on the report he'd been typing, then went to the evidence room, checked out the evidence folder with

Biggers's money and phone, told the dispatcher where he was going, and headed back to the police station in Jubilee.

━━━━━━━━

Danny Biggers was in misery. They took him to surgery to stitch up his wounds. Not because they were serious enough for surgery. It was just to keep the Glass family from finding him and finishing him off. After they stitched up his arms and legs, and shot him full of antibiotics and painkillers, they moved him to a different floor of the hospital.

Danny knew he had a guard at the door, and that the federal marshals would show up to take his ass back to prison, but he doubted he would be there long. He'd just added about a lifetime of years to his sentence with another violent assault, and now kidnapping, which was a federal offense.

He thought of Lindy waiting for him to show up at Fuzzy Fridays and the years of confinement he had ahead of him now. Lindy wasn't the faithful kind, but then neither was he. He'd given up worrying about what he couldn't control, so he turned his face to the wall and closed his eyes.

Piece-of-shit car.

Stupid kid.

Fucking dog.

Damn Cameron Pope to hell.

He was drifting in and out of dreamland from all the opiates in his system when the door to his room flew open and two men in dark suits walked in. He knew before they opened their mouths they were feds.

Then they flashed their badges and proved him right.

"Daniel Lee Biggers. I'm Special Agent Howard, and this is my partner, Special Agent Pickard. We need to talk to you."

Biggers eyed them closely. Howard was built like a linebacker and bowling-ball bald. Pickard had pale-green eyes and a scar across his right cheek.

"I'm not talking to anyone without a lawyer," Danny muttered.

"That's your right," Howard said. "But you need to know that a lawyer can't save you or change one aspect of the justice that's coming to you. You have just added robbery, theft, another four counts of violent assault, and one count of kidnapping to your sentence, and it'll be up to the judge how many years they add on to all of that for participating in human trafficking."

Danny's gut knotted. "I didn't traffic anybody," he muttered.

"That's because you got caught in the process," Howard said. "Lindy Sheets has been visiting you in prison."

Danny frowned. "So what? She's my girlfriend. I'm allowed visitors in prison."

Then Pickard unloaded.

"She's also a prime suspect in a human-trafficking ring. And you just kidnapped someone else's daughter and got caught on your way to meet Lindy Sheets at a drop-off location. Don't bother denying it because we traced your texts to her from the phone you had on your person. You thought you were going to sell the little girl for big money, didn't you?"

"I got nothin' to say to you," Danny said.

Pickard snorted. "Biggers, you're obviously not very smart. Mean. But not very smart. You need to be grateful you got caught, because if you'd made the drop expecting to get paid for the kid, you would have gotten a bullet in the back of your head for your trouble. That's how this gang works. They promise big money for kids, teenage boys, and pretty women, and kill the person who delivers them. They're eliminating the middle man, selling to an Asian and European market, and keeping all the money."

Danny's stomach roiled. "You're lying."

Howard shrugged. "No, we're just stating facts. And since you are now linked to one of their contacts and got caught, your life isn't worth two cents, and I doubt hers is, either."

Danny broke out into a cold sweat. "You gotta protect me."

"We don't 'gotta' do anything but send you back to jail," Howard said. "Unless you want to help us catch them. But that's up to you. Still want to talk to that lawyer? Or do you want to wait for the other shoe to fall?"

Danny groaned. "What do you want to know?"

"Why did you go back to the house of a woman you'd raped?"

Danny's shoulders slumped. "I didn't know it was her. I just went to pick up the kid and take her to a drop-off."

"Why would they want an escaped prisoner to do that? They had to know the authorities would be looking for you."

Danny's eyes narrowed, and then he sighed. He'd gotten himself into this, but he wasn't taking the rap for anyone. He didn't know anyone but Lindy, and he had no loyalty to her.

"I might have mentioned something to Lindy about the riot and escape before it happened. She might have mentioned something to the effect that if I made it out, I should give her a call. She had a job I could do to make some quick money to disappear. So I made it out. I called her. But when she told me what the job was, I almost turned it down. I didn't want anything to do with snatching a kid, and I damn sure wasn't moving up to murdering parents to do it. And then she said, 'Ten thousand dollars.'" He paused, groaning as a ripple of pain rolled through him. "I grew up in this area. I know the mountains. I know every shortcut and switchback to be taken to get over the mountains to the drop-off point. And I thought I could do it and get away."

"Except you didn't," Howard said. "You stole a piece-of-shit car. You came face-to-face with a woman who already knew who you were. You left her alive, and from the sheriff's report, her brother and his dog ran you to ground on that mountain and caught your ass. And you've made yourself a liability to the crooks who trusted you. So you weren't so smart after all."

Danny was bordering on tears. "You have to protect me."

"You'll be behind bars. That's protection," Pickard added.

Danny shouted. "No, dammit! You know they can get to me there, too. Don't take me back to where I was."

"No worries on that. You lost your lease on ever being incarcerated in medium security again," Howard said. "Kidnapping is a federal offense. You'll be doing time in a federal prison."

Chapter 4

LINDY SHEETS WAS GETTING NERVOUS. SHE'D WAITED AT Fuzzy Fridays until sunup. Danny wasn't answering the texts she'd sent, and he should have been here by now. Something had gone wrong. It was time to let Boss know. She made the call. He answered on the second ring, and as always, just the sound of his voice made her shudder because she'd witnessed what he was capable of.

"What?"

"Something's wrong. Biggers didn't show and he's not answering my calls."

"Then dump your phone and get out of the state. When you get settled, contact me. If he's been captured with the kid, you're linked to the kidnapping by being the drop-off contact, and that links you to me."

"We don't know that! He might be in hiding. And don't talk to me like I'm expendable! You know me and you owe me. I don't rat on anybody!"

"And I don't take chances. Do what I said," he countered.

Lindy's stomach pitched. She had to disappear. This man didn't leave loose ends. Anywhere. She disconnected and drove home. Dropped her phone down a storm drain, packed her clothes, left her car locked up in the parking lot of her apartment building, and started walking, pulling her suitcase behind her as she went.

———

It was nearing ten the same morning when Liz Caldwell came out of her room. She was still in her pajamas and a housecoat, and rubbing sleep from her eyes as she headed for the dining area to see if the breakfast buffet was still on the sideboard.

To her delight, it was still there, and warm. She got coffee, bacon, and a flaky croissant, and carried it all to the table.

Her mother walked in just as Liz was taking her first sip of coffee and frowned at the food on her daughter's plate.

"Good morning, darling. Don't you want some eggs with that? A portion of protein is important, too."

Liz picked up a strip of bacon. "Protein, Mother. As you suggested," she said and took a big bite.

Patricia rolled her eyes and poured herself a cup of coffee before joining Liz at the table.

"Aren't you having anything?" Liz asked.

"I've already eaten with your father. I'm just rambling about up here, trying to decide what to do with myself," she drawled, and then rolled her eyes. "I mean, there's so much culture and charm in this place, I simply can't decide."

Liz laughed. She knew her mother hated it here. New York City or London or Paris were places more suited to Patricia Caldwell's tastes.

"Did you hear all the sirens in the night?" Liz asked as she kept eating.

Patricia rolled her eyes. "I would have had to be deaf not to. God knows what was going on up there. Your father said police cars and ambulances went up the mountain and then came straggling back later."

Liz shrugged. "Accidents can happen anywhere, Mother. And people get sick or hurt, regardless of their bank accounts."

Patricia shrugged. "I suppose. I'd love a swim, but I'd rather lick boots than mingle with the tourists in the hotel pool. I don't know why your father is so dead set on living here. We could still own this and live elsewhere. Even if it is the penthouse, living on the premises makes me feel so… innkeeper's wife."

Liz said nothing. Her mother's dissatisfaction with life had little to do with where they slept and more to do with herself. If her daddy wasn't so rich, her mother would be long gone, chasing rainbows for the next best thing.

━━━━━━

Marsh Devon was at the heliport seeing his investors safely off, and nursing a hangover headache. Thankfully, the big chopper was already coming in for a landing, and then they'd soon be gone. Three were flying back to Boston, and the other two would be going on to New York City. It had been a successful meeting for Marsh. He was in the planning stages to develop new off-campus housing in

Lexington, near the University of Kentucky, and now he had the capital to follow through.

The day was sunny but cold, and Marsh was dreading spending another winter in these mountains. He loved the snow and he loved to ski, but this wasn't a place for skiing. The mountains were heavily forested, the area didn't get that kind of snow, and even more to the point, cutting down even one tree around here could get a man arrested. If it wasn't for the year-round music venues, the upcoming holidays, and the charm of the village shops, there would be no winter tourist trade.

But his son, Michael, had several years of hotel management under his belt now, and Marsh was hoping to put Michael in charge of Hotel Devon, leaving himself free to set up residence in Lexington to oversee the new housing development going up. There were standards he wanted to maintain in this hotel, and keeping Michael in charge would assure that. The more tourists he drew away from the Serenity Inn, the better he liked it.

Jack Barton was the other hotelier catering to tourists, but his location was two miles outside of Jubilee and geared to the budget tourists. He'd bypassed the restrictions that came with doing business with PCG Inc., the corporation that owned the land on which Jubilee was built, and bought land on the highway outside of their holdings.

He'd built tiny cabins for family sleeping accommodations rather than just another high-rise hotel, and this past year, he'd expanded his camping area for RVs and travel trailers. Come next spring, he was planning to develop an on-site water feature of some kind. Maybe a large pool with a water slide and a concession area. He was the new kid on the block but determined to suck up some of the profits from the Devons and the Caldwells.

His living quarters were in the attached log house at the back of the office. He'd just come up front to open the office and check new online reservations when the door opened and two men in dark suits walked in. Before he could speak, they flashed their badges and introduced themselves.

"Mr. Barton, I'm Special Agent Howard, and this is my partner, Special Agent Pickard. We need to ask you some questions."

"Of course. Take a seat," Jack said, and then frowned. "So. The FBI? What's going on?"

"We just have a few questions. It won't take long."

Jack shrugged. "Ask away."

"Do you do long-term rentals in your tiny cabins?" Howard asked.

Jack frowned. "What do you mean by long-term?"

"Someone renting on a monthly basis," Howard said.

"Not in the tiny cabins. I'd have to check registration about the camping areas."

"Would you do that, please? We'll wait," Pickard said.

Jack turned to the computer, pulled up registration

records, and began scanning through the list. "I have one campsite registered to a college student who's been here since the first week of July. He spends most of his time in the woods studying something or other."

"What's his name and where's the campsite located?" Pickard asked.

"Kevin Vanzant. He has a travel trailer set up at Campsite 22 at the north end of the property."

"How do we get there?" Howard asked.

"Just follow the road in front of this office and take the north fork that goes into the forest beyond the cabins. The sites are numbered. Stay on the main road and you can't miss it."

"Would you be willing to rent one of the cabins on a monthly basis?" Howard asked.

Jack shrugged. "Sure, but there's no price break for a long-term rental. Cabins are $125 a night and sleep four. A mini-kitchen/living/dining area. A single bathroom. One queen-size bed downstairs. Twin beds up in the little loft."

"Do you have problems with people who leave without notifying you, or people who skip out without paying up?"

"Occasionally, but they all leave a credit card number at the office when they register, so we just charge them and email them a receipt."

"We're going to need a list of those names from this past July to date."

Jack frowned. "That will take some time."

Howard nodded. "We want to visit Campsite 22 and

talk to Mr. Vanzant, so we'll stop back by the office on our way out, okay?"

"Yes. I'll have the list for you then," Jack said, and was already searching back files as he heard them drive away.

———

Pickard was driving toward the RV park, and Howard was riding shotgun.

"What do you think?" Howard asked.

"If this Vanzant dude seems sketchy, I think we need to get an undercover agent in here. According to the info I have pulled up here, when Biggers first attacked Rachel Pope, she was still living at home with her mother. Biggers has been in prison for four years. He wouldn't know where Rachel was now, and why would he care? I think somebody sent him for this specific kid."

Howard nodded. "I agree, and I think our undercover needs to be female. If there's a branch of the trafficking ring working out of this isolated tourist attraction, a single female suddenly appearing on her own should be the lure we need to catch them in the act."

They drove until they reached the campsite and saw the setup of Vanzant's travel trailer, but neither he nor his vehicle were anywhere to be seen.

The trailer was locked. They poked around outside to no avail, then went back to the office to pick up the list, then headed back to the chopper. They needed to get back to the office to run the names on the list through NamUs, the National Missing and Unidentified Persons System database, and also get background on Kevin Vanzant.

―――――――――

It was nearing sundown when Kevin Vanzant returned to his trailer. He'd been in Jubilee most of the day, completely unaware he'd caught the attention of the FBI.

Out of habit, he dumped his camera and laptop inside and then went back out to check the trail cameras around his camp. It wasn't unusual to catch people walking along the paths or the occasional visit from Jack Barton, the owner of the campground, but he was completely unprepared for the two men in dark suits who appeared on camera poking around outside the trailer and then actually trying the locked door.

At that moment, the hair crawled on the back of his neck. Men in black? All that was lacking from their wardrobes were Ray-Bans. He saw them pause to look around the area and then get back in their car and drive away.

"Shit. What was that all about?" he muttered, then reset the camera and ran into the trailer.

He spent the next few minutes going through everything inside, looking for hidden cameras or anything they might have bugged, but found nothing suspicious and nothing had gone missing.

Then he sat down on the corner of the bed and made a call. It rang twice before the call was picked up.

"Yeah?"

"It's me, Boss. Are we on the radar?"

"Why?"

Kevin quickly related what he'd seen.

"I'm already on that. If you are, we'll let you know," Boss said.

Kevin sighed. "Okay, thanks. I just—"

The line went dead in his ear.

━━━━━

Lili Glass woke up in the ICU crying for her mother.

It was the best news Rachel and Louis could have received. Within a short time, Lili had been moved into a regular room, and from there into her mother's arms.

Rachel sat down with her in one of the recliners, wrapped Lili up in a heated blanket, and rocked her back to sleep, while Louis left the room to make some calls. This was the news their family had been waiting for, and Cameron was the first person Louis called.

━━━━━

It was nearing 2:00 p.m. and Cameron had been up for hours. He'd tried to go back to sleep after he got Ghost home from the vet, but it wasn't long before he heard Ghost whining and knew he was in pain. After that, he got up and had been up taking care of the dog ever since.

One look in the mirror was all the proof he needed to know his face was too cut up to shave, and the shadow of black whiskers on his face just added to his lone-wolf persona. Lili was in God's hands. Ghost would heal. His face would heal. He'd shave off the whiskers, and life would go on.

It was just after lunch when he took Ghost outside and settled him on the back porch, then headed to the woodpile beside the old barn and started chopping up blocks of wood for firewood. He'd been at it for almost an hour when his cell phone rang. When he realized the call was from Louis, he swung the ax down into a block and answered.

"Hello?"

"Cam, it's me, Louis. Lili woke up, crying for her mother. She's going to be okay. The doctors have moved her out of the ICU. We wanted you to be the first to know."

"Thank God, and thank you for letting me know. I know you're going to be inundated with visitors now. I'll wait until you get to bring her home to come get my hug."

"Awesome," Louis said. "By the way, how's Ghost?"

"Not his usual self, for sure. He has stitches in his foot, so I'm babying him for a while."

"Bless that dog," Louis said. "You take care of your baby and we'll take care of ours, and when Ghost can handle it, bring him with you to see Lili. She loves that dog almost as much as she loves you."

Cameron was still smiling when Louis disconnected, then he let out a whoop.

"Hallelujah!" he shouted, and then grabbed the ax, yanked it out of the wood, and kept on working.

Ghost's head came up, but he didn't move. He was

waiting for orders. When they didn't come, he laid his chin back on his paws, his eyes following every swing of the ax and every step Cameron took.

———————

Cameron stacked what he'd cut, stored his tools, then grabbed an armload of firewood and headed for the house. It was a couple of hours before sundown and the air was noticeably colder than it had been earlier. Cameron hadn't seen a weather report all day, but from the looks of the sky, they were in for some rain. Ghost stood as Cameron came up the steps and hobbled into the house behind him. Cameron kicked the door shut and kept walking, carrying the wood into the living room and stacking it by the fireplace before starting a fire. He added a couple of logs to the flaming kindling, turned up the thermostat to warm up the house, fed Ghost, then went to clean up.

Ghost was back in his bed by the fireplace by the time Cameron came to the front of the house again. He paused to check the bandage, then stroked the big dog's head before going to the kitchen to make himself something to eat.

He was living a solitary existence by choice, but there were times, like today, when he missed his parents and the family they had been.

At this time of day his mother would have had supper cooking, and his dad would be coming in from the barn with a bucket of fresh milk to be strained. Rachel would have been playing in a corner with one of the barn cats, hoping their mother didn't notice she'd dragged it in the house again. Looking back, Cameron realized their mother always noticed. She just didn't always say anything about it.

But that was then, and this was now. His dad had died almost ten years ago, and his mother just before Lili was born. Cameron came home to this house after his second tour of duty ended and never went back.

He turned on the television in the kitchen, pulled out a cast-iron skillet, washed a couple of potatoes, and sliced them up to fry. While they were cooking in the hot oil, he grilled a hamburger steak, got a container of deli coleslaw from the refrigerator, then sat down at the table, keeping an eye on the news as he ate.

When they segued into a commercial with a lead for the story up next, he heard them say "Danny Lee Biggers, escaped prisoner" and "kidnapping," and looked up. His heart sank. It was inevitable that they would drag up the past. The sensationalism of a rapist returning to the scene of the crime was too big to ignore.

Just as he'd feared, they started with the backstory, then segued into the escape and everything that had ensued afterward. What Cameron hadn't expected was so much focus on Lili's rescue. Much emphasis had been given to the families on Pope Mountain who took to the woods with their hunting dogs to track Biggers down, and that the child's uncle, Cameron Pope, and his dog, Ghost, were the ones who found Biggers and rescued Lili.

He changed the channel and got up from the table. He'd lost his appetite and he still had to clean up the kitchen.

The Caldwells were having drinks in the den before dinner and watching the national newscast. Ray was waiting for stock market reports when they heard the journalist on air mention Jubilee, an escaped prisoner, a kidnapping, and a dramatic rescue.

Their conversation ceased.

"That must be what all those sirens were about last night," Ray said.

Patricia shuddered. "These mountains and the people who live up there give me the creeps."

But when the story began, prejudice was put aside by the horror of what had happened. As for Liz, once she heard Cameron Pope's name and his part in the rescue, she drifted off into a fantasy of her own where Cameron Pope's mad race up the mountain had been to save her. They would make passionate love afterward, and—

She sighed. Through all of her daydreams and hot flashes about having sex with the man, her fantasies never took her past the sex. Everything faded after that. It was absurd that she was so fixated on him when they'd never even been introduced. Even when she was making love to Michael Devon, she closed her eyes and pretended he was Cameron Pope.

And then she realized her father was talking to her.

"So, my darling daughter, what do you think?" Ray asked.

Liz blinked. "Think about what?"

Ray frowned. "You didn't hear a word I said. I repeat, I would like you to accompany me to a dinner in Frankfort tomorrow night. We'll take the chopper, of course, which means your mother won't be going. It's kind of a big deal for the Serenity Inn. Our chef is receiving his third Michelin star rating."

"Oh. Sure, I'd love to," Liz said. "Do I get to dress up?"

"No ball gown, but definitely after-five wear," Ray said.

Liz smiled. She did so like to sparkle.

The rain came, just as Cameron suspected. He woke to the sound of it hitting the roof and got up to look out. Ghost barely stirred as Cameron pulled a blanket up over the dog's back.

It was just after midnight.

The house was chilly, but instead of turning up the thermostat, Cameron put a log on the still-glowing embers in the fireplace and then moved to the front windows. Rain was pouring off the roof and running in rivulets down the gentle slope of the clearing. Everything in the forest had taken shelter, and he couldn't help but think how lucky they were that it hadn't been raining when Biggers took Lili. Tracking in this downpour would have been impossible.

And then he caught a glimpse of his own reflection and almost didn't recognize himself. Some days he felt a thousand years old and on others barely out of his teens.

As his focus shifted back to the rain, he remembered

it had been raining the morning he left Angel asleep in her bed. The trip back to the front lines outside of Kabul had been endless and full of regret. He would be sorry for the rest of his life that he never said goodbye and that he didn't know her last name.

Suddenly Ghost was beside him. He whined and then bumped his head against the back of his master's leg.

"It's raining like hell, boy. You sure you want to go out in this?"

Ghost looked up.

Cameron opened the door and out Ghost went, disappearing into the downpour. Cameron left the door ajar and ran to get a towel, and when Ghost came back, he mopped him up as best he could, then settled him down in his bed by the fire to finish drying. Sleep, it seemed, had abandoned the both of them, but Cameron was too antsy to watch TV, and he didn't want to read.

Instead, he poured himself a shot of whiskey and downed it neat, then pulled a throw pillow and a big blanket from the back of the sofa and curled up on the floor beside his dog. The heat from the fire felt good on his feet. Ghost whined again, and Cameron guessed walking out in the rain had hurt his paw.

"I'm sorry, boy," he said softly, then thrust his fingers through the thick ruff of fur at the dog's neck and stared into the fire.

Finally, his eyes closed, and when he woke again, it was morning. The rain had stopped and water was dripping from everything in sight.

Special Agents Howard and Pickard had made a discovery. Five of the names from Jack Barton's list were on NamUs, the national missing and unidentified persons registry. Three of the names were before Kevin Vanzant's arrival at the campground. Two since, or three if you counted the recently rescued baby. Vanzant's presence could just be coincidence, but the fact that all of them had passed through Barton's property, or from the community of Jubilee, now made the agents suspicious of the owner as well.

Initially, they were confused as to why someone had yet to make a connection between all these missing people and Jubilee, until they dug further and found out that Jubilee was not the last place the missing people's credit cards had been used. Each of those who'd gone missing had purchases on those cards in other parts of the state, supposedly after they'd left the area.

But Howard wasn't convinced.

"What if this is just a ploy?" he asked. "What if these women have been sold into human trafficking? Their luggage and personal effects would have gone with them. I know this is a long shot, but Jubilee would be a mecca for that. What if the gang took the women, then used their clothing and credit cards to mislead the authorities on their last known locations? They could dress up females of the gang and send them to different places across the tristate area to use the cards, and no one would ever know all the women had actually gone missing from here."

Pickard blinked.

"If that's happening, it's brilliant. But how do we prove this? Capturing Biggers has spooked the people we've had under surveillance in Frankfort. All of a sudden, they're nowhere to be found. And I just got info that Lindy Sheets's car is still parked at her last known residence, but her personal belongings from that room are gone. We're either going to find her body, or she's on the run."

Howard frowned. "This changes everything. We need someone on-site in Jubilee. A new face in a town full of strangers will go unnoticed. I need to call the director."

Chapter 5

RUSTY CALDWELL WAS IN THE HOT TUB ON THE BACK DECK of her Virginia town house with a glass of wine in one hand and a pimiento cheese sandwich in the other. When she'd first returned home, she'd slept for sixteen straight hours before making herself get out of bed, and then reality set in.

Since she hadn't been home in days, no laundry had been done, and there was no food in the refrigerator. She was too sore to even think about going out, so for the past week, she'd shopped online and had the groceries delivered.

Being the loner she was had merits, but the downside was having no one for backup. Her mother had been gone for six years. She'd died from a heart attack, and her father died last year from cancer. Her extended family consisted of her dad's brother, Ray, his wife, Patricia, and their daughter, Liz, who was five years younger than Rusty. The two families had never lived close to each other, and losing her parents had not changed that, so when Rusty needed downtime, she spent it alone.

This particular downtime was meant for healing and she was taking full advantage of it, soaking in the hot tub with a facsimile of cheese and wine.

The water was hot and bubbling, and she groaned with

appreciation as she shifted position and took another bite, then chewed and swallowed before washing it down with another sip.

On a good day, she would not have taken food to the hot tub, or gulped wine like it was water, but this wasn't a good day. She finished the sandwich in record time and emptied her glass, then leaned back and let the heat and the jets do their thing.

She'd been in a bad spot on this job and, not for the first time, had come far too close to being sent home in a body bag. The job was her life, and her life was the job. It was all she had going for her. There were no personal relationships. Not now. Not ever. But she was beginning to regret that.

She leaned back in the tub and closed her eyes, remembering the soldier boy and their one night long ago.

She'd never believed in love at first sight until him. Her biggest regret was not asking where he was from, or finding out his last name, and when she woke up the next morning and found him gone, she knew he'd taken part of her with him. So she buried herself in the job to the point of obsession, traveling wherever she was sent, pushing herself to the limits of endurance, always in the hope she'd see him again. Maybe in an airport or another hotel lobby.

She knew he'd been going back to a war zone. But she'd never let herself believe he died there. She always pictured him going home. She needed that fantasy—to believe he was still alive somewhere. Then when she was at the point of breaking from the loneliness of her life, she would dream of him again, and it would be enough.

Finally, the timer on the hot tub went off. She turned loose of wanting the impossible and climbed out, leaving wet footprints on the tile as she went back inside. The body aches were better. The hunger pangs had been momentarily assuaged, and she had sanctuary.

Hours later, she was caught up on laundry, paperwork, and bills, and was sitting cross-legged on the floor in sweatpants and a long-sleeved tee, scanning social media.

Her stomach growled, reminding her that her cheese sandwich and wine were long gone. So she reached for the phone, ordered her usual from the Chinese restaurant down the street, then went to the living room and refilled her wineglass. Two was her daily limit, and food was coming.

She settled herself into an overstuffed recliner and turned on the television, then scanned the channels for HGTV and settled in to watch a house being remodeled. It was mindless entertainment that required nothing but intermittent attention, which suited her mood.

When her order arrived, she carried it to the kitchen, opened up all the little boxes and filled her plate with some of everything, ignored the chopsticks and grabbed a fork before going back to the television to eat. It smelled divine, tasted delicious, and she ate with all the focus she gave to a weeklong stakeout.

She was down to breaking open the fortune cookie when her cell phone rang. One glance and her eyebrows arched. It was a call from her boss. She set the plate aside to answer.

"Good evening, sir," she said.

"Good evening, Agent Caldwell. I trust you're getting some rest."

"Yes, sir," Rusty said.

"I know you've just come off a stressful situation, and this is very short notice, but we have a problem. I understand you have close relatives who live in a place called Jubilee, Kentucky."

"Yes, sir. My uncle and his family. The town is something of a tourist attraction. He runs a big hotel there."

"And do they live there year round?" the director asked.

"They did. I assume they still do, but I've never visited them there. In fact, I haven't seen them since I joined the agency. We stay in contact by texting and the occasional phone call."

"I see. Well, we have this situation, and we need someone on-site. It's strictly information gathering. No strenuous or subversive work. Nothing like your usual assignments. Just you on holiday, checking out the sights, and no one would be the wiser."

Rusty stifled a sigh. When duty called, and all that. "Yes, sir. Of course," she said.

"Excellent. You'll be working with Special Agents Howard and Pickard out of the Frankfort office. Howard will be calling you with details of what's going on, what they need, and giving you the lowdown on their case."

"Yes, sir. Do you have any idea of when I am expected to arrive?"

"Probably yesterday," the director said, and then chuckled.

"Then I'd better call Uncle Ray and let him know that his prodigal niece will be paying them a visit," Rusty said.

She noticed the fortune cookie as she disconnected and broke it open. The moment she read it, a wave of foreboding washed over her.

An unresolved issue from your past awaits conclusion.

She'd had too many scary moments from her past, and bad people who'd escaped justice. The last thing she needed was a repeat of one of those. And she needed to call her family in Jubilee to see how they felt about an unexpected guest. She glanced at the time. Just after 9:00 p.m. Unless the family's living habits had changed, their night was still young.

―――――――――

The nightlife in Jubilee was just beginning. Music venues were in full swing. The hotel bars were packed with people drinking and watching televised sports on big-screen TVs hanging from every wall.

The hotels with indoor pools were full of families and screaming children. If it hadn't been for the soundproof walls in the penthouse above it all, Patricia Caldwell would have been on the next plane to New York.

Normally, she would have had her husband and daughter for company, but they'd gone to Frankfort for the award banquet. And because she was afraid of flying in helicopters, she was alone tonight.

She'd eaten dinner and was on her second chocolate martini with her feet to the fire and leafing through a magazine. Some people took a second helping of pie. Her desserts included alcohol. It seemed like a fair trade. But because of the cold weather tonight, she'd abandoned the balcony for the warmth of the gas logs. She was eyeing the hair color on a model in the magazine, wondering if she was too old to try something that outrageous, when her phone rang. She answered it, assuming it would be Ray or Liz, telling her they were on their way home.

"Hello."

"Hello, Aunt Pat, it's me, Rusty."

Patricia's boredom immediately shifted to joy. "Rusty! Darling! How wonderful to hear from you. How have you been?"

Rusty grimaced. "Wonderful" didn't quite cover it. Her family knew she worked for the government in DC, but they thought she was a paper pusher, and that's how she left it.

"Oh, you know! A little of this and that. How are Uncle Ray and Liz?"

"They're at a banquet in Frankfort. Business, you know. They'll be sad to know they've missed your call."

"Actually, the main reason I'm calling is I'm on leave right now because of a wreck I had a few days ago."

"Oh my God! Are you okay?" Patricia cried.

"Luckily, yes. I'm just sore all over. Lots of trips to the hot tub, taking it easy at home. Stuff like that. But since this time off was doctor-recommended, I decided to use some vacation time, too. I was thinking about heading up your way. It's been so long since we've actually seen each other, and you all *are* my only living relatives. I was wondering if—"

"Yes! Yes! You must come recuperate with us! It will be wonderful to see you again. We live full-time in the penthouse. It's quite spacious and we have empty guest rooms just begging for company. I'm afraid there's no airport here. The closest one is in Bowling Green, but we could pick you up."

"Thank you, but that won't be necessary. I know there are heliports in Jubilee. I have access to helicopters whenever the need arises," Rusty said.

Patricia shuddered. "Better you than me. I'll get on an airplane and fly halfway across the world without blinking an eye, but I can't even look at a helicopter without losing my mind."

Rusty grinned. She'd forgotten how dramatic her aunt was, and then she realized Pat was still talking.

"At least let us know when you plan to arrive. We can pick you up," she said.

"Oh, I don't expect anyone to take care of me. I'll have a rental waiting and drive myself to the inn. That way I can explore the town and the mountains at my leisure," Rusty said.

"Whatever you wish, my dear. I just can't wait to see you again," Patricia said.

"I'm looking forward to the visit, and thank you for allowing me to invite myself. Have a good night, and I'll be in touch with a day and time."

"Of course. Safe travels and all that," Pat said, and disconnected.

Rusty laid her phone aside and leaned back. She felt a little guilty about the deception of her reason for visiting, but she was looking forward to seeing them and curious to see if her cousin, Liz, had finally matured past her need to dominate center stage.

A couple of hours later, she got a phone call from Special Agent Jay Howard. After a lengthy conversation, he sent her files on the human-trafficking gang, what they needed from her, and contact information to keep them informed at every step. And in return, she got the chopper ride to Jubilee, saving her countless hours of flying and driving time.

———

Patricia broke the news to her family the next morning at breakfast. "Rusty called last night. She's off work for a bit as she recuperates from a wreck, and said she was thinking of coming up this way to visit. Of course, I immediately invited her to stay with us while she's in the area."

Ray grinned. "That's great news! We haven't seen her in ages, but is she okay to travel?"

"Apparently," she said. "At any rate, Liz and I will have all kinds of time to baby her."

Liz frowned. "I don't babysit."

Ray gave his daughter a look. "I think you will find time to at least welcome her to our home and restrict your selfishness for the time she's here."

Liz gasped. "Daddy! I'm not selfish. I'm just not cut out for bedpans and bandages."

"Oh, for the love of God, Elizabeth! She's arriving via helicopter…on her own…hiring her own rental car, and simply spending time with us. Nothing is being asked of you other than to be kind and welcoming," Patricia snapped.

Liz flushed. Her parents rarely disapproved of anything she did, and she'd obviously stepped on touchy nerves this morning, so she turned on the tears. "I am sorry I offended you," she said.

"You should be," Patricia said, and poured a little more syrup on her waffle to finish it off.

At that moment, Liz's phone signaled a text. She glanced at caller ID, then stood. "Excuse me. It's Michael," she said, and left the room with her nose in the air.

Ray frowned. "Sleeping with the enemy," he muttered.

Patricia rolled her eyes. "Michael Devon is not the enemy. His father owns a business we compete with, that is all. And who else would Liz associate with here? Jubilee, Kentucky, is hardly rife with people of her class."

Ray frowned. "Money does not establish class. Behavior does," he said. "If you'll excuse me, I'm going down to the office. You know where to find me if the need arises."

Patricia sighed. She'd just irked her husband again, and she was alone. Then her mood brightened. Rusty was coming, and within the hour she received a confirmation text.

Arriving early afternoon tomorrow. Will text to let
you know when I'm on the ground. Can't wait to
see you.

———

Michael had invited Liz to lunch, which meant sex for dessert, and she was going through her closet, trying to find something to wear. Finally, she chose one of her new winter sweaters paired with gray slacks and black ankle boots, and matching black lace lingerie to go under it all.

She liked Michael a lot. Sometimes she thought she was in love, but she always loved sex. He was slim and fit, and had thick blond hair with a tendency to curl, and pale-blue eyes that melted when she stripped for him. And he was the only son and heir to the Devon fortune. All check marks in Liz's credit column. The only mark he had in Liz's debit column was he didn't have Cameron Pope's bad-boy cachet, but Cameron didn't know she existed, so there was that.

After giving herself a final look of approval, she left the penthouse and drove to the Hotel Devon then sent Michael a text.

I'm in the parking lot, starving for Cajun food
and you.

Michael was just coming out of a meeting when he got Liz's text. He read it as he walked, smiling all the way to the elevator. He could just as easily skip the shrimp and settle for extra time with Liz, but he knew his girl. She had a healthy appetite for food, for sex, and for life in general.

He wanted to marry her but he'd never asked. He'd felt her resistance to a commitment more than once, and Michael didn't like to be told no, so he was biding his time and enjoying her company for now.

He approached the exit, frowning slightly when he saw her parked at the front entrance blocking the flow of traffic as if she owned the hotel, which was typical. But the smile she gave him as he came out of the building annulled his disapproval.

"Hello, you!" Liz said, as Michael got into her sports car, then leaned over and kissed her square on the mouth.

"Hello, you," he said, and ran a finger up the inseam of her slacks.

"Ready and waiting," she drawled, then laughed. "Buckle up, big man! Cajun Katie's, here we come."

Two hours later, they were naked as the day they'd been born and going at it like rabbits in one of Jack Barton's tiny cabins. They always chose the one farthest from the main office, because Liz Caldwell had a tendency to scream when she came. Only this trip out, she'd had a little too much to drink with lunch, and her hidden fantasies about Cameron Pope turned into words spilling out of her mouth.

"Oh God! Oh God! Harder, Cam, harder!" she moaned. Then all of a sudden, everything stopped. Her eyes flew open. Her face flushed a dark, angry red. "Why did you stop? You ass! I was almost there!"

Michael was still inside her, hard and throbbing, but the look on his face suddenly scared her. "You bitch!" he whispered. "You cheating little bitch!"

Liz gasped. "What the fuck are you talking about? I don't cheat on you with anyone!"

He grabbed her by the throat with one hand and squeezed just enough to make her choke.

"What's the matter with you?" Liz shouted. "Why are you acting like this?"

"You called me Cam. 'Harder, Cam, harder,'" he whispered, and then turned loose of her as if she was filth and rolled off. "Go fuck yourself, Elizabeth. My stud fees are too high for a whore like you."

There was one moment of sheer terror, and then Liz countered with an assault of her own. She shoved him aside and leaped from the bed. "You're an ass. A complete and utter ass! I said, 'Harder, damn…harder!' I don't even know anyone named Cam."

"You know Cameron Pope!" Michael shouted. "You talked about him twice during lunch!"

Liz rolled her eyes and began grabbing for her clothes and yanking them on.

"His name was mentioned regarding that horrendous kidnapping and the escaped prisoner incident, which, if you'll remember, you brought up! You introduced the subject, not me! I just responded to the conversation, Michael Devon. And I'm over this. Put your dick back in your pants and get your shoes, or I swear to God I'll leave you to walk back into Jubilee on your own."

Now Michael was completely convinced he was wrong and started trying to backpedal. "Look, Lizzie, you have to see it from—"

Liz moved until she was only inches away from his face. "Nobody calls me Lizzie, and *no*, I don't have to do anything! *You* look at my neck. If there are bruises there and Daddy asks, I'm telling him where they came from, understand?"

They dressed in silence, both of them reeling from the shock of what just happened. Liz had bluffed her way out of what she'd done, and Michael was groveling all the way out the door.

Liz slammed herself into the driver's seat and drove Michael back to the Hotel Devon. He opened the door to get out, but then couldn't bear to leave her angry with him. He reached for her arm and began pleading his case again.

"Liz, I'm sorry. I'm so sorry. It's just…I love you…and hearing that shattered me. Please forgive me."

"Get out, and close the door!" Liz snapped. As soon as he did, she spun out on the pavement and never looked back.

By the time Liza got back to the penthouse, she found a note from her mother.

Gone shopping for Rusty's arrival. See you at dinner. Mom.

Relieved she didn't have to face her mother in this emotional state, Liz crumpled up the note, took a sleeping pill, and put herself to bed.

Cameron worked in his office all morning answering email. As CEO and the head of PCG Inc., it was his job to stay on top of the owners' interests and to ensure their anonymity. The need to be wary all started when locals began offering their homemade goods for sale in Jubilee. It was a shock to everyone when the trade took off like fireworks, and when outsiders began flocking to the town wanting to buy property and get in on the opportunities, the landowners knew their only recourse was to band together and incorporate the joint land at the foot of the mountain.

John Cauley and Marcus Glass had been on the board for years as the representatives from their families, and Cameron's mother, Georgia Pope, was the representative from the Pope family. But his mother's sudden passing required another member of the Popes to sit on the board, and Cameron, newly home from Iraq, was voted in as their representative and then voted CEO by the board, giving him the job of liaison between PCG Inc. and their lawyer in Frankfort.

Cameron took the role seriously. It was important to everyone on the mountain that turning Jubilee into a tourist attraction did not destroy their way of life or the natural beauty of the surrounding area.

The hoteliers who'd come into the area years earlier thinking to buy up land from local hillbillies and make a killing had a rude awakening when they learned the land was already owned by a corporation. They didn't know the corporation consisted of the people they looked down on. All they knew was land was not for sale, and if they wanted to build a hotel, they would pay a goodly sum of money for a one-hundred-year lease on a set number of acres. No more. No less. And they would pay the corporation a monthly percentage of their earnings. Like rent. If they ever decided to sell the business, then the new owners would have to renegotiate their own terms.

Ray Caldwell ranted against the restrictions, but the company lawyer based in Frankfort was firm. If Caldwell didn't like the deal, he was free to build his hotel elsewhere. Just not in Jubilee. Ray knew there was big money to be made in a place like this, and he finally agreed.

Marshall Devon had his own come-to-Jesus moment when he was confronted with the same deal. Take it or leave it. But Marshall was a gambler, and he took it. The ensuing years had proved extremely profitable for all concerned, and the people on Pope Mountain appreciated the irony of being the anonymous landlords.

The individual businesses down in Jubilee were also housed in real estate owned by PCG Inc. And even though a majority of the businesses were owned and run by people from the mountains, they willingly paid "rent" and got their money back and then some through annual dividends. It was the best-kept secret in town.

───────

Cameron finished the business end of his day just after lunch, then loaded Ghost up into his Jeep and drove to town so Sam Carson could check the dog's paw and change the bandages. He was hoping the wait at the vet clinic wouldn't take long. When he pulled into the parking lot, there were only two other cars. He breathed a sigh of relief.

Ghost sat up and looked out the windshield and then back at Cameron and whined.

Cameron chuckled. "Yes, Sam is going to mess with your paw, but I'll be right there with you, buddy. Okay?"

Then he grabbed Ghost's leash and clipped it to his collar before opening the door. Cameron was still restricting Ghost's running and jumping, so he lifted the dog out and then walked him into the building and up to the front counter.

The receptionist looked up and smiled. "Afternoon, Cameron."

"Afternoon, Amber. Ghost is here for an after-surgery exam and to get his bandages changed."

"Have a seat. Doc Carson will be with you shortly."

Cameron sat, and then Ghost sat down between Cameron's knees, his ears up, his focus entirely on the girl behind the counter.

Cameron leaned over and patted Ghost's head. "She's one of the good ones, pal. At ease."

Ghost went from sitting to lying down, but he wasn't comfortable in this place and did what came natural— guarding the human he loved most.

After Sam checked out the injured paw and Leslie put on a new bandage, Cameron headed downtown to Granny Annie's Bakery. He left Ghost in the Jeep and was on his way inside when he met Patricia Caldwell coming out carrying a large box.

Their gazes met, but before she could decide if she disapproved of the big man's unshaven appearance, Cameron stopped and backed up. "Ma'am, let me get that door for you," he said and held the door as she passed.

Patricia smiled. "Why, thank you."

"Yes, ma'am," Cameron said, and went inside.

He caught a glimpse of his own reflection in the glass display cases and frowned. No wonder she'd given him a disapproving look. He looked like an outlaw. Scratches or not, it was time to get rid of the whiskers. But first things first. He headed to the display case to get cookies for Lili.

Annie Cauley was his mother's youngest sister and the owner and head baker of the bakery. When she saw Cameron moving toward the cookie case, she wiped her hands and headed that way.

"Afternoon, Cam."

Cameron smiled. "Hey, Auntie. I need some cookies for my best girl. Maybe some of those pumpkin-shaped sugar cookies. Make it a dozen so there's enough to go around."

"How's she doing?" Annie asked as she began boxing up the cookies.

"Well, thanks to Uncle John for being the one to find the kidnapper's abandoned car, we were able to find her in time. It was touch and go for a bit, but Rachel says she's good. I haven't seen her since they brought her home from the hospital. I'm on my way there now."

Annie Cauley was proud of her husband's part in the rescue.

"I told him afterward it was the hand of God leading him to it," she said, and kept boxing up cookies, then put them on the counter and rang them up. Cameron paid, then leaned over the counter to kiss her cheek as he picked up the box.

"Thanks, Auntie."

"You're welcome, sugar. Give them all my best."

Minutes later he was in the Jeep and headed out of town. He passed his drive on the way up to his sister's house, but once he arrived, instead of Rachel it was Louis's father, Marcus, who answered the door.

"Cameron! Good to see you, son. Come in, come in."

"Did I come at a bad time?" Cameron asked.

"Not a bad time, but everyone in this house is asleep but me," Marcus said, and chuckled. "Louis changed his shifts to days and so he's gone, and I'm here until he comes home in case Rachel needs something."

Cameron handed him the box of cookies. "Then I won't stay. I brought Lili some cookies from Granny Annie's Bakery, but there's plenty for everyone. Give the girls my love."

Marcus nodded. "I sure will, but are you sure you won't come in?"

"Ghost is in the Jeep. We've been at the vet and I need to get him home."

"Is he doing okay?" Marcus asked.

"Yes. His paw is healing. It's just hard to keep him off it."

"Understood," Marcus said, and waved as Cameron drove away.

⸻

Rusty Caldwell was packing, but her mind was already on the info she'd received and the case she'd be working. She had a file and a photo of a man named Kevin Vanzant, and a photo and a file on Jack Barton, a man who owned a campground where Vanzant was staying. Human trafficking had become a lucrative business around the world, and she'd encountered aspects of this before. But abducting children to order was horrific from every angle. It took a special kind of evil to take photos of other people's children, assemble them catalog-style for anyone willing to buy a child, then send someone to snatch them from their beds, like shopping for food off the shelves. It was black market—under the table, no questions asked—high-caliber theft.

She kept thinking of the harrowing rescue of the toddler Danny Biggers had kidnapped, and what might have happened if he'd gotten away with her. The details in the file indicated citizen participation in the hunt, and that a member of the child's family, an uncle, had been vital to the retrieval. She wanted to find a way to meet and talk to him without giving herself away.

Biggers had finally given a statement after his capture, but it was sketchy. He might have said something to the man in the heat of capture that would be vital to their case, but turning a conversation with the uncle into a subtle inter-rogation could be tricky. She needed to run it by Howard and Pickard first to make sure they hadn't already talked to him, so she stopped what she was doing and made a call.

———

Jay Howard was at his desk when his phone rang. He frowned when he saw caller ID. Caldwell wasn't even on-site and she was already calling? He wondered what was up.

"This is Howard."

"I have a question," Rusty said.

"Shoot," Howard said.

"I got the file on Vanzant and Barton, but what about the uncle who caught Biggers? Did you interview him when you were in Jubilee?"

"No. His name is Cameron Pope, and he's the one who ultimately rescued his niece. You're surely not suggesting he'd be part of the kidnapping?"

"No. I was thinking more along the lines of what trans-pired between him and Biggers before he left him tied to the tree. If I've understood Biggers's priors, he already had a history with this family. So there had to have been words between them when Pope ran him down. Right?"

Howard was silent a moment, and then he sighed. "Good catch, Caldwell."

"Thanks. My question is about the man himself. I'd like some background on Pope before I get there. Can you get something to me today?"

"Yes. I'll do it myself. It was our miss. Give me a few."

"Thanks," Rusty said, and disconnected.

Howard immediately turned back to his computer and ran a background check on Cameron Pope. It didn't take long for the info to come up, but when he saw the man was an army vet, he dug deeper and pulled up the history on his military service. "I'll be a son of a bitch," Howard muttered, and rocked back in his chair.

The man was a war hero. Two tours in Iraq and Afghanistan. Special Forces. Some serious commendations that could not be acknowledged due to national security, and the man had a security clearance equal to his own.

Howard printed out the info and hand-carried it down the hall to his boss. If Pope was willing, this could change the whole aspect of Caldwell's presence.

Chapter 6

Unaware he was on the FBI's radar, Cameron got Ghost inside, settled him in his bed next to the fireplace, then changed into work clothes. When he headed out the back door, Ghost followed.

Cameron didn't want him messing up the clean bandage and settled Ghost on the porch with orders to stay, then began carrying wood to the back porch and stacking it by the door.

He made three trips before he was satisfied he had enough and was on his way inside with Ghost when his cell phone rang. He tossed his work gloves on top of the washing machine, then answered.

"Hello?"

"Hello. This is Special Agent Jay Howard calling for Cameron Pope."

FBI? Cameron frowned. "Speaking."

"Mr. Pope, we're looking into the kidnapping of your niece, Lili Glass, and we're well aware of the part you played in rescuing her from the kidnapper, Danny Biggers. We're also aware of the history between your family and Biggers."

"Sir, if you don't mind, just cut to the chase. Biggers is back in custody, so what is it you want from me?"

Howard was taken aback by Pope's immediate grasp of the call. "Uh… Okay. Cutting to the chase now. Would you be willing to aid one of our agents in gathering information about an ongoing human-trafficking gang operating in your area?"

Cameron was floored. "Are you telling me there's a serious threat of an organized gang in the area?"

"We believe so strongly enough to send in one of our best undercover agents to investigate. Your military record and the security clearance you hold qualifies you to operate on behalf of your nation's best interests, and your knowledge of the area would be vital to our agent. The agent will be arriving in Jubilee tomorrow via private chopper as a regular tourist and staying at the Serenity Inn. The owner is a relative."

Cameron took a deep breath.

"I don't run in Ray Caldwell's circle. I wouldn't even qualify as a friend. But if that doesn't confuse the issue, then yes, I will do everything asked of me."

"Excellent!" Howard said. "Special Agent Caldwell is the person you'll be working with and will be the one to contact you. I understand you live up the mountain from Jubilee."

"Yes, sir. My home is about two miles up."

"Maybe your first meeting to square things away with Caldwell could be on your grounds? Caldwell will get directions from you and drive up to meet you at a date and time agreed upon between the two of you."

"Yes, sir. Understood," Cameron said.

"Thank you," Howard said. "You have served your country proudly in the past, and we are well aware this is out of order to ask it of you again."

"Not at all, sir," Cameron said. "My people have lived on this mountain since the early 1800s. The fact that Jubilee has turned into a tourist attraction is probably responsible for attracting the people you're looking for. I'll do anything to help clean them out."

"Then I'll inform our agent, and thank you again."

"Don't thank me until they're in your custody," Cameron said.

The call ended, leaving Cameron in a state of disbelief. So Danny Biggers's presence in Jubilee was not by chance after all. He'd come on someone else's orders.

———

Rusty was already packed.

She'd kicked back in her recliner with the television on, absently scanning social media on her laptop while waiting for the national news.

When her cell phone rang, she quickly picked it up.

"Hello."

"Agent Caldwell, I have the info you requested," Howard said.

"Rusty, please," she said.

"Yes, ma'am. But your request for info on Cameron Pope has shifted our plans somewhat."

"What do you mean?" she asked.

"I'm sending files and information. You'll understand as you read. Just know that he has agreed to work with you. We believe his presence will be valuable in gaining you easy access to people and places. If there are locals aiding the trafficking ring, he'll likely spot them before you do."

Rusty groaned. "Why would you saddle me with a civilian?"

"He's ex-Special Forces. His security clearance is on a level with mine. Read the file."

Rusty blinked. "You're kidding."

"Not even a little bit," Howard said. "He's awaiting your contact. He knows the cover you're going in under. What he doesn't know is that you're a female. I thought I'd save that surprise for you."

Rusty rolled her eyes. "You are too kind."

She could hear Howard chuckling as she disconnected. But now she was beyond interested to read Pope's file. It also added an issue to her visit with the family. She had to figure out how to explain him to her aunt and uncle without raising eyebrows and questions she couldn't answer.

Curious to see what Cameron Pope was about, Rusty went to her email, downloaded the files Howard sent, and then opened the first one. It was a general background check that didn't raise any flags. And then she opened the file with his military record and the first thing she saw was his picture and she forgot to breathe.

Oh my God! It's you! You did make it home.

Tears spiked. She inhaled slowly, her fingers trembling as she began to scroll through the pages, from his first tour through his second tour and everything in between. The redacted parts gave her chills. Those were the stuff spy movies were made of, and he'd survived them. And now he was back where he'd been born. It's what she'd dreamed for him all these years.

According to what she'd just read, he wasn't married and never had been. But that didn't mean he didn't have a significant other. The thought crossed her mind to call Agent Howard and tell him that she knew Cameron Pope, that they had history, but she didn't. The fact that they did have a history could solidify their cover and go a long way in explaining them being together during her stay—but only if there was no one else in his bed.

She couldn't imagine a man like him alone, and if there was a woman, she was going to have to face that, and the woman, and pretend their one night meant nothing, when in fact it had been everything.

She'd never been afraid of starting a new case before, but she was now.

What was their first face-to-face going to be like?

If he didn't remember her, she would die where she stood.

Cameron's night had been filled with anxiety and even a small measure of guilt, and he'd awakened to the same sense of dread. He was sickened by the thought of an active human-trafficking gang using Jubilee as their shopping ground, and had to accept that when the corporation went into the tourist trade, it made Jubilee a draw for this kind of crime.

They might never have known it was happening beneath their noses had it not been for Lili's kidnapping. But now that he did, he took it as his duty to do what was asked of him to put the traffickers behind bars.

The first meeting with the federal agent would happen today, and the hours of waiting for his arrival made Cameron feel like he had felt on active duty when they were going out on patrol. The tension of not knowing what they would encounter. Would it be someone they could trust? And then accepting as they left camp they might not make it back.

Sunlight was coming through a crack in the curtains when he finally got up. His movement set Ghost in motion, which meant grabbing shoes and a sweatshirt to go with his pajama bottoms. He turned up the thermostat on their way up the hall, then let Ghost out the back door for his morning patrol.

Cameron stood out of the wind next to the house, watching Ghost marking his territory and sniffing around the yard, and when the hair rose on the back of the dog's neck, Cameron knew he'd caught the scents of uninvited rabbits and raccoons and the occasional deer that had invaded his space as they'd slept.

Finally, the cold air ended Cameron's patience. There would be no long morning runs until Ghost's paw was healed, so he called him back inside, put out his food, then left him eating as he went into the living room to rekindle the fire.

He started the coffee maker, then headed for the bathroom to shave. He wasn't sure if he'd healed enough to do this, but his whiskers were thick and they itched. And every time he looked at himself in the mirror, that dark growth of whiskers reminded him of missions he'd rather forget.

He started with the electric razor, set the guide to leave a shadow of beard in case there were scratches still in the process of healing, and it worked. In a few more days, he would be able to get a clean shave.

He showered quickly, then dressed in jeans and a red plaid flannel shirt before heading to the kitchen. One breakfast and two cups of coffee later, he began dusting the furniture, then cleaning and mopping the floors. By the time he was through, the house smelled like lemon oil and the floors were shining. After that, it was a matter of sitting and waiting for the federal agent to make contact, so he went to the office to work.

A car picked Rusty up at her home in Arlington just after daybreak and delivered her to the waiting chopper. She hadn't slept enough last night to count, but when she had, she dreamed of her soldier.

Only now her soldier had a name.

Cameron Pope.

She liked the sound of it and how it felt rolling off her

tongue. This was going to be the most momentous day of her life. Either it would be heaven or it would be hell, and in the midst of all this angst, she and Cameron Pope both had a job to do.

She took her seat and buckled in and, as always, said a prayer. Unknown territory was always a risk, and strangers only made it worse. Who to trust? Who might put a knife in her back? It appeared the Company decided to trust Cameron Pope, and she'd trusted him enough for one night to give away her heart. Piece of cake.

Many hours and multiple stops to refuel later, they were skimming over the stunning beauty of the Cumberland Mountains surrounding the town of Jubilee. From the air, the forest seemed impenetrable until they began their descent. It was then that she was able to see the road winding up the mountain—like a long black snake. But was it in search of prey, or looking for a place to hide?

She kept searching for signs of habitation as she gazed down into the treetops, looking for rooftops and chimneys. She did see occasional wisps of smoke rising above the treetops, but the forest was too dense and the population within it was too well hidden.

Knowing Cameron Pope was down there somewhere made her heart skip. She was physically closer to him now than she had been in five years, and still a bit shocked by the odds of this reunion.

She needed to contact him today and get him up to speed, then set up a time when they could begin some subtle investigations. But once she got to the penthouse it was going to be not only awkward but also impossible to turn around and walk out today. Her only option was to see Cameron first. She had his contact info in her phone, so as soon as the chopper set down, she sent him a text.

> This is Caldwell. I'm on the ground. Text me directions to your residence. Touching base with you first.

By the time she got unloaded and retrieved her rental car, she had directions to his home. She sent him a thumbs-up emoji to indicate message received, then put his address in her GPS and started driving.

She was slightly surprised by the number of tourists in this obscure location at this time of year, but as she drove through the streets, seeing the charm of the little shops and the big music venues, she began to understand the draw.

People were everywhere and taking photos of everything. Posing in front of a blacksmith at his anvil and in front of carvings of black bears outside of restaurants and Native American regalia in the windows of other shops advertising handmade jewelry from early-day tribes that had once been in the surrounding areas. It was a feast for the eyes, and unfortunately an apparent resource for human traffickers.

As she started up the mountain, the frenetic pace from down below fell away. It became obvious how valuable privacy was to people here, and that the forest that appeared so wild and impenetrable from the air felt like a refuge.

She'd been driving for about fifteen minutes when her GPS suddenly signaled a left turn. She tightened her grip on the steering wheel as she made a quick left up a wooded drive and began watching for a house.

It was smoke rising from the chimney she saw first, then the chimney itself, then the shake-shingled roof of a sprawling single-story house with a covered porch that ran the length of the structure and a large carport on the nearest end. The forest-green Adirondack chairs spaced out along the porch were just begging for company, and the man of her dreams was just inside. It didn't feel real.

Rusty pulled up and parked, thinking this place had everything a wounded soul needed to heal.

Peace. Solace. Shelter.

She pocketed her phone and keys and got out, then paused, overwhelmed by the moment. It felt like the hotel lobby and hiding behind the potted palm all over again. She couldn't see him. But just like the last time, she felt him before he ever knew she was there.

———

Ghost heard the car and was on his feet and at the door before Cameron could get out of his chair, but he quickly followed. No need scaring off the fed with a yeti-sized dog before they ever said hello.

He paused at the door and laid a hand on the dog's back.

"Ghost. Sit."

Ghost sat, then looked up at Cameron, awaiting further orders.

Cameron opened the door and stepped out onto the porch, then stopped abruptly.

A woman! The fed was a woman!

He saw wild red curls flirting with the wind, and then her face. Stunned beyond the ability to speak, he could only watch as she began moving toward him. Then she paused, and when she stopped, he came off the porch and down the steps toward her in disbelief.

"You," he whispered.

Rusty sighed. He remembered. "Hello, Soldier Boy. Long time no see."

"Oh my God. Angel. How did you find me?"

She extended her hand. "Special Agent Rusty Caldwell. I believe you're expecting me?"

He shook his head in disbelief. "Is there someone waiting for you back home?"

"I've been waiting for you," Rusty said.

He groaned, and then swung her off her feet and into his arms, remembering everything. How they'd laughed. And talked. And how she felt against his body, and the deep moan in her throat when she came.

Her lips were cold against his mouth, and then they were warm and soft and inviting. She was water to a dying man, and he didn't know how thirsty he'd been.

All of a sudden, there was a bump against Cameron's leg, and he remembered Ghost. He buried his face against Rusty's neck and then put her down.

The moment Rusty felt solid ground beneath her, she looked down, saw the dog and the bandage on his paw, and gasped. "Cameron! Your dog is immense! He's so beautiful, but what happened to his paw?"

"He cut it on something when we were running Biggers down," Cameron said.

Rusty's eyes widened. "Right! He helped you find your niece."

Cameron nodded. "This is Ghost. He came back with me from Iraq." Then he knelt beside the dog. "Hey, buddy, this is my Angel. She's yours to protect, like you protect Rachel and Lili, okay?"

"What do I do?" Rusty said.

"Just hold out your hand palm down and let him get your scent. If he licks it, you're in."

"And what if he doesn't?" Rusty asked as she knelt, then held out her hand.

Ghost sniffed it, smelling Cameron on her, and the human scent that belonged to her, then ever so gently licked her skin and bumped the bottom of her palm with his nose.

Cameron laughed. "Damn. I might have known. He loves who I love, so he's already courting your attention. That's your permission to pet him."

Rusty looked up. "Loves who you love?" she said, then slid her hand over the top of the dog's head, rubbing gently between his ears. "Hello, beautiful. You are magnificent. I'm so pleased to meet you."

Cameron was as surprised by what he'd said as she

seemed to be, but he also wasn't going to explain or deny it because it had felt right when he'd said it. Instead, he pulled her to her feet. "Okay, fine. Ghost adores you, now back to me. Come inside out of the cold."

Rusty threw back her head and laughed. This was the man she remembered. Witty, sexy, and unfiltered. She walked into the cabin with Cameron's arm around her and Ghost leading the way. It was the safest she'd felt in years.

"I can't believe you're really here," Cameron said, and pulled her down onto the sofa beside him, while Ghost moved back to his bed.

Rusty nodded. "*You're* surprised? Imagine my shock when Agent Howard sent me your files and I saw your picture. The first two things that went through my mind nearly put me off this case. I was afraid you wouldn't remember who I was. Then if you did, afraid you already had someone special in your life."

Cameron reached for her hand.

"The only woman in my bed is the Angel I dream about. I never imagined I would see you again, and yet I couldn't let go of the memory. Do you… Did you ever…?"

Rusty shook her head. "I knew when I woke up in that bed alone the next morning that you'd ruined me for wanting another man. Then my life got crazy and a little too risky for personal relationships."

Cameron frowned. "Since you've read my file, you know a whole lot more about me than I do you. Is all of your work undercover?"

She shrugged. "I go where I'm ordered. I was sent here

on the pretense of recovering from a car wreck so I can investigate without raising suspicions, and that's what my family believes. I *am* recovering, but it wasn't from a car wreck. I made a jump over the side of a really big yacht into a moored speedboat two decks below while being shot at. I escaped, but I'm still recovering from the hard landing."

Cameron went still, looking at her again as the stranger she really was. "What the hell were you doing?"

"Getting the goods on pirates killing rich people for their yachts. They were using the boats for everything from gunrunning to smuggling to drug runs in and out of the Bahamas. Let's just say backup arrived in the nick of time."

Cameron stared, listening to the nonchalant tone of her story but very aware of what she wasn't saying, and watching the way the sunlight coming through the window had caught the fire in her hair. So she was as fierce in life as she was in bed.

"Then mission accomplished," he said, and saw a flash of her relief in her eyes as she nodded.

"You'll have to trust me on this case," Rusty said.

He nodded. "I'm good at following orders."

Rusty glanced at the time. "I have to get to the hotel now. My family is bound to have seen the chopper bringing me in. They know I'm renting a car. I don't want them worrying before I even show up." She leaned across the sofa, put her arms around his neck, and kissed him hard. "Damn, but I hate goodbyes. I need some time to settle in and check out some stuff. I'll keep you abreast as I do what I need to do, then let's meet somewhere in Jubilee as if by accident. We need to establish a history so no one thinks it's strange when we start seeing the sights together."

"I'd be more than happy to repeat what just happened in my front yard," Cameron said.

Rusty grinned. "At least keep it within the limits of propriety."

"Yes, ma'am. Duly noted."

"Not 'ma'am.' Darling or sweetheart or just Rusty will suffice. I'll tell Aunt Pat and Liz I want to see the sights and talk them into taking me to lunch somewhere. I'll let you know where we'll be, then you show up and play the surprise to the hilt. Our story can be our truth, that we met in the Hyatt Regency in Herndon, Virginia, when you were shipping out, and then we lost touch when we went our separate ways. And just so you know, I consider your sudden appearance back in my life as the gift it is."

"I won't have to fake that," Cameron said. "I'm already there. I'll walk you back to the car."

"I need to say goodbye to Ghost. I don't want him to forget me."

"No worries about that. You're officially in his database."

Rusty knelt beside Ghost and gently stroked the top of his head. "Goodbye, you big beautiful thing."

Ghost whined and licked her fingers, then watched intently as they walked out.

Cameron had his arm around her all the way to the car. The silence between them was heavy with unspoken promises and the reluctance to let go of something they'd just regained.

Her hand was on the door handle when she turned and buried her face against his chest. He wrapped his arms around her and pulled her close.

"I don't want to let you go," he said.

Rusty looked up. "And I don't want to leave."

He sighed. "Sometimes being responsible sucks eggs."

Her eyes wrinkled at the corners as she smiled.

"Can I quote you on that?"

He slid his hands beneath her hair, tilted her head up enough to meet the kiss coming at her, and the world fell away. He might have laid her down in the leaves right then and there but for the assignment they'd been given. What was between them came second to the evil hiding in the town below, and that was what stopped him.

Cameron cupped her face again.

"You have to promise me something."

"If I can," Rusty said.

"Don't walk out on me like I did you. I can't lose touch with you again."

Rusty laid her hand over the steady thump of his heart.

"I promise."

The look that passed between them was enough for Cameron to finally let her go, then he stood watching until she drove out of sight before going back inside.

Rusty was riding the same wave of disbelief. Finding her Soldier Boy was the upside of this case. Now all they had to do was break this gang wide open before anyone else disappeared.

She drove all the way back to Jubilee before she called the penthouse.

Patricia answered on the second ring.

"Hello?"

"I'm in Jubilee, Aunt Pat, but I had to wait to collect my rental. I am on the way to the hotel now."

"Wonderful," Patricia said. "We'll be watching for you out front. Pull into valet parking and we'll take care of the rest."

"Will do. I can't wait to see you," Rusty said, and disconnected.

As it turned out, she didn't need GPS to find the Serenity Inn. It loomed above the skyline of Jubilee like the Eiffel Tower. All she had to do was keep driving toward it. Traffic was steady, and the sights were intriguing. But knowing what was happening beneath the excitement and glitter in this town took a lot of the joy out of sightseeing.

A few minutes later, she reached her destination, pulled up at valet parking and got out. She was opening the trunk to get her luggage when she heard someone calling her name and turned around.

Ray and Patricia were walking toward her, and Ray was issuing orders as he went. A valet gave her a receipt and parked her car, while a bellman grabbed her bags and headed for the lobby.

Rusty was engulfed in hugs and sympathy for her aches and pains, and then they took her inside and into their private elevator all the way to the penthouse, with the bell-hop and her luggage in the corner behind them.

When the doors opened, the bellhop took her luggage into the foyer and then at Ray's instructions down the hall to her bedroom, leaving Liz the last one to greet her.

"Rusty! You look amazing! Long time no see," she said, and gave her cousin a careful hug. "I know you're recovering, so I hope I'm not squeezing anything that hurts."

"I'm just a little bruised and bent but not broken," Rusty said. "And speaking of looking good. You grew up into a beauty. Life appears to suit you."

Liz grinned. "I try."

Ray shook his head. "She tries us all," he said, which made everyone laugh, and then he added, "But she's also the light of our lives, so she's always forgiven." The bellhop reappeared, and Ray let him back on the elevator, then held it for himself. "Rusty darling, I hope you'll forgive my hasty exit, but I have a meeting in my office in a few minutes. I'll see you at dinner and we can catch up then, okay?"

"Absolutely, Uncle Ray. I didn't come here to be entertained. I had a chance to touch base with all of you again and I selfishly took it. We'll talk later."

Ray stepped inside the car and then he and the bellhop were gone.

Pat turned toward her niece and, for the first time, saw the shadows in her eyes. "Oh, darling, you're exhausted, aren't you? Would you like some food and then a rest?"

Rusty sighed. "I would love that, but I want to wash up first."

"Of course. Your suite is down that hall, last one on the left. It has a grand view of the mountains, if you like that sort of thing," she added.

"I do like them. I saw them as we were flying in. They're magnificent. I won't be long," Rusty said, and then shouldered her purse and headed down the hall.

Her knee and ankle were stiff from all the flying, and she was limping ever so slightly as she walked away, but the women noticed it.

"She's limping," Patricia said. "She needs a go in the hot tub later. If you don't have anything planned with Michael tonight, maybe you could join her."

Liz frowned. "I'm not talking to Michael at the moment. He was an ass, and I'm making him sorry."

Patricia arched an eyebrow. "You know best, I'm sure," she said. "Come help me set out some food."

Lindy Sheets made it as far as Detroit before she stopped running. She needed to sleep before she crossed the border into Canada. She still had family there and visited at least once a year. No one in the organization knew Lindy held dual citizenship in the United States and Canada. She had an active Canadian driver's license and passport in her maiden name, Melinda Lehigh, and went back and forth between countries at least twice a year, so she felt safe in crossing that border. It was time to go home and get lost there. But for now, she had a semi-safe place to rest, and there was always tomorrow for moving on.

——————

Danny Biggers had been born on the far side of Pope Mountain into a family of poverty and hardship. He was far too young when he wound up on his own and looking for a place to belong when he fell in with the wrong crowd. He was already lost when he happened upon Rachel Pope coming out of a store in Jubilee. He followed her car up the mountain just to see where she lived and considered the flat tire she had a stroke of luck. When he pulled up behind her, she thought he was going to help. And he did. He helped himself to her, and left her lying in the ditch beside her car and never looked back.

He hadn't counted on being caught, but it happened, and he damn sure hadn't counted on going to jail for a simple fuck. But he had, and considered it nothing more than adding to the résumé of his life. But finding out she was the mother of the child he'd been sent to snatch left him reeling, and it had been all downhill from there after he got caught.

He thought he'd seen and done it all until federal marshals drove him through the gates of this prison. This was serious shit, and hard to tell who was more dangerous—the inmates or the guards.

He was sorry all the way to his soul that he'd ever laid eyes on Lindy Sheets, and even sorrier that he'd been duped by the big story she'd spun. It was a toss-up now as to how long he had left to live.

He'd talked to the feds. Told them everything he knew and knew that if the gang found out, they would never let it pass. The feds said they would protect him, but they couldn't. Not even in here. He wasn't safe. If the big boys wanted him gone, they would find a way to make it happen.

━━━━━━━

Rusty had eaten, rested, and then at Liz's invitation gone with her to the spa down on the third floor. Liz had one of the hot tubs reserved, and after her initial shock at seeing the number of fading bruises on Rusty's body, they settled in and were enjoying the bubbling jets of hot water.

"This feels wonderful, Liz. Thank you for coming with me," Rusty said.

Liz grinned and gave one of Rusty's dangling curls a gentle tug. "Of course. Selfishly, I'm loving this, too, because I never do this alone. I do not mingle in a tub of water with total strangers."

"Aunt Pat doesn't enjoy hot tubs?" Rusty asked.

Liz rolled her eyes. "Mom doesn't enjoy catering to tourists. She'd rather be one, walking the streets in Paris or London."

Rusty grinned and changed the subject. "So, catch me up. What have you done with yourself since college?"

"Wasted an entire year of my life here with Mom and Dad," Liz muttered.

Rusty glanced at her, and then looked away. "You don't know how fortunate you are to still have them."

Liz blinked. Rusty was an adult but technically an orphan.

"Shit. I didn't think," Liz mumbled.

Rusty shrugged. "It is what it is. And we both grew up as the 'only child,' so there's the reality of no siblings for backup when life happens."

Liz sighed. Rusty had just handed her a reality check.

"I have a degree that lends itself to being an event planner. If I was smart, I would be interning with the one here, but that would mean showing up for work every morning and working all hours. And Mom is already so miserable here that I let her dissatisfaction color my decisions. Instead of using my degree, I've become her companion and 'best friend.'"

"Do you have a significant other?" Rusty asked.

"I date Michael Devon. He's the son and heir of the other big real-estate developer in Jubilee. Marshall Devon owns Hotel Devon, which is Dad's biggest rival here in town. However, Michael and I had a fight the other day, so for the time being he's on my shit list."

Rusty laughed, but she was thinking of Cameron as Liz kept talking.

"Dad's other competition in Jubilee comes from Jack Barton, who rents tiny cabins and campsites about two miles outside of town. I know nothing about his family."

"But there must be some good-looking locals who are single," Rusty said.

"I don't see the point of meeting or falling for some hillbilly. I would never live that kind of life. I guess I am my mother's child after all. What about you? I know you work for the government at the national level, but exactly what do you do?"

"Oh, I'm just a paper pusher," Rusty said, and changed the subject. "I saw some really interesting shops as I was driving through town. I can't wait to soak it all up. I know you're probably bored with all of that by now, but I'd love to take you and Aunt Pat out to lunch sometime. Maybe in a day or two. I need time to settle in and get my bearings."

Liz beamed. "I love going out for lunch. Do you have a dislike for any certain foods?"

"No. I'm game for pretty much anything. You pick, and make sure it's something your mom will enjoy. I don't want her suffering with the masses on my account."

Liz giggled. "Deal. We'll run it by Mom later."

Rusty sighed and leaned back in the water. *Problem solved.*

Chapter 7

THEY SOAKED IN THE HOT BUBBLES UNTIL THE TIMER WENT off, then went back to the penthouse and spent the rest of the evening playing cards and having margaritas with Aunt Pat. By the time Patricia had downed her second drink, she was waxing sentimental about the old days when Liz and Rusty were children, and how much fun the brothers and their wives had together before life took them in separate directions.

She was on the verge of getting teary when Rusty realized it was time to redirect the conversation and started talking about fashion and hairstyles. Liz flashed Rusty a grateful look. It wasn't long after that when Ray appeared.

"Wow. I'm a lucky man. Just look at the three beautiful women in my life!"

Patricia beamed as Ray circled the room, greeting each of them with a quick kiss on the cheek, and then he announced, "Dinner will be here within the hour. Filet mignon, buttered asparagus, and potato croquettes, along with an array of desserts. I'm going to wash up and change out of this suit and tie. Be right back."

A short while later, they were seated at the dinner table, waiting for the waiter to finish his service. As soon as he was gone, they began eating and sharing the events of their day with each other.

Finally, they were finished but for dessert. Rusty chose a ramekin of crème brûlée. Liz and Patricia opted for napoleons, while Ray chose chocolate cake.

"Goodness, Raymond! That slice of cake is huge," Patricia said, frowning as he shoveled in a bite with great enthusiasm.

Liz giggled. "Mom's right, Dad. It's not really a slice. It's a wedge about the size of a doorstop."

Laughter erupted.

Rusty couldn't help but have a few moments of regret. Their family banter made her miss what she'd lost when her parents died—the fun of being able to laugh with, and laugh at, the people you love most.

Ray waved a fork in the air to punctuate his rebuttal.

"You go right ahead and laugh all you want. I'm not one bit sorry I've made a pig of myself tonight, and I'm going to blame it on celebrating Rusty's arrival."

"Oh great! Blame me for the gluttony," Rusty said.

When they all burst into more laughter, Rusty felt it all the way to her toes. The perfect ending to a perfect day. It couldn't have been any better.

━━━━━━

Rusty went to bed that night with a sense of homecoming. She wasn't sure whether it was because of being with her family or finding Cameron again, but whatever it was, it felt right.

Just before she turned out the lights, she sent Cameron a text.

See you in my dreams.

She got a quick response.

But I want you in my arms.

Rusty shivered.

Soon, Soldier Boy.

And once again, he responded.

You're worth the wait.

She smiled, sent a heart-shaped emoji, then laid down the phone and turned out the light.

———

Kevin Vanzant was in his travel trailer at the campground, uploading images from the SIM card of his camera and drinking a beer as he waited. He was all locked up for the night. His car was locked. The trail camera across the road was on, and the security light at the edge of the road illuminated his campsite.

He'd already showered and shaved in the wet bath and

had a blanket wrapped around himself as he sat at the computer. The night was cold and the three-quarter moon was shining its own brand of light upon the earth.

"Too fucking cold for this shit," Kevin muttered as a gust of wind rocked the trailer.

As soon as the upload was complete, he sent a backup file to his other laptop, then shut everything down and went to bed. He thought briefly of Leslie Morgan, the local girl he'd been seeing for the past few weeks, then the two men who'd prowled around his campsite a couple of days earlier, and knew it was time to get out of Jubilee while the getting was good.

———————

Lindy Sheets had been busy. Tomorrow was go-day. Her bag was packed and she had everything lined up, including all of the identification she needed to cross the border and a rental car with Canadian license plates from Budget Rental.

Even though Boss had told her to get lost and he'd be in touch, she knew better. He would be looking for her, all right, and by now they would know she was running. The urge to sleep in her traveling clothes was so strong, she got sick to her stomach just thinking about closing her eyes.

The lights were off in her motel room, and she kept moving from the bed to the window long enough to peer through the curtain, then back again. Finally, she just threw up her hands, put on her coat, grabbed her purse and suitcase, and ran, leaving the room key on the bed. The door locked behind her as she headed toward her rental car. She threw the suitcase in the trunk, her purse in the seat beside her, and started the engine.

Moments later, she was pulling out of the motel parking lot into the ever-flowing traffic. She'd already signed in to Nexpress on her burner phone, so she was good to go as she headed for the Detroit-Windsor Tunnel.

Traffic was heavy, but while it was beginning to snow, the weather didn't faze her. She'd grown up in the North. What scared her were the people who would be looking for her. As soon as she reached the tunnel snow would not be an issue, and when she came out on the Windsor side, she'd be in Canada.

═══════════

Danny Biggers was asleep in his cell when something banged against his door. His heart was hammering as he rolled out of bed and crouched down in the corner. Someone was in the corridor rattling keys.

Oh God. Oh shit. A guard. If they've sent a guard to do me, I'm a dead man.

And then another inmate yelled, "Shut the hell up out there."

And then one by one, the men in the cells began banging, and cursing, and shouting, and Danny heard footsteps moving away.

He crawled back into his bed, then sat with his knees

doubled up against his chest and his back against the wall and never took his eyes off the door.

By morning, there was only one thought in his head.

I am going to die here.

———

Rusty woke up to the sound of rain blowing against the windows and rolled over to see what time it was. Just after 5:00 a.m. She pulled the covers up over her shoulders and then lay there planning out her day.

If it quit raining, she intended to get her car and drive around Jubilee. She needed to get a feel for the way the town was laid out and check out Hotel Devon and Jack Barton's campground before she hooked up with Cameron. On her own, she'd just be another tourist. But once people began seeing them together, the anonymity of being a stranger would be gone.

The rain ended before morning, leaving the sun to rise on a drippy landscape. But that didn't deter Rusty. She was up, dressed, and making herself a cup of coffee in the kitchen when Ray walked in.

"Good morning, sweetheart. You're an early bird," he said, and gave her a quick hug.

Rusty resisted the urge to lay her head on his shoulder like she used to do with her dad, and smiled instead. "I am. I can't wait to do a little sightseeing this morning and check everything out. Jubilee is an amazing place."

"You should wake Liz. Make her go with you," Ray said.

Rusty laughed. "I don't think poking the bear is a good idea. Besides, this way I can dawdle to my heart's content. I'll write her and Aunt Pat a note and tell them where I've gone."

Ray made himself some toast and coffee, and while he was checking the Dow, Rusty left a note and slipped out. She retrieved her car from valet parking and headed into town.

At the same time she was turning a corner on Main Street, Kevin Vanzant was leaving the campground on his way into Jubilee with his camera in the seat beside him. He had a full day of work ahead of him and no time to waste, because when the job ended here, so did his paycheck.

As usual, he first scoped out the areas in Jubilee with the heaviest foot traffic, but it was breakfast time, and most of the people on the streets now were going in and coming out of restaurants, so he parked on a side street and walked to the fountain in the center of town and sat down on the concrete bench surrounding it. The sound of bubbling water was pleasant, and he liked watching the birds coming in to drink.

As soon as he got settled, he took the lens cap off his camera, snapped a couple of shots to check the focus, then began scanning the people on the street for likely subjects.

An hour passed and the foot traffic was becoming heavier. He left the fountain and began moving along with the flow, following prospects into the stores, then out again, waiting for the opportunity to get a full face shot without their knowledge.

He was walking down Boone Avenue when a pretty, dark-haired girl came out of a candy shop, wearing hiking gear and carrying a backpack slung over one shoulder. She was window-shopping as she made her way through the crowds and didn't know a man was walking toward her, photographing her every move.

Kevin was so focused on the girl with dark hair that he didn't see the redhead watching *him* from across the street, or notice the frown on her face.

———

Rusty had spotted the man with the camera over fifteen minutes earlier and thought he looked familiar. Then as she got closer, she recognized Vanzant from the photo in his file. At that point she began following him from the other side of the street, and the first thing that struck her was that he was on the hunt. He was leaning slightly forward as he walked, with both hands on the camera hanging from around his neck. Every now and then he would pretend to pause to take a photo of some building, when she knew it was actually of the person in front of the building. The fact that they were all young, attractive women was not lost on her, either.

Then she saw a beautiful, dark-haired girl walking toward him and made a bet with herself that he'd snap a picture of her, too. When he did, she grabbed her phone and began videotaping him until he'd passed her. Then Rusty ducked into a store before he spotted her.

She paused in a corner of the store to view the video she'd just taken. It made the skin crawl on the back of her neck. If girls had been going missing from Jubilee, and Vanzant was in town taking pictures of young women he didn't know, then Special Agents Howard and Pickard's suspicions were right. He might be part of the reason for the women's disappearance.

She glanced at the time. It was nearly noon. Time for her to get back to the inn and send this info to Frankfort, then play nice with her family for a while. So she slipped out of the shop and returned to where she'd parked. Knowing there was a predator in Jubilee made her antsy enough to keep looking over her shoulder until she was in the car. Then she sent a text to her Aunt Pat to let her know she was on her way back.

━━━━━━━━

Kevin Vanzant was tired and hungry. He'd stopped in at the Ragin' Cajun for a bowl of gumbo and a basket of shrimp before going back to the campground, but his timing was off. It was noon, and the place was packed when he walked in. There were people in the lobby waiting to be seated, and he was debating about going somewhere else when he heard someone call out his name. He looked across the dining area and saw Leslie Morgan wave at him and point to the empty chair at her table.

Grateful for the offer, he told the hostess he was joining his friend, so she led him across the dining room and put a menu at his chair.

"Hey, Leslie," Kevin said as he shed his coat and camera and sat down in a chair beside her.

"Hi, you," Leslie said.

"Your waiter will be with you shortly," the hostess said, and walked away.

"Thanks for the seat," Kevin said. "I was too hungry to leave town without getting something to eat."

Leslie smiled. "Happy to share the space, and it's good to see you. I haven't heard from you in a while. Guessed you were busy."

"And you would have been right," Kevin said. "Trying to wind everything up. How's the cat and dog business?"

She grinned. "Scratchy and barky."

Kevin chuckled, and when the waiter swung by, he gave his order.

A short while later, Leslie's food came.

"Don't wait on me," Kevin said. "Eat while it's hot. You have to get back to work, and I'm on my own time clock."

Leslie picked up her sandwich and took a bite. "Umm, I've been thinking about this all morning. Shrimp po'boys are the best."

They talked as she ate, and when his food came, they spent more time eating than talking. They were almost finished when Leslie's phone signaled a text.

She glanced down, checked the message, and then sighed. "Gotta go. Emergency coming in. Great seeing you," she said, and left money on the table for her tab and tip.

"Oh. Yeah, sure. Take care," Kevin said, and watched her go, then finished up his meal and headed back to camp.

Rusty got back just in time to have lunch with the family. While she was poking around in Jubilee, she'd purchased presents for them from different shops. Homemade fudge for Uncle Ray, a jar of local honey for the breakfast table, and bars of handmade soaps for Pat and Liz. They were surprisingly pleased by her choices, which made her happy, and when they opened the box of fudge and passed it around the table in lieu of a dessert from their chef's kitchen, she sampled a piece, too.

"Ooh, this is good. Really creamy," Rusty said. "It reminds me of the fudge my mother used to make at the holidays."

"It's wonderful," Patricia said.

"It's going right on my hips," Liz drawled, and licked her fingers. "What's on your agenda for this afternoon?"

"I'll be in my suite for a while. I need to check in at the office," Rusty said.

"I have a hair appointment this afternoon," Patricia said.

"And I'm getting a mani-pedi," Liz added.

Ray grabbed a second piece of fudge. "And I'm going back to the office. Thank you for the goodies, Rusty."

"You're welcome, Uncle Ray. See you later," she said, and left the dining room.

As soon as she got to her suite, she uploaded the video to her laptop and then sent it in an email to Agent Howard. After that, she kicked off her shoes, crawled up into bed with the laptop, and began to work.

It wasn't long before she got an answer from Howard.

> Good work, Caldwell. I want you and Pope on Vanzant. If he's part of the trafficking pipeline, we need firm proof. Stay in touch.

Rusty went through her other email, then began making notes about Vanzant, Barton, and the Devon families, just to see if there were any connections between them and the girls who'd gone missing from Barton's campground.

━━━━━━

Cameron was tying up loose ends today. He'd already stopped by Rachel's to let her know an old friend was in town, and Rachel was immediately curious.

"I didn't know you had *old friends*, she drawled.

Cameron gave her a look. "Don't make a big deal out of anything. I am not a monk. I'm just picky, and she's the one who got away. We're exploring our options."

Rachel laughed. "Explore away, Big Brother. I would love to see you happily married."

"Right now, I'm just looking for 'happily.' 'Married' isn't part of our discussions."

"Whatever," Rachel said. "Am I going to get to meet her?"

"Sure."

"What's her name?" Rachel asked.

"Rusty."

Rachel rolled her eyes. "Rusty what? Rusty Nails? Rusty Pipes?"

Cameron laughed. "You're quite the comedian today. It's Caldwell. She's Ray Caldwell's niece."

Rachel's eyes widened in surprise. "Jesus, Cam! Isn't she a little out of your league?"

"She's nothing like them," Cameron said. "And that's all I'm going to say about her. You'll have to judge her for yourself when you two meet."

"Okay, fine. Is Rusty her real name?"

Cameron blinked. "I have no idea."

Rachel grinned. "Then her other attributes must have taken precedence over tiny details like names and stuff."

"Ghost and I are leaving now," Cameron said. "Give Lili a kiss from me when she wakes up," he said and got up, which was Ghost's signal to lead the way to the door.

Rachel followed. "Don't leave mad."

Cameron just shook his head. "You have seen me mad. You know damn good and well this isn't it. I have stuff to do. Guy stuff."

"You're going home and falling asleep by the fire, aren't you?" she said.

He grinned. "Most likely. Love you, Sis. Take care. Tell Louis I said hello."

She hugged him. "I will. Drive safe."

Then she stood at the door and watched him drive away before closing the door, all the while wondering what kind of a woman Rusty Caldwell must be to have captured Cameron's interest.

By bedtime, Rusty had gathered quite a file on Kevin Vanzant and was awaiting further information from the home office on Jack Barton. She sent Cameron a text.

> Still running down a couple of leads. Did the home office send files to you? You need to know what I know about all this.

A couple of minutes later she got an answer.

> **Yes. Reading through them now. What the hell with all the women going missing from Barton's camp?**

She replied to his text.

> That's part of what we're here to do. To find out. Get caught up on the info and we'll talk tomorrow. I wish you were here.

When he responded, she smiled.

> **Yes, ma'am. I wish I was there, too. I miss your face. Sleep well, love you.**

Rusty sighed. She missed his face, too. Then she crawled into bed, pulled up the covers and fell asleep.

The vet clinic had been closed for a couple of hours when Sam Carson got called out on an emergency at the McCoy farm up the mountain. Two bulls on neighboring farms had gotten into the same pasture and had a terrible fight before their owners got them separated and penned up. But John McCoy's bull had suffered injuries serious enough to need stitches to stop the bleeding.

Sam arrived on scene in a timely fashion and was in the barn with McCoy and his sons, Rob and Lee, and the injured bull. He had just sedated the bull and they were standing back, waiting for him to drop, when the bull took a sudden leap forward and swung his head, hitting Sam in the chest with a blow that lifted him off his feet and slammed him against the wall.

Sam came down hard, twisting his knee as he landed, then couldn't get up.

"Oh shit! Boys! Grab the doc," John yelled, and got between his bull and the downed vet while his sons pulled Sam out of the pen.

Sam was out of danger now, but the damage had already been done. He knew he had a broken rib because he'd heard it snap, and his knee was throbbing and already swelling. It hurt to inhale, but he didn't think his lungs had been punctured.

And to top it all off, the sedation he'd injected into the wounded animal kicked in. The bull was down and still bleeding profusely.

"Doc! Doc! Are you okay?" John cried as he climbed over the corral.

"Not really," Sam said, "but let's get bully-boy stitched up before I pass out."

"Oh man, I'm so sorry," John said. "Tell us what to do to help."

"Help me back in the pen, and somebody get my bag," Sam said, and they all raced to get him situated.

Following Sam's instructions, John sluiced and cleaned the cut on the bull with antiseptic, then Rob and Lee held the loose skin together so Sam could stitch it. By the time Sam finished, he was in a cold sweat from the pain, and the bull was beginning to wake up. He gave the animal an injection to offset the sedation and then they cleared out of the pen.

"Get me and my stuff back to the truck," Sam said. 'I'm leaving medicine for you to administer for six days. Keep him penned up until the wound is well, and get your damn fence fixed. We don't want to be doing this again anytime soon."

John shook his head. "The boys are driving you to the ER, and they'll park your truck at your place before they go home. You're not going to be driving it for a while."

Sam didn't have any breath left to argue.

He spent the night in the ER, and an ambulance took him home around daybreak. Now he was laid up at home with a swollen knee and a cracked rib. He tried to get a substitute vet in to cover for him, but none were available until tomorrow, so he called Leslie.

She answered her phone as she was walking to her car to go to work.

"Hello?"

"Leslie, this is Sam. I had a run-in with a bull out at John McCoy's last night. I have a broken rib and a swollen knee, and I can't get anyone in to sub for me until tomorrow."

"Oh, Sam! Oh no! I'm so sorry. What do you need me to do?" she asked.

"Just leave the Closed sign up, but if you wouldn't mind going by and putting a sign on the door letting everyone know the clinic will be open tomorrow, I would really appreciate it. And call Amber and let her know you both have the day off. Allan Morris out of Bowling Green will sub for me tomorrow."

"Will do, but are you okay to be at home on your own? Is there anything you need me to pick up for you? Any food or medicine?"

"No. I'm all set, and I can order in food."

"Okay, but if something comes up, I'm only a call away," she said.

"I know. Thanks, Leslie."

The call ended as Leslie was getting in her car. She rushed around doing everything Sam asked and drove back home for a couple more hours of sleep. She was drifting off when it dawned on her that she could pay a visit to Kevin today.

They'd been seeing each other off and on for almost five weeks, although their dates had been spur-of-the-moment and random. He had his research and she had her job, and she already knew he'd be leaving the area before the end of the year. He was sort of cute and seemed really nice, and it was hard to find someone to date when you were related to over half the population.

She fell asleep thinking of how fun it would be to surprise him.

―――――――――

Kevin Vanzant was in his bathroom, shaving. The battery-powered razor was doing its thing, but it had been so long since he'd had a haircut that he'd gone the ponytail route.

He wasn't Hollywood handsome, but his blue eyes and broad shoulders were a draw, as was his easy laugh. He could get a girlfriend when he wanted one, so he wasn't hurting for female companionship, but he was sick of this place. Sick of this little travel trailer and all these damn trees. If it hadn't been for Emily, he wouldn't even be here, but he was making some spare change, and his time was nearly over. Only a couple more weeks and he'd be gone.

He'd made all his usual rounds in Jubilee yesterday and then spent this morning on a "walk" around the campground, seeing who was new and who was gone, and had plans to spend the rest of the day in the trailer organizing photos from the past few days and saving them to his laptop.

He stopped to eat a sandwich about midday and drank his last beer with it, then took the SIM card from his camera and popped it into a port in the laptop and began uploading all of the images into a new file. He was entertaining himself watching TikTok as he waited for the upload to finish, when he heard a car drive up.

"Who the hell?" he muttered, and stayed seated, hoping whoever it was would just go away. And then he heard a couple of knocks at the door and Leslie's voice.

"Hey, Kevin! It's me, Leslie!"

He frowned, then got up and opened the door. "Uh... hi! What brings you out here today? I thought you were at work."

Leslie came in talking, explaining about what had happened and how she came to have the day off, and then hugged him.

"I thought if you were free, we could do something together."

He frowned. "Gee, I wish I could, but I'm really busy today. I have tons of data to sort today. I'm really sorry. That would have been fun."

Leslie sighed. "I should have called," she said, and then turned toward his desk and the open laptop and saw a wall of faces on the screen. "What's all that have to do with your research?"

Kevin's heart skipped a beat. The only thing he'd been warned about this job was keeping it on the down low. "Oh, that's just some random pics I took while I was in town the other day. It's a way to make a little extra money. You know how people are...always wanting special photos."

Leslie saw the panic in his eyes and knew he was lying.

"Nobody hires people to take pictures of them on vacation. They use their own cell phones for that," she said.

Kevin shifted his panic into defense. "Are you calling me a liar?"

"Did you hear that word come out of my mouth? I just made an observation for which you seem to have no answers, and I'm sorry I bothered you!" Leslie snapped.

She turned to walk away and he grabbed her by the arm.

"Where are you going?" he asked.

She twisted out of his grasp. "You're busy, remember?"

Kevin reached for her again, but she ducked beneath his arm and ran out of the trailer with him right behind her, yelling at her to stop.

And then all of a sudden Jack Barton was rolling up in his golf cart, and Kevin froze while Leslie kept going. She jumped in her car, made a U-turn at the campsite, and sped past Jack without looking back.

Kevin was pissed and Jack Barton was approaching. He had no option but to hear him out.

Chapter 8

JACK WAS EMBARRASSED AND APOLOGETIC AS HE APPROACHED the travel trailer.

"Sorry. I didn't mean to intrude. I'm just making the rounds to notify all of the active campsites that we'll be closing up for the winter by the end of the month. I can help you find a new location, though."

Kevin shoved his hands in his pockets and made himself smile.

"No thanks. I'll figure it out. I'm just sorting data anyway."

Jack knew from the way Vanzant was shifting from one foot to the other that he was hiding something, and he didn't like secrets, but Vanzant ended the conversation by returning to the trailer and firmly shutting the door.

Jack was already bothered by the fight he'd witnessed, but this odd comment didn't set well with him, either. He jumped back in his golf cart and sped away.

———

Leslie was hurt and confused. She'd just seen a side of Kevin she didn't know existed and it scared her. For a moment there, she'd felt threatened. Like he wasn't going to let her leave. Jack Barton's arrival had given her the opening she needed to get away.

She kept looking in her rearview mirror all the way back into town, afraid she'd see Kevin driving up behind her, but it didn't happen. Her day off had taken a really nasty turn, and she didn't quite know what to do with what she'd seen. Something about it didn't feel right, although there really wasn't anything to tell. It wasn't illegal to take pictures of tourists in a town full of them. But instead of going home, she drove through Jubilee and headed up the mountain. She needed her mama's arms around her, and Granny Cauley's wisdom to settle her nerves.

By the time Leslie pulled up in her parents' drive, she was feeling easier. She'd never been scared like that before. Her arms were still tingling from the grip he'd had on her, and she needed hugs to replace the fear.

Their old hound, Blue Boy, was lying on the front step, but when she got out of the car, he managed to raise his head and bugle once to let everyone know there was a visitor in the yard.

Her father came out on the porch as she was walking across the yard and then came down off the steps to greet her.

"Hey, sugar!" Wade said, and wrapped his arms around her. "Come in out of the chill. Your mom and Granny are cooking up a batch of pear preserves."

"I can smell it from here," Leslie said, and walked inside with her daddy's arm around her shoulders.

"We're in the kitchen!" her mother shouted.

Wade walked in with Leslie. "Look who's here, Granny."

Sheila Cauley looked up, pleased by her granddaughter's unexpected visit.

"Hello, sweetheart," she said.

"Hi, Granny. It smells good in here," Leslie said.

Rita took one look at her daughter and frowned.

"What's wrong? Why aren't you at work?"

Leslie slid onto a stool at the kitchen island. "Dr. Sam got hurt last night so we closed up for the day."

"Okay," Rita said. "But why do you have that look in your eyes?"

Leslie sighed. "I guess because Kevin Vanzant just scared the crap out of me and I ran home like the big baby I am."

Wade's smile went south. "Are you talking about the college boy you've been seeing? The one who's been staying out at Jack Barton's campsite?"

Leslie nodded. "Since I had the day off, I drove out to see if he was working at the campsite today instead of traipsing through the woods as usual. He was there and acted all weird when he saw me. We had a discussion that turned sour, and as I was getting ready to leave, I saw his laptop was open and the screen was covered with photos of women and children. All close-ups of their faces. He lied about why he had them and I called him on it. When I started to leave, he grabbed me and wouldn't let me go. I jerked free and ran out of the trailer with him right behind me. Then Jack Barton drove up in his golf cart, and I kept running. But I had a weird feeling and kept looking behind me all the way into town. Did I overreact?"

Rita was horrified. "No, you didn't overreact. No man should put his hands on a woman like that."

Wade was furious. "I'm going to have a talk with him."

Leslie shuddered. "No, Daddy. Just let it go. I don't want anything to do with him again. Anyway, he's leaving soon."

Wade didn't comment further, but he didn't like the implications of those photos on the laptop, and after Leslie had gotten all of that off her chest and settled into helping with the canning, he left the house and headed for his workshop. He wanted to call the police and have them check the man out, but if he did, then that would involve Leslie, and she'd already made her feelings clear. And then he thought of PCG's board of directors. They dealt with the business of Jubilee, and Cameron was the CEO, so he called him.

Cameron was reading through the files Agent Howard had sent, trying to catch up on what Rusty already knew. There were so many levels of concern within the pages, but nothing concrete or any one person to point to. The one certainty was the subterfuge and intensity to which people had gone to hide how many women, all tourists, had gone missing from Jubilee.

He was deep in thought when his phone rang and Wade Morgan's name came up on caller ID.

"Hey, Wade."

"Cameron, got a minute?" Wade asked.

"Yes, sure. What's up?"

"Leslie just came home all upset and worried. She dumped a story on us that I don't like, but she won't let me go to the police with it. Said she doesn't want anything more to do with the man, and stirring this up will just involve her again. I need someone else to know this besides me."

"What happened, and who's the man in question?" Cameron asked.

"A guy named Kevin Vanzant. He has a campsite out at Jack Barton's campground, doing some kind of research."

The hair stood up on Cameron's neck. He'd just read that name as someone the feds wanted checked out.

"How is Leslie involved with him?" Cameron asked.

"They've been seeing each other off and on for a few weeks. Nothing serious. But it all blew up on her today and she left his campsite running." Then he related everything Leslie had told them, including the fear that Kevin might follow her.

"She said the argument started over the photos?" Cameron asked.

"Yes."

"And when she tried to leave, he wouldn't let her?"

"Right, until Barton showed up. She left while they were still talking. Does this all sound as shifty to you as it did to me?"

"Something seems off, for sure," Cameron said. "Leave this to me. I know some people. We'll check him out and he'll never know it, and Leslie will be in the clear."

Wade sighed. "Thanks, man. I really appreciate this."

"Just tell Leslie to stay away from the campground and him. I'll be in touch."

"Will do," Wade said, and disconnected.

Cameron's gut knotted. "And so it begins."

———

After Wade's phone call, Cameron needed to talk to Rusty, but calling her was risky in case she was with her family, so he sent a text.

> Word from the mountain. Kevin Vanzant, the camper at Barton's campground outside of Jubilee, has a laptop full of strangers' photos. Close-ups of young women and children's faces.

Once he'd delivered the message, it was up to Rusty as to how to act on this. He also had to find a way to caution Rachel about being vigilant without scaring her more than she already was. After calling her to make sure a visit was okay, he put two cookies and a dog biscuit into a baggie, then left the cabin with Ghost at his heels. They drove up the mountain to Rachel's house. As he was getting out, Rachel opened the front door, holding Lili, and when the toddler saw Cam and Ghost, she started waving and chattering. "Unca Cam…Unca Cam."

Cameron was smiling as he came up the steps. "The best welcoming committee ever," he said as he leaned down to hug his sister, but when he did, Lili abandoned her mother and climbed into his arms.

Rachel laughed. "I guess I know where I stand." Then she knelt, stroked Ghost's head, and then hugged him. "You are our hero, too," she said, and led the way indoors.

The moment they sat down, Lili turned in Cameron's arms and patted his face.

"Cookie?"

Cameron glanced at Rachel before he answered, and when she nodded her approval, he put Lili down on the floor and pulled the bag out of his pocket.

"One for Lili," he said, and handed it to her. "And one for Mama, 'cause we love her."

Lili beamed, bounced over to where Rachel was sitting, and laid a cookie in her lap.

"Wuv her," she said, and then went back to Cameron and climbed back up in his lap before taking a bite of her cookie.

"Do I get a bite?" Cameron asked.

"Get a bite," Lili said, and shoved it under Cameron's nose.

He took a little bite and then rolled his eyes in pretend ecstasy. "Mmmm, good," he said.

"Mmmm, good," Lili echoed, then eyed Ghost lying at Cameron's feet and pointed. "Ghoss bite?"

Cameron pulled the dog biscuit out of his pocket. "Ghost eats this kind."

"I do Ghoss," Lili said as she bailed out of his lap again, took the treat, and held it under Ghost's nose.

"Bite?"

Ghost gently took the treat from her baby fingers and then chewed and swallowed.

Lili laughed. "All gone."

Cameron sat her back in his lap before she started feeding her cookie to Ghost, because sugar wasn't on his menu. As soon as she settled and started eating her own cookie, he was finally able to talk to Rachel.

"Lili looks great. Is she all better?" he asked.

Rachel nodded. "Yes, and with no lingering aftereffects."

"How about you?" Cameron asked.

Rachel touched the back of her head. "Staples will be out next week. Headaches are down to about one a day. We're getting back to normal."

Cameron hesitated briefly, then went in headfirst. "I have a gut feeling that your normal is just an illusion."

Rachel frowned. "What do you mean? What do you know that I don't?"

He shrugged. "Nothing specific, but I keep going over what you said about Biggers being shocked to see you when he broke into the house."

Rachel's eyes narrowed, and Cameron knew she was thinking back to that moment.

"Yes, I know he was. He came in all wild and running, then saw my face and froze. He said, 'You!' like it was a question of disbelief, and then I rushed at him and the fight ensued. But what are you getting at?"

"If he didn't know who lived here, it also means he didn't know the kid he came after was yours, and he didn't care if he left you dying to get her. It wasn't just a random kidnapping. You're too far off the beaten path for him to just 'hope' there's a kid living here he can snatch. He broke out of prison, so someone had to scope you out first to send him here. And that begs the question, out of all the babies within a fifty-mile radius of Jubilee, why Lili?"

All the color faded from Rachel's face.

"What are you saying?"

"Be careful. Don't assume anything. Be wary of strangers."

Rachel's eyes welled. "You're scaring me."

"I'm sorry, honey. But I'd rather you were scared than dead. I'm going to do a little digging on my own, but for now, you and Louis keep this to yourself. If there's something shady going on in Jubilee, as the CEO of the family corporation I take it as part of my duty to root it out."

Rachel had a knot in her stomach, but her brother's steady gaze and calm voice were enough to settle the panic. "I never thought of what happened in this way. It's an eye-opener, for sure, and I won't let down my guard again," she said.

"You didn't let down your guard to begin with," Cameron said. "You were invaded. There's a difference. And there's a whole mountain full of people like you who won't put up with that shit."

Oblivious of the seriousness of the grown-ups' conversation, Lili shoved the last bite of cookie in her mouth, wiped her hands on Cameron's shirt, and slid out of his lap.

He grinned at the look of horror on his sister's face, and the moment passed. He left a short while later, satisfied that he'd put Rachel on alert without giving anything away, and went home.

Kevin was antsy. He'd been here six months without having an issue, and in the space of ten minutes Leslie had walked in on him and seen stuff she shouldn't have, then accused him of lying, which was the truth, and before he could stop her and explain, Jack Barton arrived and he lost the opportunity to smooth it all over.

However, Barton's notice about the camp closing gave him the perfect opportunity to bring his little side job to an end. He just needed to call Boss and let him know. He'd never met the man and had only spoken to him a couple of times on the phone. He sat down on the sofa, made the call, and waited as it began to ring. Just as he thought it was going to go to voicemail, there was a gruff voice in his ear.

"What?"

"Uh, Boss, it's—"

"I know who it is. I recognize the number. What do you want?"

Kevin was taken aback by what sounded like anger in the man's voice, then began to explain. "The owner of the campsite was just here. He's shutting down for the winter soon. And people here are getting a little nosy. I think it's time to pack it in and head home."

"You don't quit me," the man said.

Kevin froze. "Uh, sorry. You misunderstand. I have more than paid back the favor you did for me. My job isn't secure here anymore. I have one more file to clean up and send to you. You can send my last paycheck to my bank account as usual."

"Ah, I see," the man said. "When do you plan to leave?"

"I'll get your file to you tonight. Then I'll spend tomorrow packing up camp and leave the following morning."

"Yes. One must always tie up loose ends."

"Yes, sir, and thank you again for the opportunity."

Kevin went to the desk after the call ended and began cleaning up photos and making a new file. As soon as he finished, he hit Send. Then, as was his habit, he saved the same file to another laptop he kept hidden in the trunk of his car. He wasn't convinced that sending anything to the cloud was completely protected, so this was his way of not losing valuable data in case one laptop got fried.

As he was planning his next move, he got a call and smiled when he saw caller ID. It was Emily. "Hey, sugar. How's it going?"

"I'm on my way back to Jubilee. I'm so weary of this shit."

"No worries. I just spoke to Boss and let him know Barton is shutting down the campsite for the winter. I sent him the last of the files and told him we were even. I still have to pack up, but when I leave, you're going with me."

"Oh my God! Thank you, baby, thank you. I haven't had a drop to drink since all this happened, and I can promise on my life, I will never drink again."

He heard her crying and winced. It had been a long haul to get past this. "It's okay. You and I are good. I'll talk to you soon. Drive safe."

"Yes, I will. Later," she said, and disconnected.

Kevin rocked back in the chair, relieved this was over, and then looked out the window, surprised it was already getting dark.

He began turning on lights inside, then sat down to a cold supper of saltine crackers and sardines, and washed it down with a lukewarm Mountain Dew. As soon as he'd finished, he gathered up the garbage and carried it down the short drive to a covered trash can and headed back to the trailer.

He was on the bottom step and opening the door when he heard a twig snap behind him and then someone call out his name.

"Kevin Vanzant."

He turned around, looking out into the night.

"Who's there?"

He heard the shot at the same time he felt the blow to his chest and fell backward onto the steps. Dead before he'd landed.

A dark figure emerged from the trees, walked up to the trailer, propped a rifle against the side of it, then went inside, sidestepping Kevin's body. He dragged the body the rest of the way inside, took the laptop and the phone beside it, then turned out the lights and shut the door as he left.

━━━━━━

Rusty was at peace with herself in a way she had never been before, and it had nothing to do with visiting family and everything to do with finding Cameron.

She'd spent most of the morning working and then part of the afternoon back in the hot tub. When she got back in her room and saw his text about Vanzant and the photos, she immediately forwarded it to Agent Howard.

Within minutes, he texted her back.

> **Message received. Our boy is paying off. We may need to move you from undercover to active investigation with him as your liaison to the community, but that's yet to be decided. Continue as planned.**

She sent a text back to Howard that she'd received the message, then sent another one to Cameron.

> Good lead! Talk to you tonight.

Hyped from the sudden activity involving their investigation, Rusty went to shower and get ready for her evening with family, then checked her computer for updates and emails before going to join them.

Her aunt Pat was in the library playing bartender. Ray was in his easy chair by the fireplace with a gin and tonic in one hand and his phone in the other, arguing vehemently with someone. Liz was sitting near the floor-to-ceiling windows overlooking downtown Jubilee, stirring her drink with her finger.

Patricia saw Rusty walk in. "Good evening, darling. Did you have a good rest?"

"Yes, thank you. Nothing is ever so wrong that a good dip in a hot tub won't fix it," she said.

Patricia laughed. "Would you like something to drink?"

Rusty plopped down on the sofa. "Hmm, I took a pain pill earlier, so just sparkling water for me tonight."

Patricia frowned. "Oh, honey, are you still in that kind of pain?"

"Just my knee, but I'm doing exactly what the doctor said. Light exercise, water therapy, and rest when I feel like it."

Patricia brought her drink and kissed the top of Rusty's head before sitting down beside her. "So, we're still on for lunch tomorrow?" she asked.

Rusty nodded. "Yes! There are so many little nooks and crannies in this town that intrigue me. I want to try the Back Porch. Liz says the food is good."

Liz smiled. "It's fine dining, hillbilly style. The food is good, but the decor is very rural in design. Wooden tables. Red-and-white oilcloth table covers. Salt and pepper shakers shaped like mini-mason jars, and the drinks are served in wide-mouth pint canning jars."

Patricia rolled her eyes. "It's a little too quaint for my taste, but Liz is right about the food. And we're still on for eleven thirty?"

Rusty nodded and took a sip of her water.

Ray finally hung up and then downed the rest of his drink like medicine.

"Ray, honey, is everything okay?" Patricia asked.

He frowned. "Yes, nothing drastic. Just an employee

issue. One of my best hostesses took personal leave again and I didn't know it. She does this randomly. If she wasn't so good at her job, I'd let her go."

Rusty frowned. "I wonder why? Where does she go?"

"I have no idea," Ray said.

"What is her name?" Rusty asked.

"Emily Payne."

"Do you have a photo of her?" Rusty asked.

Ray paused, then gave Rusty a long look.

"I imagine we do," he said slowly. "Why?"

Rusty shrugged. "Force of habit.. Sometimes I do research for cases. I just thought if there was anything shady, and you were worried, I could—"

Ray's eyes narrowed thoughtfully. "Meet me in the office after dinner. I'll print out all the info we have on her."

"Okay. Can't promise a thing, but being proactive always makes me feel less anxious about things," she said.

"Enough about all this business stuff," Patricia said. "I'm going to check on dinner. Liz, stop moping about Michael. Either call him or kick him to the curb."

Liz frowned. "Mom! Really? I am not calling him. He'll grovel back on his own or he won't."

Patricia left the library, and a few moments later, Liz followed.

Ray glanced at Rusty again. "You're quite the paper pusher, aren't you?"

Rusty stood. "I am what I am, Uncle Ray."

Ray nodded. "I will stow my curiosity and questions," he said, and got up and hugged her. "I'm so glad you're here."

"So am I, Uncle Ray. So am I," she said, and hugged him back.

They walked to the dining room together.

The hotel staff arrived with their food, set it all on the table, filled their wineglasses, then disappeared, leaving them to dine.

As soon as they were gone, Ray lifted his glass.

"A toast to our Rusty. To you, dear niece, and for total healing while you are with us."

"To Rusty," Liz and Aunt Pat echoed.

The clink of glasses one to the other and the smiles that came with them were balm to Rusty's solitary life.

"Thank you," she said, and took a quick sip. "Dinner looks and smells amazing, and prime rib is one of my favorites," she said.

Ray beamed. "Our chef just won another Michelin star. We're very proud of him and our kitchen. Enjoy!"

And so they did, chattering among themselves as they ate.

"I'm getting the good out of the hot tub," Rusty said.

Patricia nodded. "It's good for sore muscles. It'll help you heal faster."

"I have plenty of those, but it is very relaxing. I could get spoiled to this," Rusty said.

Ray glanced up. "I keep meaning to ask. How did you come to rate a flight in on a government chopper?"

Rusty blinked. *What happened to no more questions?*

Ray continued. "A member of our security staff saw it coming in. He recognized the pilot and knows he flies people from the Department of Justice all over the country."

"Yes, well, I had my accident on company time, and my boss set up the flight. I didn't question the offer," Rusty said.

Ray nodded and continued to eat, but he was remembering one of his last conversations with his brother before he died. Something about Rusty and the risks her job entailed. At the time, the comment hadn't really registered, but now he was thinking there was more to her than met the eye.

His security officer had been very forthcoming about how the DOJ operates, and Ray was absolutely certain they didn't spend government money sending clerks and secretaries on vacation to visit family, even if they had been hurt on the job. He watched her curiously as dinner continued, but didn't pry about her personal life again.

Rusty felt her uncle's gaze more than once, but she never acknowledged it. She just rode out the evening with all the poise and grace she could manage, and felt guilty for the lie between them.

After dinner, she followed Ray to his office and waited while he printed off all the info he had on Emily Payne. He handed it to her without comment.

"It's probably nothing, or it's a guy," Rusty said, and left with the papers.

The plus side of this evening was knowing where they were going to lunch tomorrow, and as soon as she got to her room, she hurried through the sitting area to her bedroom, turned on the television for noise, then shut herself in the bathroom and called Cameron.

It was nearing 10:00 p.m. when Cameron's cell phone rang. When he saw the number come up, he answered quickly.

"Hello, Angel."

Rusty smiled. "Hey, Soldier Boy. I wanted to touch base with you about tomorrow...and I also wanted to hear your voice before I went to bed."

"I wish you were in my bed," he said.

An ache went through Rusty in waves. "I wish I was, too. Soon," she said.

"Very soon, please. Now tell me where you're going, and when do you plan to arrive?"

"A place called the Back Porch around eleven thirty."

"Okay. I'll be there," Cameron said.

"I can't wait! Oh...your info about Kevin Vanzant is timely. We need to check him out as soon as possible. And I have a bit of news that may or may not have anything to do with what I'm here for, but Uncle Ray has a hostess who goes AWOL periodically with no warning. Nobody seems to know where she goes, and she doesn't explain herself when she comes back. I got all the info Uncle Ray had on her from her personnel file. I'm checking her out for his peace of mind. He wouldn't want someone working for him who was also doing anything illegal, but right now, I'm checking on any and everything weird that's going on here."

"Damn it," Cameron said.

"There's no reason yet to assume it's connected to these people," Rusty said.

"I don't like coincidences," Cameron said.

"Right. Neither do I. But back to tomorrow. Liz says the menu is varied and the ambiance will set Aunt Patricia's teeth on edge."

Cameron chuckled. "Liz is your cousin, right?"

"Yes. You don't know her?"

"I know *of* the whole family, but I can't say I've had the pleasure. We don't exactly have the same circle of friends."

"Well, you'll meet them tomorrow. And just for the record, I was never the debutante. I served pizza and waited tables through college, and my training after college had nothing to do with trips to Europe and more to do with the Body Farm and Quantico."

"My kind of woman," Cameron said. "I'll be on my best behavior and—"

A sudden ache washed through her, making her voice shake. "No. I want the man who stole my heart in that hotel in New York. Neither of us was on our best behavior. We did a wild, crazy thing, and I want that man back."

Cameron felt the emotion in her voice. "Have no fear. I'm coming to get you tomorrow and lay claim to you in front of God and everybody, whether they like it or not."

Rusty shivered. "I look forward to being overwhelmed."

"I aim to please," Cameron said. "Sleep well, darlin'. I'll see you tomorrow."

Rusty's eyes welled with tears. She'd always, always wanted a man to call her *darlin'*.

"Yes. See you then," she said.

She went back to the bedroom to put her phone on the

charger, then showered and crawled into bed naked, and fell asleep thinking about what it felt like to come apart in his arms.

———————

Rusty was awake before 7:00 a.m. and full of nervous energy. Today was the launch pad for the big deception. She thought about the hot tub and then opted for the pool, wrote a note to the family to let them know where she was, and rode the elevator down to the pool level.

She was alone when she slipped into the water and started swimming laps. A short while later, an older man arrived and began swimming laps a couple of lanes over. After a quick glance to reassure herself he was harmless, she never looked at him again. Thirty laps later, she climbed out of the pool, exhausted but easier in her mind about the upcoming day, and headed back to the penthouse. It was just before eight. The elevator stopped, the doors opened, and the first thing she saw was her uncle Ray, waiting for the car to arrive.

"Good morning, Rusty! What an early riser you are! I see you've been in the pool."

She nodded. "Back home I usually go out for a run, but I'm not quite ready for that."

"I commend you for your dedication and diligence," he said. "Your aunt and cousin aren't even up yet."

Rusty laughed. "They don't have to be. I'm big enough to take care of myself."

Ray's eyes twinkled. "Yes, I see that," he said, and kissed her on the cheek. "Have a great day, honey. I'll see you later."

He went down to his office as Rusty returned to her room.

The adrenaline rush was fading as she showered and dressed for the day. The weather was sunny but cool, so she opted for a black sweater and black denim jeans. Her ankle was still too sore for the cowboy boots she loved to wear, so it was slip-on shoes for her today. She was air-drying her hair, and it was turning into a mass of soft curls against her shoulders. It was a wild, untamed look, but it mirrored how she felt.

After applying just enough makeup to take the shine off her face, she went in search of coffee and toast. She found that and the rest of her family seated at the breakfast table, still in their nightgowns and robes.

"Good morning!" Rusty said as she bounced into the room.

Both women looked up.

"Oh God! An early riser," Liz groaned.

"You put me to shame," Patricia said.

Rusty grinned. "Would it make you feel any better if I told you I've already done thirty laps in the pool?"

"Why? Just tell me why? You're supposed to be on vacation."

Rusty shrugged. "I run every morning. Or I did before I hurt my knee and ankle. It's addictive."

Liz rolled her eyes. "If I'm going to be addicted to something, I choose sex."

Rusty burst out laughing.

Patricia gasped. "Elizabeth Ann! Really? What a thing to say," and then laughed in spite of herself.

A short while later, her aunt and cousin abandoned Rusty with her toast and coffee and went to get ready for their lunch date. Rusty took her coffee back to her room to check messages and email.

She'd been on the job from the moment she'd set foot in Jubilee, and her uncle's missing hostess may have just been added to the mix. Last night she'd run a quick search on Emily Payne's credit card history, and she needed to sit down and look at the data. She also made a mental note to have Cameron scout out Kevin Vanzant's campsite after their "reunion moment" at lunch. Her thoughts were spinning as to what to do first, and they kept coming back to making love to Cameron Pope.

Chapter 9

It was go time.

Cameron was on his way into town, heading straight into his future, with Ghost riding shotgun. He'd already called in a pickup order at the Back Porch as his excuse to make an appearance. He was hungry, but not for food. For Rusty. He'd dreamed of making love to her for so long, and now that she was within reach again, he wanted her back in his bed. But want and need were two different things, and right now she was part of the walking wounded and beginning a new and dangerous case. He'd agreed to help before he knew who he'd be working with. Now all he could think of was keeping her safe from herself. Like every other young woman in Jubilee, her presence made her a target.

———

Rusty started smiling the moment they entered the Back Porch. The decor was just as Liz had depicted. The background music was bluegrass, and the waiters were wearing overalls and the waitresses were in calico. She glanced at Aunt Pat, saw the instant distaste for where they were, and hugged her.

"It's perfect, Aunt Pat! Thank you for coming."

Patricia grinned. "If I didn't love you dearly…"

"Come on, Mom. The hostess is ready to seat us," Liz said, leading the way to their table.

"Gawd. In the middle of the room?" Patricia muttered and sat down, wishing herself small and invisible as Rusty took off her coat and sat beside her.

The moment passed, and she had gotten over herself enough to go through the menu with the girls, when Liz suddenly let out a groan. "Oh crap! Michael's here, and he's coming over."

"Be nice," Patricia said. "Ladies have disagreements in private, understand?"

Rusty took quick note of the nervous expression on the man's face and felt sorry for him. She didn't have to know what had happened between them to know Liz could be a real diva.

"Liz. Mrs. Caldwell. What a nice surprise," Michael said, and gave Rusty a curious look and a smile, waiting to be introduced, which left Liz with no option without being rude to Rusty in the process.

Liz sighed. "Rusty, this is my friend Michael Devon. His father owns Hotel Devon, on the other side of town. Michael, this is my cousin, Rusty Caldwell. She's visiting us for a while."

Rusty gave him her best smile. "It's a pleasure to meet you, Michael." And then she saw Cameron walking into the restaurant and froze. "Oh my God. Oh my God!" she said and stood, staring fixedly at the man coming toward their table.

Everyone, including Michael turned around to see what had caused this reaction, and the moment Michael saw Cameron Pope approaching them, he gave Liz a hard glare.

And then Rusty started smiling and walking toward Cameron, and when he suddenly picked her up off her feet and kissed her in front of all the diners like there was no tomorrow, Patricia and Liz audibly gasped.

There they stood in the middle of the restaurant, talking animatedly in low undertones, and they kept touching each other as if reluctant to lose contact. Finally, Rusty turned and pointed toward their table, then grabbed Cameron's hand and led him over.

"This is the best day ever!" Rusty said. "Everyone, this is Cameron Pope. We met five years ago at a hotel in Virginia. He was shipping out the next day and I was in town for a meeting."

Cameron put his arm around her shoulders. "We spent every hour I had left together, and her memory is the reason I'm still single."

Rusty blushed.

Cameron pulled her closer, eyeing the people at the table and waiting to be introduced.

Rusty shook her head. "Where are my manners? Cameron, this is my aunt, Patricia Caldwell, her daughter, Liz, and Liz's friend Michael Devon. I'm just learning Cameron lives here, so you all may already know each other."

Cameron shook his head. "I know *who* they are, but we've never met."

And in that moment, Michael Devon had to accept that his jealousy of Pope was misplaced.

Patricia's eyes narrowed. "I think you held the door for me the other day as I was coming out of the bakery."

"Yes, ma'am," Cameron said, then rubbed the side of his jaw. "My face was still healing, and I hadn't shaved in a few days."

"Healing from what?" Rusty asked.

"Just a hunting trip on the mountain," Cameron said, and then paused. "Forgive me for interrupting your meal. I have a to-go order to pick up and my dog is waiting for me in the Jeep." He handed Rusty a card. "Call me. We have a lot of catching up to do."

Rusty slipped it in her pocket. "I used to pray you would make it home, and now I see my prayers were answered. I'll definitely call you later today, if that's okay?"

Cameron laughed, and the sound carried across the room, turning heads again.

"Okay? Lady, if you didn't, I'd come looking for you to find out why."

Then he kissed her full on the lips again, nodded at Michael and her family, then went up front to pick up his to-go order and walked out.

Rusty sat back down in her chair with a plop. Her cheeks were pink. Her eyes were full of tears, and her voice was shaking. "Oh, Aunt Pat. Do you believe in love at first sight?"

Patricia smiled. "I've heard it's possible."

Michael put his hand on Liz's shoulder. "Liz, I miss you. May I call you tonight?"

Liz sighed. Considering she'd just witnessed the death of her last fantasy, it was probably a good idea to pick up where they'd left off.

"I suppose," she said, and picked up her menu, leaving Michael to walk away on his own. She gave Rusty a long look and then grinned. "Well, Cuz. You're something of a dark horse, aren't you?"

Rusty shrugged. "Not really. He's the only man I ever wanted, and when he disappeared from my life, all I knew was I didn't want a second best."

Liz looked back at the menu. "What are you having... besides a hard-on for Cameron Pope?"

Patricia glared. She hated it when her daughter got bawdy.

Rusty heard jealousy in the tone and ignored her.

Their waitress's appearance ended the foolishness. They gave her their orders, then as soon as she was gone, Liz and Patricia started grilling Rusty again. Finally, she gave in.

"Look, you two. It wasn't a secret. It was a one-night stand that changed my life. I knew he was going back to war, and he knew nothing about me. We made a pact. No promises. No regrets, and no names. He called me Angel. I called him Soldier Boy. When I woke up the next morning, he was gone, and I felt like he'd taken a piece of me with him. In a way, I've been at war with myself ever since. Finding him here after all this time feels like such a gift, and to know he feels the same way is a miracle. I'm not going to dissect anything about it."

Patricia reached across the table and patted Rusty's

hand. "Understood, and just so you know, I'm happy that you're happy."

"Thank you," Rusty said.

Liz glanced up. "Finally, here comes our food. After all this drama, I could eat a horse."

━━━━━━━

Cameron left with a sandwich in a bag and new orders to follow. Not all of their dramatic embrace had been sweet whispers. After what he'd told her last night about the photos on Kevin Vanzant's laptop, Rusty was sending him on his first mission—to pay a visit to Kevin Vanzant.

He sat in the parking lot long enough to eat the sandwich he'd ordered, sharing some of it with Ghost, then tossed the trash in a garbage can and headed out of town.

He was on his way to the campground when he began hearing sirens behind him. He glanced up, saw two police cars coming up fast and pulled over. They flew past him with lights flashing and sirens screaming.

Frowning, he pulled back onto the highway. A few moments later he glanced up in the rearview mirror again and saw three more police cars behind him, running hot. As he pulled over again to let them pass, he realized these were from the county sheriff's office. Now the hair was standing up on the back of his neck. Something bad was going down and he was right behind them.

When they took the turn into Barton's campground, he did the same, and was immediately flagged down by one of the local police. Before Cameron could get out, the policeman was knocking on the window.

Cameron rolled it down. "Hey, Charlie, what's going on?"

"They found a dead body at one of the campsites."

Cameron frowned. "What happened? Some kind of accident?"

"Yeah. The dude got in front of someone else's bullet, but I didn't tell you that."

"Has he been identified?" Cameron asked.

Charlie shrugged. "Some guy doing research for a college degree. Been here all summer and now this. But I didn't tell you that, either. Understand?"

"His name wouldn't be Kevin Vanzant, would it?" Cameron asked.

"I didn't verify that, did I?" Charlie said. "This place is off-limits for now. Sorry."

"No problem," Cameron said. "I'll come back another time," he added, then backed up and headed back to town.

He knew Rusty would still be at the restaurant with her family, but this was her investigation and he had to let her know. He pulled over on the shoulder of the highway long enough to send her a text.

Cops all over campground. Dead body found.
Word is that it's Vanzant. He was shot. Local
police and county on scene. Awaiting orders.

The Caldwell girls were debating about ordering dessert when Rusty's phone began to vibrate in her purse.

"Sorry," she said. "I know I'm on leave, but my job over-rules ignoring calls." She was still smiling as she pulled out her phone and read the text. Shock rolled through her as the smile froze on her face. "I have to take this. Excuse me a sec," she said, and headed outside with the phone in her hand.

The moment she was out of earshot, she called Jay Howard.

"Hello. Special Agent Howard speaking."

"This is Rusty. We're getting word that Kevin Vanzant's body was found at his campsite a short while ago. He was shot. Cameron Pope said local and county police are both on the scene, which bothers me. If they start arguing jurisdiction, we may lose an evidence trail. What are your orders?"

"Shit," Howard muttered. "What do you suppose prompted this?"

"We know nothing beyond what I told you earlier about the photos on the laptop."

"This changes everything," Howard said. "I can't get there in time to stop the dispersal of evidence, so you are officially no longer undercover. Go in and claim the crime scene as part of an ongoing federal investigation. I'll get the team down there as soon as possible. Don't let them remove anything, and keep me updated."

"Yes, sir," Rusty said, then called Cameron. As soon as he answered, she started talking.

"Where are you right now?" she asked.

"On my way back into town."

"Come get me. Undercover is over. I've got to get to the scene ASAP."

"On the way," Cameron said.

Rusty hurried back inside and slid back into her seat and leaned forward, speaking softly.

"I'm sorry. I don't have a lot of time to explain. I'm in Jubilee as part of an ongoing investigation that just blew up in our faces. I've got to leave for a while. I'll tell you more later, but right now I've got to get to a crime scene before crucial evidence disappears."

Patricia gasped. "In Jubilee?"

Liz grabbed Rusty by the wrist. "Will you be in danger?"

"It's part of the job," Rusty said as she pulled out a handful of twenties and left them on the table. "That's enough for the lunch and tip. I have to go. Both of you go home. For now, don't talk about this to anyone but Uncle Ray."

Then she grabbed her jacket from the back of the chair, slung her purse over her shoulder and bolted.

Patricia's face had lost all its color and her voice was shaking. "She's still limping," she mumbled.

Liz was still reeling from Rusty and Cameron's reunion, and now this. She didn't know how to feel. "I called her a dark horse. I had no freaking idea how close to the truth I was," she said.

Rusty was standing on the sidewalk in front of the restaurant parking lot when Cameron drove up. He had already moved Ghost and his blanket to the back seat, so when he saw her at the curb, he braked in a skid.

She jumped in, slamming the door. She was buckling up as he sped away.

"Sorry this is blowing up so fast," she said. "Are you still going to be okay with this?"

"Absolutely," Cameron said.

Rusty nodded, then turned around in the seat to look at Ghost.

"Hey, buddy. Sorry I took your seat," she said, and held out her hand.

Ghost licked her fingers.

"You're already forgiven," Cameron said. "They have a police presence keeping people off the property. You're going to have to elbow your way in."

"Been there, done that, got the scars to prove it," she said.

"Whatever you want done on scene, Ghost and I are at your disposal."

"Special Agent Howard is sending in our crime scene team. All we have to do is secure the site and wait for them to arrive."

Cameron nodded.

Once they were out of town, Cameron floored it and had her at Barton's Cabins within minutes. Charlie was still outside the office when he saw Cameron driving in again and waved him down.

"Come on, Cameron. You can't go—"

Rusty leaned across the console, flashing her badge and ID. "Special Agent Caldwell. FBI. Pope is with me. How do we get to the crime scene?"

Charlie's eyes widened as he looked from Cameron to the woman and back again. "Uh, follow the road all the way past the tiny cabins. The campsites are beyond that. The crime scene is at the end of the road."

Cameron sped off, leaving a rooster tail of dust behind.

They found the site easily enough. It was crawling with cops and police cars.

Rusty's eyes narrowed angrily. "Talk about stomping all over the crime scene." She got out with her badge in hand, yelling as she went. "Who's in charge?"

Cameron snapped a leash on Ghost's collar and took off running to catch up.

Sheriff Woodley and Police Chief Warren were in a head-to-head argument about jurisdiction when Rusty walked up and shoved her badge in their faces.

"Special Agent Caldwell. Gentlemen, this is my crime scene."

"The hell it is!" Woodley shouted. "It's outside of Jubilee, which makes it my crime scene."

"But it is not outside the city limits," Warren said.

Rusty never bothered to raise her voice. "I don't care where the man died. The point is he's part of an ongoing federal investigation into human trafficking, and I am part of that investigation team. This body and whatever evidence you people haven't already contaminated is ours."

Woodley eyed Cameron angrily. He was already pissed at the whole Pope family for calling in civilians to search for the kidnapped child, then Pope had turned up and found the bad guy and the kid, making his office look bad. Now here he was again, on official police business, and they were questioning his jurisdiction.

"What's Pope doing here?" Woodley growled.

"He's under orders to assist me," Rusty said.

"Whose orders?" Woodley asked.

"Technically, from the President of the United States. Now, sir. If you please."

She stepped aside, waiting for them to leave.

Woodley was pissed, but he didn't have recourse. "We're out of here!" he shouted, waving his men to their cars, and they left the area.

Sonny Warren hadn't said a word since her arrival, but he knew enough not to argue with a fed, and he trusted Cameron. "Ma'am. If there's anything my office can do to aid you during this investigation, all you have to do is ask."

"Who found the body?" Rusty asked.

Sonny pulled out his notebook. "A man named Rob Daley. He was walking his dog. Said the dog hit on the odor and headed straight for the trailer. He saw the blood on the steps, knocked on the door, and when he got no answer, peeked in and saw the body. He did not go inside. He called the police. He and his wife are renting Cabin 8. They're staying through tomorrow. He's coming in this afternoon to make a statement. I'll be happy to send you a copy."

"Yes, please," Rusty said, and handed him her card for contact info. "Has anybody moved the body or been inside the trailer?"

"None of *my* men were inside, and the body has not been moved by any of us, but there's blood on the steps and it appears to me someone dragged him into the trailer, so the killer may have pulled him further inside to close the door. Jack Barton said he was a college student and had been doing research out here, but he didn't know what kind of research."

Rusty frowned. "How did County know about the body, if Daley called the local police?" she asked.

Sonny shrugged. "I wonder that myself and will be having a discussion with dispatch. My dispatcher is related to the dispatcher at County."

"Are all of you related to each other?"

"Somewhat," Sonny said. "You'll have to talk to Cameron about that. If you need anything else, Cameron knows the number." Then Warren and his men left the premises.

Rusty watched them leave and then shoved her hands through her hair, wishing she had something to pull it back out of her way.

"Okay, I need to take a look at the scene. If you don't want to—"

"I've seen dead bodies before," Cameron said. "At least this time it won't be a friend."

They walked to the front of the trailer. The door was hanging open. Ghost paused at the entrance and looked up at Cameron and whined.

Cameron sighed. "He knows the smell of death. He thinks we're going in to look for IEDs."

Startled, Rusty glanced up. "I'm sorry. I didn't think what this would resurrect for either of you."

Cameron laid the back of his hand against her cheek. "We're good, ma'am. Should the need for flight occur, just consider us your wings."

"Thank you for the backup," she said, then noticed something up in a tree just outside the tent. "Is that a trail cam?"

Cameron turned to look. "Yes, it is. Could we possibly get this lucky?"

"There may be more. We'll have to let the crime scene team know. Just give me a minute," she said, and aimed her flashlight inside.

It didn't appear as if anything had been tossed, but it was hard to tell from out here. Vanzant's car was still here, so it didn't appear theft was the issue. She aimed her flashlight on the body. From where she was standing, it looked like a clean shot to the chest. She swept the light around the interior and saw a set of keys on the table, presumably his car keys, and a wallet lying beside them.

"What's your gut telling you?" Cameron asked.

"It wasn't a robbery. They left his car. His wallet and car keys are in plain sight on the table. What I don't see is a laptop or a cell phone."

Cameron's eyes narrowed thoughtfully. "Maybe someone is tying up loose ends?"

Rusty turned. "Are you talking about the photos?"

Cameron nodded. "Leslie saw the photos, but got away. If Vanzant's error was about to reveal him as part of the gang, then the quickest way to make it all go away is to retrieve his laptop and phone and kill him, leaving nothing for anyone to trace."

"Well, I know something about Vanzant's story that isn't true. He isn't researching anything for college because he's not enrolled in one. Anywhere. He has a rap sheet for B&E and boosting cars, and he did not graduate from high school. But we can hope something pops after the crime scene techs get here. There could be evidence in his car the killer knew nothing about."

She moved away from the trailer and went back to where Cameron was standing.

Without thinking, he put his arms around her. "We're going to have a long wait. Let's get you off that sore knee. You pick. The bench at the picnic table, or sit in the Jeep?"

"The bench for now. You do what you need to for Ghost. If you want to walk him or whatever. I'm fine."

"Rusty, darlin', you're sitting in the middle of a murder scene with no weapon and a killer on the loose. Ghost and I aren't going anywhere."

When he sat down beside her, Ghost plopped down on Cameron's boot and laid his head on Rusty's foot.

"I have never had backup like this before," she said.

Cameron looked at her then. At the wind teasing the curls in her hair. At eyes bluer than the sky. At a mouth waiting to be kissed. "This day is chilly, but clear and peaceful. Here I am sitting with a beautiful woman, and there's a dead man in the trailer behind us. What's wrong with this picture?"

"I should have taken up floral design?"

Cameron slid his hand over hers. "And the world would have been far less safe. I think you're doing what you're good at, which is what matters."

Rusty curled her fingers around his hand and stared off into the woods.

Cameron knew she was bothered about having to reveal her identity in such a dramatic fashion, but nobody could have expected something like this to happen. Finally, she started talking.

"Something about this doesn't add up. If Vanzant was working for the traffickers, then why kill him? What could have triggered such a drastic decision? Just because Leslie Morgan saw the photos and told her parents, who revealed it to you, doesn't mean Vanzant would tell his boss. In fact, it would be the opposite. He would have to know a mistake like that would get him killed."

"Unless he let something slip," Cameron said. "There's something else about this situation that we don't know. Remember Leslie said Jack Barton arrived in the middle of their argument, so maybe you need to talk to him. He could know something and not even be aware that it mattered."

"I want to talk to him. Can you get a number to the office and ask him to come down here?" Rusty asked.

"Yes," Cameron said, and a short while later, Jack Barton arrived in his golf cart.

"Thanks for coming," Rusty said as Barton stopped where they were sitting.

"Of course," Jack said. "This is horrible all the way around. I can't get past knowing someone committed a murder here last night and I never heard a thing."

"I understand you witnessed an argument between Vanzant and a young woman yesterday. Could you tell me about what you saw and heard?"

"Her name is Leslie. That's all I know. But I saw her come running out of the trailer with Kevin right behind her. She looked anxious and he appeared upset. I heard him call out for her to stop, but she didn't. And then they both saw me. She kept running toward her car, but my arrival stopped Kevin's pursuit. She drove away, and he seemed embarrassed and angry. I apologized for interrupting, then told him what I'd come to say," Barton said.

"And what was that?" Rusty asked.

"That I was closing the campsite at the end of the month and wouldn't reopen until spring."

Rusty frowned. "So, you were basically giving him notice to move on?"

Jack nodded. "He didn't seem bothered by it. He said he was through with his research and planning to leave in a couple of days anyway. Then he went back inside the trailer."

"Did you think he was still angry?" Cameron asked.

"Yes, but I didn't take it as being angry with me. I assumed it had to do with what I'd interrupted. So I left," Jack said.

"Did you see any cars enter the area after dark?" Rusty asked.

Jack paused, thinking back. "Uh, I saw a couple. One was the pizza delivery car, and another car came twice, but it's the girl who delivers for Door Dash. My tiny-cabin renters often order late at night. I didn't see any cars come in after that."

"Okay, thanks. But if you think of anything else, please call me," Rusty said, and gave him one of her cards.

Jack made a U-turn and started back up the road.

As he did, Cameron's eyes suddenly narrowed. "Except for the sound of the tires on gravel, you'd never hear him come and go."

"Now there's a random thought. You're pretty good at this detective business," Rusty said, and sent Special Agent Howard a text.

> I need a full background check on Jack Barton that goes beyond the norm. Everything you can find.

She got a thumbs-up emoji back to let her know the message was received, and then sighed.

"Are you hurting or just tired?" Cameron asked.

"I'm fine. I would turn a cartwheel for anything with caffeine in it, but I'll settle for water," she said, and headed for the water hydrant.

Water gushed as she turned it on. Sidestepping the splash, she adjusted the flow, pulled her hair to one side, and then leaned over and drank from what was coming out of the tap.

Ghost walked up beside her and nosed the water pooling in the shallow concrete basin beneath.

"Good stuff?" Rusty asked, and shut off the water so he could drink without it running on his head.

As soon as he backed off, he licked her fingers, then walked beside her back to the bench. Rusty was smiling as she sat down beside Cameron again.

"How did you teach Ghost to be so polite?" she asked.

Cameron scratched Ghost between his ears. "We've spent a lot of time together."

Rusty was getting a firsthand look at the bond between them. "How did you get permission to bring a bomb-sniffing dog back with you?"

"Technically, he wasn't an American-trained bomb sniffer. We didn't bring him over. He was a starving pup who wandered into camp. I fed him, and that was that. When we'd go out on sorties, he'd disappear, and when we came back, he always found me. We found out by accident how good he was at tracking, and then it became a game with our squad. I'd hide, and they'd turn him loose and make bets on how fast it took for him to find me."

Rusty smiled. "What was his best time?"

"Under a minute," Cameron said. "When we moved camp, he always followed. He was about a couple hundred yards behind when a truck ran over an IED. He disappeared, and I feared that he'd been hit and maybe crawled off and died. But the company was in chaos. We were pulling bodies out of the wreckage and getting the ones still alive on choppers. When it got dark, we sheltered in a small village that had been evacuated. He showed up in the night, found me, and lay down beside me. After that, he became a member of the squad and sometimes trotted ahead of the convoys when we were on the move.

"After that IED exploded so close to him, we figured out he must have identified a scent associated with IEDs that meant danger to him, because he began alerting on them. When he'd get a hit, he would stop in front of the lead truck in the convoy, which meant everything came to a halt. Once he indicated the location, we had different methods of dealing with them. After that, no one questioned his value. When I headed stateside, they knew he'd never work with anyone else. He didn't belong to anyone but me. It took some paperwork to get him here, but here we are."

"Yes, here we are. You came home for peace and quiet, and wound up in this mess," Rusty said.

Cameron shook his head, then brushed a quick kiss across her lips. "There are all kinds of wars. What's happening here is a war on humanity, and my family got caught up in it. I'll do anything to make Jubilee safe again, and I'm never going to regret anything because it brought you back to me."

She wrapped her arms around his neck.

Cameron held her without talking, sheltering her from the chill.

Chapter 10

THE CORONER ARRIVED MIDAFTERNOON, AND THE CRIME scene team behind him. At that point, it was in their hands. After an initial examination of the body, the coroner gave Rusty a rough estimate of the time of death. Confirmed for her the cell phone was not on the body, and that the victim had suffered a single gunshot wound to the chest from a distance away. He told them they were probably looking at a rifle as the weapon, and then his team bagged the body and headed for the morgue in Frankfort, leaving the crime scene team on-site still gathering evidence.

Rusty pointed out the trail cams, which they confiscated, along with personal info inside the trailer. While they were going through his car, one of the techs removed the carpet in the trunk and found a second laptop in the wheel well where the spare was carried.

"Agent Caldwell!"

Rusty hurried over to see what he'd found.

"The missing laptop?" Rusty asked.

"Or a second one, like a backup," Cameron suggested.

"Why two when everything is saved in the cloud, or Carbonite, or a dozen other sites you could name for the same purposes?" Rusty asked.

Cameron shrugged. "Even if a laptop was destroyed, it would still take a second laptop to access what's been saved, and maybe he was just OCD."

"Maybe. We'll send it to the lab," Rusty said, eyeing the crime scene tech.

"Yes, ma'am," the tech said, and bagged the laptop.

It was nearing sundown by the time the scene had been processed. The car was gone. Everything had been bagged and removed and the trailer hauled off to the lab. There was nothing left at the campsite. Not even the trash Vanzant had dumped in the barrel.

Cameron and Rusty were on their way back into Jubilee, and Ghost was asleep in the back seat. Rusty was quiet as they rode, thinking back over the day. All of a sudden she sat up. It was the look on her face that made Cameron curious.

"What?"

"How well do you know Sheriff Woodley?" Rusty asked.

"Only by name," Cameron said. "He's not from here. He came to the area ten years ago, worked as a night watchman at a warehouse, and with no law enforcement experience got elected sheriff eight years ago. Why?"

"Wasn't he in charge of your niece's kidnapping case?" she asked.

"If you call his foot-dragging reaction to imminent danger being in charge, then yes."

"Tell me," Rusty said.

So Cameron began explaining how the officers had arrived on the scene and immediately began interrogating

Louis and Rachel as being guilty of their child's disappearance, when it was obvious Rachel had been attacked, and Louis had been at work when the kidnapping occurred. Then Cameron filled Rusty in on the frantic race on the mountain, with the authorities joining in the search later rather than being the ones to initiate it.

"If Louis and Rachel hadn't called on family, we would not have found Lili in time to save her life, and Biggers would have gotten away. Why do you ask?" Cameron said.

"I keep thinking about why the sheriff's office would have responded to a crime scene that is within the city limits of Jubilee. Yes, it's a couple of miles outside the main part of town, but it's still within the city limits. He was actually shouting at Chief Warren when I walked up on them, insisting it was his crime scene to process."

Cameron nodded. "Yes. I heard part of it."

"So that would be twice Woodley has tried to impede the progress of incidents either involved or suspected to be involved in human trafficking."

Her words hit Cameron like a fist to the gut. "You don't think…?"

"I get paid to think like this," she muttered, and then shoved her hands through her hair. "God! What a mess. Just in the past two weeks, a toddler is kidnapped, a woman who works at a hotel goes AWOL, and a man is murdered."

"There is nothing random about this," Cameron said.

"My thoughts exactly," Rusty said. "I have so much work ahead of me, and all I want is to go home with you and come apart in your arms."

Cameron felt the angst and longing in her words. "You have no idea how close you came to that when you showed up on my doorstep. The only thing that stopped me was knowing I'd never let you go. I honor your devotion to duty. As a soldier, it's also part of who I am. But you're always in my heart, and have been from the moment we first met. We'll find our time, honey, and it will be worth the wait."

Rusty's eyes welled as he pulled up in front of the Serenity Inn to let her out. "I don't know what you like to eat, or what kind of music you like, but I know I don't ever want to lose you again," she said.

"That's never gonna happen," Cameron said, then reached across the seat, cupped the back of her neck, and planted a kiss on her lips she wasn't likely to forget. "Sleep on that, darlin'. There's more where it came from. Call me with orders. I can meet you or pick you up at anytime, anywhere."

Rusty sighed. "Thank you. I'll see what I can find out from headquarters and call you later. Oh…about Leslie Morgan. I've kept her name out of all the photo business. You need to tell her and her family not to talk about it to anyone. We don't want the bad guys to consider her another loose end."

"Shit," Cameron said. "I'll call her dad and find out where she is and talk to her myself."

All of a sudden, Ghost poked his head in the space between them.

"Someone's jealous I'm getting all of the attention," Cameron said.

Rusty gave Ghost a big hug. "You are such a good boy. Take care of Cameron for me, okay?"

She exited the Jeep, her steps dragging as she headed for the entrance. Cameron watched until she was safely inside, then pulled up Wade Morgan's phone number and was listening to it ring as he drove away.

Wade was washing up, getting ready to sit down to supper when his phone rang. He dried his hands and then answered.

"Hello?"

"Wade, this is Cameron. Did Leslie go home, or is she still there with you?"

"She went to work today, but she's spending the night here again. Why?"

"Kevin Vanzant was found murdered today. It happened sometime last night after Leslie was there."

Wade gasped. "Oh my God!"

"I have a message for you from one of the FBI agents involved. Tell Leslie not to talk about what she saw on Vanzant's laptop, and don't any of you tell anyone else. We don't want her name even mentioned with his. It could put her in danger."

"Jesus, Cameron! What's going on?"

"I can't talk about it beyond what I've already said. And it's probably a good idea that she continues to spend the nights at your house for a while."

"Yes, of course. I'll tell her. We haven't mentioned it to anyone but you, and I'll make sure to caution her, as well. Is Leslie in danger?"

"We have no reason to think she is. It's just early days. I think they want to cover all the bases to limit leaks," Cameron said. "I'm on my way home. You can call anytime if you need me."

"Thanks," Wade said and disconnected, but he was sick to his stomach. How had everything turned so ugly so fast? Or was it always here, and the continuing rotation of strangers in and out of their little town had masked the truth?

———

Cameron pulled into the carport at his home a few minutes later, bone-tired and worried. Now that Rusty had to reveal herself to claim the crime scene, her cover was blown. Any aspect of the criminal element associated with human trafficking would not want feds poking about in their playground, which meant this could play out one of two ways.

Either they'd take her presence as a sign they were in danger and move their operation elsewhere, or they'd just decide to remove her. It would be a stupid move from a criminal standpoint, knowing an agent's death would bring the whole department down on their heads. But criminals were motivated by greed and thought nothing about taking someone out who got between them and the source of their money flow.

Special Agent Caldwell was now in their line of fire.

Rusty walked off the elevator into the penthouse, wanting nothing more than a hot bath and maybe a glass of wine. But the moment she arrived, her family came from every direction to meet her.

"You're back! We've been so worried. We heard all kinds of sirens and then nothing," Patricia said, and threw her arms around Rusty.

"She looks like hell, Mom. At least let her sit down," Liz said.

Ray appeared at the end of the foyer. "Wine in the library, then a hot bath for you."

Rusty was full of guilt and regret as she walked with them into the library, then plopped down in the first chair she came to.

"I'm so sorry. None of this was supposed to happen," she said.

Ray handed her a glass of red wine. "It's your favorite," he said, gently pushing a wayward curl from the corner of her eye.

She took a sip, then looked up at the trio standing around her. "Right now, this looks like an inquisition, and I feel like I need to give my name, rank, and serial number, then clam up."

"Oh! Sorry," Ray said. "Everybody! Sit."

They crowded together on the sofa across from where Rusty was sitting, anxiously waiting for her to explain.

They were so dear to Rusty, and she felt like she'd

betrayed their hospitality, but this had to be said. "I am limited as to what I can tell you, but it's fair to say I am not a clerk for the government. I am an undercover agent for the FBI and have been since college."

Patricia gasped. Liz was in complete shock, and Ray nodded.

"I thought as much," he said.

"I knew you suspected something," Rusty said. "I did get injured. But not in a car wreck. I was on the job. I have been off duty recovering. And then I was ordered here. I was never supposed to reveal myself. It was just an info-gathering mission. I'd be safe, undeterred, and still get to see my family."

"What's going on here, or can you say?" Ray asked.

Rusty glanced up. "I'm getting to that. I was told before I left home that I would be working with a civilian familiar with the area. I balked. No agent wants that. But orders are orders. I arrived. My contact was going to meet me at lunch today. I didn't know it was going to be someone I knew. Someone I fell in love with five years ago."

"Cameron!" Liz said.

Rusty nodded.

"Why him?" Ray asked.

"Because his security clearance is as high as mine. Because he was special ops all through his tours of duty. Because he's badass. None of which I knew until I read his file."

"I may have to revise my rather prejudiced opinion of the locals who live up the mountain," Ray muttered.

"At any rate, the reunion was a shock for both of us, and before we could even meet to coordinate anything, a person of interest was murdered at Jack Barton's campground last night. His body was discovered this morning, and my hasty exit from lunch was Cameron calling to tell me about it. I had to notify my superiors. And because we needed to claim the crime scene to gather the evidence ourselves, I had to blow my cover. I officially identified myself to Police Chief Warren and Sheriff Woodley to claim the scene for the FBI."

"Murdered! Oh my God!" Patricia cried. "What's happening here? First that baby getting kidnapped, and now this!"

Ray was frowning. "And my missing employee? That's why you asked for her info, wasn't it? You want to know if her disappearance is part of this."

"We have to follow all leads to eliminate what doesn't fit," Rusty said.

"What do we need to do?" Ray asked.

"It is imperative that you say nothing about any of this. I've probably said more than I should, but I've unintentionally involved you by my presence. I'm guessing my boss will be moving my ass out of here ASAP."

"Where will you go?" Patricia asked.

"Wherever they tell me to go," Rusty said. "I can't talk about anything else, and please forgive me. Now you know why I've absented myself from family gatherings for so long. Mom and Dad knew my status, but never anything more, and they never asked."

Patricia leaned back against the sofa. Tears were rolling down her face. "I always said this place is awful. I want to get away from here."

Rusty sighed. "Unfortunately, Aunt Pat, what's happening here is small potatoes compared to what's already happening in the big cities. And not just across our nation, but across the world. Nowhere is really safe anymore. You have to always pay attention."

Liz's eyes widened. "What are you saying? What's the big secret?"

"I'll answer that, and you won't have said a thing or have to confirm or deny," Ray said. "The first thing that came to mind was human trafficking. Now. You go run yourself a tub full of bubbles and soak to your heart's content. We'll have dinner in an hour."

Rusty gave him a grateful glance, then took her wine with her as she limped out of the room.

She started water running in the tub, added lavender-scented bath salts, and then made a call to Special Agent Howard.

"Hello, Caldwell."

"Sir," Rusty said. "This is just a quick call to update you. We bagged all the evidence on the murder scene. It was definitely not a random robbery. The only things taken after Vanzant was killed were his phone and laptop. There was a second laptop hidden beneath the wheel well of his car, and Vanzant had a trail cam on his campsite. If we're lucky, it caught the killer. Everything is at the lab in Frankfort, including the deceased's vehicle. I blew my own cover doing this, and I no longer feel comfortable staying here with my family in the hotel. There are too many strangers coming and going here, and I may have become a target. I can't put my family or innocent people staying here in danger. If you still want me on-site, I'm going to have to move my location elsewhere."

Howard frowned. "This is a problem. Let me make a few calls. I'll get you out tonight after it's dark."

"Yes, sir," Rusty said, then disconnected.

She turned off the water, then stripped and climbed into the tub. Sinking into the hot, steamy water soon began to ease her aches, while the scent of lavender swirled about her head.

She stayed in the tub until the water began to cool off, then got out and dried before dressing in sweats and returning to her family.

"Feeling better?" Patricia asked.

Rusty smiled. "Almost human again."

Liz gave her a quick hug. "You have once again reminded me of what a dilettante I have become. I don't have your guts or daring, but I feel the need to become a contributor to humanity."

"We each do what we're led to do, Cuz. You don't owe anything to anyone but yourself. Remember that."

"Dinner is on the way up," Ray said, and led the way into the dining room, then seated his girls before settling into his chair.

The food arrived and was served at the table, and then the waiter left them to enjoy their meal. They were down to dessert when she broke the last of her news.

"I have new orders. I need to leave the hotel. My presence could put all of you and the guests at the hotel in jeopardy. I'll be leaving tonight after it gets dark. The less fuss is made about it, the better for all of you."

Ray was startled. "Really? We have security and—"

"Uncle Ray. You don't want your guests in any way involved in this investigation. I know what I'm doing. Uncle Sam trusts me to do my job. You have to trust my instincts, too."

"Done," Ray said. "And don't wait so long between visits next time."

"Absolutely," she said.

"You can't leave without eating your dessert," Liz said. "If there's extra, I don't have the willpower to leave it alone."

Rusty laughed. "I think I can choke down that slice of key lime pie. It looks delicious."

Patricia had sniffled and dabbed at her eyes all through the meal, and now hearing this was the last straw. "Everything is just so awful and ugly, and I hate to think of you involved in it," she said, and started crying.

"Don't cry, Aunt Pat. This is mild compared to most of what I'm sent out to do, but this time I won't be alone. I'll have Cameron Pope as a partner and my backup. I won't be making some crazy call to my contact who might be hours away, hoping they can send in reinforcements in time. He'll be with me," Rusty said.

"Do you know where you're going?" Patricia asked.

"Not yet. I'll find out later. Now let's eat pie before I have to go pack," she said.

Cameron fed Ghost, then began bringing firewood in for the night, but he couldn't settle so he heated up a can of soup, made himself a sandwich, and was eating in the kitchen with Ghost lying on the floor nearby.

After spending the day with Rusty, he felt the silence more than he'd ever felt it before. He'd been alone for a long time, but never lonely. Until now.

When his phone suddenly rang, he was grateful for the interruption.

"Hello."

"Pope, this is Special Agent Howard. I just had a conversation with Agent Caldwell. You two have had quite a day."

"Yes, sir."

"Good catch on alerting us to the Vanzant murder."

"I was just following up on Rusty's orders, sir, but someone got to him first," Cameron said.

Howard was startled by Pope's reference to their agent. He called her Rusty, instead of Boss, or Agent Caldwell. "So you're getting along with Caldwell?"

Now Cameron was silent a moment. "Uh…yes. Didn't she tell you?"

"Tell me what?" Howard asked.

"It turns out our first face-to-face here was a shock for the both of us. We knew each other from before. Briefly, but memorable, if you get my drift. We lost touch over five years ago. And then she drives up into my front yard. I guess your file alerted her to who I was ahead of time, but

I knew nothing until she arrived. We're both fine with this. It is not interfering in any way with the investigation. In fact, it's added a level of trust between us that would have taken months of working together to acquire."

Howard chuckled. "I'll be damned. She's said nothing."

"On the job she's all business and doesn't miss a thing," Cameron said.

"I don't question her judgment. She's earned her stripes," Howard added. "And this brings me to her concerns. She blew her own cover and knows it could be a problem. She is adamant about getting out of the hotel so as not to put her family or hotel guests in danger, and I concur, but she needs to stay in the area to continue working the case. Do you have any suggestions?"

"With me," Cameron said. "My home is two miles up the mountain and outside of Jubilee."

"You know if someone wants her gone, they won't be worried about collateral damage," Howard said.

"If I had my way, she'd never leave," Cameron said. "I can keep her safe and still help her in any way she needs."

"Well. This isn't what I expected when I called, but it's fine with me, if Agent Caldwell agrees."

Cameron smiled to himself. "Trust me. She'll agree."

"Then I'll let her know. Will you be okay if she shows up tonight? I think leaving the hotel after dark will be better than making a production out of it in broad daylight," Howard asked.

"Absolutely. Do you want me to pick her up?" Cameron asked.

"She has a rental. She may want to keep it," Howard said.

"We're partners in this, sir. What we do, we'll do together."

"Then you name a time and I'll make sure she's in the lobby," Howard said.

"She'll want to tell her family she's leaving and have dinner with them and then she'll have to pack. Just tell her to be in the breezeway of the hotel at 10:00 p.m. I'll do the rest."

"Yes, that makes sense," Howard said. "And thank you for picking up the slack here."

"Yes, sir," Cameron said.

The call ended. Cameron looked at Ghost and grinned.

"We're getting company, buddy, which means best behavior from both of us, understand?"

Ghost cocked his head sideways.

Cameron laughed. "You heard me. Best behavior."

Lindy Sheets had a one-bedroom rental in downtown Windsor, Ontario, under her maiden name, Melinda Lehigh. She'd gotten a job as a shampoo girl in an upscale hair salon, dyed her blond hair black, then shaved the sides, leaving the top in a Mohawk.

She used Transit Windsor, the bus line in the city, or walked everywhere she needed to go. It was a far cry from what she'd been doing and cost a hell of a lot less money. But she'd long ago accepted the risks when she sold her honor and humanity for the money, and this was legal. She felt reasonably safe.

Sometimes she had nightmares about the girls she'd lured into human trafficking, but she couldn't change that. What was done was done. Danny Biggers had been a mistake, but he didn't know anything about the organization or anyone attached to it—except her. It was fine until it wasn't. And then he got caught, the kid never made it to the drop-off, and Lindy became expendable.

She had eased into a routine and was getting comfortable with this life and her old identity, enough so that she quit looking over her shoulder.

The workday at Sam Carson's vet clinic was nothing short of chaotic. Working with the substitute vet was distracting, but Leslie was figuring it out. They had several emergencies involving two different surgeries that kept them running all day long. By the time she headed home, she was exhausted. But the moment she walked into her childhood home, the chaos in her life turned into a nightmare.

Her dad was sitting in the living room with a cup of coffee cradled between his palms. His thick, graying hair looked like he'd been running his fingers through it all day, and his blue plaid shirt was all rumpled. Not a bit like him at all.

"Hi, Dad. You look tired," Leslie said as she shut the door behind her.

"Hi, baby," Wade said. "Come sit with me a minute. There's something I need to tell you."

All of a sudden his rumpled appearance began to make sense. Something was wrong!

"Is everything okay? Is it Mom? Has something happened to Granny?"

"No, no. It's nothing to do about us. It's about Kevin Vanzant."

Leslie frowned as she plopped down beside him. "What about Kevin Vanzant?"

"Someone murdered him last night."

Leslie gasped. "No! Oh my God! What? Why?"

"They aren't sure. Cameron said the FBI has taken over. He's helping the agent in charge. We are not to mention to anyone about the photos you saw, or that you even knew Kevin. And to be on the safe side, they suggest you stay nights here with us until further notice."

Leslie felt like she was going to throw up. She was shaking so hard she couldn't take a good breath. "Dad! Daddy! What have I done?" she moaned, and fell into his arms and started sobbing.

"You did nothing wrong," Wade said. "Nothing. The FBI will figure it out. Now go wash your face. I'm here. You're safe. Cameron said we could call him any time we needed to. You are to go about your business as if nothing has changed. Okay?"

Before she could answer, her mother shouted from the kitchen, "Supper's ready!"

Leslie swiped the tears from her cheeks and left the room to wash up.

Wade saw the slump in her shoulders and the way her

steps were dragging. She was scared to death and there wasn't a thing he could do to make it better, except make damn sure he kept her safe.

─────────────

Rusty was in her suite packing when her phone rang. She sat down on the side of the bed to answer.

"Hello."

"It's me," Howard said. "Be in the breezeway downstairs at 10:00 p.m. You will be picked up and taken to a different location for the duration of this case."

"Yes, sir," Rusty said. "I'll be needing copies of all the test results from the crime scene, a copy of the film from the game camera, and a copy of the autopsy. Also…I still need those background checks on Jack Barton and Sheriff Woodley, and if they break the password on Vanzant's computer, let me know. He's got to have been sending files of those photos somewhere."

"I'll put a rush on as much of it as I can," Howard said.

"Do we know where Lindy Sheets is?" Rusty asked.

"No. She's still in the wind, and Danny Biggers got transferred to a federal prison. That's all for now," Howard said.

"Okay. I'll be watching for files to arrive, and in the meantime, if we have anything else to report, you'll be the first to know."

"Thank you, Caldwell. Have a good night."

"Thank you, sir," Rusty said, and disconnected, regretful of the need to relocate.

She glanced at the clock. It was already a quarter past nine. She needed to hurry so she could say her goodbyes. And since she was being relocated, keeping that rental car seemed redundant. More details to tie up and no time to do it.

Rusty was wearing jeans and a sweatshirt and pulling her wheeled suitcase behind her as she walked down the hall. She could hear voices in the living room and the sound of some television program in progress.

This sucks. It just sucks.

They looked up as she paused in the doorway.

"I'm so sorry this is happening, but it's for the best. We'll catch up later, for sure."

The three of them swarmed her with hugs and goodbye kisses, and begged promises from her to stay in touch as they walked her to the foyer and the elevator beyond.

"I'll call when I can, but don't think anything of it if you don't hear from me for a while. Staying under the radar is part of my job and I'm damn good at it, so don't worry. Oh…Uncle Ray, if you could do me a favor tomorrow, I would appreciate it greatly. These are the keys to my rental car and the key card to the penthouse. Would you call the rental agency and have them come pick up the car?"

"Of course," Ray said, then frowned. "Wait. If you're turning in the car, then how are you leaving?"

"I'm being picked up. All low-key. Just me dragging a suitcase out of the hotel. No public farewells in the lobby, okay?"

Liz threw her arms around her. "Be safe. Someday I'm

going to break down and get married and you have to be my maid of honor. I won't do it without you."

Rusty hugged her back. "Just say the word and I'll make it happen," she said, then entered the elevator, turned and waved as the doors began to close, and then she was gone.

Pat was teary-eyed and anxious. "I just don't understand what possessed her to take a job this dangerous," she said.

Ray gave his wife a quick hug. "Some people live to please themselves, and some people live to do for others. Rusty is one of the latter."

―――――――

It was five minutes to ten when Rusty exited the elevator. She paused in the hallway, looking out into the lobby, scoping out the people coming and going before heading for the exit. As she was walking, she kept thinking she should have called Cameron and let him know what was happening, then shrugged it off. They were still going to be working together. She'd call him tonight after she got to the new place.

She walked outside, pausing beneath the overhead lights at the valet station, and as she did, saw a vehicle come wheeling into the breezeway and stop right beside her. She recognized Cameron's Jeep and the big white dog in the back seat. Then Cameron emerged and came toward her.

"You get in. I'll get your bag," he said, and took it out of her hands.

"What's going on?" she asked.

"I told Agent Howard you're coming home with me."

Next to finding him again, this had to be the best news ever. Rusty climbed into the passenger seat, turned around and gave Ghost a pat on the head, and then buckled up as Cameron slid behind the wheel.

He gave her a look that curled her toes, and then they were on their way.

Chapter 11

"I'M NOT EVEN GOING TO ASK HOW ALL THIS HAPPENED. I DO not look for reasons in blessings, but you are one to me," Rusty said.

"I want to know you're safe. I want to help you clean out this wasp nest of criminal activity. And I want you," Cameron said. "It's as simple as that."

Nobody had ever said that to her, and the emotion that welled up in her throat choked off anything else she might have said. She shivered, then leaned back against the seat as the streets of Jubilee began to blur. At first she thought it was raining until she realized she was crying.

Suddenly, Ghost's big head was between the seats. He whined, then licked her cheek. That's when Cameron saw the tears. Ghost whined again.

"She's okay, buddy. She's just like us. She's been alone too long."

Then Cameron reached for her hand and gave it a quick squeeze. "If you want it to be, this trip is the beginning of us and the end of your exile. But only if you're ready. Otherwise, we're still going to make a crackerjack team. Oh…and I have a really important question."

"Ask," Rusty said.

"Is Rusty your real name?"

It was the last thing she expected him to say and it made her smile. "No. My name is Faith."

Cameron felt the word as she spoke it. It fit, because it was how she made him feel. Like he could believe in something good again. "It's beautiful, like you," he said.

Rusty sighed. "It's a good thing we're on the same side in this battle, because I'd be tempted to walk on the wild side for the pleasure of your company."

Cameron pulled a handful of tissues from the box in the console and handed them to her.

"No tears for my girl," he said softly. "You've been in my heart for years. I'm taking you to my home, and then to my bed. Can't have you crying when you walk in the door. People up here would say that's bad luck."

She wiped away the tears as they left the lights of Jubilee behind. Now the headlights were focused on the dark, winding road before them, and the looming silhouettes of the bordering trees. The farther they drove, the darker it became.

When Cameron turned left off the blacktop onto a heavily graveled road, her heart began to pound. She recognized where they were.

Almost home.

And then the house was before them. The porch light was on, and the house was lit from within. She could smell woodsmoke even before they drove under the carport. She looked at Cameron and then the dog between them and wondered if they were ready for a woman to invade their space.

Cameron parked and opened his door, then let his dog out of the Jeep. Ghost went sniffing off into the yard as Rusty got out. Cameron went to get Rusty's bag from the back of the Jeep as she began to scope out her new abode. There was nothing but trees all around the clearing in which the house was sitting.

One way in to the property.

One way out.

She saw two security cameras just beneath the eaves of the porch, and when she gave the house a closer look, realized the shutters weren't just decorative. If the need arose, they could actually be closed. In the dark, in the cold, the house now took on the aspect of a bunker. Cameron Pope may have come back from the war, but he'd brought some of it with him.

And then he was at her side. She looked up just as his head came down. His lips were cold, but his breath was warm on her face. "You're safe here, darlin'. Come inside."

She followed him to the side door. He put her bag down long enough to unlock the door and whistle for Ghost. The dog loped across the yard and up the steps, then ran into the house in front of them.

Cameron saw the surprise in Rusty's eyes as Ghost charged past them. "He's cleared the perimeter. Now he's clearing the way to make sure it's safe to go inside. After you."

The warmth inside welcomed her like a big hug. Cameron locked the door behind him and started down the hall.

"I have a spare room. I am not assuming you will want to sleep with—"

"You should assume that," Rusty said.

Cameron grinned. "Then I'll take your bag to the spare room so you can unpack there. We'll call it your dressing room."

"Works for me," Rusty said. "As to this sleeping arrangement, how's Ghost going to feel about—"

"His bed is by the fireplace. He'll be fine," Cameron said. "Follow me. I'll show you the lay of the house as we go. Nothing is off-limits to you."

Rusty followed, admiring the width of his shoulders and the steady stride of his footsteps rather than the rooms they were passing. That she was even here felt surreal, and all she wanted was to come undone in his arms.

"This used to be Rachel's room when she was a kid," he said, as he flipped a light switch, put her bag on the bed, then pulled the curtains to shut out the night. "I'll leave you to unpack. Oh, and there's an extra bathroom across the hall if you want to put all of your stuff in there. However, I would not take offense at sharing the shower in my bedroom."

Rusty was taking off her coat when he said that. She glanced up, saw the look on his face, and tossed her purse on the bed.

"How long are we going to dance around the obvious?"

Cameron took off his coat and threw it on the bed beside hers. "Since you're under my roof, I know I'm not waiting five more years. I'm going to throw a log on the fire and settle Ghost. The door to my bedroom is open. I want you. I will always want you. But it's going to be your call. I take nothing that isn't given."

Then he turned and walked out of the room, leaving the decision up to her. As far as Rusty was concerned, that decision had been made when they met. Now was about catching up.

She walked up the hall, made a quick left into the room with the open door, saw the king-size bed. Her hands were shaking as she began taking off her clothes. He made her ache.

When she pulled back the covers of his bed and slid between the sheets, she caught the faint scent of his aftershave and shivered. The sound of his footsteps as he walked up the hall matched the drumbeat of her heart.

Cameron came through the doorway with his boots in one hand and his shirt in the other and saw her lying in his bed.

"Dream come true," he said softly, then closed the door and turned out the lights. Within moments he was lying naked beside her. "Are you still—"

"Protected? Yes."

He raised up on one elbow and cupped her cheek, then threaded his fingers through her wild, unruly curls.

"Magic, just like you. Fire that doesn't burn," he whispered, and then centered his mouth on her lips and set a fire of their own.

It was just like before. Every move instinctive and familiar, mapping the curves of her body with his hands and then his mouth, feeling the hammer of her heartbeat beneath his palm. Hearing her sighs, and then the moans.

Rusty's arms slid around his neck as he moved between her legs and then he was inside of her. So big. So hard. She wrapped her legs around his waist and rose to meet the thrusts and lost her mind.

They made love again, and then again before she fell asleep. Exhausted. Satiated. Held like the precious treasure she was to him, safe within his embrace. He was lying on his side, thinking of the task ahead of them when he closed his eyes. And slept.

———

Cameron woke before dawn. The door to his room was open. The covers were thrown back on Rusty's side of the bed and she was gone. He bailed out of bed, pulled on a pair of sweats, and walked out into the hall.

The scent of fresh coffee drew him toward the front of the house where he found Rusty sitting cross-legged on the floor in front of the fireplace with a mug of coffee at her knee. A fresh log had been laid upon last night's embers and was already burning. She was checking messages on her phone with one hand and scratching Ghost's head with the other.

He had to grin. Her hair was a tangle of curls. He'd done that. And she had a very satisfied expression on her face. He was responsible for that, as well. God, how he loved her.

"I see you have tamed the other male in this house."

Rusty looked up, beaming. "Good morning, sweetheart! I didn't mean to abandon you. I'm just used to being up early and wanted to let Agent Howard know the transfer of residence had happened."

"And Ghost and I are usually up by now, too. Before he hurt his paw, we ran every morning."

Rusty nodded, but she just kept staring at him, and then blurted out a statement he wasn't expecting. "You are such a stunning man," she said.

"Uh… Thank you, baby."

"I just wanted you to know. You make me feel wanted. You make me feel beautiful."

Cameron knelt beside her and cupped the back of her neck. "Because you are wanted. Because you are beautiful. Five years ago you gave me everything. We were strangers, and yet I held onto that memory, because even then you mattered that much."

Ghost whined.

Cameron sighed. "I better get some shoes on and take him out. You can fill me in on developments at breakfast."

"Okay," she said, and when Cameron stood, she lifted her hand for a boost.

With one tug, she was on her feet and in his arms. The kiss was hard and quick. His hug was enveloping, and then he left to get a shirt and some shoes, then came back on the run.

Ghost was waiting at the door.

Cameron frowned. "Usually he wants to go out the

back. I guess we'd better see what's interesting out front first this morning," he said, and opened the door.

Ghost shot out the door and bounded down the steps just as a deer disappeared into the trees.

Cameron looked back at Rusty and smiled. "A deer. An invader to him, and now it's gone. I think we're safe," he said, and shut the door behind him.

Rusty went to the window. Cameron was standing in the middle of the yard watching Ghost, who had his nose to the ground and was moving in circles. She shook her head, marveling at the bond between them, and went to get dressed.

As Rusty changed into jeans and a sweater, the urge to take everything off and go back to bed with Cameron was overwhelming. Staying on task here was going to take some self-control, but the luxury of seeing him day in and day out was going to be worth it.

She was tying the last tie on her sneakers when she got a text from her uncle Ray.

> **My missing hostess showed up today, typically apologetic and claiming a family emergency. I'm about to have a come-to-Jesus meeting with her.**

Rusty's eyes narrowed thoughtfully, and then she sent a follow-up text.

> If you would send me a list of all the dates she's disappeared and the dates she came back for

the last six months, I would appreciate it. Just
email it to me. Oh...and don't fire her. I need to
know where to find her if the need arises.

Ray responded: **Will do.**

Rusty was satisfied to know Emily Payne was back, so
she hadn't been a victim. But she still needed to be cleared
as a possible person of interest. She tossed her phone on
the bed and went to find a hair tie and get her hair away
from her face. She was getting ready to take her laptop to
the kitchen and update Cameron as they ate when her cell
phone rang.

It was Special Agent Jay Howard.

"Good morning, sir," Rusty said.

"Morning. Good to know you've settled in. I want to
touch base with you about a couple of things before you
begin your day. We've discussed your continuing presence
in Jubilee but think it would be advantageous for everyone, including the police chief and the sheriff, to think that
you're gone."

"Yes, sir, but is there a reason?"

"I've just sent you a big file on the local sheriff, Rance
Allen Woodley. He's from Chicago, and I'm curious as
to how he wound up this far south. I want you to apply
yourself to every aspect of him. You'll also receive updated
information on the Jubilee police chief, Sonny Warren, and
you have the list of missing women. See if anything clicks."

"Yes, sir. Oh...the missing hostess from the Serenity
Inn showed up this morning, but I've asked my uncle for

a list of all the dates she went AWOL during the past six months, just to see if there's any connection on the time-line," Rusty said.

"Good idea," Howard said. "Let me know what you need and keep me informed."

"Yes, sir. I will," Rusty said, and disconnected.

She pocketed her phone and grabbed her laptop as she left the room.

As soon as Cameron came back, she began sharing everything she knew while he made them scrambled eggs and toast, reading aloud some of the new info Howard had just sent.

Cameron was surprised. "So they're investigating the local sheriff and police chief?"

"So it appears," she said. "At least eliminating them as suspects."

"Right," he said.

He carried two plates of food to the table, then refilled their coffee cups before he sat down.

Rusty took a bite of the eggs and toast and then gave him a thumbs-up.

"I love spicy eggs. These are delicious and you can't make them too hot for me."

"Good to know," Cameron said, and scooped up a bite for himself.

"Oh! One more thing," Rusty added. "They want the public to think I've left the area, so I'm guessing I'm house-bound here for the time being. Please don't let that inter-fere with whatever you need to do on a daily basis. I'm not in danger. And if people think I'm gone, then no one comes looking."

Cameron nodded. "Yes, that makes sense. Ghost and I will make a grocery run into Jubilee later today. If you need stuff, write it on the pad on the counter. I'll pick it up for you."

"Okay," she said, then spread jelly on her toast and finished eating. "You cooked. I'll clean up."

"Thanks, honey. I have some business to take care of online, and then I'll make that grocery run."

Rusty hesitated. There was something she was curious about, so she just came out and asked. "What, exactly, do you do now? Or are you pulling retirement?"

"I didn't serve long enough," Cameron said, and then hesitated. Nobody outside of the families on Pope Mountain knew about PCG Inc.

Rusty saw him hesitating. "I don't mean to pry. It doesn't matter. That was pure curiosity and it's not my business."

Cameron sighed. "It's not that. I'm the CEO of a corporation. PCG Incorporated, to be exact. It's just that nobody outside of the families up here knows about our connection to the corporation."

She frowned. "PCG Incorporated. Is that manufacturing? And why would it matter if people knew?"

"This is between you and me and no one else. Okay?"

"Sure, but if it bothers you to break a confidence, I'm fine with not knowing," she said.

"I live in the hope that one day you're going to marry me and live here. If that happens, you'll have to know then. All spouses do."

Rusty put the dirty dishes into the sink and plopped down in his lap.

"Did you just kinda-sorta propose to me?"

He grinned. "Probably."

"Then when you do get around to a for-sure proposal, the answer will be yes," she said.

He laughed and planted a kiss on her lips that left her breathless, then cupped her face.

"PCG stands for Pope, Cauley, and Glass. The three 'first families' of Pope Mountain. Our ancestors have been here since the 1800s. When locals began building little shops down the mountain about sixty years ago to sell their homemade goods and food, they never expected the tourist trade to blow up like it did. So to protect ourselves from less-than-desirables setting up shop there and protect our privacy up here, we incorporated the land in the valley. No one has a business in Jubilee without the board's approval, and we own the land and the buildings. People lease places to open their businesses, but there's no land for sale."

Rusty frowned, trying to absorb what he was telling her. "Wait. What?"

"Basically, we own the town of Jubilee, lock, stock, and barrel. The hoteliers have one-hundred-year leases on a set amount of land. They built their hotels on our land and pay a percentage of their monthly profits to the corporation. Like rent. If they decide to sell the hotels, then the new owners would have to sign a whole new agreement with the corporation. The people on Pope Mountain may come off as hillbillies, but they're drawing quarterly dividends from a very profitable business, and have been for years. We made a pact when the corporation was created. Nobody outside the family circles knows. The hoteliers don't know. They think it's some big-city corporation."

Rusty's mouth opened, then she shook her head and smiled. "That's freaking brilliant. I've taken vows of loyalty and secrecy. I know how to keep my mouth shut."

He hugged her. "Now you understand why I immediately agreed to help a federal agent with the human-trafficking investigation. We don't want anything like this entrenched in Jubilee."

"Yes. I understand why this is so personal to you, even over and above your niece's kidnapping," she said. "You go do you. I'm going to clean up in here and then get to work myself."

She got up from his lap and began clearing the table while Cameron went down the hall to his office. She was glad he'd confided in her. It explained a lot.

Ray Caldwell was furious, but kept his anger intact and Rusty's request uppermost as he waited for Emily Payne to come to his office. He didn't know what she was up to, but if Rusty was investigating her, it couldn't be good.

Moments later there was a knock at his door.

"Come in!"

Emily Payne came in, smiling and walking with that little bounce in her step as if she didn't have a care in the world. "Good morning, Mr. Caldwell. You wanted to see me?"

Ray pointed to the chair across from his desk.

"Sit down, please."

Emily's heart skipped. Ray Caldwell was frowning.

"I'm really sorry I didn't think to—"

"I've heard it all before," Ray snapped. "You've already said it wouldn't happen again, and yet here we are. Just know that I'm docking your next paycheck for every day you've missed work for the past six months. Maybe that will remind you who's the boss around here. And if that puts you in the red, we'll just hope you've saved up enough money to get by until your next paycheck, okay?"

Emily gulped. "Uh… Exactly how many days will that—"

"Twenty," Ray snapped. "We're done here. Go back to work."

Emily's eyes welled. "Yes, sir. I'm sorry."

Ray said nothing.

She slipped out of his office far less bouncy than when she'd entered.

Ray was still frowning when he went back to work.

———

Danny Biggers wasn't sleeping. He was a walking zombie, just going through the motions while waiting for the end to come. The key rattling at his cell door happened every morning around three. He knew guards were making the rounds, but they weren't jiggling their keys like that at every other door. It was a warning that he was being watched.

Yesterday he'd passed out during exercise time on the grounds and woken up in the infirmary with an IV in his arm.

Joseph Weller, the prison doctor, asked Danny if he was sick, and Danny just shook his head.

"Something is wrong. Your pulse is slow. Your blood pressure is low. Are you passing blood?" Dr. Weller asked.

Danny shook his head again.

Weller frowned. "Something is wrong. If you don't talk to me, I'll wind up having to run a dozen tests on you to see what's happening here."

"I'm just waitin' to die," Danny said.

Weller frowned. "From what?"

"Payback. I'm a dead man walking, and the suspense of when it happens is sucking the life out of me one minute at a time."

"Who wants you dead?" Weller asked.

Danny shrugged. "Got no idea. I just pulled a job for someone and got caught. Them people don't leave loose ends."

"What people?" Weller asked.

Danny looked up at the doctor as if he'd lost his senses. "Didn't I just say I don't know? I can't sleep. I can't eat. I just wish it was over."

"I'll talk to the warden," the doctor said.

Danny scoffed. "Just let it be. I've done things. Bad things. I always knew I wouldn't live to be an old man. The sooner my heart quits, the sooner my misery ends." Then he turned his face to the wall and closed his eyes.

Dr. Weller had seen plenty in his years on the job, but he'd never seen anyone this young so ready to die. In a way, it was almost as if Biggers was willing himself dead before anyone got to him. Like he needed to beat them to the punch.

Weller checked the drip in the IV, then went in search of a nurse.

"I want you to keep an eye on the inmate in Bed 12. He should be on suicide watch. I'm going to speak to the warden."

"Yes, sir," the nurse said.

Weller left the ward. The nurse pulled up a chair and sat next to Danny's bed. But the warden was unavailable, so Weller left a note saying they needed a meeting, then went back to his office in the infirmary.

———

Boss was in a mood. Everything had been running like clockwork until the bungled kidnapping of that kid. He'd lost the chance to make a fortune and was still furious about how it had gone down. He knew Biggers was back in prison. But he didn't know where Lindy Sheets was, and that bothered him. Part of him wondered if the feds already had her and were keeping her under wraps. But then if they did, and she'd talked, they would already have been on his doorstep.

He couldn't concentrate on work and hadn't been sleeping. He'd popped a couple of uppers before coming to work, and now it felt like he was coming out of his skin. He'd just refilled his coffee when the burner phone in his desk began to ring. He jumped up and closed the office door, then unlocked the drawer and grabbed the phone.

"What?"

"It's me, Dewey. We can't find a trace of Lindy Sheets anywhere. It's like she dropped off the face of the earth."

Boss frowned. She was a loose end, but she was smart. She'd read between the lines of their last phone conversation and done a runner.

"Where's her car?" he asked.

"Still at her old residence," Dewey said. "Just sitting there in the parking lot with the doors locked and the key in the ignition, waiting for someone to heist it. Her clothes are gone, but all of her shit is still in her old apartment. She don't wanna be found."

Boss sighed. "Fine. Whatever. As long as the feds don't have her stashed somewhere, we're good."

"So do you want me to keep looking?" Dewey asked.

"No. We have business to attend to and orders to fill. Get back to regular business. I'll be in touch."

"Yes, sir," Dewey said.

The line went dead in Boss's ear. He put the phone in his desk, locked the drawer, and then went back to work. It was just as well she'd skipped out, and she knew better than to talk. But her absence did leave a hole in his organization. He needed to replace her, and soon.

Liz was meeting Michael for lunch. It was their first date since the debacle at the tiny cabins, but she wasn't having sex with him today, no matter what he was expecting. She was getting ready to leave and went to tell her mother goodbye. To her surprise, she found her mother in her bedroom, packing.

"Mom! What are you doing?" Liz asked.

"I'm flying to Philadelphia to stay with Penny for a while. I'm so unnerved by all that's been happening here that I just can't bear to stay a moment longer," she said.

"So you're abandoning Dad and me just like that?" Liz asked.

"Oh, you know your dad. He's always busy, and you have Michael. I just need to get away for a bit."

"I might have liked to go to Philadelphia, too. The least you could have done was invite me," Liz muttered.

Patricia paused. "Well, do you? Want to go, I mean?"

Liz shrugged. "No."

Patricia beamed. "See? All that angst for nothing. I love you to bits, but you're so dramatic," she said, and fastened the latch on her suitcase and put it on the floor by the other two.

"Three bags?" Liz asked.

Patricia frowned. "Stop being so critical," she said, then kissed Liz on both cheeks. "I'll call when I arrive. Love you, darling. Take care." She waved absently as she picked up the house phone and called down to the front desk. "Yes, this is Mrs. Caldwell. Please send someone up to the penthouse for my luggage, and make sure the car is waiting. I have a flight to catch in Bowling Green."

Liz rolled her eyes and walked out of the room. She rode the elevator down, picked up her car, and took off toward the Hotel Devon while Patricia Caldwell was leaving Jubilee.

━━━━━━━━

Rusty was in the living room with her feet turned toward the fire and her laptop in her lap. The house was mostly quiet, although she could hear the murmur of Cameron's voice coming from his office.

She was looking at the file the feds had collected on Jack Barton, and specifically the women who'd gone missing after staying in tiny cabins or one of the hotels in Jubilee. She was trying to establish if there was a matching timeline from when they disappeared to the next time their credit cards were used. As best she could tell, the timeline for the next use of the cards was always less than five days after their "departure" from Jubilee, and each card was only used once. After that, the trails went cold, and the women disappeared.

Once she had that spreadsheet finalized, she began entering the dates that Emily Payne had gone AWOL, then compared them to the last time the missing women's credit cards had been used.

As soon as she was finished, she leaned back and began

studying the spreadsheet as a whole, and what she saw made her skin crawl. Emily's absences coincided every time with the use of a missing woman's credit card.

"Holy shit," she muttered, then looked up as Cameron entered the room.

"What holy shit did you uncover?" he asked.

"Come look at this," Rusty said. "I'm about to send this to Agent Howard, but I want your feedback to make sure I'm not reading too much into this."

Cameron sat down on the sofa beside her and leaned over as she turned the laptop toward him. "Okay, what am I looking at?" he asked.

"These are the names and dates of the women who've gone missing from Jubilee in the past six months. The next date beside their names is when their credit cards are used again. See? All within a week of their disappearances, and then they're never used again and the women have disappeared. And then here are all of the dates Emily Payne, the hostess from the Serenity Inn, went AWOL."

Cameron frowned. "That can't be coincidence. Not every time."

"My feelings exactly," Rusty said. "I don't have enough to arrest her, and we don't want to question her until we do for fear she'll disappear for good. I'm sending all this to Jay Howard. They can investigate this in depth. They'll need to pull security footage from the most recent places where the credit cards were used to see if the woman using them could be the same woman in different disguises. All it would take is a wig with the right hair color, sunglasses, and makeup to match the driver's license photo, and the groundwork is laid to draw the authorities away from Jubilee."

Cameron eyed her with renewed appreciation. "When your uncle mentioned his hostess's habit of coming and going without notice, you suspected a connection. You're pretty darn sharp, lady."

Rusty smiled. "Dad used to say I was going to make one hell of a mother one day. My kids would never be able to lie to me and get away with it."

Cameron went still. "You want babies."

Rusty noticed it was a statement and not a question, then frowned.

"Well, yes. Don't you?" she asked.

"I want everything with you," Cameron said, and kissed her before reluctantly pulling back. "I'm ready to leave. Is there anything you need?"

"Just you, but we'll save that for later," she said.

"You have my number in your phone. Call if you remember something you want me to bring home. I'm taking Ghost by the vet's office first in hopes his paw has healed enough to get the stitches out and his ratty bandage removed."

She nodded, then put her laptop aside and leaned over to give Ghost a quick kiss between his ears.

"You are such a good boy," she said, and got a lick on her cheek. Cameron stood up, prompting her to add, "Drive safe, you two. I'm about to light a new fire under Howard and Pickard, and then we'll see where we go from there."

Chapter 12

JAY HOWARD WAS AT HIS DESK GOING THROUGH MORNING email when Rusty's call came through.

"Good morning, Agent Caldwell. Thank you for letting me know your relocation went smoothly. What's up?"

"Maybe the missing hostess, Emily Payne, being a connection to the trafficking gang, or maybe not. But Cameron and I both agree this goes way beyond the percentage of coincidence. I'm sending you a spreadsheet you need to look at. All of the info will be included in the email. If you can find footage from security cameras to back this up, you might hit the jackpot. And regarding the new suspect, she's about to get raked over the coals by my uncle today, but I asked him not to fire her. We need to be able to pick her up for questioning without having to put out a BOLO on her to do it."

"Excellent work," Howard said.

"I have a photo of Emily Payne from her personnel file. I'll include it in the file I'm emailing to you. I'll be in touch if we find anything else," Rusty said.

"Caldwell."

"Yes, sir?"

"Are you getting along okay with Pope?"

"Of course," Rusty said. "Why wouldn't I?"

"I hear he's got a dog the size of a bear."

"Yes. Ghost. He's not quite that big, but I like dogs. We're all one big happy family here, so butt out...sir."

Howard laughed, and he was still laughing when she hung up in his ear.

Rusty rolled her eyes. They knew. They all knew. Whatever. If things went the way she hoped, this was going to be her last case. Finding Cameron had made her realize her life was worth more than the money they paid her to put it at risk. She gathered up the files she'd created, attached them to the email, and hit Send.

She went to the kitchen to refill her coffee cup, then came back to the sofa, opened up the file on Sheriff Woodley, and started to read.

———

Liz and Michael were having lunch at the Hotel Devon in the penthouse where Michael lived with his father, Marshall. Marshall came into the residence long enough to greet Liz and remind Michael of a two o'clock meeting later, and then he was gone.

Michael seated Liz, kissed the side of her cheek, and then took the chair opposite her.

"You look beautiful, Liz."

"Thank you," Liz said.

She couldn't help but preen a little at the compliment, but she wasn't going to make this easy. He'd put his hands around her neck. He was lucky she hadn't gone for his balls.

As soon as they were both seated, the waiter served their food, left dessert on the sideboard, and exited the penthouse.

"Looks good," Liz said, eyeing the cold shrimp salad and white wine, then put her napkin in her lap and picked up her fork.

"I've missed you," Michael said. "I miss us."

Liz swallowed the bite she was chewing and pointed at him with her fork.

"You miss the sex," she said.

He shrugged. "Well, yes…that's part of it. Don't you?"

"I'm still dealing with the ugly threats you made to me," she said, and popped a shrimp in her mouth.

He flushed an angry red. "I've apologized for the misunderstanding several times. You either choose to accept it and quit harping about it, or you don't and this doesn't work anymore, because I will not grovel."

She calmly chewed and swallowed, then took a quick sip of the wine. "I didn't ask you to grovel, Michael. In fact, I haven't asked you for anything, have I?"

He sighed. "No."

"Then consider this starting over, because you broke 'us.' Now we just have to decide if there's anything left to repair," she said.

Michael stared at her as if she was a stranger. "You've changed," he said.

She shrugged. "I have come to realize what a shallow life

I was living. Rusty showed me that without even trying. I admire her greatly. I always have. I'd just forgotten how really special she is."

He blinked.

"Speaking of Rusty, I've been hearing rumors," Michael said.

"If the rumors are that she is smarter and prettier than me, then they're all true," Liz said. "Anyway, she's already gone, and Mom took off for Philadelphia this morning. One of her little trips she takes when she can't stand the sight of Jubilee another moment."

"I'm sorry," Michael said.

"Oh, don't be. Dad and I get along just fine. In fact, I've been thinking about hitting him up for a job. Maybe interning with our event planner. I feel like I've been wasting my degree just sitting around with my mother, getting my nails done, my hair done. Makes me feel like a toy in the house for her amusement." She poked at her salad again, spearing another shrimp. "This shrimp salad is delicious. Good choice, Michael."

Pleased that he'd done something right, he smiled. "I'm glad you're enjoying it. The entree is a petite filet mignon with a black pepper and caper sauce, and seared garlic-butter fingerling potatoes."

She smiled. "You turned lunch into a mini surf and turf. I like it."

"I aim to please," he said lightly, and the meal continued.

Cameron walked into the vet clinic with Ghost on a leash, waved at Amber, the receptionist, to let him know they were there, and then took Ghost to the far end of the room to wait. He looked up as Leslie appeared, escorting a woman to the door who was carrying her cat in a crate. The cat was hissing and spitting at everything in sight, and the woman was talking baby-talk to the cat as they went.

The look on Leslie's face was comical. It was all Cameron could do not to laugh.

As soon as the woman exited the lobby, Leslie turned and waved. "Hi, guys. We'll be with you shortly." Then she grabbed the next chart from the desk and looked up. "Charlie Pug is next."

A teenage boy stood up with an old, wheezing pug cradled in his arms and followed her back into an exam room.

Ghost looked up at Cameron.

"You're fine, buddy. Just relax."

Ghost lay down at Cameron's feet and gave his bandaged paw a lick.

"No licking," Cameron said, and laid a hand on the top of Ghost's head.

About fifteen minutes later, the teenage boy and Charlie Pug exited the lobby, and Leslie pointed at Ghost. "The Terminator is up."

Cameron laughed. The nickname fit. Ghost stood up as if he understood the summons and walked beside Cameron all the way into the exam room. Now that they were alone, Leslie's demeanor shifted, and Cameron could tell how bothered she still was about her involvement with Kevin Vanzant.

"You okay?" Cameron asked.

She shrugged. "As good as someone can be in my situation," she said. "You're here about removing stitches, right?"

"If the doctor thinks the foot is well, definitely," he said.

She nodded. "Then we'll need Ghost up on the exam table."

Cameron lifted him up just as the vet entered the room, and removed the leash.

Alan Morris stopped in the doorway, staring in disbelief at the size of the dog standing on his exam table.

"Doctor Morris, this is Ghost, and his owner, Cameron Pope. Dr. Sam performed surgery on the bandaged paw several days ago. They've already been in once to have the wound site checked and bandages changed. Cameron is hoping to get stitches out today."

"Well then, let's see what we can see," he said. "Cameron, can you get him to lie down for me?"

"Ghost. Down," Cameron said.

Ghost went flat.

"The exam table isn't really big enough for him, but I'll hold onto him so he doesn't roll off," Cameron said as he gently scooted Ghost onto his side, then stood behind him, with one hand on his belly and the other on his head. "Stay."

Ghost stayed.

"I'm impressed," Morris said. "Do we need to muzzle him before I start?"

"No. You're good," Cameron said, and began lightly scratching the spot between Ghost's ears.

Morris removed the bandages, then gently parted the pads on the dog's toes.

Ghost whined.

"You're okay, buddy. Lie still. You've been dying to lick this foot ever since you hurt it. Let's get this over with."

It was the calm, even tone in Cameron's voice that steadied Ghost's composure. He didn't know the strange man, but he knew his master and that was enough.

A few minutes later Doctor Morris was pulling out the last stitch and then flushing the foot pad with antiseptic. "That should do it," the vet said. "It was a pleasure to meet you and Ghost. He's magnificent."

"Thanks," Cameron said as he lifted Ghost off the table and clipped the leash back to his collar.

Leslie walked them through the lobby and then opened the door for them.

Cameron paused. "Take a breath, girl. You're okay."

Her eyes welled. "Thank you."

"Tell your family I said hello."

"I will."

Cameron's next stop was the supermarket, but the gathering clouds looked like imminent rain, which meant no time to waste. He wanted to finish and go home, and the thought of having someone to go home to left an immediate lump in his throat.

He reached the parking lot, found a spot close to the entrance, and left Ghost in the Jeep, then locked him in. Not so much to protect the dog but to protect anyone who might be stupid enough to think about opening the door with Ghost on guard.

He grabbed a cart, checked the list, and then started

shopping. He was in and out in less than twenty minutes. Ghost was asleep in the passenger seat and woke up when Cameron put the groceries in the back. The clouds were growing darker and he could hear thunder rumbling.

Ghost whined as he got in.

"I know. I heard it. It's thunder, not bombs. You're fine," he said, and stroked the big dog's head. "Next stop, Granny Annie's Bakery."

As luck would have it, there were several empty parking spaces in front of the store. Cameron wheeled in to the curb and parked, then got out on the run.

His aunt was in the back of the bakery and Laurel, her oldest daughter, was waiting on customers. He walked straight up to Laurel while other customers were still scanning the bakery case.

"Hi, Cam!"

"Hey, Cuz… I have an order to pick up."

"I think Mom has it ready to go. Just a sec," she said, and went into the kitchen. She came back moments later with a sack.

"A sour-cream brownie cake with chocolate ganache?"

"That's it," Cameron said, and handed her a card.

Laurel looked over his shoulder as she swiped the bank card. "Looks like it's gonna rain. Drive safe going home."

"I will, thanks. My best to Doug and the girls," he said as Laurel returned his card and scooted the sack across the counter.

Moments later he was out the door and running for the

Jeep, and none too soon. A big clap of thunder announced the storm's arrival.

Ghost whined and then turned and jumped into the back set and lay down on the floor.

Cameron sighed. "You're okay, buddy. Just one more stop and we'll be done."

Emory's Barbeque was the last public business at the foot of the mountain and it had a drive-through. It was already beginning to rain as Cameron pulled up to the speaker.

"Welcome to Emory's. How can I help you?"

"This is Cameron Pope. I'm picking up an order to go."

"Yes, sir. Drive on through."

Cameron turned on the windshield wipers as he stopped at the pickup window with his card in his hand. After he'd paid, he set the bag of food on the front floorboard and sped away.

The rain was really coming down now but they were headed home.

Ghost was sitting up in the back seat, and as Cameron glanced up in the rearview mirror and saw the glint in the dog's eyes and the way his ears were on alert, he laughed.

"Smells good in here, doesn't it, boy? Let's go see Rusty. We don't want to keep our girl waiting, right?"

Ghost barked.

———

Rusty was so involved in the file she was reading that she didn't know clouds were rolling in until a big clap of thunder made her jump.

She looked out the window, saw the dark sky and the wind beginning to blow, and glanced at the time. Surely they would be home soon, unless Cameron had had to wait a long time at the vet.

And even if it rained before they got home, the carport was deep enough to unload groceries without getting wet. She got up, slipped her feet into some shoes, and put on her jacket, then went outside and sat down on the front porch.

She could tell how strong the wind was from the way the treetops were whipping, but there were so many trees around the cabin that they partially blocked the blast below. When the first raindrops fell, they splattered like broken eggs on concrete. But as they came faster, it turned into a downpour, blowing the rain halfway across the porch and close enough to where she was sitting that she could feel the spray blowing against her face and flashed on the spray from the speedboat blowing in her eyes. Only this time no one was shooting at her, and she wasn't lost anymore.

She stayed outside, with her feet up in the chair, a willing witness to the storm. This was what life out here would be like. No big shopping centers. No traffic noise. No people unless you went looking for them. She'd never known a simplistic life, but God knew she was ready for one. And she'd live under a rock if Cameron Pope was with her.

A sudden clap of thunder made her look up, and as she did, she saw the Jeep barreling toward the house.

Thank God.

She waved and then darted inside, running toward

the side door to help carry. The moment she opened the door, she saw Ghost. And when he saw her and the open door, he shot out of the back seat and into the house, then began dancing around her feet for a welcome-home pat.

Rusty laughed and gave him a quick hug. "I see! I see! The bandages are gone. You're ready to run, aren't you, boy?"

Cameron came in grinning. "You are the best thing ever to come home to," he said, then set the bags from the bakery and the barbecue on the counter and gave her a big kiss. "Your face is cold, darlin'. How long have you been sitting outside?"

"I don't know… Since it started raining. I like thunderstorms. They're wild and cleansing…blowing away the cobwebs in my thoughts, I guess."

Cameron grimaced. "Ghost hates them. He thinks the crashes of thunder are bombs. He's been in the front seat, and the back seat, and on the floorboards in the back ever since it started."

"Oh, bless his heart," Rusty said, and then looked around. "Where did he go?"

"Probably under my bed. I need to bring in the groceries and then I'll go check on him."

"I'll help," Rusty said, and followed him to the carport.

They brought everything inside in one trip. Rusty began pulling things out of bags while Cameron put them away.

"Something smells so good," Rusty said.

"That bag is smoked ribs and sides, and the other bag is

a chocolate cake from the bakery. As soon as I find Ghost and get him settled, we can eat."

As Cameron predicted, the dog was under the big four-poster, shaking. Cameron got down on his knees and peered under the edge of the bedspread.

"Come here, boy. Come on. You're okay. I'm okay. It's just rain."

Ghost whined.

Rusty dropped to the floor, then went flat on her belly. Before Cameron knew it, she was halfway under the bed with the dog, coaxing him in a soft, quiet voice. "You don't like that noise, do you, baby? But it's cold under here. Come get in your bed by the fire and I'll bring you a treat!"

Cameron rocked back on his knees, watching, falling deeper in love with every second seeing her and Ghost together. But it was the word *treat* that got the dog's attention.

Rusty began backing up, still saying, "get a treat," and Ghost came crawling out on his belly and then went straight to Cameron and laid his head on Cameron's shoulder.

Cameron gave the big dog a hug, then led him to the living room as Rusty bolted for the pantry. Ghost was in his bed by the fire and Cameron was on the floor with him when Rusty plopped down beside them.

"I don't know how many he can have, but he's a giant and these are tiny and he's scared, so I brought four."

Cameron grinned. "He will be delighted. You promised them, so you should give them to him."

The delight on Rusty's face was evident as she picked up the first little bone-shaped treat.

Ghost took it from her fingers like a proper gentleman, but once it was in his mouth, it disappeared in one crunch. He looked at her again because he knew there were more. By the time the last treat was gone, the dog's anxiety had eased. Cameron pulled an old quilt from a basket on the floor and covered him up.

"They make thunder shirts for dogs. Supposedly, the pressure of the shirt around the dog helps with anxiety, but they don't make them big enough for Ghost, so I use the weight of this old quilt, and it seems to work the same."

"People don't think about animals with PTSD, but it should be obvious. Abuse is abuse. War is war. Suffering is suffering, whether we walk on four feet or two. He's lucky he has you," Rusty said.

Cameron kept stroking Ghost's head as they talked. "And I always think I'm the lucky one to have him."

Rusty nodded. "He was every bit a soldier with the rest of you."

Cameron was leaning against the sofa as he sat and suddenly reached for her and pulled her close. When she laid her head against his shoulder and snuggled down, he felt a slight shift in his world, as if everything had suddenly found true center.

So this is how love works. Feeling whole.

They sat by the fire while the wind blew and the rain came down, both lost in thoughts of all that they had endured and the randomness of fate that brought them together again.

Finally, Cameron shifted and then gave her a quick hug. "Are you ready to eat?"

"Yes, but will Ghost be okay?" she asked.

"If he's not, he'll follow us into the kitchen and that will be fine, too. Come on, honey. You can tell me what you've been digging into while I was gone."

They began pulling out the food and getting flatware and plates like they'd been doing it together all their lives. The ease with which they'd entered each other's lives was seamless.

"I've been reading the files on Sheriff Rance Woodley. Outwardly, there doesn't seem to be anything to explain his irrational behavior about the kidnapping and the murder other than he's just as ass."

Cameron grinned. "Some men are."

"And women," Rusty added, and licked barbecue sauce off her thumb before carrying her plate to the table.

Cameron followed and sat across the table as they began to eat. After a few bites, Rusty picked up the conversation again.

"Back to Woodley," she said. "He was born in Chicago. He has a high school education. He's had factory jobs, been married and divorced, no children, no family. He moved to this area about ten years ago, got a job as a night watchman at a warehouse, and two years later, went through CLEET training and got himself elected sheriff. With no prior experience. How does that happen?"

Cameron shrugged. "Look at where we are. The Cumberland Mountains in rural America. Likely ran without an opponent. It happens."

"Good grief," Rusty said, and popped a french fry in her mouth.

Cameron frowned. "You said he'd been married?"

"Yes, divorced right after he came here, but before he ran for sheriff."

"Was she a local?" Cameron asked.

Rusty looked up. "I don't know. I'll dig into that and see where it goes. I think her name was in the report somewhere."

They finished their meal, cleaned up the kitchen, and went back to work. Rusty shared her files with him, and they both settled down with their laptops and began to read.

═══════════

The rain put a damper on downtown businesses. Tourists were either holed up in their rooms or in bars and restaurants, waiting for it to pass.

Marshall Devon was watching it pour from his office and thinking what a miserable day this was. Michael was out there somewhere running errands, and he wished now that he hadn't insisted they all be done today, then shrugged it off. It was days like these that would harden his son for the daily grind. He needed Michael ready to take over here when he made the move to Lexington. He was contemplating going up to the penthouse and calling it a day when his cell phone rang. He picked it up from his desk, saw Michael's name on caller ID, and answered.

"Hello."

"Dad, I'm okay, but I just had a wreck. I was stopped at a red light when a car fishtailed in the rain and rammed into the side of my car."

"Oh my God! Michael! Where are you?"

"At the intersection of Main and Boone. Wreckers are on the way. The police are here."

"Sit tight, Son. I'll be right there," Marsh said, then grabbed a raincoat from the closet in his office, took the car keys from his desk drawer, and ran.

———

Just hearing his dad's voice was reassuring, but Michael couldn't stop shaking. It was all from the adrenaline crash and the shock. He'd never seen it coming. One moment he was just sitting, waiting for the light to change, and then impact! It slid his car all the way into moving traffic. It was only by the grace of God that neither of them were hit by other cars, and now traffic was at a standstill and being rerouted as he waited.

He wanted to call Liz, but after their lunch today, he realized they had a long way to go to get back to where they'd been. And so he sat, waiting for his dad to arrive. When he finally saw the dark-green Jaguar coming up the street, he grabbed his things and got out in the downpour, then called out to the officer nearby. "Officer! That's my dad coming to pick me up. Is it okay to leave my car?"

"You'll need to leave the keys in it," the officer said.

Michael gave him a thumbs-up and then started running through the rain.

Marsh had pulled over to the curb and unlocked the door when he saw Michael coming toward him. Just the sight of his son upright and in one piece was a relief. And then Michael opened the door and all but fell into the car.

"Thanks for coming, Dad," he said, and dropped his briefcase on the floor between his feet.

"My God, Son. Of course. Are you sure you're all right? I could run you by the ER just to make certain."

"I think I'm okay, but my head is throbbing. From whiplash, I think," Michael said.

Marsh gripped his son's arm and gave a quick squeeze. "Then I'm taking you to the ER. You are so very precious to me. Is it okay for us to leave the scene?" he asked.

"Yes. They've already taken our statements. The other dude knows he was at fault. We've exchanged insurance info and IDs," Michael said, but his eyes were welling with sudden tears. He knew his dad loved him, but he'd never been one for displays of affection, which made what he'd just said more meaningful.

"Okay. To the ER we go. Did you call Liz?" Marsh asked.

Michael's father knew nothing about the fallout between him and Liz, so Michael lied. "No. I didn't want her out in this weather."

"Oh, right!" Marsh said, and took the next street left to get to the hospital.

As he turned, Michael pointed. "There come the wreckers."

"They'll have the cars out of the intersection in no time. We'll check with impound tomorrow and deal with all of that then. Just rest easy."

Michael groaned. "What a mess," he said, then leaned back and closed his eyes.

His trip to the ER was tedious. They took him straight back into an exam room, but then wheeled him to X-ray. By the time the ER doctor came back to read the X-rays, Michael was getting stiffer, and the pain in his body was increasing by the minute.

"Mr. Devon, you don't have any broken bones, but you did suffer whiplash and a slight concussion. You will need to take it easy and rest for the next few days. I'm going to suggest a cervical collar for the next week at least. It will give the strained muscles in your neck and shoulder time to heal. You can remove it to shower, but otherwise keep it on until you contact your regular doctor later in the week."

"Yes, sir," Michael said, and then sighed. *What a hassle.*

"Can he take anything for pain?" his father asked.

"I'm preparing a prescription for muscle relaxers. It's only good for three days' worth. After that, over-the-counter pain meds will be fine. Take care leaving the building. The rain is still coming down," he added.

A few minutes later, they loaded Michael into the Jaguar and headed back to Hotel Devon. "I'm dropping off the prescription on the way home. I'll have them deliver it to the hotel. You need to get in bed," Marsh said.

"Thanks, Dad," Michael said, but the urge to cry was huge.

He knew it was shock and an adrenaline crash, and knowing Liz had him on a kind of probation made him anxious. What if she never forgave him? God. What a fucking mess he'd made of everything.

Chapter 13

THE SPREADSHEET RUSTY EMAILED TO JAY HOWARD HAD become their new lead. They had teams pulling security footage from the most recent locations where the credit cards had been used, then comparing those with charges from Emily Payne's personal credit cards on the same days, trying to put her in the same cities, in the same areas, on the same days. And another team was researching every aspect of Emily Payne's life.

What turned up was shocking.

Howard opened an email from one of the research teams, then shifted his glasses and leaned forward so that he was looking through the bifocals to read it.

"Yes! Hell yes!" Howard crowed.

Pickard was coming back to his desk with a fresh cup of coffee when he heard his partner's shout.

"What? What did we get?" he asked.

"Check this out," Howard said. "Emily Payne spent time in a drug rehab facility at the same time that a young man named Kevin Vanzant was there, and the team has already verified it's the same Kevin Vanzant as our murder victim."

Pickard grinned. "That is not a coincidence."

"No, it's not. And that's not all. We have video of a woman in a clothing store four days ago using a credit card belonging to one of the missing women. Then we pick her up again on video in the parking lot. We got a good shot of the car tag. It's registered to Emily Ann Payne. And Emily Payne used her own credit card for gas right after she left the mall. We need to pick up this Payne woman for questioning."

"Do we want to involve Chief Warren?" Pickard asked.

"Only as far as asking him to use one of their interrogation rooms for the questioning," Howard said. "You go tell the boss where we're headed. I'm calling for a chopper. We'll pick her up after we get there."

"Do we involve Agent Caldwell in the interrogation?" Pickard asked.

"No. We don't want anyone knowing she's still on-site gathering info," Howard said. "But we need to make sure she is on the job. Do we have Ray Caldwell's contact info?"

"Yes, because that's where Rusty was staying," Pickard said.

"Call him. Tell him we need Emily Payne brought to his office in about an hour."

Pickard nodded, pulled up the phone number they had on record, and made the call.

━━━━━━━━

Ray Caldwell was in the same mood that Marsh Devon had been, standing at the windows in his office and watching it rain, when his phone rang. He glanced at the time, wondering if it might be his wife letting him know she'd landed, then realized it was too early. He turned and picked up the call.

"Hello?"

"Mr. Caldwell, this is Special Agent Pickard from the Frankfort office of the FBI. We have a request."

Ray was suddenly focused. Whatever this was, he suspected Rusty was involved. "Yes, sir. How can I be of service?" Ray asked.

"You have an employee at your hotel named Emily Payne. Is this right?"

Ray's gut knotted. "Yes, I do. She's a hostess."

"Is she at work today?"

"Yes, she'll be on duty until 6:00 p.m. today," Ray said.

"Excellent. My partner and I are coming in on a chopper to pick her up for questioning. Rather than cause a scene in your hotel, it would be helpful if you'd have her brought to your outer office and have one of your security guards stay with her until we arrive."

Ray was startled, but immediately agreed. "Yes, sir. I can do that. Does she know about this?"

"No, and don't tell her."

"It's raining pretty steady here," Ray added.

"It's already clearing here. We'll be flying behind the moving front, but thank you for your concern. See you soon."

"Right," Ray said, and hung up. His gut knotted as he glanced at the time, then made a note to himself. Something told him he was about to be minus a hostess again.

Back in Frankfort, an FBI chopper was warming up at their heliport, and Howard and Pickard were inbound. As soon as they arrived and boarded, the pilot lifted off.

———————

The dining area was finally clearing out from the lunch rush, and Emily was among the workers helping gather up menus, changing tablecloths, and readying the dining area for the evening meal.

She was still a little rattled about the money being docked from her paycheck and trying to decide if she should just cut her losses and move on or stick it out. But most of the decision was not hers. She'd gotten herself in deep to a man she was afraid to cross, and the next time he called, she was going to have to tell him the ultimatum she'd been given. But she'd have to wait. He always called her from burner phones, and she didn't even know his name. He was just Boss.

She had just returned a stack of menus to the front desk when a member of hotel security approached her. "Emily, Mr. Caldwell wants to see you," he said, and slipped his hand beneath her elbow.

Emily's heart sank. *Oh crap! He's going to fire me after all.*

She walked beside the guard to the elevator, and when the doors opened and he got on with her, shock rolled through her.

He's actually escorting me up!

As soon as they reached the third floor, they got off together and walked into the outer office.

"Take a seat, please," the guard said.

Emily sat and then watched the guard walking to the door, but then he stopped and turned around, taking a stance as if he was blocking her escape. She had an overwhelming urge to run. What on earth could they possibly know?

———

Chief Warren received a heads-up about the inbound chopper a few minutes before it landed. The rain was down to a drizzle, but something must be important to fly in this weather. He didn't know what was happening, but he guessed it still had to do with the campground murder. He didn't know that Rusty Caldwell was no longer in residence at the hotel and half expected her to show up for the FBI agents' arrival. But when she didn't, and the chopper landed and unloaded the agents, he put on his hat and his rain slicker and went out to greet them.

"Welcome back to Jubilee," he said, and shook their hands upon approach. "I assume it's business? I thought Agent Caldwell might be on hand to greet you, but she's not."

"Oh, she's no longer in Jubilee," Howard said. "We are going to the Serenity Inn and pick up a woman for questioning. We'd like permission to use one of your interrogation rooms for the process."

"Absolutely," Sonny said. "Do you need a ride to the hotel to pick her up?"

"That would be helpful," Howard said. "And an extra car to transport her back here."

Sonny flagged down two of his men. "Paulson, I need you to drive Special Agents Howard and Pickard to the Serenity Inn. And Williams, we'll need you to take your patrol car to bring in a suspect."

"Yes, sir," they echoed.

The agents got into Paulson's patrol car and Williams followed. It didn't take long to get to their destination, and as soon as the cars pulled up in the breezeway, Howard and Pickard got out.

"We won't be long," Howard said as they turned and walked inside.

Within seconds, a security guard who'd been awaiting their arrival saw them getting out of the cop car, called Ray to let him know they'd arrived, then flagged them down and took them straight up to Ray's office.

Ray was aware Emily was in place, but he waited until the agents were on the premises to leave his office. And the moment he walked out and saw her, he knew she was scared. He just didn't know what she'd done.

Emily stood. "Mr. Caldwell?"

Ray motioned for her to sit back down and then stood with his arms crossed, waiting. Moments later, his security chief walked in, followed by two men in dark suits. One bald and stocky. One with a scar on his face. They looked like they meant business.

Howard went straight to Ray. "Mr. Caldwell. I'm Special Agent Howard. This is my partner, Special Agent Pickard. Thank you for your cooperation."

"Of course," Ray said.

Then both agents turned and approached Emily where she sat.

"Are you Emily Ann Payne?"

She nodded.

They flashed their badges. "I'm Special Agent Howard. This is my partner, Special Agent Pickard. We are taking you down to the local police station for questioning regarding the murder of Kevin Vanzant and the disappearances of several women who've gone missing from Jubilee during the past six months."

Emily gasped and then leaped to her feet. "Kevin's dead? I didn't know! I didn't know!" she wailed.

She started crying as they were reading her rights and then walked her out. They took her down in a service elevator and out a side door to the police cars, while Ray watched from his windows above. He was still in shock that he'd had someone on the premises actually connected to all this.

———

Emily was in hysterics all the way to the station. Who murdered Kevin? Was it Boss? Was she next? She didn't know what to think or how to move forward. She needed a lawyer, but the shit she was in was deep, and if she had a snowball's chance in hell of getting out of this alive, she was going to take it.

By the time they walked her into the local police station, past the curious eyes of locals in the lobby and into an interrogation room, she was shaking so hard she could barely stand. She stumbled twice going in and would have fallen but for the officer beside her. As soon as she was seated, they removed the cuffs.

Both agents sat down across the table from her, started a recorder, stated the date and time, and introduced themselves and the woman they were interrogating before beginning.

Agent Howard began the questioning. "Miss Payne, do you understand why you are here?"

"You said Kevin was dead. I didn't know. I've been gone," she said.

"Yes, we know. Your absences from your employment at the Serenity Inn happen to coincide with the disappearance of women who have gone missing from Jubilee."

Shock registered. "Wait! What? I don't understand what you're talking about!"

"Yes, you do. We already know your part in this. Human trafficking is a federal offense. You're going down for a very long time, Miss Payne. It would help your case if you are straight with us from the start."

"No, no, I don't understand," she kept saying.

"Then understand this. Someone murdered Vanzant at his campsite, dragged his body back into his trailer, stole his laptop and his phone, and disappeared. We already know he was trolling women for a human-trafficking website. And we know that because he kept a backup on a second laptop. We don't need his phone to know who he called. We've already gotten a search warrant for the records. We already have the man in custody who stole a baby they were going to sell. We already know who the kidnappers' contact was, and there is a warrant out for her arrest. You and Vanzant were part of the team. You were in collusion with someone and we want to know who's running the show."

Emily froze. "I don't know about this stuff. I wasn't part of that. I bought things with stolen credit cards to keep from going to jail. Do I need a lawyer?"

"What do you mean, to keep from going to jail?" Pickard asked.

Emily started crying. "I never wanted to do this. But I was going to lose my license if I got a third DUI on my driving record. I'd just gotten an apartment in town and a job at the Serenity Inn. Kevin came to visit me. He had his travel trailer and parked it at Barton's campground. We'd been in Jubilee partying up into the night, and we were on our way back to his place when these lights came on behind me."

"Was it a county patrol car or a city patrol car?" Pickard asked as he handed her a handful of tissues.

Emily shrugged as she swiped at her eyes. "I don't know. It was after midnight and dark on the highway. All I saw were the flashing lights behind me and then this guy at the window asking for my ID and stuff."

"Then what?" Howard asked.

"He made me get out. I couldn't walk a straight line. He gave me a Breathalyzer test which I guess I failed. He kept looking at me, walking in a circle around me like he was sizing me up. Then Kevin, who was in the back seat, wakes up and gets out of the car. The cop gets all freaky and pulls a gun on Kevin, makes him sit down on the side of the road. Then he puts me in cuffs, and Kevin in cuffs, and makes a call. I'm still crying and begging him to let me go. He's talking to someone but I can't hear. Then he shoves the phone up to my ear and there is this guy on the phone telling me if I do a favor for him that he'll make sure the charges go away. I didn't understand exactly what he'd asked, but all I cared about was not getting a third DUI."

"What was the cop's name?" Howard asked.

Emily frowned. "I don't know, and he never wrote me a ticket so it wasn't like I would see it later after I sobered up. Oh. Wait. When he made that phone call, I heard him say, "Hey, this is 'Bear.'"

"And that's it? They just let you go?"

"No. He took all of my contact information and told me I would be getting a call, and that I better not ignore it or I'd be sorry. That plenty of women disappear and no one ever sees them again. It scared me. Kevin and I went on to his travel trailer and slept it off. We woke up to a phone call, and three weeks later, I did the favor."

"How did that happen? Did you meet up with someone to get the stolen cards?" Howard asked.

"No. The card and ID were shoved under the door to my apartment when I got off work. There were written instructions to dress up as close to the woman in the photo as I could and go to Frankfort to buy something with the card, then afterward burn the card and the ID and donate the purchases somewhere in Frankfort. Only it didn't end after one favor. It was like a snowball rolling down a hill, and I was caught in it and couldn't get out. That's all I did. And I didn't know what it meant."

"You could have gone to the police," Pickard said.

Emily looked at him like he'd lost his mind. "It was a cop that got me into this. Why would I trust another one to get me out?"

Pickard realized what he'd said when he got that "look" from Howard, but he ignored the faux pas and kept questioning. "How did Kevin Vanzant get mixed up in this? He wasn't driving."

She shrugged. "I don't know. I was drunk, remember? But the cop saw all of his cameras and Kevin was a witness to what had taken place. I know they took his information just like they took mine. But he got a call almost immediately. Something about taking pictures of tourists. They gave him a photo op, and they gave me the shopping deal. I know he got paid money to do that. I don't know if he ever figured out what was going on, but I didn't ask questions. Once we got involved with the boss, we were not supposed to know each other." She started crying all over again, and they paused, giving her a moment to pull herself together.

"I called Kevin while I was on the way home the other day. The last thing he said to me was that it was almost over. He said Mr. Barton notified him that he was closing down the campground for the winter, and when Boss called, Kevin told him he was done. I don't know how Boss took that. But Kevin told me when he left, I was going with him. We were going to disappear."

She dropped her head and began to sob in earnest.

Pickard sighed.

Howard glanced at his partner and ended the recording. "Emily Payne, you are under arrest for…"

She blanked out on the rest of what they were saying, and when the cuffs fastened around her wrists again, life as she'd known it was over.

They walked her straight to the chopper from the station and flew her back to Frankfort.

Jail. Arraignment. Sentencing. It was all in Emily's future, while Kevin Vanzant was still in a drawer in the morgue.

———

The rain ended before nightfall, and during that time, Rusty had been backtracking on Rance Woodley's ex-wife, Melinda Lehigh, a native of Michigan. She found her in census records. In school records. The marriage license to Rance Woodley and divorce papers three years later. Then employment records off and on and another marriage a few years later to Thaddeus Sheets, and again, a divorce two years later.

Rusty read past the second husband's name without it registering, and then all of a sudden, she went back and read it again. Melinda Sheets. Lindy Sheets? Could she possibly be one and the same?

"Oh my God," she muttered, and typed the name Lindy Sheets in credit ratings and job searches and then hit Search.

There were many Lindy Sheets in the system, but only one with the maiden name of Lehigh, and Sheriff Woodley had been married to her! A Lindy Sheets was connected to the attempted kidnapping of Cameron's niece. And Sheriff Woodley had dragged his feet long and hard before instigating a search for the missing child.

Rusty jumped up from the sofa.

"Cameron! Cameron!"

Cameron was on the back porch watching Ghost make his evening rounds when he heard her shouting. He turned and opened the back door. "Out here!" he said.

Rusty came flying through the kitchen. "You will not believe what I found!" she cried as he walked inside.

"What?"

"Woodley's ex-wife was Melinda Lehigh before they married. Melinda Woodley remarried a few years after their divorce to a man named Thaddeus Sheets. Melinda Sheets? Maybe Lindy Sheets? Lindy Sheets was Danny Biggers's contact in the kidnap attempt on your niece!"

Shock rolled through Cameron so fast he couldn't think. And then it hit him.

"Is Woodley part of this?"

"I'm not even going to pretend this is a coincidence, but I can't make that judgment. I'm dumping this back in Howard and Pickard's laps. They've been working on this cell for over a year. I'm a newcomer to this case."

"Son of a bitch," Cameron muttered.

Rusty grabbed his arms. "I know this is personal. I know Lili almost died. But you can't act on this info. You can't confront him. Do you understand? I did not confirm Woodley is connected to the trafficking. Only that she is his ex-wife. He may just be part of the chain and he may not."

Cameron took a deep breath and then nodded. "Yes. Understood."

Rusty tightened her grip on his arms. "I'm so sorry. I can't imagine how this must feel. It's so personal. That baby was stolen from her home. You found her. You held her little body. You didn't know if she was going to live. I get it. But we'll take them down. We will. It's happening. We just have to do it right so no one gets off on technicalities. That's my world. That's how my job works."

Cameron reached out and pulled her close. "It's okay. I'm okay. I'm not going to lose my shit. Military training frowns on soldiers losing their shit."

Rusty knew he was trying to lighten the moment, but she could tell he was moved. "We'll get them and with your help. You've been pivotal in helping me do this, and now you're providing an alibi for my absence," Rusty said.

At that moment, her phone rang. She looked at caller ID. "It's Howard. I need to answer."

Cameron turned her loose and walked back out onto the porch to call Ghost in as she picked up the call.

"Hello, this is Rusty."

"Agent Caldwell, we're calling to let you know all of your work on Emily Payne paid off. She was doing exactly what you guessed. We have security footage. We have more credit card usage to back it up. She and Kevin Vanzant were in drug rehab together. When she found out he'd been murdered, she unloaded. I'll send you details, but we wanted you to know."

"That's wonderful, sir. But I have more info and I'm handing it over now. Make what you will of it."

Howard hesitated. "Yes... Okay. What's up?"

Then she repeated what she'd just told Cameron. "Lindy Sheets was Danny Biggers's contact on the kidnapping of Lili Glass. And if you remember, Woodley dragged his feet big-time before starting a search. I'm not saying he's connected...but she is his ex-wife."

"Oh my God. That's huge. Okay. We'll take that from here and do the diligence needed to find the link. Good job!"

"Thank you, sir. And good job on getting Emily Payne in custody."

She hung up and dropped her phone back in her pocket, then went outside, walked up behind Cameron, and wrapped her arms around his waist and laid her face against his back. She could feel the tension in his muscles and wished she could make this easier for him.

"Do you know how much I love you?" she asked.

He went still, then turned in her arms and cupped her face.

"As much as I love you?" he whispered.

Rusty smiled. "Probably."

"Ah...God," he muttered, and kissed her forehead, then the tip of her nose, then settled his mouth on her lips and let go of everything but the feel of her in his arms.

It was the sound of something running that made them stop and turn around. Ghost was coming out of the woods like his tail was on fire, and Cameron's first instinct said danger.

"Get in the house," he said. He stepped inside the door and pulled a rifle from a rack on the wall and then ran back out onto the porch. "Ghost! Inside!" he yelled, but it was an unneeded warning. Ghost was already on the way and in midleap over the steps when a black bear came lumbering out of the woods.

"Oh my God!" Rusty cried. She grabbed Ghost by the collar and held on as Cameron fired a shot up in the air.

Ghost immediately turned toward Cameron. His instinct to protect was stronger than his initial fear, but Cameron slammed the door shut between them and fired again.

The second shot stopped the bear's full-on attack. The animal paused, rocking back and forth on its feet, its big head hanging toward the ground and swinging from side to side. And that's when Cameron noticed the broken shaft of an arrow in the bear's shoulder and the fur on that leg matted with blood.

"Oh hell, it's wounded," Cameron muttered. His shoulders slumped as he walked to the edge of the porch and raised the rifle. As he did, the bear turned sideways, as if about to retreat. Cameron couldn't let it leave suffering like this, saw his chance for a double-lung shot, and squeezed the trigger.

The bear dropped, and then Cameron walked off the

porch and out to where the animal was lying and put a second shot in it.

It was done.

Rusty was watching, wide-eyed and sick at what just happened, and Ghost was growling.

Cameron eyed the broken shaft, then pulled up the number for the Kentucky Department of Fish and Wildlife and made a call.

"Department of Fish and Wildlife. David Andrews speaking."

"David, this is Cameron Pope. I just had to put down a wounded bear that was after my dog. It's a really big one. Someone shot it with an arrow and let it get away. It looked like it was pretty bad off."

"If you'll give me directions to your property, we'll send someone out to recover the carcass."

Cameron gave him directions from Jubilee.

"Okay, got it," Andrews said. "We should be there within the next couple of hours."

"Thanks," Cameron said, then turned and walked back toward the house. He saw Rusty's face at the window and Ghost standing right beside her and sighed.

As soon as he got inside, he went straight to Ghost and began running his hand all over the dog to make sure he hadn't been attacked.

"How did you get in trouble so fast, buddy?"

"That was scary," Rusty said. "Does this kind of thing happen often?"

"No. I'm too close to Jubilee for animals like that. But

it had been wounded. There's a broken shaft from an arrow sticking out of its shoulder, and it looked in rough shape. No telling how long it's been suffering like that, either. It was probably hungry and smelled Ghost. Ghost has never encountered a bear up close before, and I'm glad he didn't decide to challenge him."

"Poor thing," Rusty said.

"Yeah, it's bear-hunting season right now through the first week of November and someone shot it and let it get away."

"Good lord. I'm going to need different survival skills for the mountains," she muttered.

He grinned. "You've got me."

"When we have children, I'm going to need to know there's at least a six-foot fence around this backyard or they're never setting foot out of this house to play."

He laughed. "That can be arranged, although you should know that I'm the third generation of Popes to grow up in this house and none of us were ever attacked or threatened by wild animals. Just dodged a few snakes. We did some running away from switches to our backsides from time to time, but no bears."

Rusty looked at him, trying to imagine him as a little boy and growing up here, then nodded. "I won't argue. This is your world I'm walking into. I'll figure it out."

"I called Kentucky Fish and Wildlife. They're sending someone to retrieve the carcass, but it'll take a while for them to get here."

Rusty plopped down in one of the kitchen chairs and

slowly exhaled. "I'm going to take a break from work for a bit. I don't think I could concentrate if I had to. I need a drink."

"I have beer and straight whiskey."

"I'll take a shot of the hard stuff…and a piece of cake," she added.

Cameron threw back his head and laughed.

"Ah God…cake and whiskey. I had no idea you were such a connoisseur."

"I've made do with less in far worse situations," she muttered. "And Ghost is pretty frazzled, too. I think he needs a treat."

"Yes, he *was* flying when he came out of those trees. I don't know what kept him from attacking that bear. That would have been his first reaction if I'd been there."

"But you weren't, which proves how smart he is," Rusty said. "He had the good sense to know he was on the lower end of that food chain." Then she reached for Ghost and scratched his head between his ears. "Didn't you, boy? Smartest dog ever…yes, you are."

Cameron got two shot glasses out of the cabinet, pulled down the bottle of whiskey beside them, and carried them to the table. He poured two shots, then cut two slices of the chocolate cake from his aunt's bakery, grabbed a couple of forks, and they were good to go.

Rusty lifted her glass. "To being alive," she said.

The smile slid off Cameron's face. "To being alive," he said softly.

The glasses clinked, and then they downed the shots in one gulp.

Rusty shuddered as it went down, and then picked up her fork and took a bite of the cake.

"Much better," she mumbled as the chocolate melted on her tongue.

Cameron watched her get up and go to the pantry to get Ghost a little treat and thought how easily she'd wrapped them both around her finger.

"Everything is better with you in my life," he said.

Rusty looked up. "Not to wear out an old movie line or anything, but you had me at hello. Don't lose me, okay?"

Suddenly there was a lump in Cameron's throat. "Don't be afraid of love, baby. I will never hurt you."

Rusty's eyes welled. "I'm not afraid of you. I'm just overwhelmed by what you make me feel. I have a reputation. Cold-as-Ice Caldwell. Reckless Rusty. And you remind me I'm a woman first. It's taking some getting used to."

"Just so you know, you make me forever grateful I was born a man."

She focused on his steady gaze and almost smiled. "I'm pretty happy about that myself," she said, and took another bite of cake.

"Now that we have that settled," he said, downing the rest of his cake, "want coffee?"

She nodded.

And so they sat talking through the next hour without looking out the window again. The bear's carcass was a sad reminder of the damage people do.

When the Fish and Wildlife truck finally pulled up into Cameron's drive, it was hauling a front-end loader on a flatbed trailer. He went out to meet the workers and directed them around to the back of his house.

Rusty watched from the windows as they used the front-end loader to pick up the carcass and move it into the bed of the truck. Then they reloaded their equipment and drove away.

Rusty was sitting on the sofa watching TV when Cameron came back into the house carrying an armful of firewood. He stacked it by the fireplace and stirred the fire that was burning, then sat down beside her and made one call. The phone rang three times before the call was picked up.

"Hello?"

"Uncle John, it's me, Cameron."

"Hello, Cam. Good to hear your voice. Everything okay?"

"I just wanted you to know so you can spread the word a bit. I had to put down a wounded black bear that was after Ghost today. It had an arrow in its shoulder that had broken off. It looked like it had been wounded several days ago. I know it's bear season, but our people know better than to let a wounded animal get away like that."

"Oh damn. Bears don't usually go that far down the mountain, which shows how hungry and desperate it must have been. That sounds like something some younger kid would do. I'll put out the word and make sure the men who bowhunt have a talk with their boys."

"Thanks, Uncle John. I appreciate that."

"Sure thing. Say…I heard you were involved in helping out the feds with a murder investigation."

"Not really involved like you mean. They just keyed in on my military background and asked for a little help. And they've got it all under control now, so I've stepped back."

"Good to know," John said. "Anytime you're up this way, stop by. Annie will cook us up a steak and some of her fine biscuits."

"Thanks. I just might take you up on that, but I'll be sure to let you know first. Take care."

"You too, son," John said and disconnected. Ghost walked up between Cameron's legs and whined.

"Okay, let's go see what you stir up this time." Then he slid his hand on Rusty's knee. "Get a jacket and come outside with me. Dusk on the mountain has its own kind of magic."

Rusty quickly obliged and then walked out onto the back porch and watched while Cameron went with Ghost all the way out to where the bear died. The big dog circled the spot with his nose to the ground, and once he was satisfied the danger was gone, he meandered a little more to do his business before Cameron walked him back to the porch.

Rusty was sitting on the top step. Cameron sat down beside her as Ghost flattened out on the step beside them and sat with his head up, still sniffing the air.

"Watch the sky," Cameron said, and as she did, she became aware of all the birds flying in to roost and caught glimpses of night birds taking flight.

A rabbit darted into the underbrush and disappeared, and a few moments later, a fat raccoon waddled out from the other side of the yard.

Ghost whined.

"No. Stay," Cameron said, and put his arm around the big dog's neck.

"It's like watching the shift change. Day workers go home. Evening shift comes on," Rusty whispered. "And it's so quiet."

He nodded.

"Remembering all this kept me sane when all we heard were bombs and gunfire and all I could see was sand."

Rusty leaned her head against his shoulder and slipped her hand beneath his elbow.

"I've never been rooted to a place like you have. We moved all the time and always lived in cities. Nothing meant home to me but my parents, and they're gone. I've been homeless in my heart for a long time."

"Not anymore, you're not. And you're inheriting a family bigger than anything you could imagine, too."

"I can't wait to meet them all," Rusty said.

"Rachel knows there's someone. She's dying to meet you."

"Really?" Rusty said, but when she looked up, Cameron was blurring in the twilight. She clung to him a little tighter, almost as if she was afraid he'd fade away.

"Yes, really, but you have nothing to worry about. She's going to be crazy about you, and I'm going to make a bet right now that when Lili sees you, she's going straight for your hair. Your red curls will be a magnet. We just need to make sure she doesn't have cookie hands when she does."

Rusty smiled. "Cookie hands?"

"She's our little cookie monster, and I've fostered that. Her uncle Cam knows not to show up without cookies."

"What a wonderful thing. I can't wait to meet them all," Rusty said.

Cameron nodded. "Louis and Rachel are crazy about each other, and Lili is the jewel in their crown."

Rusty sighed, imagining a female version of Cameron and wondering if Lili was like that. One day they'd make their own brand of Popes and watch them grow up while she grew old with this man. She couldn't think of anything better.

"Well, it's full-on dark out here. I guess we better go inside. Are you hungry?" he asked.

"No. I'm calling the cake and whiskey dinner, and no more work. Not today. I'm tired of thinking."

"Come to bed with me," Cameron said. "You won't have to think about anything except how good it feels to come apart in my arms."

Rusty blinked. "I don't know if my heart can take another ride like the one it had today, but I'm willing to test it."

"You know the way. I'll be right behind you," he said.

Rusty walked inside and up the hall, while Cameron got a rawhide chew and took Ghost to his bed in the living room and gave it to him. Ghost plopped down with the chew and never looked up when Cameron left the room.

Rusty had her shoes off and was taking off her jeans when Cameron walked in and shut the door.

"Let me," he said as he knelt at her feet and pulled off

her jeans. She braced her hands on his shoulders as she lifted one foot out and then the other.

Then he spanned her waist with his hands, shoved her sweater up above her panties, and kissed the satin-soft skin on her belly. When his tongue slipped into her belly button, she tangled her fists into his hair and held on, moaning as he lit nerves all the way to her core. All of a sudden her panties were a pool of silk at her feet and he was taking her sweater off over her head. He unfastened her bra with one hand and slid it off with the other.

Weak with longing, Rusty fell onto the bed behind them, then lay watching as Cameron stripped. He was already hard and blatantly erect as he slid onto the bed beside her and took her into his arms.

He heard her sigh right before he kissed her, and then fell into her spell.

He couldn't kiss her enough, touch her enough to ease the ache, to quell the need he had to be inside her. When she reached for him, he obliged, moving up and over her and slowly tested his welcome. She was hot and wet and waiting as he slowly slid inside.

Rusty shuddered from the sensation, then put her arms around his neck, taking his full weight upon her.

After that, it was all about the rhythm and the ride.

Chapter 14

PATRICIA CALDWELL LANDED SAFELY IN PHILADELPHIA. The weather was wet and the streets were covered in slush, but she didn't care. It was a busy, bustling city with history and culture and shops and fun places to be, and she was in her element.

While she was waiting for a taxi to take her to her sister Penny's home, she sent a text to Ray and Liz, letting them know she had landed safely and was waiting for a taxi, then dropped her phone in her purse without waiting to see if they would answer, because she didn't care. For the time that she was here, she wanted to forget Jubilee, Kentucky, existed.

———

Ray got her text as he was finishing up a staff meeting and read it after they were gone. He was relieved to know she'd landed safely and resigned to her absence. At least she wouldn't be constantly bemoaning her place of residence. The penthouse would never be special enough because of the geography of where it was, and that was how Patricia Caldwell rolled.

He picked up his appointment book and began looking to see what was on the agenda for tomorrow when someone knocked at his door.

"Come in!" he said, and then smiled when Liz walked in. "Hello, darling! What a nice surprise! To what do I owe the pleasure of this visit?"

Liz plopped down in one of the chairs by his desk, straightened her blouse, sat up straight, then folded her hands in her lap. "I've come to apply for a job. I have a degree that I'm not using, and if Mr. Devlin, your event planner, is willing to mentor me, I would love to intern."

Ray's smile widened. "Honey! That's wonderful! At this moment, Gerald does not have an assistant, and he would be grateful. He's actually mentioned the need for one before. I just never pursued it. And interning is the obvious way for you to begin."

Liz resisted the urge to clap her hands. "Thank you, Dad! I know there are perks of being the daughter of the boss, but I appreciate the opportunity."

Ray laughed. "You're welcome, and out of curiosity, what prompted this?"

Liz didn't hesitate. "Rusty. She's so smart and so driven and gives so much of herself in the service of others. She made me feel like a slug without even knowing it."

"Ah…yes, I can see that," Ray said.

"I miss her," Liz said. "And now that Michael and I are kind of at odds, I feel like I have no purpose."

Ray frowned. "Have you two decided to call it quits?"

"No, but we're at a rebuilding stage, I would say."

"I heard he was in an accident earlier today. Someone broadsided him downtown during the downpour. Do you know how he is?" Ray asked.

Liz gasped. "Oh my God! I didn't know that happened! He didn't call. I can't believe he didn't—" And then she took a deep breath as her eyes welled. "I need to check on him. I'm going up to make some calls. You can tell me about my work schedule and all that tonight at dinner, okay?"

"Absolutely," Ray said. "It'll give me time to speak to Gerald and give him a heads-up about you interning with him. Oh…I got a text from your mother. She said she landed safely and was waiting for a taxi."

"Yes, I got one, as well. She's in her own world. I didn't bother responding. Thank you for the opportunity and for letting me know about Michael," Liz said, and then gave her dad a kiss on the cheek and left the office.

Ray watched her go and then reached for the phone. This horrible day had just taken a remarkable turn to the good.

But for Liz, her day was shattered. She couldn't get to the penthouse fast enough. She went straight to her room, crawled up in the middle of her bed, and called Michael.

His phone rang and rang, and she was imagining all kinds of horror scenarios about him too injured to speak, or in a hospital bed unconscious, until she finally heard his voice. It was a little slurred and raspy, but it was proof he was alive.

"Hello?"

"Michael! Oh my God! I just found out about your wreck! I'm so sorry. How badly were you hurt? Are you at home or in the hospital?"

Michael sighed. This. Her voice. Tinged with panic and concern. That's what he needed to know. She still cared.

"I'm home. Nothing broken. Whiplash. Slight concussion. Just hurt all over," he mumbled.

"Oh, honey. I'm so sorry," she said, and started crying. "I'm so sorry you didn't feel like you could call me. And that's my fault. But I do care about you. I do love you. I'm supposed to start work with our event planner tomorrow, but as soon as I get off work, maybe it would be okay if I came to see you?" she asked.

"Of course you can," Michael said. "It will be something to look forward to. I'm so glad you called. Love you."

"Love you, too," Liz said. "Rest well."

As soon as the connection ended, she fell backward on the bed, curled up on her side, and cried until her eyes were burning and her throat was raw. She was ashamed of herself. Of her lies. Of the fantasy world she'd indulged in. It was dishonest and destructive, and she'd almost destroyed her relationship. She hadn't known how much he meant to her until this brush with death.

She spent the rest of the evening going through her closet, sorting out clothes that would be proper outfits to go to work in, and when Ray came home, dinner soon followed. They talked and planned all the way through the meal and up until they went to bed without once mentioning Patricia's absence.

Bottom line. Liz would start work tomorrow. She called herself an adult. It was time to start acting like one.

———————

Jack Barton was getting negative feedback about the murder on his property from paying guests and hoped closing the campsites down now would give the public time for the horror of that to fade. Few locals ever used the campsites, and by next year, the new tourists who arrived would be unaware of the history.

He went out on his golf cart the next morning to turn off water access to the campground to protect from frozen pipes during the winter. And when he drove all the way to the last site, he got out and removed the last bits of crime-scene tape.

———————

It began to snow in the night, and when everyone on Pope Mountain woke up the next morning, there was an inch of the white stuff all over the trees and the ground.

Ghost had been born in heat and sand, and even after all the years of living on the mountain with Cameron he still didn't love the snow, so when Cameron took him out to do his business he ran out to pee, made a quick sweep of the yard because it was his duty, and bolted inside without any kind of urging.

Cameron laughed. "He so does not like snow. He'll tolerate the cold weather, but snow messes with his chi."

Rusty gave Ghost a quick pat on the head as he trotted through the kitchen, but when he smelled the bacon she was frying, he turned and plopped down beside the table. She smiled, then turned her attention back to the stove and the skillet.

"How are we doing the eggs?" she asked.

"Just scrambled for me," Cameron said, as he went to wash up.

Rusty cracked five eggs into a bowl, whipped them with a fork, and then as soon as the last of the bacon was done, poured off the drippings into a can sitting by the stove and cooked the eggs in the same skillet.

They made their plates and took them and their coffee to the table where a stack of fresh toast was waiting.

"You cook eggs like my mom did. Seasoning them with the bacon drippings. Heaven on a plate, sugar. Thank you," he said.

"Everything should be cooked in bacon drippings," Rusty said.

Cameron grinned. "I won't argue with that."

They ate like they made love, with gusto and an appreciation for the opportunity, and then dawdled over extra toast with jelly and a second cup of coffee.

Cameron had just swallowed his last bite of toast when his cell phone rang. He glanced at caller ID and frowned. "I need to take this," he said, and got up and walked out of the room, talking as he went.

Rusty cleaned up the dishes, wiped down the counters, and then went to her bedroom to get a load of clothes she needed to wash. She had them in the washer and was adding detergent when Cameron came looking for her.

"Trouble on the mountain. Someone broke into Leo Duroy's house. He's one of our elders and is in the hospital recovering from surgery. His wife died over a year ago, so the house was unoccupied. Shit like that doesn't happen up here. Neighbors went over to tend his chickens and discovered the break-in. They've called the sheriff, but they both have to go to work, so they called me because everybody up here knows I don't punch a time clock. I don't know how long I'll be, but you can reach me by phone, okay?"

"Absolutely," Rusty said, and then she added, "Just a thought. If you rule out everybody on the mountain, then that leaves a good number of people who work at the hospital who also know his home is vacant. Orderlies, janitors, nurses, aides, lab techs, and the list goes on and on. Suggest to Woodley that he immediately check the pawn shops and see if any of what's missing has been pawned by any locals. If Leo Duroy has had flowers delivered, check florists. They would know he was in the hospital, too. They should all have video of stuff being pawned…unless the thief takes it out of town."

Cameron started smiling as she kept talking.

"Dang, woman. You're sharp enough to draw blood. And if Woodley balks at the suggestions, I'll take the list of stolen property to Chief Warren and have him check."

Then he gave her a big hug and kiss and went to look for Ghost as he got his coat. A few minutes later they were gone.

Rusty was still savoring that kiss when she took a cup of coffee to the living room, then went to get her laptop. She noticed Cameron had added a fresh log to the fire, and snuggled down in the chair. When she opened her laptop, there was a new file waiting, so she went to work.

———————

Cameron had been waiting at the house for over an hour before Rance Woodley arrived with a deputy, and during that time it had continued to spit snow—tiny little specks of frozen ice so light they weren't heavy enough to fall, just floating about in the air.

They arrived in two patrol cars, making new tracks in the snow, and seemed in no hurry as they sauntered up to the porch steps and knocked on the door.

Cameron watched through the window and waited until they knocked before answering. He knew by the look on Woodley's face that he was not happy he was there.

Woodley was taken aback and immediately went on the attack. "What the hell are you doing here?" he said.

Cameron held the door open as they stomped inside, tracking snow that quickly melted into droplets on the floor.

"The neighbors who called this in both work in town. They had to leave so they called me. They told me they found blood on the kitchen floor, so it had to belong to the thief or thieves because Mr. Duroy has been gone for almost two weeks. They left me a list of what they know for sure was taken and just asked me to wait for the law to arrive."

"Oh, yeah, well then," Woodley muttered. "So where did they break in?"

"Back door," Cameron said. "If you'll follow me, you'll see where they jimmied the lock and see the blood drops begin from the threshold and go all the way across the floor. Looks like one of them might have fallen coming up the steps. There's blood on the porch, as well. They did all this before it snowed, because the only footprints you'll see in the yard belong to the neighbors who were feeding Duroy's chickens and gathering eggs for him. I feel bad for Leo. The thieves trashed the place. Some of this stuff they destroyed belonged to his deceased wife. These little figurines they broke and the jewelry missing from her jewelry box were all he had left of her."

Woodley pointed at his deputy. "Get photos in all the rooms. I'll call in the crime scene team. We'll dust for prints and get some blood samples. Probably some damn kids from up here, since everybody knew he was gone."

Cameron turned and glared. "We don't steal from each other up here."

"Bullshit," Woodley said. "Teenagers these days will take anything that's not tied down."

"And you'd be wrong," Cameron said. "There's a whole other group of people who know Leo Duroy was not in his home."

"Like who?" Woodley asked.

"For starters, all the people who work at the hospital.

Everyone from janitors to doctors, nurses, aides, the pharmacy techs and lab techs would all know the old man and it wouldn't take much digging to find out he lives alone. Hell, he probably told them in passing. Check pawn shops in the area. Here's the list of stolen property with descriptions. I'm getting out of your way now. If you need me, I'll be outside."

Woodley was irked with himself for popping off to Pope because he knew the man wasn't someone he could bully or back down, and the fact that Pope had been hanging out with the feds made him nervous. There were things about this man he didn't know.

"You can go on home. We've got this," Woodley said.

Cameron stared at him, and knowing all he did about this man and his past, it was all he could do to keep his composure.

"I'll be outside in the Jeep with my dog. And when you're done, I'll lock up," he said, then walked out, leaving Woodley to his business.

―――――――――

Rusty received an email from Jay Howard with the trail cam video attached and the comment that they didn't ever get a good enough view of the killer's face to identify them. They wanted her and Cameron to take a look before considering it of no use. After two hours of reviewing the same grainy footage over and over until she'd given herself a headache, Rusty had nothing to add.

The video was all birds and wildlife, and Vanzant in and out until Leslie Morgan drove up and went inside. Then it showed Jack Barton arriving on the golf cart in the middle of Leslie's hasty retreat, Kevin talking to Barton, then disappearing inside the trailer for hours afterward.

She fast-forwarded it after that until it began to get dark. At that point, she saw Vanzant come out of the trailer carrying a sack of what looked like garbage. He walked toward the end of the drive, dumped his trash, and headed back toward his trailer. She saw him walk all the way back to the trailer and open the door to go inside. He was partway up the steps when he suddenly turned to face the road. He was still silhouetted by the light inside the trailer, but she could see his mouth move as he spoke—like someone had arrived and called to him.

Even though she knew he was about to be shot, she still jumped when the bullet's impact threw him backward into the trailer. All of a sudden, she saw the back of someone's head come into view of the trail cam and what appeared to be a male figure advance toward the trailer. He was wearing a dark hoodie and carrying a rifle. He was average in height and weight and had an odd stride that tilted slightly to the side as he walked.

"Oh my God, there you are!" she muttered, and leaned forward, praying he would turn around. Instead, he propped the rifle against the trailer and stepped up, then over the body, and went inside.

She watched as Kevin's body was dragged all the way in and out of sight, and then just before the man came out, he turned off all the lights inside the trailer and emerged in shadows. The missing laptop the man held clutched against his chest was the most visible thing about the footage because it was silver and reflected the light from the security light at the end of the drive. He picked up his rifle, but instead of walking back toward the camera, he turned sideways and walked toward the trees and out of range. It was a dead end, in more ways than one.

All she could do was hope Cameron would see something she didn't.

It was almost noon by the time Cameron and Ghost left Leo Duroy's to go home. He was fed up with Woodley and Woodley knew it, but they kept their distance from each other until the sheriff and his crew finally left the scene.

Leo's only relatives lived on the other side of the mountain, and one of the neighbors who'd discovered the break-in had called them. They showed up as Cameron was getting ready to leave, horrified by what had happened. He gave them all of the info he had, a copy of the list of stolen items, and the name and number of the sheriff who'd investigated. It was all he could do. The rest was their responsibility.

The drive home was actually calming. Traffic on the road had worn the snow down to blacktop, leaving a clear one-lane set of tracks right down the middle. The snow-covered trees were picture-worthy, and the faint scent of woodsmoke from the chimneys of houses all over the mountain permeated the air enough that he could smell it inside the Jeep even with the windows up.

About three miles from home, a huge buck darted out of the trees and across the road in front of him and disappeared into the forest on the other side, but not before Ghost had spotted it and set up a continuous bark and howl until Cameron had to make him stop.

"Ghost! No. Lie down!" he said loudly.

Ghost gave Cameron a you've-got-to-be-kidding look but obeyed, leaving Cameron shaking his head.

"Yeah, you're ready to take on a buck from a moving car, but you ran from a crippled bear, thank God. What am I going to do with you," he muttered.

Ghost whined.

Cameron reached over and scratched him between the ears. "You're not in trouble. And you're right. He was beautiful, but not as amazing as you."

Ghost laid his head on his forepaws and sighed.

They made the rest of the drive home in silence. When Cameron pulled up beneath the carport and parked, the urgency of seeing Rusty again kicked in.

He got out and Ghost followed, then had to make the rounds in the snow to do his business. Cameron heard the door open behind him as he waited at the edge of the carport, and then Rusty came out. Her smile was the welcome-home he'd been waiting for.

"Everything go okay?" she asked.

"More or less," Cameron said. "I hope Woodley follows

through and actually does police work instead of looking to pin it on the first kid he sees so he won't have to work at it."

"I have video from the trail cam. But unless you see something neither I nor the home office can see, it's a bust."

"Really? Damn it. I was hoping for better," he said.

"So were we all. I won't say any more. I just want you to look at it with fresh eyes."

He nodded and pulled her close as she leaned against him, then Cameron told her about Ghost and the deer and made her laugh. It was her laughter that caught Ghost's attention, and he came bounding toward her with his mouth slightly open and his tongue hanging out the side, smiling like a big goofy kid.

"Hi, buddy!" Rusty said. "Let's go inside. It's cold out here."

Ghost knew "go inside" and headed for the door.

"He's probably hoping for a treat. Ever since your arrival, he has decided he is marvelous enough to deserve one every time you smile."

Rusty laughed again, and when she did, it echoed within the clearing and went straight into Cameron's heart.

He followed her inside, as smitten as his dog, and knew exactly what treat he wanted, too, but that would have to wait.

As soon as Ghost settled himself, they made sandwiches and took them to the table, then Rusty turned her laptop toward Cameron so he could watch the trail cam footage while he ate. She had it fast-forwarded to the place where Leslie Morgan arrived at the trailer, and then started it.

She sat quietly as she ate, watching how intently he

looked at the screen and thinking how much he'd come to mean to her. It was sad to know that neither of her parents would ever know him, but then she would never know his parents, either. They'd been the ultimate loners until their paths crossed, and some things were meant to be. She got up to refill his drink and later cleared away their empty plates, and he still hadn't moved.

Then all of a sudden his posture changed. He leaned forward and stopped the video, studied it for a few moments, rewound it a couple of seconds back, then started it. She saw his pupils widen and knew he'd just witnessed Vanzant getting shot. At that point, she held her breath because she knew the killer would already be appearing on the scene.

Cameron leaned back, watching as the killer was moving toward the trailer, and then pointed.

"His gait."

Rusty's heart skipped. She'd noticed that but had no reference point to make it important.

Cameron moved the video back a few frames and sat watching the killer appear, then backed it up and watched it again, and again, and this time all the way through.

"His hand."

"What about his hand?" Rusty asked.

"See how he's holding that laptop?"

She moved around behind him and leaned over until their cheeks were almost touching.

"You mean clutched against his chest?"

"No. With a thumb and three fingers. He's missing his little finger."

"I completely missed that," she said.

"And his gait."

She nodded. "Yes, he kind of leans to the right a little. Like maybe his back is crooked or something."

"No. One leg is shorter than the other. I know who that is! It's Dewey Zane."

"Who's Dewey Zane?" she asked.

Cameron hit Stop on the video and shoved his hands through his hair in disbelief. "He works at a bar called Fuzzy Fridays on the other side of the mountain. He's one of Rance Woodley's hunting buddies."

Rusty gasped. "Woodley again! And Fuzzy Fridays was the drop-off location for Danny Biggers. I need to get Howard on the phone. I want you to talk to him."

Cameron nodded as Rusty grabbed her phone and made the call.

———

Jay Howard was away from his desk. Pickard was manning the phones and had just taken a big bite of chicken chow mein when his partner's cell phone rang. When he saw who was calling, he quickly chewed and swallowed before he answered.

"Caldwell, it's me, Pickard. Jay's away from the desk for a minute. Will I do, or do you want me to take a message?"

"You'll do," Rusty said. "Cameron recognized the man on the trail cam video. Here, I'm going to let him talk to you." Then she put the phone on speaker and laid it between them on the table.

"Okay, Pope. I can't wait to hear how you identified anyone from that footage," Pickard said.

"Because it's somebody I've known all my life, that's how," Cameron said. "When the man walks out of the trailer carrying the laptop, if you pay attention to the way he's holding it, you'll see he's missing his little finger."

Pickard nodded. "Missing a finger? How the hell did we miss that?"

"Also, he has an odd gait when he walks, right?" Cameron added.

Pickard frowned. "Yes, we noted the gait but that may or may not have been a permanent thing…you know… sprained knee or ankle, something like that."

"No. It's because one leg is shorter than the other. I know a man who's missing a little finger and has one leg shorter than the other. His name is Dewey Zane. He works at a bar called Fuzzy Fridays. It's just over the switchback on the other side of Pope Mountain."

Pickard was excited and they could hear it in his voice. "Fan-freaking-tastic," he said.

"That's not the best part," Rusty interjected. "Drive in the last nail, Cameron."

"He's Rance Woodley's hunting buddy," Cameron said.

Total silence, and then Pickard whistled softly beneath his breath.

"Jay just walked into the office. I'll fill him in. We'll review the footage again and then get a search warrant on the Dewey Zane residence in hopes we find the murder weapon, and take an arrest warrant to go with it. Keep all this to yourself. We still don't have enough to pick up Woodley, but if he gets word Dewey's been arrested and he's guilty of what we suspect, he'll run."

"Yes, sir," Cameron said, and then he and Rusty heard Howard's voice in the background.

"What's happening? What did I miss?" Howard asked.

"We'll be in touch," Pickard said, and disconnected.

Rusty saw a look of satisfaction sweep over Cameron's face and laid her hand on the middle of his chest. The heartbeat was as steady as he was.

"Good job, partner."

He took her hand, lightly rubbing her knuckles and thinking how delicate she looked, yet how very, very tough she was. "You were right. We're on the right track. We'll get them out of Jubilee for good, won't we, baby?"

Rusty nodded. "And we're not going to let up until they're all under arrest. This isn't just a little gang. This is big business, and someone with a hell of a lot of money and clout is running it. So far we've been fishing the little floaters with cane poles and bobbers, but I want the big fish. The bottom feeder. I want the boss."

Chapter 15

Liz Caldwell was a fish out of water, but she already knew she was going to love this job. Gerald Devlin was welcoming and patient and soon figured out that Liz wasn't just playing. She was in the middle of setups for a thirty-member book club hosting a visiting author at the inn and not messing around, pulling folding chairs and tables off of racks and helping with the placement of them around the ballroom. Making sure the PA system was in place and live at the podium where the author would be speaking.

When Gerald realized the flowers had yet to be delivered, he gave her the job of a follow-up call to the local florist to see what was wrong. She handled it quietly and competently, and within the hour, all of the arrangements had arrived.

When one of the workers missed getting the legs locked on a folding table and it went crashing to the ballroom floor, she raced over and helped him right it, without making a scene. Despite the slight chill in the ballroom, by the time the setup was finished the room was comfortably warm, and Liz had beads of sweat running down her back.

"Good job!" Gerald told her. "I'm going to wait until the hostesses arrive and make sure everything is to their liking, so why don't you take an early lunch, and when you come back, just come to the office. We'll go over the way we take on clients, how we price, contact numbers within the hotel, and who we outsource to."

"Yes, sir," Liz said, and left the ballroom almost bouncing with every step and thinking *So this what it feels like to be productive.*

She grabbed a salad and a sandwich from one of the cafés on-site and carried them up to the penthouse to eat. The quiet engulfed her as she stepped off the elevator. The realization that she was lunching in the penthouse while other workers went to break rooms was not lost on her. But her truth was her truth, and she wasn't going to apologize for it.

In the middle of her meal, she thought of seeing Michael later and wondered what she could take him as a gift, then discarded the thought. This visit was for forgiveness…not the time to come bearing gifts.

As soon as she finished, she changed from flats into sneakers and went back to the conference center, then down the hall to Gerald's office. They spent the afternoon going through a binder he'd made for her containing rules and contact numbers.

As soon as her workday ended, she hurried upstairs to change her clothes and sent her dad a text telling him where she was going, then called downstairs to valet parking. By the time she reached the valet stand, her car was waiting.

She got to Hotel Devon, called the penthouse to let them know she'd arrived, and they sent the elevator down to get her. But the moment she stepped into the car, her emotions got the better of her. She had tears in her eyes when she exited the car.

Della, the Devons' maid, was waiting for her in the grand foyer and welcomed Liz with a smile. "Good evening, Miss Caldwell. May I take your coat?"

"Good evening, Della. Yes, thank you," Liz said, and unwrapped the scarf from around her neck and slipped out of her coat.

"Mr. Michael is looking forward to your visit. He's in his suite. You know the way," Della said, and hung the coat and scarf in the guest coat closet as Liz moved toward the hallway to her left.

Michael's suite was the first one on the right. She knocked lightly. Heard him call out "Come in," and then opened the door and went in.

Michael was in pajamas and lying down, but he was pale, and the neck brace he was wearing was scary.

"Oh, Michael. You poor darling," Liz said and hurried to his side, then knelt on the floor beside him. "I want to hug you, but I'm afraid to touch."

Michael managed a weak grin and then made a joke. "I look better than I feel."

"Oh lord," Liz said and clutched his hand. "Tell me how this happened."

And so Michael told it from beginning to end, all the way to his dad coming to his rescue and the hours in the ER before he got to come home.

"Was the man who hit you injured, too?" she asked.

"No. He was braced for impact. I never saw him coming and caught the brunt of it, I guess. Anyway, the car is totaled, but I'm still in one piece. And you're here, which means everything to me," he said.

"This has been a horrible eye-opener for me. The mere thought of losing you for good hit home. I have been an utter ass. I am so sorry. I love you. I don't want us to be mad like this ever again."

"Deal," Michael said. "Now tell me, how did your first day at work go? I've met Gerald Devlin. He seems nice enough. Do you like working for him?"

That opened a floodgate of information and excitement from Liz he did not expect. He listened to her and then finally lost track of what she was saying and just listened to the excitement in her voice, and watched the way the right corner of her mouth turned the tiniest bit up when she rolled her eyes, and fell the rest of the way in love.

The next morning, just after six

Four black SUVs rolled up on a weathered, ramshackle house just off of a county road, ten miles east of Jubilee. There was a red Dodge 4x4 truck sitting in the yard, a rusting tub full of auto parts beneath a tree that had long since shed its leaves, and a meager stack of firewood near the front porch. Wisps of smoke drifted upward from a leaning chimney.

As the vehicles pulled to a stop, a murder of crows took off from the fence beside the house, and a scrawny redbone hound crawled out from beneath the porch and set to baying.

Federal agents spilled out of the cars and headed to the house with their weapons drawn, swarming the porch in such quantity it sent the hound back under.

One agent began pounding on the door, yelling, "Federal agents. Federal agents. We have a search warrant! Open the door! Open the door!"

All of a sudden the door swung inward. A skinny blond wrapped in an old blue chenille bathrobe and with her hair still in tangles was standing in the doorway, wide-eyed and shaking.

The agents pushed their way inside and slapped some papers into her hand. "We have a search warrant for this house and an arrest warrant for Dewey Zane. Is he here?"

A door opened in the hallway. A skinny, fortysomething man emerged bare-chested, wearing saggy sweatpants and a pair of dirty white socks.

"I'm Dewey Zane. What the hell's goin' on here?" he shouted.

They surrounded him and slapped him in handcuffs, with Special Agents Howard and Pickard leading the way. The missing finger and his awkward gait as he stumbled trying to get away were enough for the agents to know they had the right man. Seconds later, he was taken into the living room and shoved into the nearest chair. They put his wife, Carly, in a separate chair, but she just kept crying.

"Dewey, Dewey, what did you do?"

Dewey kept cursing and shouting, "Shut the hell up, Carly. Just shut the hell up," watching in horror as a dozen other agents began searching through his house, while an agent named Pickard informed him of the charges against him and read him his rights.

"Dewey Zane, you are under arrest for the murder of Kevin Vanzant. You have the right to remain silent. Anything you say can and will be used against you in a court of law. You have the right to an attorney. If you cannot afford an attorney, one will be appointed for you."

It was the word *murder* that got Dewey's attention.

"I don't know nothin' about no murder, and I don't know nobody named Kevin Vanzant."

"Sorry, but we know that's a lie. The whole thing was caught on a trail cam. From the time you shot him and walked into view of the camera, leaned your rifle against the trailer, and went inside. You pulled the body into the trailer, turned off the lights, and when you came out, you had Vanzant's phone and laptop. That silver laptop was shining in your arms like a brand-new baby as you came down the steps. You retrieved your rifle and walked away with the laptop and your gun."

Dewey's heart was hammering so hard he couldn't breathe right. "You didn't see me on no trail cam," he muttered.

"Yes, we did. We already have someone who can identify you from the footage."

"That's a lie!" Dewey shouted. "It was dark and you can't see nothing for the hood."

And the moment that came out of his mouth, the horror in his eyes gave it away when he realized what he'd said.

"I never said anything about the killer wearing a hoodie…did I?" Pickard said.

Carly shrieked. "You killed a man? For a laptop? What's wrong with you?" she screamed.

Dewey wouldn't look at her and dropped his head.

Moments later, an agent came up from the back of the house carrying a rifle he'd already bagged. "Same make and model," he said.

Another agent came out carrying a black hoodie they'd bagged and tagged.

Dewey's sudden interest in a worn spot on the floor was notable.

"We know it was a hit. Who are you working for?" Howard asked. "Who ordered it? How much did you get paid to commit murder?"

"I want a lawyer," Dewey said.

They got him dressed and walked him out the door in handcuffs and drove away.

Carly followed all the way to the edge of the porch, yelling and crying, but there was no one left to hear her except the hound still cowering beneath the porch.

———

The bed was warm, and Cameron's body against Rusty's back was even warmer as she slept, buried beneath the covers with his arm lying across her waist, and then suddenly the weight of him was gone.

She heard the *tick, tack* of Ghost's nails on the wooden floors and guessed Cameron had gotten up to let Ghost out. She rolled over, saw the time, and groaned. The house was chilly, but she'd already heard the central heat come on and knew Cameron would stir the ashes and put more wood on the fire.

She lay there for a couple of minutes until she felt warmth coming from the heat vents in the ceiling and rolled over to check her phone. She had a text from Jay Howard. They'd arrested Dewey Zane. Details in an email.

Elated, she got up and dressed, then grabbed her laptop to read the details of the arrest. Zane's accidental admission of guilt was icing on the cake. The only downside was Zane refusing to name who he worked for. It was a flight of fantasy to pretend Sheriff Woodley wouldn't hear the news, but she was certain they already had him staked out.

Whither thou goest, Rance Woodley, the feds are sure to know, she thought, and got up and dressed for the day.

Melinda Woodley Sheets nèe Lehigh was still in the wind, and Rusty wanted to know where she'd gone and how she was able to completely disappear. If Dewey Zane refused to tell who hired him, and they could find her, she could be the key component to either linking Woodley to the gang or clearing him.

It was midday.

Carly Zane had locked up the house after the feds carted off her husband and crawled back in bed, too scared to function. She couldn't believe what had just happened. Dewey as much as admitted he'd shot a man in cold blood, but why?

When her mother called her later to ask if she wanted to go with her to Bowling Green, Carly turned her down. She'd never lied to her mother, but she was too ashamed to admit her man had turned into a killer.

Finally she got up and dressed, then began putting everything up that the feds had pulled out—putting her house back to rights and thinking about what she'd make for supper tonight. Then it hit her.

Dewey wouldn't be there for supper.

He wouldn't be going in to Fuzzy Fridays to work evenings.

He wouldn't be going off to Barton's campground. He wouldn't be coming home. Ever.

Still holding one of his dirty shirts, she dropped into one of the kitchen chairs and started bawling anew. She was still crying when a car rolled up in front of the house.

Frightened that it might be the feds come back to take her, too, she ran to the window, then breathed a sigh of relief. It was just Rance. And then it hit her! Rance was the sheriff! He'd know what to do! He knew all about crimes and jails.

Rance Woodley was all the way up the steps, carrying a six-pack of beer, when Carly opened the door. He looked up and smiled.

"Hey, Carly. How's my best girl, and where's your lazy-ass husband? He was supposed to meet me for coffee this morning."

"Oh, Rance! Dewey's gone! The FBI come to the house before we was even out of the bed and arrested him for a murder. Said he stole a phone and a laptop and they caught it all on a trail cam."

Rance felt faint.

"Say what?"

"It's true. And before it was all over, they tricked him by talking too fast and he gave himself away. They kept asking him who paid him to do it, but he clammed up and asked for a lawyer, which just made him look guilty all over again! Why would Dewey go kill somebody for a laptop? We don't even use computers. Not even to play games. I don't understand!"

"I don't know," Rance said, then handed her the beer. "Here, you take it. I gotta go," he added and then ran back to his patrol car, made a U-turn in the front yard, and spun out as he drove away.

Carly went back inside and started to put the beer in the refrigerator, then put the six-pack on the table and popped the top on one longneck and carried it to the living room. She needed something to calm her nerves, and this was as good as anything.

But Rance Woodley could have drowned himself in a

barrel of beer and it wouldn't have changed one facet of his shock. His thoughts were in free fall as he headed back to the sheriff's office, and then halfway there made a split-second decision and took the road to Jubilee.

———————

Cameron was outside caulking the last of the windowpanes and Rusty had been with him for the better part of an hour, nailing down the loose boards on the front porch in the places he'd marked with chalk.

She was on her hands and knees about to start a new nail, but as the hammer was coming down, the nail slipped out of her grip and she hammered her thumb instead.

"Oh, crap!" she cried, and grabbed her hand and squeezed it more, as if that would actually stop the pain. "Oh my God, that hurts."

Cameron heard her cry out, saw what she'd done, and came running. Seconds later she was on her feet and in his arms.

"Oh, honey…sweetheart! I'm so sorry," he said. "Let me see."

The thumb was already swelling and turning purple around the nail bed. It was hard to tell who hurt more that it had happened, her or him, but seeing her little thumb already beginning to bruise broke his heart.

"That's enough for you," he said and took her inside, made an ice pack, and sat her down by the fire to ice her thumb.

Ghost was in the middle of both of them, trying to lick Rusty's hand and whining a little in sympathy.

"Thank you, sweet boy," Rusty said. "If love could cure, I'd already be fine." She winced when Cameron put the cold pack in her lap. "Yikes. The cold hurts, too."

"It will help with the swelling," he said. "Can you wiggle the joint? If you think it's broken, I can take you—"

"It's not broken. Just flatter than it's supposed to be," she grumbled.

"My poor baby," Cameron said. He kissed her thumb, and then kissed her. "I don't have much left to do. I'll finish up and be right back," he said.

She sighed. "You don't have to babysit me. I'm okay. Just not much of a handyman."

He stroked her cheek with the back of his hand.

"Ghost seems ready to be the babysitter," he said, eyeing how his dog had immediately plopped down at her feet. "And you make a damn fine figure of a woman, so I choose that over driving a nail straight any day."

"Yes, well…"

"No arguments, and I'm doing all the cooking and cleaning up for the rest of the week, so there's that," he said, and went back outside.

Rusty looked down at Ghost. "Thank you for giving up time with your precious boy to spend it with me."

Ghost's ear twitched, but it appeared he had nothing more to add.

Rusty leaned back in the chair and tried to ignore the constant throb, but it seemed to be in rhythm to the rise and fall of Cameron's hammer and really hard to ignore.

Finally, he'd finished and was looking down the length

of the porch, checking to make sure he hadn't missed any spots, when he heard a car turn off the road. He paused, listening, thinking maybe they'd just been turning around. But then he heard the sound of tires to gravel and knew someone was coming to his house.

He gathered up the bag of nails and the caulk gun and laid them on a little table near the door beside the hammer, then moved to the front steps to wait.

A little shock went through him when he saw it was a patrol car from the sheriff's office, and when the driver parked and got out, he was even more surprised to see Rance Woodley.

He glanced toward the window and got a glimpse of Rusty making tracks out of the living room, and then turned back to his visitor.

"Morning, Sheriff."

"Morning, Cameron. If you can spare the time, I really need to talk to you."

"It's a little cold out. Come inside," Cameron said.

Rance took off his Stetson as he followed Pope into the house, then hesitated as the white dog suddenly loomed before him.

"Lie down, Ghost. Stay," Cameron said.

Ghost dropped, but he never took his eyes off the stranger in his house.

"Have a seat," Cameron said.

Rance dropped. "I'm too rattled to beat around the bush. I just found out the FBI arrested Dewey Zane this morning for that murder out at Barton's campground. I don't even know where to start, but it puts me in a bad light. I thought I should maybe talk to those federal agents, and thought you might be able to help, since you'd worked with them some. That Caldwell woman is gone, so I don't know who to contact. Thought you could give me a name or a number to call."

"Why does it put you in a bad light, and why do you need to call them?" Cameron asked.

Rance was shaking. "Dewey is a friend. We hunt and fish together. He and Carly have been to my house for meals. He doesn't have a lot of skills, but he works hard at what he does. Hell, I even introduced him to my ex-wife about five or six years ago when she was still living in the area. She was bartending at Fuzzy Fridays, that bar at the crossroads just over the switchback on Pope Mountain. She helped get him a job there."

Cameron didn't know what to think, but he had a gut feeling they'd been chasing the wrong guy.

All of a sudden, Rusty walked into the room and Woodley jumped where he sat.

"Shit! Oh...'scuse my language. I didn't know you were still around," Rance said.

Rusty glanced at Cameron, knew exactly what he was thinking because she was of the same mind, then fixed Woodley with a look and started talking. She already knew the answer to what she was going to ask, but she wanted to see his reaction.

"You said your ex-wife got Dewey a job. What's her name?"

"Melinda Sheets now, but she mostly goes by Lindy these days. We were living around Bowling Green when we divorced. She had a good job at the time, so she stayed in the area."

"When was the last time you spoke with her?" Rusty asked.

Rance paused, frowning. "Maybe a year or so ago. I saw her in passing. Didn't really stop to talk."

"Is she still in the area?" Rusty asked.

"I have no idea," Rance said. "After she quit Fuzzy Fridays, I kind of lost track of her."

"I heard you mention Dewey Zane was your friend," Rusty said.

Rance scrubbed his hands up and down his face as if trying to wipe away the shock of what he was still feeling.

"Yeah…hunting and fishing…that kind of thing. I tried to get Dewey on as janitor at the sheriff's office, but the county commissioners didn't go for it. He has worked at both of the big hotels in Jubilee before. Mostly day labor. He works for cleaning companies around town if they call him in. Mostly like mopping floors at cafés and the like after they close. But that was all before he went to work out at the campground full time."

Rusty's heart skipped. "Zane works for Jack Barton?"

"Yes, for the last three or so years. He also works an evening shift three nights a week at Fuzzy Fridays. God. I can't believe this!"

"What's his job out at the campground?" Rusty asked.

Rance shrugged. "I don't really know. Repairing stuff.

Getting the garbage from the tiny cabins and campsites and making sure it's in the dumpster on pickup days…stuff like that. Sometimes he picks up supplies for Barton, but that's when he goes out of town."

"So, those trips… Exactly what does he pick up that Barton couldn't have delivered?"

"Again, I don't know. I guess I never really asked. Carly, his wife, might know more. Then again, maybe not. She kept crying to me this morning, asking me why Dewey would kill a man for a laptop, which is something they don't even use. Whatever he was doing, he kept it to himself."

Rusty's thoughts were spinning. She was coming to the realization that all of this *had* been a horrible twist of fate, and Rance Woodley had nothing to do with any of it. Which meant the only person still alive and on the loose who they'd identified as being part of the gang was Lindy Sheets, and she was missing.

"Tell me about your ex-wife," Rusty said.

Rance frowned. "Why?"

Now was where Rusty made the knee-jerk decision to share a piece of evidence, and she'd know by Woodley's reaction whether he'd known it or not.

"Because she was Danny Biggers's contact. She was the drop-off for the little girl Biggers snatched."

Woodley reeled as if Rusty Caldwell had just punched him in the face, then turned white as a sheet. His eyes welled, and he began to shake.

"I don't believe it."

"Oh, we have proof. That phone you confiscated from

Biggers. There were calls and texts to each other on it. She was also an old girlfriend of Biggers. She visited him in prison before the escape."

"Uh…I'm gonna be sick," Woodley whispered, and made a dash for the front door.

Cameron followed, watching as the man staggered to the edge of the porch and puked up his guts. When he finally backed away, wiping his brow and then his mouth, there were tears running down his face.

"Come inside," Cameron said. "I'll get you some water."

Woodley stumbled back inside and fell into the chair where he'd been sitting. "I'm sorry," he mumbled.

Rusty sighed. There for a minute she thought he'd been having a heart attack. Nobody was that good of an actor.

Cameron brought him a glass of water, and Woodley took a few sips and set it aside.

"And here I thought I was gonna look bad being friends with a murderer. Fuck a duck, ma'am, but I'm just gonna come out and say it. You are looking at me as being part of this mess, aren't you?"

"Now that you know why I asked about your ex-wife, tell me everything you know about her," Rusty said.

"Is she missing?" Woodley asked.

She nodded.

He wiped his eyes. "She was a good girl. I can't imagine what turned her. She's from Michigan. Her dad is Canadian, from Ontario. Her mother's from Detroit. We met in Detroit and got married there. She's from good people. She—"

"Wait," Rusty said. "You said her dad is Canadian? As in a Canadian citizen?"

Rance nodded. "Yeah. Actually, Melinda has dual citizenship. Something about where she was born, and to people who were citizens of different countries. I never do get that stuff straight."

Rusty stood, her throbbing thumb forgotten.

"Lindy Sheets has dual citizenship?" she repeated.

He nodded.

"Are her parents still alive?" Rusty asked.

"They were last time I knew," Rance said.

"Don't move," Rusty said, and handed Cameron her cell phone. "My thumb hurts too much to send a text. Would you please pull up Special Agent Howard's number? I need to talk to him before this goes any further."

Cameron slipped into his assistant role without blinking. "Yes, ma'am," he said, and did as she'd asked.

Rusty took the phone and walked out of the room, waiting for Howard to answer.

"Morning, Caldwell. What's up?"

"Rance Woodley is sitting in our living room as we speak. He came to ask Cameron how to contact the feds who just arrested Dewey Zane. He just found out about Zane's arrest and is in shock. He said Zane was his friend. They hunted and fished together, and he feared his connection to Zane would fly back on his position as sheriff."

There was a long pause, and then Howard cleared his throat. "Is he in on this call?"

"No. I've been asking him about his ex-wife, Lindy

Sheets. I'll give you the short version. He hasn't seen her in over a year, but he introduced her to Dewey Zane some years ago. She helped Dewey get a job at a bar called Fuzzy Fridays. Woodley also told us Dewey has worked all over Jubilee, but currently has been working for Jack Barton's campground every day, and three nights a week at Fuzzy Fridays. He said Dewey also makes some kind of trips out of town for Barton, but he doesn't know what they entail. He asked us why we wanted to know about his ex-wife, and I told him she was Danny Biggers's contact. At that point, I thought he was having a heart attack. He vomited off the front porch and is crying as we speak."

"Well, shit," Howard muttered.

"Exactly," Rusty said. "But Woodley did give me a very important piece of information just now. His ex-wife holds dual citizenship. Canadian and U.S. status. I'm going to let him fill you in. Give me a sec to get back to the living room."

Rusty came back into the room with her phone.

"I'm going to put this on speaker now. Sheriff Woodley, Special Agent Howard wants to ask you some questions." Then she laid the phone down on the table between them and sat beside Cameron.

Woodley scooted closer to the phone.

"Sheriff Woodley, could you please tell me about your ex-wife having dual citizenship," Howard asked.

"Yes, sir," Woodley said. "Melinda was born in Ontario. Her father is a Canadian citizen. Her mother is a citizen of the United States. Her parents still live in Ontario. Their names are Clyde and Gladys Lehigh. He worked for the

City of Windsor in their billing department and retired from that job."

"Okay, got it," Howard said. "Thank you for coming forward. This information is all useful to us, and I'll ask you not to speak of it outside this circle."

"Absolutely," Rance said, choking back tears. "I have never been so shocked as I am sitting here right now. I will do anything you need. All you have to do is ask."

"Well, if your ex-wife does happen to contact you, let us know. Otherwise, we've got this."

"Yes, sir. Thank you for being so understanding. I'm available by cell phone if the need arises."

Rusty took the phone off speaker.

"I'll be in touch," she told Howard, and ended the call.

Woodley stood. "If that's all you need from me, I'll be going," he said.

Cameron eyed Woodley closely. "Are you fit to drive?"

"Yes. I'll be okay. And I want to say right now to the both of you… It's embarrassing to admit I am sometimes out of my depth in this job. I don't understand the concept of clans. Of being so trusting and connected to each other like all of you people are on the mountain. And because I sometimes feel inadequate for this job, I overreact when it comes to defending myself, like I did at the campground. Thank you for helping me clear this with the feds."

"I appreciate your honesty," Rusty said.

Cameron walked him to the door, then stood in the doorway watching Woodley shuffle back to the patrol car and drive away.

"Well, that big bubble just popped in our faces, didn't it?" Rusty said as Cameron shut the door.

"That's for sure. What next?"

"Back to the drawing board. I'm going to go back over Emily Payne's arrest statement and Jack Barton's files. He has just become the daily special. It's time to start digging deeper."

"I suspect Dewey Zane is going to get grilled again, and this time when they throw out the name Jack Barton, it would be interesting to see his reaction," Cameron said.

"Yes, I'm sure the guys are already all over the new info. But in the meantime, I'm here on the spot. It may be time to come out into the open again. It might be just what's needed to shake things up."

Cameron frowned. "Shaking things up can be dangerous."

"But that's how I roll," Rusty said. "And I'm still a federal agent until this case is over."

"Then what?" Cameron asked.

"Then I'm all yours. Body and soul for the rest of my life," she said, and wrapped her arms around his neck.

He groaned as their lips met, and then lost himself in the kiss.

———

Boss didn't know about Zane's arrest.

And Carly Zane wasn't telling people what happened, but she was weighing her options as to even staying in the area.

Dewey was still in shock that there had been a trail cam

and that he'd been identified. He blamed Boss. He was supposed to know that shit ahead of time.

———————

Later that morning, Jack Barton came back from Jubilee with a sack full of groceries and realized Dewey had never showed up for work. He called his cell, but got no answer. Disgusted, he grabbed a box of garbage bags and took off in the golf cart to make the rounds.

The air was cold and the garbage smelled. He was seeing Dewey's job from a different angle and guessed he might need to raise his pay.

Chapter 16

THAT SAME MORNING, THERE WAS SOMETHING OF A TO-DO at the cell block where Danny Biggers was housed. The guard discovered Biggers's body as he was making early-morning rounds. Biggers was flat on his back on the floor in the middle of the cell. No blood. No signs of having been in a fight. Just his arms outstretched on either side, and his feet crossed at the ankles, like Jesus nailed to the cross, staring sightlessly up at the light burning in the ceiling.

His body was quickly moved off the cell block, but not before everyone there knew that he'd died. The silence was telling. It had to be someone's fault, but who?

The warden had to report to the feds. The report went up the chain of command until all of the agents were edgy. This was another broken link to the human-trafficking gang, and they were thrown back to the beginning of the case as if the last two years had never happened.

Who'd gotten to him?

What were they missing?

It would all come down to the autopsy as to how he died. But it wouldn't tell them who had done it.

Rusty was still nursing her swollen thumb and in a mood. She'd reread Emily Payne's arrest statement, and there was something about it that kept bugging her.

Cameron had made them a late lunch and they were just finishing up when she got a text.

"Now what?" she muttered, juggling the phone and swiping the screen at the same time as Cameron got up to refill their coffee. She read the brief text and then sent back a reply.

> Are you kidding me? Lord. Let me know what the autopsy determines. Do I need to go hunting?

Howard sent back a reply.

> **Not yet. Wait. We think we located Lindy Sheets living in Ontario as Melinda Lehigh. We don't want to spook her.**

Rusty sent back an OK emoji and then shoved the phone across the table so Cameron could read the message, and the shock was real.

"Whoa! Biggers was found dead in his cell? Looks like loose ends are getting tied in a very ugly manner. What if we never figure out who the boss is?"

"Well, that's not going to happen. They're going to pick up Lindy Sheets and scare the crap out of her. Once she knows she's the only one still on the loose who can identify the boss—assuming she knows who he is—she'll talk to stay alive. And Biggers being found dead may be what scares Dewey Zane into talking, too."

Cameron sighed. "You're right. This was just a kick in the teeth I didn't see coming."

She could see the wheels turning. "In my business, you have to be patient. In your world, death was swift and ugly. And on another note, the ham sandwiches are good."

He blinked. "Uh… If that was your attempt to distract me, it's not going to work."

"Sorry. So what would distract you?"

"You could dance naked hanging onto the bedpost of my bed or…ride with me down to Rachel's house to deliver some wood."

Rusty laughed. "Oh my God. It's not the weather for stripping naked. I choose Rachel."

"Good answer. I'd just as soon not leave you on your own," he said.

"Do we have cookies?" Rusty asked. "I understand that's required to set foot in their house."

"Yes, we do. And remind me to take dog treats, too, or Lili will try to feed Ghost cookies. She likes to share."

Rusty shivered from the excitement, but there was also just the teeniest bit of worry. She'd never had a meeting-the-family moment before. "Do I look okay? Should I put on some makeup or…"

"Well, I still like you butt-naked best, but you're beautiful with clothes on, too. And don't worry about makeup. Rachel won't be wearing any, but Lili might. Only she's never going to get past admiring your hair. You're fine."

Rusty grinned. "You are good for my soul."

Cameron waggled his eyebrows. "I'm still working on being good for your beautiful body. You go do what you want to yourself. I'm going to put the dishes in the sink and load up a rick of wood. I'll come get you when we're ready to go."

Rusty bounced up from the chair and went down the hall to change her shirt. She'd dripped a little mayo on her sweatshirt and didn't want to go visiting wearing her lunch, like she used to do after her breakfast when she was little and going to school with jelly on her sleeve.

A half hour later, Cameron had the wood loaded onto a flatbed trailer and the trailer hooked up to his Jeep. Rusty went bouncing out of the back door, bundled up against the cold as Cameron was still going through the house, locking up and getting cookies and dog treats, with Ghost dancing along beside him. The dog knew they were going for a ride, and he knew there were treats involved.

Rusty opened the back door of the Jeep, and Ghost leaped inside and assumed the position. His butt was in the seat, his front legs extended all the way down to the floorboard, and if he ducked enough, his head fit just right between the seats so he could rest his chin on Cameron's shoulder.

It made Rusty laugh.

"Ghost is an open book, isn't he? There's nothing sly about him. He's all run and gun, or passed out in front of the fire."

Cameron grinned. "Nailed it," he said. "Let's go do this."

She took a deep breath. "I'm not gonna lie. I'm nervous."

He frowned. "About what?"

"Meeting your family," she said.

"Honey, they've been trying to settle me down for years. They're going to be so happy to know someone finally figured out the code that broke me that they won't know what to do with themselves."

"I didn't break you. I just unlocked the door. You let me in," she said.

He leaned across the seat, dodging Ghost's big head, and kissed her.

"Yes, I did, and it's the smartest thing I ever did."

Then he put the Jeep in gear and eased out of the yard and up the drive. He'd tied down the load, but was still going slowly enough not to dislodge it. As soon as he reached the blacktop, he turned left and headed up the mountain.

Rusty began talking about Emily Payne's arrest statement as they drove. "There's something that bothers me about it," she said. "She mentions the cop stopping her. But there's no physical description because it was dark and she was drunk. She doesn't know if it was a county patrol car or a local police patrol car. So now that we've set Rance Woodley aside as a suspect, that kind of removes the people working under him from the radar, too."

"Right. So what are you thinking?" Cameron asked.

"Maybe local cops? Emily said she heard the cop identify himself as 'Bear' to the man he called. He said, 'This is Bear.'"

Cameron frowned. "I didn't receive a copy of that statement. I don't think I knew that," he said.

"I'm sorry. I thought they were sending us duplicate files. I should have checked."

"No biggie, but this is new info to me," Cameron said.

"So, does that make any sense to you?" she asked. "Do you know any local officers with that nickname?"

"No. But we could ask the chief. Sonny might be able to help," he said.

"That's what I was thinking, but not by showing up in his office and alerting the officers that we're still digging." She sat for a moment, staring out through the windshield, and then she asked, "Do you trust Sonny Warren?"

"I grew up with him. He's a little older, but I've never had a reason not to," Cameron said.

"I think we have to ask him. And I think he's not going to like having his officers' veracity in question."

"He may not like it, but I'd bet a steak dinner he'll be professional about it."

"Yes. Okay. I know what you mean. Like he was out at the campground. He didn't like me storming in and usurping a case in his jurisdiction, but he never said an ugly word about it. And offered copies of the statements he'd already taken."

Cameron nodded.

"Then I think I need to call him," she said. "He won't know where I'm calling from, and maybe we'll get a new lead."

"Works for me," Cameron said. "And…here's our turn, and that's Louis and Rachel's house just in the trees there.

I'll pull up in the backyard and unload the wood. Likely she'll come out, but if not, we'll go inside after I'm done. And before you mention it, no, you can't help. The last thing you want is for your poor little thumb to get squished between sticks of firewood."

Rusty cradled her hand and winced. "I'm not about to argue. Just thinking about that gives me the shudders."

―――――――――

Rachel knew Cameron was bringing them wood. She'd hated to ask, but after Lili's abduction, Louis refused to work nights again and was on the day shift at Trapper's Bar and Grill. At this time of year the sun set early, and by the time he got home and their chores were done, it was dark, leaving no safe time left to cut wood. The man they'd been buying it from was out momentarily, and she'd called Cameron in a pinch, hoping this rick would tide them over until their regular supplier had a couple of cords ready for them again.

She'd been watching for Cameron, and when she saw his Jeep coming up the drive, she put on her coat and called out to her daughter, "Lili! Lili! Uncle Cam is here!"

Lili came running, her little legs pumping and her arms folded up and swinging against her body like chicken wings.

"Unca Cam! Unca Cam!" she squealed.

"We need our coats. It's cold outside," Rachel said, and zipped and snapped Lili up into her little red coat.

"Need my coat!" Lili said, patting the front of it.

"Yep. We're ready," Rachel said. She swooped Lili up in her arms and went out the back door.

Cameron had already backed the trailer to the spot where he needed to unload, and Ghost was in the yard checking everything out. They both heard the back door slam and looked up and saw Rachel coming across the yard carrying Lili.

Cameron waved.

Ghost went bounding toward them to say hello.

Rachel was smiling, and Lili was squealing in delight.

Then Rusty emerged from the Jeep, and everything after that began happening in slow motion.

Rachel saw the woman, and the wild red curls blowing in the wind, and saw the love on Cameron's face and wanted to cry.

So this is who you are. And you're so beautiful! Please like me. Please be my sister, my friend.

Lili's mouth was open in a squeal, and then she saw the stranger. She swallowed the squeal, leaned a little closer to her mama, and stared in awe.

Cameron grinned. This was "the moment," and Rusty was exactly the show-stopper he'd guessed she would be.

He dumped the armload of wood, brushed the chips off his coat and gloves, and went straight to Rusty and put his arm around her.

"Hey, everybody. Come meet my girl."

Rachel waved and kept walking toward them, but then the moment she stopped, Lili bailed out of her arms and into Cameron's like she'd been catapulted into the air.

"Lord!" Rachel gasped as she tried to grab for her, but Cameron was laughing.

"I caught her," he said, and then kissed Lili's cheek. "Rusty, this is my sister, Rachel, and this little grasshopper is Lili. Rachel, this is my forever woman, Faith Caldwell, also known as Rusty, for obvious reasons."

Rusty was still reeling over the forever-woman comment, and hoped to God that Rachel Glass liked her.

"I'm so happy to finally meet you," Rusty said.

Rachel beamed. "I'm happy to meet you, too. I was beginning to think there wasn't a woman alive who'd slow this man down."

Rusty threw back her head and laughed. "Oh lord…I didn't slow him down. I just happened to be fast enough to catch up and strong enough to hold on."

Cameron grinned.

Lili patted both his cheeks and said, "Cookies."

"Not yet, Little Bit. See all this wood?" Cameron said. She nodded.

"Uncle Cam has to unload it first. And this is Rusty. She's my friend."

"Russy," Lili said, and then reached out and patted the top of Rusty's head. "Pitty hair."

Cameron nodded. "Yes, she has real pretty hair. How about you take Mama and Rusty inside out of the cold, okay? I'll bring cookies in a minute."

"Inna minute," Lili echoed.

Cameron put her down, and when he did, she went straight to Ghost and locked her fist into his fur.

" C'mon, Ghoss. Inside now."

"As you can tell, this one thinks she's in charge. Let's go inside where it's warmer. I have coffee," Rachel said.

"I'd love some," Rusty said, and gave Cameron a backward glance as they walked away.

He was watching them go. She knew he would be. That's why she turned to look. He was waiting for her smile, so she obliged.

By the time he got the wood unloaded and went inside, Rusty was in the floor. Lili was standing between Rusty's legs and playing with her hair. Ghost was lying beside her, and Rachel was chattering away as she watched them play.

Rachel looked up as Cameron walked in, gave him a thumbs-up, and got up to hug him. "Thank you for the wood, Brother, and for the sister. I already love her," she whispered in his ear.

"You are most welcome," Cameron said.

The moment Lili heard her uncle's voice, her focus shifted. "Cookies now?"

Cameron held up the sack he'd brought with him. "Cookies now. And what do we do when we get a treat?" he asked.

"We share!" Lili cried.

Cameron pulled Rusty to her feet. "You're not gonna want to be in the floor when the crumbs fly."

Rusty laughed and sat down on the sofa beside him. She guessed the ritual being played out before her had happened countless times before, and she couldn't wait to see.

The first thing that came out of the sack was a dog treat.

"This is Ghost's treat. Remember? No cookies for Ghost."

"For Ghoss," Lili said, then held the treat out to Ghost, and as always, he took it from her baby fingers with the greatest of care, and chomped once and it was gone.

"And this cookie is for Mama," Cameron said.

"For Mama," Lili echoed, and dashed across the floor to give her mama a cookie, then came running back to Cameron.

"One for Rusty," Cameron said.

Lili giggled. "For Russy."

"Yum! Thank you," Rusty said.

Then Cameron pulled out another cookie, but Lili was already crawling up into his lap.

"This one we eat together," Cameron said, and gave it to her as soon as she settled.

Lili lifted the cookie to Cameron's lips.

"Little bite, Unca Cam."

Rusty was enchanted. "That request suggests you need to be reminded."

"I am insulted," he said, and then took a bite, and like Ghost, chewed and swallowed so fast he barely tasted it.

After that, Lili leaned back in his arms and proceeded to eat and crumble all over Cameron's lap and onto the floor.

"Why it has to be in Cam's lap, we'll never know, but I have a Dustbuster for this very reason," Rachel said.

"I think maybe Lili sees Cameron's invisible hero's cape. And you have to admit, nobody's going to try and take anything away from her with a hero that big and pretty."

Cameron frowned. "I wouldn't call myself pretty."

Rusty shrugged. "You didn't. I did it for you."

Rachel burst out laughing. "Oh my God. You're so done for, Brother, aren't you?"

Cameron sighed. "I am willingly held sway by anything she wants."

"I just want you…and world peace," Rusty said.

At that, Cameron and Rachel both started laughing, and because they did, Lili laughed too, while Ghost just kept licking up the crumbs at Cameron's feet.

Once the cookies were gone, they began saying their goodbyes. While Rusty was getting a goodbye hug from Lili, Cameron pulled Rachel aside to remind her. "Remember, there's a reason she's stayed under wraps for now. Say nothing. People's lives are at risk until we've finished what she came to do."

"Understood," Rachel said. "Be safe, both of you, and be careful. You and I are all that's left of our immediate family. I have no wish to become an orphan."

"Love you, Sis. Give Louis my best," he said, and then they were gone.

Rachel watched as they walked back to the Jeep. They were holding hands. She'd watched him leave her house countless times, but always alone. Whatever was going on, she needed them both to be okay.

"So, you survived 'the visit.' How do you feel now?" Cameron asked, as they started back down the mountain.

"Like I already belong. Thank you, darling. Loving you is the best job I'll ever have, and your family is going to be the fringe benefits I've been missing."

"I love that, and I love you," Cameron said.

"Love you more. But I hate sneaking around, which makes that all the more reason to close this case."

"Speaking of closing cases, did they find any of the stolen property from your friend's home?"

"I don't know, but I hope they find out who did it soon. If thieves find a prime location to start stealing, Mr. Duroy's home will just be their starting point. I'll give Woodley a call and see if he's had any leads."

"And I'm going to call Jay Howard and talk to him about bringing Chief Warren into this."

As soon as they got back to the house, Rusty went inside, leaving Cameron to pull the trailer into the barn.

She hung up her coat, smiled as she brushed a cookie crumb off her sweater, and then settled down in front of her laptop and pulled up the file on Emily Payne before she made the call.

It rang several times, and she thought the call was going to go to voicemail, but then he answered. "This is Howard."

"It's me," Rusty said. "I want to run something by you."

"Talk to me," Howard said, and she explained what she thought, and what she wanted to do regarding the unidentified cop and involving the Jubilee police chief.

"We have no problem with Sonny Warren. I don't see a conflict of interest here, unless he winds up being related to someone who fits into the picture."

"I agree," Rusty said.

"Okay then, go for it," Howard said. "See what you can dig up. And FYI…we have extradition papers for Melinda Lehigh. Normally this has to go through all kinds of channels, but we got special dispensation due to the gravity of the situation and the ongoing case. Canadian authorities have her residence staked out."

"Oh. Wow. So you've already located her?"

"We know where she's living. Where she's been working. And where her parents live. The Canadian authorities are watching all three locations, and whichever place she shows up at first is where she'll be picked up. They'll turn her over to us and we'll bring her back. After that, it's all about trying to crack her."

"I'd love to be a fly on the wall during that interrogation," Rusty said. "Happy hunting, and keep me updated. I'll let you know if we learn anything from Sonny Warren."

The call disconnected, and Rusty laid the phone aside and began making notes of what she wanted to discuss with the chief. She heard Cameron's footsteps on the back porch and then heard them coming into the kitchen. Moments later, he called out, "Hey, honey! Do you want something to drink?"

"A Coke on ice?"

"Coming up!" he said.

Rusty kept writing, and in a couple of minutes, Cameron set a glass of Coke down next to where she was sitting, then leaned over and kissed the top of her head.

She looked up, smiling. "Thank you for the kiss and the Coke."

"I couldn't resist. You're so damn cute when you get serious," he said.

She arched an eyebrow. "You should see me when I get mad. I'm an absolute knockout."

He walked away, laughing.

Rusty shivered. Sparring with him was almost as satisfying as coming undone in his arms. She took a sip of the Coke, then a second sip before picking up the phone to make the call to Sonny Warren.

It rang and rang, and then went to voicemail. Rusty left a message for him to call her at his convenience, and then disconnected.

Her thumb was throbbing again, so she got up to take some pain meds, heard Cameron talking on the phone to the sheriff's office, and quietly moved past as she went back to work.

―――――――

Between the fuckup of kidnapping the kid, Lindy Sheets's disappearance, and Vanzant's execution, Boss was nervous. Now Emily Payne wasn't answering her phone, and Dewey Zane was AWOL, as well. What the hell was going on? But there was still one person he knew he could count on, so he quickly made that call. It only rang once before the call picked up.

"Hello."

"Bear, it's me. The Payne woman isn't answering her phone and Zane seems to be out of pocket. Nobody is answering my calls. What the hell?"

"Shit! I thought you already knew."

Boss frowned. "Knew what?"

"The feds picked the Payne woman up the other day and flew her away in a chopper. I don't have any idea where they took her. And Zane is in federal custody for Vanzant's murder."

"What? No way! I thought that—" He stopped. "How did that come about?"

"I heard Vanzant had trail cams up around his site. One of them caught the whole thing."

"Trail cams? Why the hell did I not know about that?" Boss shouted.

There was a long moment of silence, and then Bear cleared his throat. "He was your employee. I would have assumed you did."

The subtle accusation was a slap in the face. "Don't you piss me off, too!"

"You shouldn't have threatened Lindy. She wouldn't turn on you. You should have let Vanzant leave. He didn't know the implications of what he was doing. You should have let him and the Payne woman out of the picture months ago. You brought all of this shit down on yourself," Bear said.

"You're in this as deep as I am," Boss snapped.

"I know that. And I'm still here, too, aren't I? I trust you. You should return the damn favor," Bear said, and hung up.

Boss blinked. "He hung up on me. He hung up on *me*!" He stood so abruptly the chair he'd been sitting in went rolling backward, hit the wall, and knocked a framed document off the wall.

"Son of a bitch," the Boss muttered, and hung it back up.

What he'd learned changed the whole outline of his future. The Payne woman didn't know anything, so there was nothing she could say that would hurt him. Zane was the loose cannon. He needed to make damn sure he was too scared to talk, but how? And then he remembered.

Dewey Zane was married. He needed to be reminded of all the things that could happen to his wife without him around. But first, he had a message to send.

———

Sonny Warren was downtown at the scene of a robbery in progress when his cell phone rang. One suspect was already in cuffs and in the back of a patrol car, and the second one was holed up in the bathroom of Neighbor's Gas Station, which they'd just tried to rob. He felt his phone vibrating in the pocket of his jacket, but let the call go to voicemail. They were trying to get the last perp out of the building without a standoff.

He and two officers were on-site, and he'd already been on the bullhorn, telling the suspect to come out, that they had the place surrounded. They were waiting for backup when the front door to the station began to open. They saw a gun come sliding out onto the pavement, and then the other robber walked out, hands in the air, shaking and crying and yelling "Don't shoot!"

The first thing that went through Sonny's mind was *Holy shit!* The second thought was *It's a girl!* The third thing he noticed was the size of her belly. She had to be a good six months pregnant.

His officers swarmed her and retrieved the weapon she'd discarded, while Sonny still held a gun on her. As soon as they had her in cuffs, he holstered his weapon. This was a first. And he'd bet money she was underage to boot. How the hell do kids go this wrong this fast?

An hour later, he was back in his office, still dealing with booking minors, calling Social Services, contacting court-appointed lawyers, and trying to locate parents. His phone kept ringing, and he kept not answering, with no time to deal with missed calls.

———

Rusty was digging deep, going through the minutiae of Jackson (Jack) Lee Barton's life. Fifty-seven years old. That surprised her. He looked younger.

He owned a lot of real estate. Some developed. Some still in development. He was what her daddy would have called land poor. In other words, he had more land than he knew what to do with.

On the surface, nothing looked suspicious. But that didn't signify anything to Rusty. The really good criminals always knew how to hide their dirt. So she kept looking for a trail that might lead her to some.

She kept thinking about Melinda Lehigh, and how she'd had two names and two citizenships she could legally claim. So she went back to Barton's birth certificate. If she could eliminate anything funky about that, then she could move on to looking for offshore accounts or shell companies. But what she found surprised her.

Jack Barton had been born a twin, then adopted three days after his birth. His brother had also been adopted, but not by the same family. Sad, but not unusual. She wondered if they'd ever found each other, then let that go. It had nothing to do with the current situation.

Now that she knew he was a U.S. citizen, she started looking for a big money trail. Human trafficking was a worldwide industry. Criminal, yes. But the profits were staggering, and if the gang Howard and Pickard were chasing had international ties, then the ones at the top were raking in billions.

Cameron came in and sat down, then waited until she paused and looked up before he started talking.

"Woodley said they've already located some of the stolen property. The thieves pawned it in Bowling Green. They have some grainy security footage showing two older men. No teenagers as he predicted. He apologized. I guess this Dewey Zane thing has shaken him out of taking the easy route to solving crimes."

"At least he won't be hounding kids for no reason," Rusty said.

"Exactly. Have you heard from Sonny?"

"No. He didn't answer his cell. I left a message."

"Is there anything you want me to do?" he asked.

Rusty paused. "You know that feeling you get when you know something is about to go down, but you don't have a clue what it's going to be?"

He nodded. "All too well. What's bugging you?"

"The unknown cop. The one who stopped Emily Payne. I hate not knowing who to watch out for."

"How about I take myself to Jubilee. See what's been going on in town. And if I see Sonny, I'll tell him you sent me to get a list of all the employees of the PD, including janitors. That way, he won't immediately think you're looking at his officers."

Rusty jumped up from where she was sitting and threw her arms around him.

"Yes! Thank you! That's the perfect way to approach this. If he asks, just tell him it's all related to the Emily Payne arrest, and he won't think anything of it, since he participated in that."

"You got it," Cameron said, and stole a quick kiss. "I'll bring something home for supper. Do you have a preference?"

"You don't have to do that," Rusty said.

"Honey, if you weren't here, I'd still be feeding myself."

She grinned. "Okay. But I want whatever sounds good to you. Truly. Surprise me."

Cameron grabbed his coat and car keys and whistled at Ghost.

"Ghost! With me!" he said, and opened the door.

The big dog bounded outside, while Cameron lingered for one last kiss. The scent of her was alluring. The taste of Coke was on her lips.

"Love you, darlin'."

Rusty sighed as he let her go. "Love you, too. Come home safe to me."

"Count on it. Lock the door behind me," he added.

She waved as they drove out of the yard and then did as he asked. She locked herself inside, then went through to the back door and locked that one, too, just because.

Chapter 17

CAMERON DROVE STRAIGHT INTO TOWN, WITH GHOST beside him. He went through the ATM drive-up at his bank to get cash, then parked downtown. He put Ghost on a leash and began walking around, visiting with friends and talking to tourists who wanted to talk about his dog. He never told them the truth. Not about himself. Not about where Ghost came from. He would just make a joke about everything being bigger on the mountain.

When he saw Sam Carson, the injured veterinarian, coming out of the pharmacy, he stopped to talk. "Sam, how have you been? Leslie told me about your accident."

Sam grimaced. It was still a point of embarrassment to him that he'd let a big animal get the best of him when he should have known better.

"I'm still off work until my broken rib heals a bit more." Then he reached out to Ghost and gave him a quick scratch between the ears. "Hey, boy. Long time no see." Then he glanced back up at Cameron. "Did his paw heal properly?"

"Yes, you did a great job," Cameron said. "Leslie and your sub seem to have everything under control."

"I know," Sam said. "I might be feeling a little insecure about not being needed."

And right at that moment, Ghost licked Sam's hand. Both men laughed.

"I guess that was Ghost's way of saying you're irreplaceable," Cameron said.

"I'm going to take it that way," Sam said. "Did you hear about all of the to-do down at Neighbor's Gas Station?"

"No. What happened?" Cameron asked.

"A couple of teens, a boy and a girl, tried rob it. There was quite a ruckus getting them into custody. I heard they were both underage and the girl was pregnant. Can't imagine what a paperwork nightmare that's gonna be. It's been good to see you, but I need to get home. Take care."

"You too," Cameron said, and watched Sam ease himself into his truck and drive away. Now he knew why Sonny Warren hadn't returned Rusty's call, but that wasn't going to stop him from doing what she sent him to do. "Come on, Ghost. Let's go for a ride."

They walked back to where he'd parked, and a few minutes later he was driving past the precinct, checking out the number of cars to gauge his chances of getting to talk to Sonny. He didn't see any signs pointing to turmoil, so he parked, locked Ghost in the Jeep, and went inside.

Walter Winter, the desk sergeant, was a short, stocky man with a shock of gray hair and was a year shy of retirement. Cameron had known him most of his life.

Sergeant Winter eyed Cameron's approach. He'd heard all about him being with the feds who'd taken over the crime scene at the campground, and he still didn't know what he thought about that.

"Afternoon, sir," Cameron said. "I need to speak to the chief, if he's available."

"I'll check," Winter said. He picked up the receiver on the switchboard and punched a button. "Hey, Chief. Cameron Pope is here. Says he needs to talk to you." There was a pause as Winter listened. "Yes, sir," he said, and hung up. "You can go back."

"Thanks," Cameron said, and walked toward the hallway leading down to the offices.

When he reached the door to the chief's office, he knocked, then heard Sonny's voice.

"Come in."

Cameron could tell when he walked in that Sonny Warren was frazzled. He looked like he'd been running his fingers through his hair, and there was a snap that had come undone on his shirt. But when he saw Cameron, he smiled and stood up.

"Sit down. Sit down," he said.

Cameron sat. "From the gossip in town, I hear you've had quite a day, so I'll skip the chitchat and get right to the point. Agent Caldwell has a task that you can easily fulfill for her. She needs a list of names of every employee who works at the PD. Not just officers…but support personnel included…like janitors and cleaning services."

Sonny frowned. "What the hell does she need with that?"

Cameron leaned forward. "I don't know for sure, but I'm thinking it still has to do with why they arrested Emily Payne."

The frown slid off of Sonny's face. "Oh! Right! Sure, I can furnish that easily enough." He spun around in his chair to face his computer and began typing on the keyboard.

Cameron could see the cursor sliding down a list of files on the screen until it stopped at one. Sonny clicked on it. From where Cameron was sitting, he could tell it was some kind of spreadsheet, with names and the addresses and contact information for each employee.

"I'll just print off a copy for her," Sonny said, then got up and walked across the room to the printer.

It spat out five sheets of paper. Sonny took them back to his desk, eyed them once making sure the list was up to date, and then handed it to Cameron.

"I hope this gives her the answers she's looking for. I'd like to bring an end to whatever the hell is going on here, because I *know* something is. Tell her if there's anything I can do to help, just let me know."

"Will do," Cameron said as he stood. "I'll see myself out."

Sonny followed him to the door, frowning as he watched Pope striding up the hall and out of sight. "Yep. Something is going on for sure," he muttered, then went back into his office and closed the door.

Cameron folded the pages lengthwise and put them in the console, then gave Ghost a gentle stroke across his head and down his back. The muscles rippled beneath his hand, a reminder of the big dog's size and endurance. But for Cameron, Ghost was still that stray puppy who'd wandered into their camp, filthy and starving. They'd both come a long way from that day, but they'd done it together.

"Well, what's for supper, big guy? Rusty said we have to choose."

Ghost's ears twitched at the sound of her name. He looked up at Cameron and whined as if to say "Don't lay this on me, pal."

Cameron laughed, then backed away from the curb and drove away.

———————

It was Melinda Lehigh's day off. She'd gotten her brows waxed, had lunch out at a diner she liked, then shopped for groceries before heading for the bus stop. The bus was just pulling to a stop when she arrived and ran to get on, juggling her purchases as she climbed in, then flopped down in a seat near the front.

Ten minutes passed, and she was thinking about making spaghetti and meatballs for dinner and wondering what to wear to work tomorrow, when she realized the bus had reached her stop. She gathered up her things, shouldered her handbag as she disembarked, and headed home. The air was cold enough it made her eyes water, but the streets and sidewalks were clear.

Her apartment was less than a block away, and she was thinking about a hot cup of tea when all of a sudden multiple police cars came flying at her from all directions, with lights flashing and sirens screaming.

They all skidded to a stop, and when police began spilling out of the cars and shouting at her to drop her things and put her hands in the air, she started screaming, "What's happening? What's happening?"

They were restraining her and shouting back, "What's your name? State your name!"

She took a breath, her voice shaking as she answered, "Lehigh. Melinda Lehigh."

"Melinda Lehigh, you are wanted by the United States of America for questioning regarding murder and human trafficking. You are being taken into our custody and will then be transported to the border and handed over to the FBI." Then they cuffed her and put her into the back of a patrol car.

She looked back as they were driving away. Her groceries were scattered everywhere. There would be no hot tea. No spaghetti and meatballs for her dinner. She wouldn't show up for work tomorrow, and they'd wonder for a while what had happened, where she'd gone, and then forget she ever existed. She was sick-to-her-stomach, out-of-her-mind petrified. She didn't know how they'd found her, but she knew why it was happening. She wasn't nearly as smart as she'd thought she was, and that was her revelation.

─────────────

It was almost sundown when Cameron pulled in beneath the carport. He came in the side door with a sack full of fried catfish, hush puppies, and coleslaw, and the list of names Rusty wanted, while Ghost was making the rounds in the backyard.

"Something smells good!" Rusty said as Cameron put everything on the counter.

When he saw her walk in, he swooped her up in his arms and nipped the lobe of her ear, then buried his face in her curls as she was laughing.

"You are a crazy man," Rusty said, and slid her arms around his neck.

"You make me crazy," he whispered, then kissed her senseless.

It might have gone way past just kissing had Ghost not decided he wanted back in the house. He was standing at the back door, barking.

Cameron groaned as he pulled away. "I am being paged," he said. "Hold that thought."

He let Ghost in and fed him, while Rusty began getting out plates and flatware. They filled their plates from the to-go containers and carried them to the table, then Cameron went back to get the list.

"Oh, you got the list!" Rusty crowed, as he laid it beside her plate. "Way to go!"

"They had an attempted robbery in town at one of the gas stations. I think that's why you never heard from Sonny. I didn't even mention to him that you'd called. I just told him I was running an errand for you. He bowed up a little about the list. And then I told him I thought it had something to do with the Emily Payne arrest. After that, he was fine," Cameron said.

"I'll run through the list later and see if anything pops. For now, we eat this wonderful food before it goes cold."

Agents Howard and Pickard learned of Biggers's death about the same time they found out Melinda Lehigh, a.k.a. Lindy Sheets, was in custody. They celebrated her arrest by paying a visit to the jail where Dewey Zane was being held. Their thinking was that if Zane knew Biggers was dead, he might be willing to talk. They had no idea Zane had already had one visitor while he was in jail: his wife, Carly. And she had received a threat she couldn't ignore.

She and Dewey were talking in whispers, trying to get said what had to be said without being overheard. Tears were rolling and Carly was wiping snot and shaking so hard she could barely breathe.

"They said if you talked, they would sell me. That there was nowhere I could go that they couldn't find me. They said they'd turn me into an addict and men would fuck me till I died."

Dewey's blood ran cold. The horror on her face. The tears swimming in her eyes. The words cut to the heart of his very soul, and he knew Boss meant it.

"Oh my God, sugar, oh my God. I'm so sorry," Dewey whispered.

"Sorry ain't gonna save my life," Carly said.

Dewey swallowed past the lump in his throat "I won't

talk. That ain't ever gonna happen. I love you. I'll die to keep you safe."

Carly Zane was shattered. She loved Dewey with all her heart, and had since the day they'd met, but she didn't trust him anymore, and she damn sure didn't trust the man who'd threatened her to keep his word and leave her alone even if Dewey didn't give him up.

"I love you, too," she said. "I wish that had been enough."

She ended their visit and walked back to their old red truck and drove away from the jail. All of her clothes were in two suitcases in the back seat. She'd withdrawn what money they had from their bank account, plus the little cash stash they'd kept in a box under the bed. She drove out of the city and kept driving into the west, straight into the setting sun.

So by the time Howard and Pickard arrived a few hours later, Dewey was mute. The sight of the two agents who'd arrested him didn't even make him blink. Their news that Danny Biggers was dead didn't even faze him. No matter how they worded the questions, he never changed his answer.

"I got nothing to say."

They left, more frustrated than when they'd arrived, only to learn his wife had visited earlier.

Pickard was frustrated. "Damn it. Something spooked him. Maybe her life was threatened. If he talks, she's dead."

Howard nodded. "Definitely a possibility."

"We've still got Lindy Sheets," Pickard said.

"Somebody's got her," Howard muttered. "But I'm not

counting on anything until she's sitting across the table from us in an interrogation room."

⸻

Cameron emerged from the shower with a towel wrapped around his waist, only to find Rusty sitting on his bed with a bowl of popcorn in her lap, watching a show on TV. Ghost was standing beside the bed with his chin on the mattress, watching every bite go in Rusty's mouth.

He sighed. What a beautiful sight.

Rusty looked up. "Lord. You sure did get all the good from your DNA. Good thing I'd already swallowed my last bite or I would have choked on it."

"He's begging, isn't he?"

She looked at Ghost and nodded. "I wasn't certain he could have popcorn. I told him we had to wait and ask you. So he's waiting."

Cameron laughed. "He can have some."

"Thank God," Rusty said. "Just look at that face." Then she took a single piece of popped corn and leaned over and kissed his head. "Good boy for waiting. He said yes." She held it out, and Ghost licked it out of her fingers and swallowed it whole. She shook her head. "You don't even know what you ate."

Cameron laughed again, then dropped the towel and put on a pair of sweats and crawled up onto the bed beside her. He reached for some popcorn, then leaned back against the headboard.

"What are we watching?"

"*The Last of the Mohicans*. Daniel Day-Lewis version. It always makes me cry."

"Then why watch it, honey?"

Rusty shrugged. "I don't know. Maybe because the good people in the movie never backed down."

"Like you. Indomitable," he said.

Her eyes suddenly welled. "Cameron..."

"Don't cry. You'll wash all the salt off the popcorn," he said, then leaned over and kissed her. "Umm, salty," he whispered.

Ghost barked.

"I think he just asked for another bite," Cameron said.

Rusty picked out three kernels and gave them to him one at a time.

"Enough, Ghost. Lie down," Cameron said.

The dog flopped down on the floor at the foot of the bed and closed his eyes.

"Now...where were we?" Cameron asked.

"At the best part. The waterfall. That's where Hawkeye says to Cora Munro, 'Stay alive! Whatever you do, stay alive! I will find you!' And then he and Chingachgook and Uncas leap into the water."

Cameron couldn't take his eyes off her face. The passion and animation were palpable. She was amazing and a mystery, and he loved her to the depths of his soul.

"Why is it the best part?" he asked.

She shrugged. "It's so romantic, and yet so horribly frightening, both for the ones who are leaving, as well as the ones left behind to be captured. The faith she had in him to find her makes me cry. She is a strong woman who knows her heart."

She leaned her head against Cameron's shoulder and handed him the bowl of popcorn.

"You don't want any more?"

"I don't want to eat now. I'm getting ready to cry."

"Oh my God," he said softly, and put his arm around her and pulled her close.

They watched the rest of the movie in silence, and when it was over she sighed, satisfied with the emotional journey she'd been on.

"I have to take Ghost out. Want something to drink, honey?"

"Yes, but I'll come with you," Rusty said. "I need to fill you in on stuff."

"You'll need shoes and a coat. It's really cold out. It'll probably snow again before morning."

She scrambled to get dressed properly, then followed them out to the back porch. The area was lit by a security light, but Cameron had been right. It was cold. He pulled her into the shelter of his arms as they watched Ghost make the rounds.

"Howard sent a text. They have Lindy Sheets in custody. She probably won't be back in the States until sometime tomorrow. Dewey Zane isn't talking. And they're still waiting for the autopsy on Danny Biggers."

"Anything new on Jack Barton?" Cameron asked.

"No. I can't find anything. They haven't uncovered

anything, and I went through the list you brought home. There's nothing on any of the employees to indicate they might be connected to Barton, and nothing suspicious about any of the officers on the force," Rusty said.

"We still have Lindy Sheets," Cameron said.

"Right. We still have her."

"You know... This whole gang has been about people representing themselves as something they're not. Vanzant wasn't really a student doing research. Emily Payne was masquerading as someone else. Lindy Sheets pretending to befriend girls who were alone. What if that cop who pulled Payne and Vanzant over wasn't really a cop? Emily said she didn't remember anything about the cop car. What if it wasn't a cop car and only had the lights and siren? What if he's just part of the gang...masquerading as a cop just to pull women over?"

Rusty stilled, and then turned in his arms and looked at him.

"Oh my God! Yes! And the reason Emily Payne didn't go missing like all the others was because Vanzant was in the car. And the fake cop didn't see him until after the stop had been made. Her begging for mercy gave him the idea that she could be coerced. So he called his boss for orders, and this is what happened? Having one single woman go missing is one thing. But having a couple go missing could double public interest and a police presence!"

Cameron nodded. "But again...the unknown man."

"Yes. That unknown man," Rusty muttered.

After a few minutes more, Ghost was called back to the

house. They bedded the dog by the fire, added a log to keep it going, and took themselves to bed.

This mess was a puzzle best left for another day.

———

Lindy Sheets was back in Detroit. She recognized the city as they sped through on their way to the airport. She was loaded onto a jet in the middle of the night, accompanied by four agents, two of which were females, and handcuffed to her seat. She tried asking questions, but no one was talking to her other than to bring her food or take her to use the restroom. Finally, she gave up to the inevitable, leaned back in her seat, and closed her eyes.

When she woke again, they were landing.

"Where are we?" she asked.

"Frankfort, Kentucky," one of the agents said.

"I want a lawyer," Lindy said.

"One will be waiting for you at headquarters."

"I need to pee," Lindy said.

"We'll take you before you leave the plane."

She frowned. "Do I get breakfast somewhere? I haven't eaten since noon yesterday."

"You'll get what is coming to you," the agent said.

Lindy frowned. That cryptic comment could mean anything, but she quit asking questions because she wasn't liking the answers.

Special Agents Howard and Pickard were waiting when a van arrived with the agents and the prisoner. They escorted her into the building in leg irons and handcuffs and walked her back to an interrogation room.

Lindy was immediately alarmed. They hadn't bothered to jail her…or book her. Or give her time to talk to her lawyer. She felt like she was being railroaded, but since she knew she was guilty as hell, she decided to stay quiet until she saw how this was playing out.

In the interrogation room, she was cuffed to the table, and then all of the agents walked out, leaving a guard standing just inside the door, staring at her. Her heart was pounding. Her belly growled.

And then the door opened and a stranger walked in. "Melinda Sheets? My name is Darrell Holder. I'm your court-appointed lawyer."

A guard walked in behind Holder carrying two cups of coffee and a small bag of doughnuts and set it all down on the table between them.

"Compliments of Uncle Sam," Holder said. He pushed one cup of coffee within her reach, laid a napkin in front of her, and opened the sack. "Help yourself. We can talk while you eat."

Lindy took several sips of the coffee before reaching for a doughnut. They were simple glazed doughnuts, but they were like manna in her mouth. As soon as her initial hunger was assuaged, she began to speak.

"What are they charging me with?" she asked.

"For starters, human trafficking. Attempted kidnapping. Abetting the escape of a state prisoner, and—"

She interrupted. "I had nothing to do with that prison riot or the escapees. I heard about an attempt being planned, but I had no idea they'd make good on it. I was contacted after it happened."

"You promised Biggers a job if he got out. We know that because he told us, and you knowingly withheld information about a planned riot."

She frowned. "Biggers talked about his business? So what? He knows nothing about me. Whatever he said is a lie, and you can tell him I said so."

"Biggers is dead," Holder said. "He died in his cell. Because whoever is left out there is still calling the shots."

Lindy's lips parted, only nothing came out but a grunt.

Holder leaned forward. "You need to tell me everything. I don't want to go to trial without knowing where all the skeletons are. The background I was given on you is that you work for a human trafficking ring. You were Biggers's contact. You were waiting for him at a place called Fuzzy Fridays but he never showed. He said you promised him ten thousand dollars for a three-year-old child named Lili Glass. But the feds are telling me that the gang you are associated with always paid for their deliveries with a bullet to the back of the head."

Lindy groaned. They knew more than she'd thought.

"Who's your boss?" Holder asked. "You have to help me help you, or you'll be going down for all of this on your own."

"I want a deal," she said.

"They'll have to hear everything you know to see if it's worth making a deal."

Lindy popped the last bite of doughnut in her mouth, chewed, swallowed, and washed it down with coffee.

"What would be my best offer?" she asked.

"You're looking at a minimum of twenty-five years to a maximum of life, and if they designate each sex trafficking case separately, you might never see outside again."

Lindy reached for a second doughnut. "I'll tell them what I know for the minimum sentence with a chance of parole."

"Well, they won't promise you anything. The final decision will belong to the judge. Otherwise you'll just go to trial and suffer the consequences of twelve angry jurors knowing you participated in selling young women as sex slaves and kidnapping babies to sell on the black market. They'll crucify you."

She took a bite, chewing as she thought, then shrugged. "I'll talk to them up to a point, but until I know what they can offer me, I'll take my chances because there is no paper trail to tie me to any of this."

"They have Biggers's phone with your texts on it. You're nowhere near in the clear. Just remember that," Holder said, then signaled to the guard they were ready for the agents.

She finished the doughnut and the coffee, then took the second cup and held it between her hands to warm them. Even though the room was warm enough, she felt cold all the way to her bones.

Chapter 18

As soon as they got the nod, Howard and Pickard entered the interrogation room, carrying file folders. They sat down opposite Lindy and her lawyer, pressed Start on the recorder to tape the session, and only then did they look up and make eye contact with Lindy.

Howard began the interview. "Special Agent Howard and Special Agent Pickard are present in the room, along with Darrell Holder, the court-appointed lawyer for our detainee, Melinda Sheets." Then he eyed Melinda. "Please state your full name for the recording."

"Melinda Renée Sheets."

"You have been read your rights prior to this interview. Do you understand that anything you say that is being recorded today can be used against you in a court of law?"

"Yes, I understand," Lindy said.

"Is it true that you hold dual citizenships? One in Canada, one in the United States?"

"Yes."

"And for the record, would you please state the name under which your Canadian citizenship is recognized?" Howard said.

"Melinda Renée Lehigh. That's my legal maiden name."

"And what name is your U.S. citizenship under?"

"The same."

"And you'd been married twice? First to Rance Woodley, then to Thaddeus Sheets in later years, and at the present you are a divorced woman. Is this correct?" Howard asked.

"Yes," Lindy said.

"Thank you," Howard said and then fired the first volley. "What was your relationship to Danny Biggers?"

"Just someone I knew," she said.

"You visited him in prison," Howard said.

She shrugged. "There's no law against that."

"No, but there are laws against human trafficking and kidnapping. We have the phone records between you and Biggers in which you text directions to a specific home to snatch a child, the meeting places and money offered for the delivery of said child, a three-year-old girl named Lili Glass who was stolen from her home by Danny Biggers with the intention of delivering her to you at a bar called Fuzzy Fridays near Jubilee, Kentucky."

"No comment."

Then Agent Pickard stepped in.

"When the drop didn't happen, why did you run?" he asked.

Lindy shrugged. "No comment."

"Who were you running from?" Pickard asked.

"No comment."

"Then let me make a few comments that might encourage you to reconsider your silence. We know you are a member of a human trafficking ring. We know you are the lure. The hunter. You lead innocent young women into traps and those women are never seen again. But we also know what happens to people within your organization when the deliveries are made, and what happens to those people when they fail. Who's your boss, Melinda? You weren't just running from the law. You were running from your boss because you left evidence behind tying you to Lili Glass's kidnapping. Your boss doesn't like loose ends, does he?"

Lindy looked at her lawyer, then back at them. "You don't have anything but a few texts and the word of some hookers. That won't stand up in court."

"Oh, we have plenty. You weren't your boss's only loose end. Kevin Vanzant is dead."

Lindy gasped before she thought, and then tried to cover it up.

"I don't know anyone by that name," she said.

"How about Dewey Zane?" Howard asked. "He killed Vanzant under orders, and he's sitting in prison awaiting trial, given he lives long enough to get there. Your name is on the boss's hit list, too, isn't it? That's why you ran. Emily Payne has been arrested. And now we have you, and don't assume you'll be safe in jail, because Danny Biggers was found dead in his cell in a federal prison and we're still trying to find out who got to him. So you're not safe. You'll never be safe as long as your boss is still out there giving orders to tie up his loose ends."

Lindy's head was spinning. *Oh my God, oh my God. He's wiping out everyone connected to him, and he'll walk away without a worry.*

She looked at Holder. He nodded.

"I want a deal," she said.

"You give us everything. Names, contacts. Money drops. The people who bought the women. The parents who knowingly bought stolen children. We want it all, and in return the judge will take your cooperation into consideration when you're sentenced. It's either that or a cell in hell."

"One question," she muttered.

Howard shrugged. "You can ask."

"How did you find me?" Lindy asked.

"Your ex-husband."

Lindy rolled her eyes. "Rance Woodley? I'd almost forgotten he existed."

"Your ex-husband is an officer of the law. You're involved in human trafficking right under his nose, and you forgot? You're two kinds of stupid, lady, and that was your mistake, too," Howard said. "Now start talking. We need your boss's name. Where he keeps his records. Where he banks the trafficking money. Who else is a part of the ring."

"I need to pee," Lindy said.

"Then talk fast, because you're not leaving this room until your confession and information is on record."

"That's not fair," she whined.

"That's probably what all of your victims thought when they got drugged and turned into prostitutes."

Holder frowned. "You have options. Make a choice," he reminded her.

Lindy chose to talk.

It was nearing 3:00 p.m. when Rusty's cell phone rang. She'd been cleaning and rearranging the pantry for over an hour, and Cameron had gone outside with Ghost, and then went after him when the dog flushed something out of the bushes and chased it into the barn.

Rusty wiped her hands and then grabbed her phone from the table. "Hello."

"It's me," Howard said. "Lindy Sheets talked. It's Jack Barton. I'll fill you in on all the details after we get there, but we're still more than thirty minutes out, and we have info Barton just bought a plane ticket online to Malaysia. He may already be spooked. The last thing we need is for him to disappear like Lindy Sheets. I need you and Pope at the campsite ASAP. Detain him for questioning, and ask Chief Warren and some of his officers for backup. We'll land at the campground."

"Yes, sir," Rusty said. She dropped the phone in her pocket and ran outside, calling Cameron's name.

Cameron had Ghost by the collar and was already leading him out of the barn. The critter he'd cornered in the barn had been a porcupine, and Ghost had come close to having a mouth full of quills.

He was giving Ghost a talking to when he heard the back door slam and saw Rusty running out. He could tell by the tone of her voice that something was wrong. He turned loose of Ghost's collar and shouted, "Ghost! Go home!" and started running, with Ghost leading the way.

Ghost met Rusty in the yard, and Cameron was two steps behind.

"What's wrong?" he asked.

"Howard called. Lindy talked. It's Barton, and we have to get to Barton's campground now. They think he may be planning to bolt. Howard and Pickard are coming in by chopper. They want us to detain him for questioning until they get there."

"Then we're going in armed. Meet me at the Jeep," he said.

They both raced into the house, Cameron going one way, Rusty another. She came running with her cell phone, her coat unzipped, leaving her handgun and shoulder holster in full view.

Cameron was loading Ghost into the Jeep when she jumped into the front seat. And while he was speeding down the drive, she was calling Sonny Warren's cell.

Cameron was already on the blacktop and flying down the mountain when Warren answered.

"Chief Warren speaking."

"Chief, this is Agent Caldwell. I need backup."

She began explaining what was happening, and by the time she hung up, Cameron was already in Jubilee and on the street heading out of town.

They were on the two-mile stretch leading out to Barton's campground when they began hearing sirens behind them. "We need to get there before Barton knows those sirens are for him," Rusty said.

Cameron tightened his grip on the steering wheel and stomped the accelerator. One mile passed. The wheels were humming. The scenery was a blur, and then the campground came into view and Cameron slowed down enough to take the turn.

Barton was outside, throwing suitcases into his SUV when he saw them, and the moment he saw Rusty's face, he turned and ran for the office.

"He knows!" Cameron said as they skidded to a halt, but Rusty was already out of the Jeep and running with her weapon drawn.

"Shit!" Cameron muttered, and opened the door. Ghost bolted after Rusty before he could stop him, and the race was on.

Jack had his desk drawer open and was reaching for his handgun when Rusty leaped into the doorway, still running, with her gun aimed straight at his chest.

"Hands up!" she shouted. "Now!"

"Like hell!" Jack yelled, and pulled out his weapon.

He didn't see the dog until it was too late.

Ghost cleared the desk running, hit Jack hard against his shoulder, then clamped his teeth into the side of Jack's face.

Jack screamed out in pain as the gun went off.

Cameron crossed the threshold just as the gun discharged. He saw Rusty on the floor and for a second thought she'd been hit, until she rolled to her feet and grabbed Jack's gun.

"I've got the gun. Call Ghost off!" she shouted.

Jack was screaming, "Get him off! Get him off!"

"Ghost! Down! Down!" Cameron commanded.

Ghost dropped, blood dripping from his jaws, awaiting orders.

Rusty took a deep breath, pulled out the handcuffs she'd brought with her, and had Jack on his belly and cuffed, facedown on the floor, just as backup arrived.

Chief Warren was the first one in the office, followed by three of his deputies.

"Jesus," Warren muttered.

"We had a difference of opinion," Rusty said. "Would you please call for an ambulance?"

"Absolutely," the chief said, and stepped outside to make the call.

Cameron was still trying to wrap his head around watching the woman he loved chasing a bad guy with a gun. He'd heard the tales, but seeing her in action was startling.

"Are you okay?" he asked.

She nodded. "I ducked."

Sonny Warren was back in the doorway. "Ambulance is on the way."

"Thank you," Rusty said. "There's a chopper inbound. Make sure your patrol cars are out of the way enough for it to land."

"Right," Warren said, and waved a couple of his officers over to move their cars.

Jack was shaking from the pain. "I need to call my lawyer," he kept mumbling.

"Does he know how to sew up your face?" Rusty asked.

"No, but—"

"Then first things first, hot shot," Rusty said. "The EMTs will patch up your face. You'll go for a ride with the good guys for a change, and then you get to call your lawyer."

Jack groaned. He was getting too light-headed to argue and passed out from the pain.

Rusty felt Barton's pulse. It was strong and steady. "He's okay," she said.

"I hear the ambulance. It'll be here shortly," Cameron said.

Rusty leaned against the desk and holstered her weapon, thinking finally this was over. Yet even as she thought it, something felt undone.

As the ambulance came nearer the siren got louder, and Ghost whined and stood up.

"Maybe you should put him in the Jeep," Rusty said. "The place is going to be a madhouse."

"Exactly my thought," Cameron said. "Ghost. With me."

Ghost looked at Rusty to see if she was coming.

Cameron sighed. "Ghost. With me. Come on, boy."

The dog turned and followed Cameron out of the office, and then hopped back up into the Jeep. Cameron grabbed a bottle of water, poured some in a bowl he kept in the Jeep, and watched the dog drinking.

"Wash that blood out of your mouth real good, boy. That was a bad man you took down."

Ghost was still drinking when Cameron locked the Jeep. He was halfway back to the office before he realized he was still carrying his rifle, and then shrugged and kept it with him anyway.

The ambulance was pulling into the driveway. It was the same team who'd come after Lili. Billy, Fagan, and B. J. Kelly. When Billy and Fagan jumped out with their bags and went inside, Kelly followed.

Rusty looked up as the medics entered, and saw the older man behind them looking in horror at Barton, who still lay in a growing puddle of blood.

"Is he dead?" Kelly asked, and then he saw the gun in Rusty's holster and started toward her.

Three steps forward and he was in her face. "You killed him!" he shouted, then doubled up his fist and hit her on the jaw, knocking her unconscious. He grabbed her weapon and began waving it at everyone in the room. "Back off! All of you, just back off or I'll kill her!" he shouted.

"Kelly! What the hell?" Warren shouted and pulled his weapon, and when he did, every officer with him did the same.

Now there were six guns all aimed at B. J. Kelly, and it didn't seem to faze him.

Cameron came in the door, saw the guns trained on

Kelly, Rusty unconscious on the floor, and B. J. Kelly with a gun aimed at her back.

"You don't want to do this!" the chief shouted. "Put the gun down and we can talk."

"She killed Jack. She didn't have to kill him," B. J. kept saying.

Every fiber of Cameron's being went right back to war. The rifle was in his hands. He swung it up, aimed straight at Kelly's shoulder, and fired.

Kelly flew backward, hitting a chair and then a file cabinet. The gun was on the floor, and Cameron kicked it out of the way as he scooped Rusty up in his arms.

"Now you can talk to him," Cameron said, and carried Rusty out of the building.

"Williams. Get the gun," the chief ordered, and then ran over to where Kelly was lying.

"I'm bleeding. Help me," Kelly moaned.

The chief frowned. "You didn't have to do this. Agent Caldwell didn't even fire her weapon. Barton isn't dead. He just passed out because Pope's dog bit him in the face." Then he looked up at one of his officers. "Call for another ambulance."

Rusty came to as Cameron was carrying her out of the office. She saw a muscle jerking at the side of his jaw.

"What happened?" she asked, and then felt pain in her jaw. "Who hit me?"

"The ambulance driver, but I have no idea why," Cameron said, then put her down long enough to open the door to his Jeep and sat her down inside.

Ghost poked his head between the seats and began licking her cheek where she'd been hit.

"Thank you, buddy, but I'm okay," Rusty said, and stroked his head once to reassure him. As she did, she realized her gun wasn't in her holster.

"My service weapon. It must have fallen out."

"No. Kelly took it off you after he knocked you out. He thought you killed Barton. He was waving it all over the place, threatening to kill you."

Rusty's eyes widened. "Why would he care what happened to Barton?"

"Don't know," Cameron said.

Rusty frowned. "What happened to Kelly?"

"I shot him. He'll live."

And then she heard the inbound chopper and looked up above his head.

"The cavalry has arrived," she said.

"They can pick up the pieces of this mess," Cameron said. "As soon as you clear it with them, I'm taking you home."

"I won't argue with that," Rusty said. "But I need to talk to them first."

"Fine. But I'm right beside you," he said.

Rusty slid out of the seat and leaned into his embrace.

"I wouldn't have it any other way," she said.

The chopper was coming in for a landing when Pickard looked down.

"There's an ambulance on-site."

Howard frowned. "Maybe it was called in with the backup," he said, and then they were on the ground and he saw Rusty Caldwell standing near the office with Pope's arm around her.

"Don't shut down. We won't be long," Howard said.

They got out running, ducking their heads against the flying dust as they headed to the office.

"You missed all the shouting," Rusty said as they arrived.

Cameron gave her a look. "So did you."

Rusty shrugged. "He's right. I was somewhat unconscious for a while. You'll have to get the lowdown from Cameron and the police chief."

Howard frowned. "Did you get Barton?"

"Uh, technically, Ghost got Barton."

Pickard blinked. "A ghost?"

"Not a ghost. My dog, Ghost," Cameron said. "Barton's inside getting patched up. Ghost rearranged a little bit of his face."

"Jesus," Howard muttered, and walked inside, his eyes popping when he saw Barton flat on his back getting bandages on his cheek and another man bloody and unconscious on the other side of the room.

Barton was moaning and cursing. "You shot Bear. You sonsabitches shot my brother."

Rusty froze. "Bear? Oh my God! The unknown man is Barton's twin!"

Jack Barton heard her. "Yes, he's my twin. We found each other through a DNA test site. He's why I bought land here. Why I built the campground. So we could be together... And you killed him."

Chief Warren toed the heel of Barton's shoe.

"Well, it's obvious you two are brothers. You both seem to be missing a measure of good sense. Kelly tried to kill a federal agent, thinking you were dead, when you were only dog bit. And you're threatening and cursing a blue streak about your brother being dead, and he's just unconscious from a shoulder wound. You need to stop talking while you're still ahead," Warren drawled.

Rusty moved into Barton's line of sight.

"Chief Warren is right," she said. "We already knew a man named Bear was responsible for getting Emily Payne and Kevin Vanzant sucked into your gang. And God only knows how many other innocent women he dumped in your lap. But we didn't know who Bear was...until now. He was the last unknown, and you're the one who gave him up."

Howard waved an arrest warrant in Barton's face and read him his rights, and then they pulled him up to his feet as the second ambulance rolled onto the scene.

The second EMT crew came running into the building, unprepared for the scene before them, then saw B.J. Kelly on the floor and raced toward him. They dropped to their knees beside him. One was cutting off his shirt to get to the wound, while the other paused long enough to ask, "What happened?"

"He tried to kill a federal officer is what happened. And when the son of a bitch comes to, he'll be under arrest for his participation in a human trafficking ring," the chief said.

Both Billy and Fagan were in shock. B.J. Kelly was their friend. He'd been the ambulance driver in Jubilee for years. To learn he'd been mixed up in something this ugly had them rattled to the core. They gathered up their equipment and stood up without looking at where Kelly was lying.

"Mr. Barton is all yours, officers. Good enough to travel," Billy Jackson said.

"Plenty well enough to make the ride to a prison hospital," Fagan Jennings added, and they left the site and headed back into town, leaving the two other EMTs working on stabilizing Kelly enough to transport him back to the hospital.

"I'm taking Rusty to the ER to make sure she doesn't have another concussion," Cameron said.

"Yes. Absolutely," Howard said. "Good job, both of you. We've got this covered now. We'll be in touch," Howard said.

Cameron didn't respond, and Rusty wasn't going to announce her resignation in the middle of a takedown. It seemed a little tacky.

She was grateful for Cameron's steadying arm as they went back to the Jeep, and when he started the engine, she leaned back against the headrest and closed her eyes as they drove away.

"I'm so sorry, darlin'," Cameron said. "I should have been there."

Rusty reached for him. "You were there. You and Ghost saved me. Then she sighed. "I'm going to be sucking my food through a straw again."

"We'll be fine. As long as I know you're okay, I don't give a tinker's damn what we eat."

Ghost whined.

"I think Ghost just voted against soup," Rusty said.

Cameron shook his head. "He's sad because he smells your hurt."

"Oh my God," Rusty whispered. "Are you serious?"

Ghost's head appeared between the seats again, and once again he nosed her cheek.

"See? He can smell the hurt," Cameron said.

Too moved to speak, Rusty wrapped her arm around the big dog's neck and hugged him.

"I am the luckiest woman in the world. My two best guys saved my life today."

―――――――――

It was after dark by the time Cameron got Rusty home. The good news was she had not suffered a concussion, and her jaw was intact. But her entire head was throbbing to the point that it hurt to blink.

She staggered when she started to get out of the Jeep, and seconds later she was in Cameron's arms. "I've got you, darlin'. Let's get inside out of the cold,"

Ghost shot into the house first and did his usual run-through, then went back to the fireplace and flopped down.

"What do you need first?" Cameron asked. "Food? A shower? You name it and I'll make it happen."

"I just want to go to bed," Rusty said.

Cameron carried her all the way through the house to his bedroom, put her down on the side of his bed and went to get her pajamas. When he came back, she was trying to get out of her shoes.

"Let me," he said, and gently began stripping her down, then dressing her for bed as if she was a child.

She pointed to the bathroom. "I need—"

"Can you walk?"

She nodded and went to wash up, then took some pain meds while he was pulling back the covers. When she came out, he was waiting for her.

"You are my love, but you're also my best friend," she mumbled as she climbed up onto the bed and stretched out.

He tucked her in, then leaned over and brushed a kiss across her forehead.

"Sleep, sweetheart. I'll be in later."

"I'm fine," she mumbled.

Cameron sat on the side of the bed for a few moments, looking at every nuance of her face, touching the tumble of curls lying on the pillow beneath her head, waiting for her breathing to shift. Waiting for her body to relax.

And when he was certain that she was okay, he left the room.

Ghost was lying in the hall, waiting.

"She's okay, boy. Wanna go outside?"

Ghost jumped up and trotted to the back door. Cameron turned on the porch light as they walked out, and then he sat down in a chair beneath the light as Ghost began to make his rounds, sniffing bushes, sniffing the woodpile, trotting in circles as he traced the tracks of random animals that had crossed into his territory.

Cameron didn't know he was crying until the tears turned cold on his cheeks. He swiped them away with the heels of his hands and drew a deep, shuddering breath. He'd never loved this hard before. Not in this way. And she'd dodged death twice today…both times at the hands of brothers.

God, please…this has to be enough.

He needed her in his life like he needed to breathe.

As he was sitting, his cell phone rang. It was Howard.

"I'm checking in to make sure she's okay," he said.

"No concussion. No broken bones. But she has the headache from hell and staggers when she walks. I just put her to bed."

There was a long moment of silence, and then Howard sighed. "I didn't think it was going to get that bad that quick."

"You can't predict stuff like this," Cameron said. "But having this happen on the heels of still healing from the other case she was on has really taken it out of her."

"Thank you for stepping up," Howard said.

"I'll never regret that. It brought her back to me," Cameron said.

"Is the agency losing her?" Howard asked.

"You'll have to ask her that," Cameron said.

"Understood. I'll send details later. We've found records that might help us locate some of the women who were sold. That would be the icing on the cake, but that's all on us. We think we've located the money trail. Oh, and tell her that Danny Biggers's autopsy was inconclusive. There is no reason for why he died, other than the doctor at the prison said Biggers wanted to. We're sending our best wishes for her to get well soon."

"I will tell her," Cameron said.

The call ended, and so did Ghost's sortie into the wilderness behind the house. Cameron whistled, and Ghost came running. Cameron leaned down and hugged him.

"Thank you for saving our girl," he said softly, and buried his face in the fur on Ghost's neck.

———

The house was quiet.

Rusty's sleep was restless, likely from the pain, but Cameron wasn't sleeping at all. He was on alert with every uneven breath she took, every tear that rolled down her cheek, and every moan that came from between her lips.

She woke up with a jerk, mumbled something about "hitting the deck," and then fell back to sleep.

Cameron got up, stirred the embers in the fireplace, and added another log. Ghost opened one eye long enough to see what was happening and huffed softly as if he was acknowledging his master's presence, then snuggled deeper into his bed.

Cameron covered him with the old quilt again, and then went to the kitchen and made a cup of coffee. When he looked out, the ground was white and the air was full of snowflakes so huge they looked like feathers. He stood at the window, watching the snow spinning into an eddy beneath the security light and drinking coffee simply for the boost of caffeine. He'd sleep when she was well.

It was just after sunup, but Cameron's phone was on fire. After a half-dozen texts and three phone calls, all from family, the secrecy of Rusty's presence and what had been happening in Jubilee was unraveling. But it didn't matter. His entire focus was on the woman in his bed.

The snow was still falling but lighter now, and Ghost was thoroughly disgusted by the depth of it to the point that he'd cut his ramblings short and meandered only far enough away to do his business before running back to the house.

Cameron was watching from the back door, and when Ghost started running, he opened the door and stepped back, knowing the moment the dog's wet feet hit the floor he was going to slide.

Cameron grinned. "Nice landing," he said, and shut the door.

He grabbed a towel and began digging the snowpack

from between Ghost's toe pads, then gave him a chew bone for his troubles.

Ghost trotted off with it hanging from his mouth like a big cigar.

A few moments later Cameron heard footsteps, and then Rusty walked into the kitchen. She was wearing her heaviest sweatshirt and oldest jeans and thick fuzzy socks with her house slippers. Her curls looked like she'd combed them with her fingers and called it done, and the side of her face where Kelly hit her was purple and the eye above it was turning black.

"Ah God…honey. If you'd looked like that yesterday, I wouldn't have stopped at winging him," Cameron muttered, and wrapped his arms around her. "Want some coffee?"

She nodded and slid down into a chair at the table.

"How about oatmeal? I made some, and you won't have to chew," Cameron said.

Rusty nodded again. She could talk, but every time she opened her mouth, her jaw popped so hard it felt like it was falling off her face, so it wasn't worth the pain.

Cameron brought the hot cereal to the table. It had a pat of butter melting on top, and he set a bowl of brown sugar and a carton of half-and-half in front of her to let her do her thing.

She gave him a big thumbs-up and doctored the cereal to her liking, then opened her mouth just enough to slide in the first bite.

"Ummm. Thanks," she said.

"Just eat. I'll talk."

She nodded and took her second bite.

"So here's the scoop," Cameron said. "Various scenarios of the truth are all over Jubilee, but close enough not to be libelous."

She smiled at the phrasing and then winced and nodded instead.

"Agent Howard called me last night after you were asleep. He thinks they're going to be able to locate some of the women who were sold, or at least a starting point to finding some. He also said they've found a money trail. I'm paraphrasing here, but he kind of apologized for sending you into a volatile situation. He thought they'd get Barton before that happened. He thanks you, and he'll be in touch."

She rolled her eyes and shook her head. "I'm done," she mumbled.

Cameron sighed. *Thank you, Lord.*

"I'm not going to pretend that's not the best news I've ever heard, because that would be a lie. I'm not sure I'd survive long watching you running into burning buildings instead of away from them. And yes, that was an analogy, but you get my drift."

"Not sure I'd survive it again, either," she said, then finished the oatmeal and carried her bowl to the sink, then went back to the table and plopped down in Cameron's lap. "You. Me. No more wars," she said.

Cameron cupped the back of her head and laid his cheek against the curls.

"You. Me. Forever after?" he said.

She met his gaze.

"Deal. Love you," she said, then winced again. "Ice?"

"Yes, for your jaw?"

She nodded.

"Go find a comfortable place to be. I'll bring it to you."

She hugged him, then chose the sofa in the living room and stretched out by the fire. He was moments behind her with one of the ice packs he kept in his freezer. He had wrapped it in a hand towel.

She laid it on the side of her face, but she could tell he was at war with himself. He couldn't fix her, but he didn't want to let her out of his sight.

"Do what you need to do," she mumbled.

"I need to do for you, because right now you hurt my heart," Cameron said, then unfolded the blanket from the back of the sofa and covered her up. "I think we need to let your family know you're okay. I'll call them for you if you want."

She gave him a thumbs-up and closed her eyes.

"TV, please?"

He picked up the remote and hit Power, then put it in her hands and walked out of the room to make the call.

Chapter 19

LIZ CALDWELL WAS ALREADY AT WORK, BUT RAY WAS STILL in the penthouse.

The town was buzzing with news about the arrests and the shootings, and the stories ranged from the absurd to horrific. He couldn't focus enough on work to bother going to the office until he'd heard from Rusty, and he didn't know if it was kosher to call her first.

Patricia was due to come home today, and he could only imagine the fit she was going to have when she found out about all this. When his phone rang, he didn't recognize the number, but at this point screening calls was the last thing on his mind.

"Hello, this is Ray."

"Mr. Caldwell, this is Cameron Pope. Rusty wanted me to call and let you know she's fine. All of the bad guys have been rounded up."

"Thank God. I've been worried sick, but where is she? Why didn't she call?" Ray said.

"She's at my house. She has been working from here ever since she left the hotel. We were in on the episode out at the campground. Rusty has a sore jaw and a black eye, so talking is not on her agenda right now.

But nothing is broken, and other than being miserable, she's fine."

"Thank you, Cameron, thank you. I feel like I can breathe now. Please give her our love, and ask her to let us know before she leaves town again."

"She's not leaving. And since her father isn't alive to hear this, I'm asking you. I'm going to marry your niece, and I'm asking for your blessing. She's put her life on the line for Uncle Sam for the last time."

"This is wonderful news! And of course you have my blessing. Welcome to the family," Ray said.

"And welcome to mine," Cameron said.

Ray laughed. "I suspect you have us outnumbered, but Rusty never wanted to be an only child. She will be elated."

Cameron laughed. "She hasn't met them all yet, and some of them are characters, but there's not a bad one in the bunch. And they're going to love her. With all her heart and fire, she's going to fit right in."

Ray was still chuckling when he hung up, but it felt like a weight had just lifted from his shoulders. He dropped his phone in his suit coat, patted his pocket to make sure he had his key card, and headed for the elevator.

Just as he reached the foyer, the door opened in front of him and one of the bellhops emerged pushing a luggage cart full of bags, packages, and suitcases, with Patricia right behind him.

"Darling!" Patricia said, and threw her arms around Ray's neck as the bellhop pushed the luggage cart down the hall to the master suite. "I've missed you terribly. I can't wait to tell you what we did and the shows we saw while I was gone."

Ray shook his head, smiling wryly. "You didn't miss anyone. You called me once and Liz twice, and wait until you hear what all you've missed while you were gone."

Patricia blinked.

The bellhop came back with the empty luggage cart, got on the elevator and went down, leaving them staring at each other in the foyer.

"What do you mean? Oh, never mind. Liz will tell me. I'm going to wake her up. She'll be furious but she'll get over it. I brought prezzies."

"Liz is at work, and I have a meeting in fifteen minutes. I'll be back to have lunch with you later. We can talk then. Love you, darling. Don't work too hard unpacking."

Patricia was aghast. "What do you mean, Liz is at work?"

"Oh, she came and asked me for a job while you were gone. She's interning for my event coordinator and loving every minute of it. And Gerald says she's doing a bang-up job. Gotta go." He paused and looked at her again, only closer, then gave her a long, lingering welcome-home kiss. "You've lost weight. I love that shade of blond in your hair, and you look sexy as hell. Hold that thought."

Patricia's cheeks were burning but there was a twinkle in her eye.

"Well then," she said, and turned around to face the empty penthouse, then decided it felt so good to be home it didn't matter if she was alone.

Cameron had one other call to make, and that was to Leslie Morgan.

He knew she'd already be at work, but she would be hearing all the gossip and he wanted her to know that she was safe.

He pulled up the number to the vet clinic and called the office.

"Carson Veterinary Clinic. This is Amber."

"Amber, this is Cameron Pope. Is Leslie at work?"

"Yes, she is."

"I need to give her a brief message, but if she's busy she can call me back."

"It's kind of slow this morning, Cameron. She's just down the hall. Hang on a sec."

Moments later, Leslie picked up the call.

"This is Leslie."

"Hey, Leslie. This is Cameron. I just wanted you to know you're in the clear. You can go back to your place anytime you want. All the bad guys are in custody in other parts of the state."

"Oh, thank God," Leslie said. "That's the best news I've had in a while. Thank you so much for keeping my name out of all that and for letting me know."

"You're welcome, and my best to your family."

"Hey, Cam, one other thing."

"Yeah, what's that?"

"Is it true about you and the pretty redhead?"

"I don't know what you heard, but she's in my life and not going anywhere, if that's what you want to know."

Leslie smiled. "Yes. That's what I heard. Congratulations."

"Thanks. Take care," Cameron said.

"You too," Leslie said. She shivered as she laid down the phone, so grateful that the nightmare was over, and in that moment she heard Granny Cauley's words. *And this, too, shall pass.*

Rusty wrote her final report on the case, including the important part Cameron Pope had played in helping solve it, and sent it to Agent Howard. Then she wrote her letter of resignation, signed it personally, and faxed it to her superior in DC. The feeling afterward was of relief. There was no one left to whom she owed allegiance but the man who held her heart.

She sent a text to Liz to tell her she was okay, that she was recovering from a slight injury that made talking a little uncomfortable, and she'd be in touch.

A few minutes later, she got a text back from Liz.

What the hell, Rusty? Do you still have all your teeth?

Rusty laughed out loud, and then groaned from the pain of movement, took a selfie of her face, and sent it to Liz.

For your eyes only.

Liz sent back a series of emojis registering shock, tears, and added an eye roll for good measure.

Oh. My. God. You freaking rock. Love you.
Oh. You'll be proud of me. I'm interning with
the event coordinator at the hotel. Don't tell
anyone, but I love it. Even getting up early to
go to work. You were a terrible influence on
me. I have become an adult.

Rusty sent her a big heart emoji that ended their conversation, but it felt good to have their family connection again.

There were things she had to do to cut her last ties with the past, and one of them was closing up her apartment. But she had friends in high places and numbers to all the good moving companies and considered that inconsequential. What she did want was the rest of her clothes. She'd only packed for a quick trip, not for the rest of her life, but that was all for another day. Today was for ice on her face, and soup in a bowl, and snuggles beneath the blankets and quilts from the generations of Popes who'd come before.

It was daunting to realize she was going to become part of the history of this place. That she and Cameron would be adding to the next generation of Popes on Pope Mountain. She'd always wanted to leave her mark on the world in some way, but she'd never thought her red hair would be part of her legacy. Redheaded babies on the mountain were going to shine like new pennies, considering the number of people she'd met with Indian black hair and dark eyes.

She took the ice pack to the kitchen to refreeze it, then went back to the living room, crawled back beneath the blanket, and closed her eyes.

She was almost asleep when she heard Ghost's nails clicking on the floor, felt his nose against her sore cheek, and then a gentle lick.

"Thank you, buddy," she murmured.

She didn't know when Cameron came in to stir the fire, or that it had started snowing again. And for the first time in her adult life, she was not on alert for sounds that didn't belong. She would never have to call for backup or put herself in danger to right a wrong again. She had a one-man army and a Ghost, and they'd given her a home.

———

Rusty's first meeting with Cameron's family came with a black eye and a bruise on her face the size of B. J. Kelly's fist. Once word got around that Cameron was marrying a fed, they all made excuses to come meet her. Back in the day, they'd hidden their stills of moonshine from federal agents, and the old ways of distrust still ran deep.

Until they saw her.

She delighted them and then entranced them. She'd been a real-life, gun-toting warrior just like Cameron, only prettier. And now she was marrying into their family and becoming a Pope.

And as Wade Morgan said when he met her, "New blood makes the bloodline stronger. Can't wait to see the first redheaded baby."

Every day after that, someone found a reason to come to Cameron's place. And every day, Rusty met another uncle, or two sets of cousins, or someone's grandma twice removed. She'd given up trying to remember how they were all connected. All she knew were their names and that Cameron belonged to them, which meant she would, too.

Annie Cauley, Cameron's aunt, stopped by on her way home from the bakery one evening with an apple tart. She trudged through the snow to the front porch with it still warm in the box and beamed when Rusty came to the door.

"Evenin', honey. I'm your Aunt Annie. Cam and Rachel's mama was my oldest sister."

"You have the bakery in town!" Rusty said. "Come in out of the cold."

Annie wiped her feet and handed over the tart after Rusty closed the door.

"We're in the kitchen," Rusty said, and led the way.

Ghost was lying against the back door like a guard doing sentry duty. He wagged his tail when he saw their guest but didn't bother getting up.

"Hi, Auntie," Cameron said. "What did you bring?"

"Apple tart, but now that I see your girl's poor face, I should have brought custard," she said.

"No, no. I'm not so sore now. It looks worse than it feels," Rusty said. "This is much appreciated."

Annie Cauley paused, giving Rusty a long silent look, and then nodded approvingly.

"You have grit, girl. I can see it in your face. You don't look away from someone staring, and it's apparent you don't run from a fight. I see your heart." Then she shifted focus to Cameron. "It took you forever. We were beginning to think you were gonna let the Pope name die."

Cameron grinned. "Thank you for your candor."

Rusty liked this woman on sight. "We'll do our best not to let you down," she said.

"No pressure or anything. Just a fact. And speaking of facts, when's the wedding and where's it gonna be held?" Annie asked.

Cameron slid his arm around Rusty's shoulder.

"We decided the week before Easter…at the ballroom at the Serenity Inn. Ray Caldwell and his family are all the relatives Rusty has left. We'll need all that room for friends and family."

"Grand idea," Annie said, and then reached for Rusty's hand and clasped it between her own. "Just remember… marrying my nephew lands you square in the middle of the biggest clan in Kentucky. We mind our own business, but we're always there for each other, and if you need a simple hug or some help, all you have to do is call. Now I better get home. John will be wanting his supper."

"Thank you for the apple tart," Rusty said. "And since you offered, I'll take a hug before you go."

Annie threw her arms around Rusty and held onto her like there was no tomorrow, then did the same to Cameron.

"Your mama would be so proud of you, Cam. But since she's not here, I'm gonna be proud of you for her. You two go on about your business. I'll just let myself out."

Cameron walked her to the door anyway, then waved as she drove away before coming back inside.

"I just love her," Rusty said.

"So do I. Of all my mother's siblings, Annie is the most like her. Now, where were we?" he asked.

"Peeling potatoes and carrots to put in with the roast," Rusty said.

"And apple tart for dessert. I call this a good day," he said.

"I call every day with you a good day," Rusty said, and took the kiss coming at her square on the lips.

The turmoil in Jubilee had passed, and while wedding plans continued, life had taken a nosedive for a few former residents. After a brief and final message from Agent Howard, Rusty and Cameron learned the fate of those they'd taken down.

Once the details of Emily Payne's involvement within the gang were made known, and the level of pressure and coercion that had been used upon her was taken into consideration, her charges were dropped to theft and credit card fraud.

Dewey Zane's fear for his wife ended when he learned Barton and Kelly were both behind bars. And when Carly quit calling, he knew she was gone. He also accepted he would likely die in prison and that made him sad, but it was nothing less than he deserved.

Just before Christmas, and acting on behalf of his client, Jack Barton's lawyer contacted a Realtor. Barton's Tiny Cabins and Campground was officially for sale.

Lindy Sheets's willingness to cooperate with the FBI in taking down the rest of the gang didn't impress the judge who ultimately sentenced her. By their count, she'd participated in the kidnapping of more than 143 women from across the country, knowing full well they were being sold into sex slavery, and the kidnapping and selling of more than a dozen children under the age of four. She wound up sentenced and buried so deep in the prison system that she was never going to walk the streets a free woman again.

Kevin Vanzant's body was buried in a cemetery in his hometown, beside the parents who'd kicked him out before he turned sixteen. The irony of his final resting place was lost upon humanity. He hadn't mattered to anyone before, but in the grand scheme of things, it was God who took him home.

Epilogue

RUSTY WOKE BEFORE DAYBREAK.

She was getting married today!

She rolled over, scooted up closer to Cameron's backside and slid her arm around his waist, and buried her nose in the middle of his back, waiting for the rumble of his laughter, and it came.

"Woman, you breathe on me like Ghost does. What do you want?"

"You," Rusty said. "Make love to me while I'm still wild and single. Tonight I'll be sleeping with a married man."

Cameron was still laughing as he rolled over and kissed her, and then the last laugh died as he took her hard and fast.

Between one second and the next, he was inside her. All thought vanished. For the next few minutes, there was nothing that mattered but the rhythmic motion of man to woman chasing that shattering blood rush.

His hands were tangled in her hair.

Her legs were locked around his waist.

Sweat was running down his back when he heard her gasp. When he felt her tense, he opened his eyes. She was looking at him, her gaze locked on his face as the climax washed over her. He saw her pupils dilate, then contract before she closed her eyes in silent ecstasy. He let go and came inside her.

When Cameron's heartbeat finally leveled, he rolled over onto his back, taking her with him.

"I will never take this or you for granted. You…Faith Caldwell, I adore. You, I honor. You, I love. We may be making this legal today, but I've been yours since the first time I laid eyes on you."

Rusty cupped his cheek, feeling the stubble of black whiskers beneath her palm. "After you were gone, all I did was pray you would live to come home. I never imagined I would see you again…or that you would become my anchor, and the love of my life. Fate led me straight to your door, but you're the one who kept me. And while this was a glorious way to wake up, we have stuff to do. Are you sure Ghost will be okay here on his own this afternoon?"

"Absolutely. He'll get a bone to chew on and his bed to wallow in. And when I tell him to stay, he stays. He's done it plenty of times before. Besides, since we're honeymooning at home, we'll be back before dark."

The ballroom had been set up like a church, with chairs in rows like pews and a podium for Brother Farley, the preacher who would be performing the service. He was the pastor of the Church in the Wildwood, the only church on the mountain. It had served the people in the hills since the early 1900s, and Farley was the latest in a long line of preachers who'd gone before him. He'd met with Cameron and Rusty more than once and, at their request, agreed to come down the mountain just for them to perform this ceremony.

There was a backdrop of leafy greenery in the ballroom that had been set up on either side of the pulpit. And baskets of flowers in abundance—all in blue, white, and spring greens, the bride's chosen colors.

The aisle they'd created between the seating was covered in a long carpet of green, with standing baskets of flowers in the bride's colors on either side of the doorway where the guests would enter.

Leslie Morgan was manning the table with the guest book. She'd been seated just outside the ballroom doors and was excited to be participating in the event.

The wedding was Rusty's gift from Ray and Patricia, and her aunt had been in her element with planning and designing, leaving Liz and her boss in charge of the setup and the party afterward.

Guests had begun arriving just after one thirty, and the seating in the ballroom was filling up. One side was reserved for Cameron's family, with overflow to be seated in the back rows on the bride's side.

Michael Devon was there as Liz's date and was seated on the bride's side of the aisle.

Cameron and his entourage had dressed in a hotel meeting room just off the ballroom, while Rusty was dressing in the penthouse, unaware Cameron had asked Special Agents

Howard and Pickard to let her fellow agents know she was getting married and to RSVP to him with a head count.

As of today, thirty-four federal agents from both DC and Frankfort would be in attendance on her behalf.

It was a surprise he couldn't wait to reveal.

Patricia had teared up a dozen times while helping Rusty and Liz get ready and finally pulled herself together with a shot of whiskey.

"You were a beautiful baby, and you're an equally beautiful bride," Patricia said. "I love your dress. It's siren sexy, yet equal parts traditional and daring…just like you. Not a lot of lace. A neckline to die for, and a slightly naughty slit on the skirt, but not too high. Just enough to make a man wonder."

Rusty laughed. "I love you, Aunt Pat."

Patricia grinned. "I love you, too. Now let's get this veil pinned somewhere within those glorious curls and we'll be finished, and none too soon. We need to head downstairs."

As if on cue, Liz came out of her bedroom. "Mom, please zip me up."

Patricia fastened her daughter's dress, too, and then gave her a quick hug.

"You look beautiful. Both of you. And as I just told Rusty, I love these slim, fitted dresses. No lace and ruffles. No petticoats to fluff. Now…do we have everything? What about the flowers?"

Liz waved her mother out the door. "The florist is waiting downstairs with everything. You go ahead and take Daddy with you. He's in the living room, pacing. An usher will seat you, and Daddy will stay out in the hall to wait for Rusty, like we practiced."

"Okay, okay. Love you both," Patricia said, and left the room.

Liz reached for Rusty's hands and gave them a quick squeeze.

"I am sorry it took an accident to get you back in our lives, but I'll be forever grateful you found your forever man waiting for you here."

"Cousins by blood. Sisters of the heart," Rusty said. "Let's do this."

They headed for the elevator, then had a couple of minutes to wait for it to return. By the time they reached the ballroom floor, the last of the guests had been seated and were inside and waiting.

Ray Caldwell was with Gerald Devlin, the event planner. When Gerald saw the girls arrive, he waved them over, then eyed the florist as she handed Liz her bouquet, filled the flower girl's basket full of flower petals, and handed Rusty her bridal bouquet.

"Perfect," Gerald said. "You're all here. The flowers are done. The pastor is in place. The groom just walked into the room and is waiting at the altar. Liz, go find the best man… What's his name again?"

"Louis Glass," Liz said.

"Yes, yes, find Louis, please, and get in line. The flower

girl is waiting impatiently with her mother. We need to get this show on the road before she plants the petals in one of the urns."

Lili Glass had just turned four and was so delighted with her dress that she thought she was the one getting married. Then suddenly having flowers in her basket had shifted her focus from bride to fairy.

As everyone began to take their places, Ray slipped his hand beneath Rusty's elbow. As he did, she saw her father in his face and blinked away tears.

"My darling niece...you are such a beautiful bride. Thank you for this honor," Ray said, and kissed the back of her hand.

Then the doors to the ballroom opened.

The music began, signaling the beginning of the ceremony.

Liz and Louis went down the aisle side by side, but Rusty was looking for the man standing tall beside their tiny preacher.

This was happening! It was really, really, happening!

She noticed a large number of people who'd been seated on the bride's side of the aisle, but all she saw was the back of their heads so she assumed they were just more of Cameron's people.

Lili took off down the aisle toward her Unca Cam, waving and smiling, and then the people began turning toward the aisle to watch, delighted by the tiny girl throwing flower petals on the "green grass" and in wild abandon up in the air. By the time Lili reached the altar, her hair was as adorned as the aisle.

But it wasn't until Rusty and her uncle moved toward the entrance that she finally saw the strangers' faces. Only they weren't strangers. They were her people! The agents she'd known and worked with from the home office in DC. Even Howard and Pickard were there.

She leaned over, whispering, "Look, Uncle Ray. Those are all people from the FBI. Agents I once worked with. How did they know?"

"Cameron invited them. It was a surprise for you," he said.

Her eyes welled. "There are days when I'm certain I do not deserve him."

"No way," Ray said. "He is a good man. He asked my blessing for this marriage months ago, and he is exactly who you deserve."

And then the music changed.

"I believe this is our cue," he said as the notes of the "Wedding March" rolled out into the hallway.

Clutching her bouquet with one hand, Rusty slipped her other hand beneath his elbow, and then they crossed the threshold into the ballroom.

For the first time in years, she was pain-and-bruise-free, walking down that aisle with her chin up and her curls bouncing, walking toward the soldier boy who waited for his bride.

Once she reached his side, everything faded into the background but him. He took her hands and then winked as he turned to face her. Brother Farley was talking, his voice rising and falling in grandiose rhythm as he spoke, but she was waiting for her turn. And then it came, repeating the words the little preacher gave her.

"I, Faith, take thee, Cameron…"

Cameron was watching her face as she gave him her heart, absorbing all of the love she was vowing and the trust she was giving and waiting his turn. When it came, he too repeated the words Farley gave him in a clear, sure voice that echoed out across the ballroom just like an echo from the hills.

"I, Cameron, take thee, Faith…"

And it was done.

They cut cake and posed for pictures, and then the music began.

The first dance was theirs.

They'd never danced together before.

But it soon became evident that he danced as skillfully as he made love. When that song ended and another began, the first in a long line of friends appeared.

A big man in a too-tight suit tapped on Cameron's shoulder.

"Mr. Pope, my name is Browning. I have worked with your wife. Might I steal her away just for a moment?"

Cameron grinned. The look on Rusty's face was worth losing her to the next dance.

"Yes, you may, but take good care. I want her back."

Browning smiled. "The last time I saw this lady, she

was being chased by a boatload of pirates. It does my heart good to see her so happy."

Then he whisked her out of Cameron's arms and began their dance.

"You look lovely, my dear, and it's obvious you are happy. And may I say you have chosen quite a man. I know people who know him. When he served, he was hell on wheels in his own right. They talk about him and this dog when he was in country. They were quite a pair."

Rusty laughed. "You mean Ghost? He came home with Cameron. He's still doing his thing, too."

Browning laughed. "Wonderful! Wonderful! I did not know this!"

Halfway around the floor, Jay Howard cut in, and then Dan Pickard, and then her old boss from DC. She danced with men who'd rescued her and men who'd been her backup.

She danced with men from the mountain while Cameron swept their ladies around the room.

She danced with her uncle, and teenage boys with the last name Glass, and young men who were part of the Cauleys, and got hugs and best wishes from all the women from the Pope family, and ate cake and drank champagne until she was giddy.

When it was time to throw her bouquet, the single women gathered. There was a moment when she would have sworn she heard her mother's laughter, then she turned her back to the crowd and gave her bouquet a toss. But she threw it so high and so far that it overshot the women and came down within the men— straight into Michael Devon's hands.

He blushed and then laughed and marched it through the crowd of people slapping him on the back in good-natured teasing and handed it to Liz. She took the bouquet with a curtsy.

Then Cameron walked out of the crowd as more music swelled.

It was a waltz, and he'd come to claim his bride.

He took her in his arms and whispered in her ear.

"The last dance is mine."

Then he began turning her and dipping her in rhythm to the music, circling the floor with her, watching the light catch in her hair, and then disappear into the fiery depths.

As the music played on, more couples joined them.

Ray and Patricia. Liz and Michael. Louis and Rachel. Leslie with her father, Wade. John dancing with his Annie, and more couples joined them until it appeared as if the ballroom floor was spinning clockwise on its own.

And while no one was looking, Cameron danced his bride out of the ballroom all the way to the elevator and slipped her out of the hotel.

Night met them on the road up the mountain, pulling them farther, guiding them higher into the darkness, with music and memories still spinning in their heads.

The motion-detector lights came on as Cameron pulled beneath the carport.

Ghost began barking.

Cameron circled the car to help Rusty out, then walked

with her to the door. The moment it swung inward, Ghost shot past them and out into the backyard to make his rounds.

"Tradition, darlin'," Cameron said, then swept her up in his arms and carried her across the threshold and into the kitchen.

Their running shoes were tucked neatly beneath the kitchen table, and the jacket she'd worn outside to do morning chores was hanging from the back of a chair.

Ghost came bounding in behind them, making his run through the house to clear their path as Cameron put her down and closed the door.

Thank you, Lord, Rusty thought, and looked down at the gold band on her left finger, and then the matching one that he wore.

Their rings. A symbol of unbroken eternity, and she was counting on this and him for at least that long.

Cameron winked and gave her hand a soft tug.

"Rusty, darlin', welcome home. It's time to put a log on the fire and a dog in his bed."

She raised up on her toes and kissed him. "Thank you for the welcome. I am happy to be here," she said and followed him into the living room, watching as he went through their nightly routine before walking back into her arms. "You dance as beautifully as you make love. Can we do it again?"

He winked. "Resume the position."

She put one hand on his shoulder and the other on his waist, laughing as he two-stepped her down the hall and straight into bed.

"First things first," he said.

The lights went out and the clothes came off before they tumbled into bed.

Love came easy, because they'd been this way before.

Read on for an early look at

A thrilling new romance from Sharon Sala

Chapter 1

SHIRLEY WALLACE WOKE UP ON THE KITCHEN FLOOR WITH her son, Sean, hovering over her. He had a phone in one hand calling for an ambulance, while holding a kitchen towel pressed against the top of her head with the other.

The taste of blood was in her mouth.

Her body was one solid pain, and it hurt to breathe.

She could hear the frantic tone in his voice, but she couldn't focus enough to respond.

"Yes, yes, she's breathing and starting to regain consciousness, but she's bloody as hell, and I don't know where all the blood is coming from. Yes, I know who attacked her. Her husband, Clyde. No, I don't know where he is. Just hurry."

The 911 dispatcher's voice was calm and quiet even as he was dispatching emergency vehicles to the address.

"Sean, stay on the line with me until help arrives," he said.

"Call my brother," Sean said. "His name is Aaron Wallace. He's an officer with the Conway Police Department."

That was the last thing Shirley heard before darkness claimed her.

The next time she woke up, she was in the ER.

"Shirley! Can you hear me? My name is Dr. Malone, and you're in the ER"

"Where's my son?" she mumbled.

"He's just outside this room. You're safe. He's safe, and we're going to make you better."

———

Sean was frantically pacing outside the exam bay when he heard the sound of someone running up behind him. He turned to look, then breathed a sigh of relief. Aaron was here!

"How is she?" Aaron asked as he slid a hand across his brother's shoulder.

Sean shuddered. "I don't know. Jesus, Aaron. He's never hurt her like this before. I came in from running errands and found her like that. Her face is bloody and swollen. She's bleeding from both ears, and from a huge cut in her scalp, and she has broken ribs, for sure. Scared the hell out of me. Have they found Clyde?"

Aaron lowered his voice. "He's in jail. They're processing him now. Mom got off lucky. Clyde walked into a Quick Loan and shot two people dead. He's high as a kite and talking out of his head."

Sean froze, unable to believe what he was hearing. "What?"

Aaron gripped his brother's shoulders. "Our father just murdered two people in cold blood. Shit has hit the fan. Have you called Wiley? Does B.J. know?"

Sean's eyes welled. "Oh, my God. No...not yet."

Aaron nodded. "I'll do it. And I'll call the school for B.J. Did he ride his Harley this morning?"

Sean nodded.

"Okay. You just stay here with Mom. I'm going outside to make some calls."

It was the beginning of the end of life as they'd known it.

———— · ————

Within a week of leaving the hospital, Shirley Pope Wallace had filed for divorce. By the time Clyde Wallace's trial came to court, their names and faces were as well-known as his, and they were being judged and found guilty of nothing but bearing his last name.

The Conway, Arkansas police department decided it would be in the public's best interest if the son of a killer was not on their force, and despite an exemplary record, they let Aaron go.

Aaron's wife, Kelly, couldn't handle the pressure and filed for divorce two months before their first anniversary. Again, it was nothing Aaron did. She just didn't want to be associated with the crime.

Clyde was in prison for life, and so, it would seem, was his family.

Sean lost clients through the IT firm he'd worked for and was scrambling to make ends meet. And Wiley was reduced to a DoorDash delivery driver instead of the law enforcement job he'd been hoping for since graduating from the police academy.

B.J finished his senior year of high school but skipped the ceremony, unable to face the shame.

Shirley was let go from her job as a receptionist in a dental office and removed from being a volunteer storyteller at a local library. She finally found a job as a dishwasher in a small Mexican restaurant and was grateful for it.

Then one day, about a year after Clyde's imprisonment, Shirley got a phone call that changed their world.

———

It was the first week of February and Shirley's day off. She was doing laundry when her phone rang. She recognized the area code, and without looking at the number just assumed it was her mother, Helen, calling from Kentucky.

"Hello."

"Hi, Shirley. This is your Aunt Annie."

Shirley was a little surprised but pleased to hear from Annie. She was one of her deceased father's sisters, and she adored her.

"Hi, Auntie! It's good to hear your voice."

"Well, sugar, I'm not calling with good news," Annie said. "I'm so sorry to have to tell you, but your mother passed away in her sleep last night."

Shock rolled through Shirley in waves.

"No! Oh, my God, no! I just spoke to her day before yesterday. She was in good spirits and said she was feeling fine." She started crying. "Mom was my touchstone to sanity."

"I know. I'm so sorry, Shirley," Annie said.

Shirley was sobbing now, struggling to catch her breath. "Why didn't Mom let me know she was failing?"

"She wasn't. Not in the way you mean. Helen never looked at life like that. She just got old, and she was ready to go," Annie said.

Shirley moaned. "But I could have been there to help."

Annie hesitated before answering. "Honestly, I think Helen knew you already had more on our plate than you could say grace over. This was how she wanted it, and you have to honor that."

"I feel like someone just cut the rope to my anchor," Shirley said, then wiped her eyes and blew her nose. "So, what do I need to know? What do I need to do? I can't be there before tomorrow at the earliest."

"No, no. No need to hurry here at all," Annie said. "Helen always said she didn't want to waste money on some big funeral, and she didn't want people looking at her in a coffin. She wrote it all down years ago and showed me where her papers were kept. She will be cremated, and her ashes will be saved for you. She always said when you come home to claim your heritage, she wants you to sprinkle them where the mountain laurel grows. She said you'd know the place."

Shirley hadn't thought past the shock of the loss until she heard the words *come home to claim her heritage*. Her brother, and only sibling, had died in a car accident some years back, and knowing she was the sole heir to the land and the home in which she'd been raised, felt like one last hug from her mother.

"Yes. Yes, I know right where she means," Shirley said. "Thank you for calling, Aunt Annie. I am so sad right now, but the thought of going home to Pope Mountain feels like a godsend."

"I know," Annie said. "We all know what's been happening to you and your boys, and we're so sorry for your suffering. Come home, darlin'. We love you. You'll be safe here. This is where you'll heal."

"Yes, yes…I will. It will take a while, but I'll let you know. Thank you for calling. I love you too."

After the call ended, Shirley sent a group text to her sons, calling a family meeting for that evening, and after the year they'd just lived through, the text sent them all into a panic.

Getting that message from his mom stopped Aaron cold. He didn't even go back to his apartment after he got off work at the service station, and drove straight to her home, worried all over again as to what else might be happening.

His younger brothers had all moved home after the fall out to help pay the bills and look after Shirley, but the moment they got the messages, a feeling of dread came over them.

That evening they began arriving within moments of each other, leaving B.J. the youngest, to be the last to get home from his job at a fast-food drive-in. He parked his

Harley in a skid, then came running into the house, wide-eyed and pale.

"Mom! What's wrong?"

"Sit down with your brothers," she said, then drew a slow, shaky breath.

"Your grandma has died. Aunt Annie said they found her in her bed. She died in her sleep."

"Oh, Mama!" they said in unison, and jumped up and ran to her, hugging her and commiserating with her, which brought on another round of weeping.

"I'm so sorry," Aaron said. "We were all going back for Easter right after Kelly and I got married, and then Dad broke your nose, and we made excuses. We were going to go a year ago last Christmas and that shit with Dad happened and we didn't. Now this."

Shirley wiped her eyes. "Your grandma knew what was happening. She always knew. We talked weekly, sometimes more. She didn't blame us for the situation. Aunt Annie said there won't be a funeral. Mom didn't want one. But when we do go there, she wants us to spread her ashes on the mountain."

"So, we're going now? After she's gone?" Wiley asked.

Shirley swallowed past her tears. "As the only living child, I have inherited the home and land where I grew up. I own it now. We haven't been welcome in this town for a long time. I want to go home to stay, and I'm asking if any of you want to come with me. We'll be living in a home that's paid for, surrounded by family and people who love us, and there is always work to be had in Jubilee."

Sean sighed. "But Mama, what will they think of us? I mean…we'll still be Clyde Wallace's sons."

Shirley's chin came up. Her eyes were still teary, but her voice was sure and strong. "They'll think I have raised four fine sons," Shirley said. "And none of us have to bear Clyde Wallace's name or sins if we don't want to. You're not just your father's child! You're mine, too, which makes you Popes. You carry the DNA of generations of honorable men within you, and you might as well carry the name as well."

Aaron stood, his fists clenched. "I choose to change."

Sean nodded where he sat. "I choose to change."

Wiley was grim-lipped. "Hell yes, and thank you!" he said.

B.J., the youngest, had tears in his eyes. He'd known nothing but his father's abuse and rage, and now the shame of being his son. "I choose you, Mama. I always have," B.J. said.

Shirley nodded. "Then we'll do it! Since there are so many of us doing it at once, I'll contact a lawyer to get us through the process."

Within the month, it was done. They'd cut the last link they would ever have with Clyde Wallace by rejecting his name.

After that, leaving Conway was easy.

―――――

March—Pope Mountain

Shirley Pope's heart was pounding as she and her sons drove their little convoy through the bustling tourist town of Jubilee, located in the valley below Pope Mountain. She was coming back to her roots, and they were almost at the end of their journey.

Shirley and B.J. were in the lead.

Aaron was in his SUV behind his mother.

Sean was behind Aaron, driving his car, and Wiley was in his car behind Sean and just ahead of the moving van bringing up the rear.

B.J.'s Harley was in the moving van, and he'd been riding shotgun with his mother all the way.

It had been far too long since Shirley had made this trip. Her eyes were full of tears, but they weren't tears of joy. She was crying because there was no one left to welcome them home.

Even though six weeks had passed since they'd received the news, Shirley was still in shock that it had happened. Her mother had seemed invincible, even immortal, and had been Shirley's steadfast backup through her abusive marriage with Clyde Wallace. Helen had always been the gentle voice and the deep wisdom Shirley needed in times of strife.

As they were driving out of Conway, Shirley had made a call to Annie, letting her know they were on the way. But it had taken two long days of traveling before they met their moving van in Frankfort this morning to lead the way home.

This was the last leg of a long trip. They didn't know what lay ahead, but anything would be better than what they'd left behind.

Shirley's sons only knew what she'd told them about her side of the family. Thanks to their dad, their visits to Kentucky had been few and far between. But they knew their ancestors had lived in this place since the early 1800s. And they knew this mountain they were now driving up bore their family name. Here, in this place, they hoped to regain their sense of self. To be proud of who they were again. And one day, know that their mother was no longer crying herself to sleep.

From the moment they'd started up the tree-covered mountain, B.J quit talking and became wide-eyed and quiet—too quiet. After the four-lane highways and the busy streets of their city, the two-lane blacktop on which they were traveling seemed little more than a trail cut through a wilderness. Shirley was worried he was not happy about her decision.

"So, B.J., what do you think?" she asked, then heard him sigh.

"I think it feels safe here."

She smiled. "Good. Hold that feeling," she said and kept on driving. A few miles later, she began slowing down and flipped on her turn signal. "There's where we turn."

One by one, the vehicles behind her did the same as she left the blacktop and began following the gravel road up into the trees.

The house was a hundred yards back, all but buried in the woods. As soon as she passed the twin pines, she saw the house, and then gasped at the sight of a half-dozen cars in the yard and a whole row of people lining the front porch.

"Mama, who are those people?" B.J. asked, as she parked off to the side.

Shirley shivered, seeing herself in their faces. The high cheekbones. The dark hair. The women's curves. The men's broad shoulders.

"Some of our family. Look at them. That's why you're all so tall. That's where your dark hair comes from. Look at them, and you'll see yourself."

"Oh wow," B.J. whispered.

One by one, her sons parked, but when they got out, they headed straight for Shirley, as did the people coming off the porch. After that, they were surrounded, fielding hugs and handshakes.

Then one man who stood a head above the rest spoke up from the crowd.

"Shirley, I'm Cameron Pope, your aunt Georgia's oldest son. This is my wife, Rusty. Welcome home."

Shirley was crying. "You were just a boy last time I saw you. These are my sons, Aaron, Sean, Wiley, and Brendan Pope, but we call him B.J."

Cameron smiled. "Another Brendan, huh? Named after the man who started us all. Good to have some more Pope men on this mountain. I've been the only man left with that name since my father's passing."

And just like that, Shirley's sons took their first steps into the family.

Annie Cauley slipped up behind Shirley and whispered in her ear. "We cleaned the house. You have food in your refrigerator. The appliances have been serviced. John will show the boys around outside. You come in now and sit where it's cool while you tell the movers where you want to put your things. After your call, and mentioning your sons were bringing their own things, we took down the old beds in the spare rooms and stored them all in the attic. Your mom's living room furniture was past hope. She'd written in her last wishes to have it donated, so there's plenty of room now for your stuff. And don't worry. All the family heirlooms are still where she had them. The cupboard. The pie safe. The sideboard. And your great-grandpa's old secretary desk. We'll have you set up and comfy before nightfall."

Walking into the old home place without her mother to greet her was bittersweet, but Shirley took the home as the blessing it was, and by the time night fell, the moving van was long gone. All her sons had their own beds up in their own rooms, and she had her things around her again. Clothes were unpacked and put away, and they'd just sat down to supper at the kitchen table.

There were no sirens or dogs barking outside. No cars honking. No streetlights. Just the glow from the security light between the house and the barn, and their cars, lined up in front of the house like a used car lot.

Shirley looked at the faces of her sons, at the food before them, and the familiarity of the room in which they were sitting, and then she sighed.

"Well, we're here. And right now, I am at peace. Once again, my mother has saved my sanity and your futures."

"Amen," Aaron said.

"I'm thankful," Sean said.

"I'm thankful," Wiley added.

"Me, too," B.J. said, and then pointed at the platter of cold fried chicken. "Somebody please pass the chicken. I'm starving."

Their laughter was sudden, but it felt good to have something to laugh about.

The next few days were about settling in. Shirley walked the woods with her sons, showing them the woods and the creek where she and her brother had played in when they were little, and the pond where fish never quit biting. And then one bright morning, she took them to the place where the mountain laurel grew and scattered her mother's ashes.

"Love you, Mother. I'll miss you forever. Rest in the peace you have given to us," Shirley said, and wiped tears as her sons gathered around her. On the walk back, she showed them the creek that ran through their property. "This creek water is cold year-round. It comes from a long way up, out of a spring in the rocks at the top of the mountain. It runs all the way down through Jubilee, to a river miles and miles away."

"Did you play here when you were little?" B.J. asked.

Shirley smiled. "When my brother and I weren't doing chores, or going to school, we lived in these woods, waded in these waters. Pope Mountain was our playground."

Aaron saw the far-off look in his mother's eyes as she

gazed down into the swift, running water, and knew she was remembering better days.

As they began to settle in, they talked about getting chickens for a chicken coop long since empty, and after a week of sleeping in and lazy days, her sons began looking for jobs. Finding out that their relatives ran a lot of the businesses in Jubilee was a boon they hadn't seen coming.

After getting Wi-Fi and internet to the house, Sean set up his own IT office in their home and using his contacts from Conway and his online website, he began growing a new clientele.

Wiley was ecstatic when he got hired as a daytime security guard at one of the music venues, and came home beaming, carrying in uniforms, his badge, and the weapon he'd been issued.

Shirley celebrated with him, but the irony was not lost upon her of having an ex-husband serving a life sentence, and two sons who'd chosen careers in law enforcement.

B.J. got a job driving a delivery van for his Aunt Annie at her bakery in Jubilee, but for the time being, Aaron was staying home to help his mother settle in. He missed being on the force and wasn't sure where to go from here.

And then one morning not long after their arrival, Cameron called to ask if it was okay if he dropped by that evening after all of the family was home, that there was some family business they needed to know about. Instead, Shirley invited him and Rusty to eat supper with them, and they accepted.

"I haven't cooked for anyone but family in so long I've forgotten what it's like to have company," Shirley said, as she took a big beef roast out of the oven and set it on the counter to rest.

Aaron grinned. "You're a good cook, Mama, and you know it. Do you want me to put the leaf in the table?"

Shirley beamed from the compliment as she nodded. "Yes, to the table leaf. With seven at the table, we'll need it."

He went to get the leaf from the hall closet, while Shirley began cleaning fresh vegetables for a tossed salad. She had three apple pies cooling on the sideboard, a basket of dinner rolls beside it, and fresh green beans warming on the stove that she cooked and seasoned with bits of ham. All she needed was for Wiley and B.J. to get home from work, and the company to arrive.

Moments later, she heard a car driving up.

"That's Wiley," Aaron said, and then they heard the rumble of B.J.'s Harley as he pulled up to the house. "And that's B.J."

"Good. Then all we have to do is wait for Cameron and Rusty."

"What does he want to talk to us about?" Aaron asked.

"I don't know, but we'll find out soon enough," Shirley said, then winced when the front door slammed.

"Sorry!" B.J. yelled. "The wind caught it. I'm going to shower! Won't be long!"

Shirley grinned. B.J. had been slamming doors all his

life. Today it was the fault of the wind. Tomorrow it would be something else. Truth was, B.J. was always in too big of a hurry to catch it.

Seconds later, Wiley came in the back door. "Thought I'd park out back and leave room for company out front. I'm gonna change."

Now Shirley could relax. All her boys were accounted for.

"Cameron, I need help," Rusty said, and turned her back to him so he could zip up her sundress.

Cameron turned away from the dresser to come to his wife's aid. She was holding her long curly hair up off her neck so it wouldn't get caught in the zipper, and he couldn't resist a kiss below all those red curls.

"I'd just as soon be taking this off you, as putting it on," he said.

Rusty laughed. "Hold that thought and you can do that later," she said. "We don't want to be late."

Cameron grabbed the zipper tab and pulled it all the way up, then kissed the back of her neck one last time.

"Done and done," he said, as she turned around to face him. "Damn, but you are a beautiful woman, Rusty Pope."

"Flattery will get you everywhere," she said, and kissed him square on the lips before tearing herself away. "All I need are my shoes and I'm ready."

The big white German Shepherd who'd been lying in the doorway watching them dress, stood up and whined.

"Ghost is sad," Rusty said.

"He'll be fine. I'm not taking a dog the size of a small Polar bear out to dinner."

Rusty frowned. She couldn't bear it when Ghost whined. "Then he gets the big chew bone, right?"

Cameron rolled his eyes. "Yes, he gets the big chew bone. He won't miss us after that. Trust me. Ghost. Treat!" He said, and Ghost shot off down the hall at a gallop.

Rusty laughed.

"See?" Cameron said.

As soon as they gave Ghost the bone, he chomped it and carried it to his bed in the living room.

Cameron and Rusty set the security alarm, then locked up and drove away.

It took less than fifteen minutes to get up the mountain to where Shirley and her sons were living now. Just enough time for Rusty to watch the sun moving down behind the tallest treetops. It would be dark in an hour. She loved night on the mountain almost as much as she loved the man sitting beside her.

They pulled up in the yard and parked at the end of a line of cars.

"Good thing Shirley doesn't have but four sons. She'd be running out of parking space with any more," Cameron said.

They were on their way up the steps when the front door opened.

Aaron was standing in the doorway. "Welcome to the house," he said, then stepped aside for them to enter.

"Something sure smells good," Rusty said as they entered.

"Mama's a good cook," Aaron said. "We used to say that's why we grew so tall, but after moving here, I'm thinking it was DNA, not roast and mashed potatoes."

"You've got that right," Cameron said, as Aaron ushered them into the kitchen. Sean and Wiley were already there and carrying the food to the table.

Shirley met them with a hug.

"Welcome! Ooh, Rusty, I love that blue sundress. It's the perfect foil for your gorgeous hair."

Rusty smiled. "Thank you. Mom and Dad used to blame my hair color on the postman and then laugh hysterically, because no one in our family had red hair. I had to get older to get the joke."

"That hair is a country all its own," Cameron said. "It's what I saw first across a crowded hotel lobby, and then I saw her, and I was done."

"What a storybook meeting," Shirley said.

B.J. walked into the kitchen on that last comment.

"Sorry I kept everyone waiting," he said, then shook hands with Cameron and gave Rusty an appreciative glance, thinking to himself how pretty she was.

Shirley waved a hand toward the table. "Please be seated." Then she nodded at Aaron to sit at the head of the table and saw the pleased expression on his face. As soon as everyone was in their place, Shirley gave the blessing, then as the passing of food began around the table, she shifted her attention to Cameron and Rusty.

"You two are the first guests in our new home, and we are so grateful for your company."

"It's our pleasure," Cameron said.

Chatter filled the room as they filled their plates, and the boys poked fun at the size of B.J.'s helpings.

"Still growing into those long legs," Cameron said.

Shirley laughed, and as she did, realized how long it had been since she'd felt this kind of delight.

As the meal progressed, conversation turned to jobs and work. Cameron heard about Sean's IT business in their home, and B.J. making deliveries for Aunt Annie's bakery. He already knew through the family grapevine that Wiley had gone to work at the music venue for country music star, Reagan Bullard.

"So, Wiley. What do you think of Reagan Bullard? Have you met him yet?"

"Yes, I met him my first day on the job. He seems nice enough. I also heard he bought the campgrounds outside of Jubilee and is turning it into a whole new venue. Waterslides. A big swimming pool, pony rides, and a concession stand to go with the little cabins and the campgrounds and fireworks every Saturday night."

Cameron glanced at Rusty. That place held a not so nice history for them, but they'd been aware of the changes after the previous owner's arrest.

"I heard a bit about that myself," Cameron said. "A new owner will work wonders for the place." Then he glanced at B.J. "So how do you like working at the bakery?"

B.J. grinned. "I like it. Aunt Annie is awesome, and the free cookies I get are just fine too."

They laughed, even Aaron, who had been silent during

the job discussion. But Rusty had noticed his reticence and was curious about the silence.

"So, Aaron, what kind of job are you looking for?" she asked, as Shirley began serving slices of apple pie for their dessert.

He met her gaze, but it took everything within him to not duck his head in shame.

"Before Clyde Wallace's crime spree, I was a police officer for the City of Conway. After Clyde's trial and sentencing, they let me go. I always wanted to be in law enforcement. I had seven years on the force before Clyde's killing spree. After all the bad press and publicity, I guess being the son of a killer tainted the badge and screwed up public relations."

Rusty didn't blink. "Well, that sucks, but we have a lot in common. I was an undercover agent for the FBI for almost ten years. It's what brought me to Jubilee, and why Cameron and I reunited after meeting years earlier."

Aaron blinked. "No joke? A Fed?"

"I liked it, but undercover work is dangerous, and I had too many close calls. I happily gave it up just to have a family again."

Cameron had been silent through the conversation, but in a lull, he had to ask. "Have you applied for a job here with the Jubilee PD?"

Aaron shook his head.

"Why not?" Cameron asked.

"We came here to get away from being Clyde Wallace's sons. I don't want to resurrect that again with a simple background check."

Cameron frowned. "Your last name is Pope. That name goes a long way around here. Sonny Warren is the police chief. I grew up with him. He's a good man and a fair man. If you want that career, then fight for it."

"If I thought it wouldn't make trouble for us all over again here, I'd do it in a heartbeat," Aaron said.

"Every family has a cross of some kind to bear. Your reputation should have nothing to do with who you're related to," Cameron said. "Trust him. Trust us."

Aaron nodded but stayed silent.

Rusty took a bite of the pie, then rolled her eyes.

"Lord, Shirley. This pie is delicious!"

Shirley beamed. "Thanks. B.J. helped me make them. He's a good hand in the kitchen."

B.J. nodded. "I like to cook. But I like to eat better."

They laughed, and the moment passed, but after the meal was over and the table cleared, Cameron knew it was time to explain why he'd come.

"I know you're all wondering why I needed to talk to you, so I'll get right to the point. And I need to stress this, above all else…what I say to you tonight stays in the family…in this room. Everybody on the mountain knows it, but we don't talk about it, because it has to stay a secret."

It was the word 'secret' that got their attention, and in that moment, Shirley suddenly realized what this was about.

"What's the secret?" Aaron asked.

"The entire town of Jubilee is a very successful tourist attraction, owned by a company called PCG, Incorporated.

All of the businesses in town lease the property locations and pay monthly rent to the corporation. The land is never for sale, nor is the mountain on which we live. It's how we are protected from investors and outsiders wanting to clear it for their own gain. That's how it's been since my grandfather's time. And this is how it will always be. But nobody except the families involved know that PCG stands for Pope, Cauley, and Glass."

Shirley was smiling. "I've been gone from here so long I'd completely forgotten about all this."

Aaron leaned forward. "What? What are you saying?"

Cameron glanced at Rusty, and then spoke. "That we here on the mountain own Jubilee, and all of the members of those families on the mountain are stockholders. We all receive quarterly dividends from the company. Any one up here automatically becomes eligible for dividends once they reach their eighteenth birthday. Each family is represented by a family member of their choosing to sit on the board. I am, at the present time, the CEO of PCG, Inc. I was the elected member of the Pope family, and the other members of the board selected me as the CEO."

"What kind of money are we talking about?" Sean asked.

"We're in the third generation of PCG's existence. It is a multimillion-dollar company. The dividends are generous and issued quarterly, and the investments from the money grow the coffers, as well. By moving here and coming into Helen's heritage, you will receive your first checks by the end of the month. There are less than 250 people still living on Pope Mountain. The money arrives by direct deposit into your personal bank accounts, or into savings accounts per each family's wishes. In the next three days or so, I'll be needing your bank information so I can get it all to the lawyer in Frankfort who oversees the legal end of the corporation, and you will have assigned bank accounts in a bank in Frankfort. That keeps the people down below from finding out we're their landlords. This is never up for discussion. Nobody outside the families ever knows unless they marry into it."

Wiley was stunned.

Sean was grinning.

Aaron was in shock.

"Cool," B.J. said, and served himself another piece of pie.

Shirley's eyes welled. "Just one more gift from Mama," she whispered. "All I had to do was come home to claim it. I didn't remember, but she did."

Cameron nodded. "And, just so you know, if any of you ever have problems or want advice, everyone on this mountain is here for you. It's never a burden. It's our way."

About the Author

New York Times and *USA Today* bestselling author Sharon Sala has 135-plus books in print, published in six different genres—romance, young adult, Western, general fiction, women's fiction, and nonfiction. First published in 1991, her industry awards include the Janet Dailey Award, five-time Career Achievement winner, five-time winner of the National Readers' Choice Award, five-time winner of the Colorado Romance Writers' Award of Excellence, the Heart of Excellence award, the Booksellers Best Award, the Nora Roberts Lifetime Achievement Award, and the Centennial Award in recognition of her 100th published novel. She lives in Oklahoma, the state where she was born. Visit her at sharonsalaauthor.com and facebook.com/sharonsala.

UNCHARTED

The sparks are flying in this fast-paced romantic
suspense by award-winning author Adriana Anders

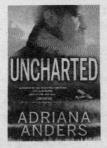

Hotshot pilot Leo Eddowes is afraid of nothing and no one. So when she's
asked to evacuate a man from the wilds of Alaska, she doesn't hesitate. But
with enemies in close pursuit and the weather turning sour, what should
have been a simple mission quickly shifts to disaster.

And there's only one way out.

When Elias Thorne disappeared, he was America's most wanted—a
criminal both hated and feared by the entire nation. He's spent more than
a decade in one of the most remote places on earth, guarding a dangerous
secret. When Leo arrives, quickly followed by a team of expert hunters, it
shakes up his uneventful existence, leaving him no choice but to join forces
with her—and run.

**"Scorching hot and beautifully emotional.
A pulse-pounding, edge-of-your-seat read."**

—Lori Foster, *New York Times* bestselling author,
for *Whiteout*

For more info about Sourcebooks's books and authors, visit:

sourcebooks.com

BEYOND POWER

Sultry romantic suspense set in Florida's untamed wilderness from author Connie Mann

Delilah Atwood barely escaped her ultra-fundamental militia family years ago. Now she's back in Florida to save her sixteen-year-old sister, and no government man is going to stop her.

A bush pilot and officer for the Florida Fish and Wildlife Conservation Commission, Josh Tanner is one of the tough cops needed to manage these rugged areas. He can't stand by and watch Delilah risk her life, but unless he can get her to trust him, she may end up being the next victim...

"Charming, exciting, and thoughtful...a strong sense of place and thrilling action."

—*Publishers Weekly* for *Beyond Risk*

For more info about Sourcebooks's books and authors, visit:
sourcebooks.com

WELCOME TO BLESSINGS, GEORGIA

Sharon Sala, *New York Times* and
USA Today Bestselling Author

Count Your Blessings
novella eBook only

You and Only You

I'll Stand By You

Saving Jake

A Piece of My Heart

The Color of Love

Come Back to Me

Forever My Hero

A Rainbow Above Us

Also by Sharon Sala

The Next Best Day

BLESSINGS, GEORGIA
Count Your Blessings (novella)
You and Only You
I'll Stand by You
Saving Jake
A Piece of My Heart
The Color of Love
Come Back to Me
Forever My Hero
A Rainbow Above Us
The Way Back to You
Once in a Blue Moon
Somebody to Love
The Christmas Wish
The Best of Me